ALSO BY OLEN STEINHAUER

THE
MIDDLEMAN

THE
MIDDLEMAN

OLEN STEINHAUER

MINOTAUR BOOKS

NEW YORK

THE MIDDLEMAN. Copyright © 2018 by Third State, Inc. All rights reserved. Printed in the United States of America. For information, address St. Martin's Press, 175 Fifth Avenue, New York, N.Y. 10010.

www.minotaurbooks.com

Designed by Omar Chapa

Library of Congress Cataloging-in-Publication Data
Names: Steinhauer, Olen, author.
Title: The middleman / Olen Steinhauer.
Description: First edition. | New York : Minotaur Books, 2018.
Identifiers: LCCN 2018004424| ISBN 9781250036179 (hardcover) |
    ISBN 9781250036162 (ebook)
Subjects: LCSH: Undercover operations—Fiction. | Terrorists—Fiction. |
    BISAC: FICTION / Thrillers. | FICTION / Suspense. | FICTION /
    Espionage. | GSAFD: Suspense fiction.
Classification: LCC PS3619.T4764 M53 2018 | DDC 813/.6—dc23
LC record available at https://lccn.loc.gov/2018004424

ISBN 978-1-250-19956-0 (signed edition)

Our books may be purchased in bulk for promotional, educational, or business use. Please contact your local bookseller or the Macmillan Corporate and Premium Sales Department at 1-800-221-7945, extension 5442, or by email at MacmillanSpecialMarkets@macmillan.com.

First Edition: August 2018

10 9 8 7 6 5 4 3 2 1

For
Margo
and
Slavica,
without whom I wouldn't care nearly as much.

If no one out there understands
Start your own revolution and cut out the middleman.

—BILLY BRAGG, "WAITING FOR THE GREAT LEAP FORWARDS"

THE BRIGADE

SUNDAY, JUNE 18, 2017

1

KEVIN MOORE leaned against the counter at Sushi Taka. He counted the rings in his spicy tuna roll—one, two, three—thinking of architecture. Then he went about the ritual: the trimming of the chopsticks, the laying on of ginger, the measured smear of wasabi. The flavor was appealing, but nothing special, not to his palate, yet he had eaten so much of this food since moving to the West Coast a year ago that by now the ritual was second nature. The joy he took in eating sushi was one of form and not content; this realization felt like something important.

He shifted his gaze to the window in front of him—watching, like always. A few minutes ago, he'd seen a homeless guy urinate against the bland office building across the street, turning to face the wall as if by this show of modesty no one would notice. But San Francisco residents had seen far worse—hadn't everyone?—so no one bothered him. By the time Kevin's phone vibrated beside the tray, number unknown, the homeless guy was long gone, and there was nothing to interrupt the steady Sunday trickle of tourists, vagrants, and hookers.

"Hello?" he said into the phone.

"Time to go, George," said a male voice.

The office building blurred. "Really?"

"Now," the caller said, then hung up.

Kevin blinked until his sight cleared, the hazy distance coming into focus again. He wasn't scared, not really, because he'd been waiting weeks for this moment. Each morning, walking to the Office Depot in the Potrero Center where he stocked shelves and tried to be patient with customers, he'd carried in him the weight of knowing that *this could be the day.* It had never been, though, and after a while he'd begun to wonder if the day would ever come. Maybe Jasmine and Aaron had been full of hot air, posers in a city of posers, and all his time here would turn out to be a waste. And now . . .

No, not fear. Anxiety, yes, but not fear.

He lifted his phone again and scrolled through contacts: MOM. He typed, *Off on trip with friends, let you know when I get back. xx.* Send. Then he took out his wallet and removed his MasterCard, the Virginia driver's license he'd never gotten around to changing, and even his library card, but he held on to his debit card. He brought everything to the trashcan and dropped in his soiled plate, the empty cup of miso soup, the cards, and his phone. As they disappeared into the darkness, an involuntary sigh escaped him. Though he knew better, he'd grown attached to the phone that had been pieced together in some Chinese sweatshop. The truth was that Kevin Moore loved the modern world even when he loathed it.

The trashcan lid snapped shut. It was accomplished.

He walked casually over to traffic-clogged Montgomery and south toward Market, past the grand columns of US Bank, and at the ATM emptied his account of $580. He pocketed the cash, then found a trashcan at the corner of Pine. *Good-bye, cruel world*—in went the debit card. He looked around, wondering if anyone had spotted his madness, but no one stared. Like a man pissing on a wall, people had probably seen this sort of thing before. They'd seen worse.

What was unexpected, though, was the feeling of lightness that overcame him. The anxiety fell away as he walked deeper into his day. A phone and a bunch of cards. So simple. Yet with a few deft moves he'd become unmoored. Who, now, was to say his name wasn't George? Who could say if he was a rich man or a poor one? Who, really, could say *what* he was? *I'm a NASA scientist,* he could say. Or: *I'm a cop.* The only thing he wasn't allowed to say was *I'm a revolutionary seeking to bury all this modern sublimity.*

At Market he joined the crowd heading down into the BART station to catch the 2:14 for Pittsburg/Bay Point. He reached the platform just in time to face the wind of the gray-hulled train before it emerged from the darkness. Despite the gusts, he was sweating, while around him people stared at little screens in their hands. Any other day, he would have been doing the same thing. One of the well-washed masses. His dizziness returned. It was the light-headedness, he understood now, of abandon. There wasn't much air up here.

He searched for a seat, but there were none available until Orinda, where he settled next to an old woman reading the Bible. He peered over her shoulder—she was somewhere in Leviticus—and when she noticed him he apologized. "Are you a reader?" she asked.

"Been a while," he said, which was true enough.

She smiled a beautiful smile and offered the Bible to him. "I got plenty of 'em."

He tried to refuse, but her insistence was so full of earnest generosity that he gave in and carried it as his only luggage when he left at Walnut Creek. He waited until the train left again before dropping it, too, into a trashcan and trotting down the stairs to reach the underpass. He leaned against a wall and untied his left sneaker, then took it off. Holding it in his hand, he walked out into the sunlight, a slight limp from his unbalanced stride, hardly even feeling ridiculous. He waited at the curb, watching. Cars came and went, but he tried not to look expectant. He used his eyes clandestinely, checking windshields, and peered beyond to the expansive BART parking lot.

He'd been told so little. Take off your left shoe and wait. Maybe Aaron would show up. Or Mother would pull up and tell him to call it a day. Anything, really, felt possible.

He guessed that fifteen minutes passed before an old GTO—must've been midsixties—pulled up. A rangy-looking white man of indeterminate age leaned across the passenger seat and cranked down the window.

Kevin said, "That you, George?"

A rough voice: "Get in."

Kevin opened the door and settled into the stink of cigarettes and fried food. George put the car into drive, and they moved slowly forward. As they exited the parking lot and continued onto Oakland Boulevard, Kevin put his shoe back on and tied it up. "So," he said. "Where to?"

"Away."

"Far?"

"How about you let me worry about that?"

2

ON THE opposite end of America, in New Jersey, a party was under way. Bill Ferris, the host, guessed he didn't know a quarter of the partygoers; and most of those partygoers didn't know that they were here to celebrate his retirement from the world of entertainment law. Some were confused by the fact that this was Father's Day, and even wished their childless host a happy one, while others—neighbors, mostly—had come solely for the free booze. Not that this bothered him. He and Gina were social creatures; they had spent decades gathering around themselves a menagerie of artists, actors, gurus, and agitators of a smorgasbord of races because this was what they most enjoyed witnessing: the descendants of Trotsky engaging one another on neutral ground.

Children were safely jailed inside a screened trampoline, while the sharp aroma of skunkweed came and went along with snatches of conversation: rising unemployment in the heartland, the latest corporate mergers, the recent acquittal of a Newark cop who'd shot and killed a black man in front of his wife and daughter, a congressional money-laundering investigation into Oklahoma City's Plains Capital Bank and Frankfurt's IfW, or *Investition für Wirtschaft,* and, as ever,

POTUS #45. A voice on the warm breeze: "Fuck this, man. I'm moving to Canada."

When David and Ingrid Parker arrived, Bill was on the front porch, signing for an emergency half keg of Shiner Bock. He kissed Ingrid's permanently flushed cheeks and asked after her health—she'd just crossed into her second trimester. "The food's staying down," she said, pushing back the long walnut hair that she'd been growing out for a year; once it was long enough she was going to donate it to make wigs for cancer patients. "What've you got to eat?"

"Everything," he assured her.

Bill had met the Parkers ten years before, back in 2007, during a month-long stay in Berlin to negotiate the minutiae of a studio buyout, and they had remained friends ever since. Ingrid had been writing grants for the Starling Trust, while David had wallowed in the dissolute life of an expat novelist. His debut, *Gray Snow,* a story of concentration camp survivors making their way home to Yugoslavia through the apocalyptic landscape of postwar Europe, had garnered impressive reviews back home, and by the time Bill met him he was working furiously on his follow-up, *Red Rain.*

David's audience had been small, but he was living the romantic exile's life, which, until 2009, was enough for him. Early that year a terrorist bomb went off in an apartment building as David was passing on the street, and his brush with mortality changed everything; all he wanted now was success. The first step was to move back to Manhattan, to the nexus of American publishing, where all doors would be open to him. At first Ingrid resisted, but David eventually wore her down. She got a transfer to the Starling Trust's New York headquarters, and they moved into an Upper East Side rental, where David spent his days hunched over a laptop, putting everything he had into his masterpiece. He was poised for success.

Which was why, after five years of hard work, he was dumbfounded when his editor unceremoniously rejected all eight hundred pages of *Balkan America.* Then Ingrid learned she was pregnant, and money became an issue. Her salary just covered their exorbitant rent, and as they ate their way through their savings they tried in vain to plan for the expenses of parenthood.

In the backyard, David stationed himself beside Bill, who was keeping an eye on some Kobe steaks. Though the rest of the party was being catered, Bill had insisted on manning the grill. They gazed down the arc of the yard to the trampoline, where a hired clown had just arrived to terrify the children of the Left, and Bill opened up about a fight he and Gina had been waging. "She wants to move south. *Florida.* Just contemplating a life in that cultural wasteland makes me sick."

David gave him an appreciative smile, but his mind was clearly elsewhere.

"What about you and Ingrid?" Bill asked.

The smile faded. "She's giving me a month."

"What?"

"To start pulling my weight."

"You still have savings, don't you?"

"We've eaten up too much."

Bill didn't say anything.

"Teaching," David said.

"The horror."

David drank again, looking out at the busy backyard. "Maybe we should just throw in the towel and move back to Berlin. Every time we turn on the news we talk about it. This country's a mess."

"Don't watch the news, then."

"Ingrid doesn't watch anything else," he said. "You know where she was after the last election? In the streets, marching around with her NOT MY PRESIDENT sign in front of Trump Tower. Screaming like a banshee. Then last week? Ran off to Newark to protest that Jersey cop who killed that guy . . . what's-his-name."

"Jerome Brown."

A shrug. "She came back filthy. I think there was blood in her hair."

"She wasn't the only one protesting," said Bill.

"Did you go?"

Bill shook his head.

"My point exactly. You and me—we're grown-ups."

Bill checked the steaks. While he wasn't looking, they had burned.

3

FIVE MONTHS ago, Kevin had first been invited *inside* after a meeting in an Oakland loft of the uninspiringly named West Coast Anarchists (WCA). A Swede named Olaf who wore a bow tie as an act of radical irony had been discussing Martin Bishop's latest diatribe, posted on *The Propaganda Ministry,* on "the pharmaceutical mafia." There were about fifteen in attendance, none older than thirty, and when a med student from UCSF tried to explain the economics inherent in drug companies' research and development, and their impact on prices, Kevin cut in with "You sound like a corporate shill. Since when is medicine supposed to be a profit industry? Make a profit on cars, sure, or toys, but hospitals and drugs, the internet and basic foodstuffs— anything that's *necessary* for living? That ain't business. It's a human right."

The med student, not used to being interrupted, had been irritated. "Then move off to a farm and grow your own fucking food."

"There's only twenty-four hours in a day, man, and this late in history I don't think we should all have to move back to the seventeenth century. Is that the promise of capitalism?"

He'd surprised himself with his outburst, and a few others looked surprised as well that the skinny black guy who'd sat silently through so many meetings suddenly had a bone to pick. Afterward, Jasmine—twenty-six, a performance artist—asked him out for a drink. "You're right, you know. He *is* a shill, and so are half of them. I'm even starting to suspect Olaf is a spy."

"Spy?" he asked, trying to appear sufficiently shocked. "For the Feds?"

"Why not?"

"Because a few millennials in a loft doesn't mean shit to them. They're looking for Russian hackers and ISIS bombers."

"Maybe," said Jasmine. "But if that's the case, they're missing out on something big, and they'll be kicking themselves later."

"Something big? Not the WCA."

"I'm not talking about those guys."

"Who, then?"

She smiled and raised her beer. "To the Revolution, Kevin. It's gonna be massive."

Aaron came along later, Jasmine introducing him at Aunt Charlie's Lounge before the drag show got under way. Aaron shook his hand cursorily, then deposited the newest issue of *Rolling Stone* on the bar and opened it to a full-page profile called "The Revolution's New Face." Though not entirely flattering, it was a revealing piece, chronicling the life of Martin Bishop, the thirty-seven-year-old from Tennessee whose youthful Baptist fervor had reinvented itself in the shape of social justice. He and his co-revolutionary, a Pennsylvania thug named Benjamin Mittag, first made a name for themselves among the progressives of Austin, Texas. A blog (*The Propaganda Ministry*—www.propagandaministry.com) with an enormous following led to a Kickstarter-funded tour of campuses around the country, "speaking truth to power." His followers called themselves the Massive Brigade.

In crowded auditoriums, Bishop held forth with religious intensity, and was compared by some to Martin Luther King Jr., though more often he quoted Thomas Jefferson's personal seal: "Rebellion to tyrants is obedience to God." The power elite, he told audiences, had built up its defenses and become so distanced from the 99 percent that it barely noticed the whimpers of those who challenged it with sit-ins and marches and T-shirts and pop songs. The elite saw nothing to fear.

"Who, then, are they afraid of?" he asked auditoriums, then pointed at the people who were hit hard by lawsuits and jail time: the chaos-makers. Hackers, whistle-blowers, and the angry mobs that actually destroyed property. "Look to Seattle! Look to Ruby Ridge! Look to the Battle of the Brooklyn Bridge!" he soliloquized to a crowd in St. Louis. Whoever opened up the ruling class to examination by the masses, whoever exposed the illusion of their authority—*those* were the ones who forced power to reveal its true face: riot police and big lawyers.

He asked the students of NYU, "Is everyone blind? The police are gunning down our black brothers and sisters! The prison-industrial complex fills our jails with the cheapest labor around, for the benefit of McDonald's and Wendy's, Walmart and Victoria's Secret. Our modern-day slaves man call centers for Verizon and Sprint. For ninety cents a day! And if you're on the outside, don't think you're off the hook. Banks steal your homes at the first opportunity. Oil companies send your kids into the desert to die for their profits! Have I got something wrong here?"

The crowd came back, as one, *"No!"*

"If it looks like war and smells like war, what is it?"

"War!"

After the St. Louis meeting broke up, thirty pumped-up Massive Brigade followers smashed their way into a Citibank branch and trashed the lobby before the police rounded them up. That was when the charge of terrorism was first raised against Martin Bishop—if not by the authorities, then by the court of public opinion and his most vocal critic on television, Sam Schumer. Every day, Facebook delivered another salacious bit of news—sometimes fake, sometimes not—about Bishop and his followers. The Massive Brigade was synonymous with "the coming unrest."

Sitting with Aaron, listening to him read out his favorite passages from the *Rolling Stone* profile, knowing instinctually where this conversation was heading, Kevin had felt a primal rush of excitement. *The Brigade.*

A manic-depressive whose moods were as unpredictable as his Marxist faith was unshakable, Aaron had worked with Martin Bishop in Austin, back in the beginning. Oh, he had stories he could tell, but they would have to wait until later. "The question I need to ask you, Kevin, is: Where do you stand?"

"Right next to you, man."

"I mean, what do you see in the future? Once we've done what we've been put on this Earth to do?"

It felt like a test, which it was, but Kevin also smelled a trick question in the works. As he glanced around the bar, where men in makeup sipped prework cocktails, he thought over conversations he'd had since landing in town and making his way through the subterranean world of utopian thought. Left, right, and everything in between. So many opinions, so many dreams of tomorrow. He said, "I'll know it when I see it."

Which, to Aaron, turned out to be as good an answer as any.

Two weeks ago, the three of them were drinking beer in Jasmine's Chinatown apartment when Aaron delivered his good news. "Word has come, comrades. We have to be ready."

"For what?" asked Jasmine.

"To disappear."

Aaron had passed their phone numbers up the ladder, and he explained that in hours, days, or weeks, word would come. They were to leave everything behind.

This was not entirely unexpected. Over the past months, as the media had worked itself into a frenzy of fear over the rhetoric that typified Massive rallies, the trouble in St. Louis, and the sporadic incidents of Massive followers in small towns being attacked by self-proclaimed patriots, it had been one of Bishop's talking points: *We have to make our own space for the dialectic. We have to create our own underground where we can defend ourselves against the fascists who run this* *country. When they come for us we'll need a place where we can escape to.* *Where we can disappear.* Until Aaron's command, Kevin had assumed Bishop had been talking about a metaphorical underground. An underground of the mind. Not, apparently so.

Aaron handed them each a piece of paper with an assigned meeting point and a signal that would identify them to their pickup. He ordered them not to share that information even with one another. "Things just got serious. Are we serious?"

"Absolutely," Kevin told him.

Jasmine, giddy, nodded and laughed.

Now, sitting in the GTO with endless highway in front of him, Kevin listened as the driver he only knew as George said, "I was up on this shit long before Bishop and Mittag."

"Sure you were," said Kevin. They were an hour into their drive, taking I-80 around the north end of Sacramento. Traffic was surprisingly light.

George gave him a look. "You don't believe me."

"I don't *know* you."

"Nineteen eighty-nine—remember then?"

"I was one."

"But you've heard of '89, right? I mean, you got yourself some kind of education, yeah? East-West? Berlin Wall?"

"Sure. I've heard of it."

"Well, I was ten. I remember all the noise and celebration. My dad was a Cold War obsessive. Dug a fallout shelter in the backyard in '82—lost my virginity in that thing, by the way." He winked. "Anyway, 1989: the Wall falls, and I remember my dad watching it on TV. Those Germans with their mullets and bottles of cheap champagne—my dad saw them and started to cry. He was so happy. Told me that the world had just changed. Wanted me to remember that moment. Enemies would become friends. Swords into plowshares. That sort of thing. I was ten, but I remember it all. I remember how excited *I* was. We were officially living in the future. Shangri-La. And then . . ." He tilted his head, cracking a vertebra. "You know what happened then?"

"Why don't you tell me?"

"Nada, sir. Not shit. You got McDonald's and a long line of salivating corporations piling into the newly free countries, scooping up land and resources. You had a lot of confused Easterners fucking over their neighbors to get rich, and quick. You had a war in Yugoslavia. You had Africa slowly falling apart. Genocide in Rwanda. They had a chance," he said, staring hard at the cars ahead, "a chance to really make something of the world. But instead it was the same old story. Greed. Nothing changed. And a decade later people were surprised we were at war all over again. It broke my dad. Hell, it nearly broke me, and I was too young to know better. A system like ours—a system that pisses away a chance for a better world, that can't see past short-term gain . . ." He sighed loudly. "Every day you see it—this week it's Plains Capital and IfW. Some rich assholes didn't want to pay their taxes, so they slipped billions to shady bankers who hid their cash in brand-new accounts opened under other people's names. If the journalists hadn't made such a stink about it, you can bet your ass there wouldn't be any investigation." He shook his head. "Doesn't matter, though. Not a single rich white man—believe me—is going to pay for it." George's knuckles whitened as he squeezed the steering wheel. "A system like that needs to be ground into the dirt."

Kevin watched the side of George's face. How old was this guy? Ten in '89—thirty-eight? With his shoulder-length unwashed hair and the cigarette dangling from his lips, he looked like he was aiming for eighteen.

"How long have you known Martin?" Kevin asked.

"Don't. Not really. Ben's my guy. I heard him speak in some dive in Toledo. His voice stripped the paint off the walls. I was in."

"I don't think I've ever heard Ben Mittag speak."

"Not anymore, he doesn't. His kind of speech? Gets too much attention from the Feds. That's what happens when you talk about shooting cops and blowing up post offices. So he stepped back so the government would stay off our backs." A grin. "Not that that helped much. But we're still here."

"So who's running things—Mittag or Bishop?"

"You want hierarchy? Join the Democratic Party." He looked into the rearview a moment, as if watching for shadows, then said, "What about you? You must've seen through the bullshit early."

"Why?"

George opened a hand, bobbed his head. "I mean, you're black. I don't have to tell you about injustice."

"No, man. You don't." He looked out his window to see a station wagon loaded down with possessions, a young woman at the wheel. Returning home from school, or escaping her life. Almost by rote, he said, "It was the realization—maybe I was thirteen—that my life was a cliché. Dad spending his life in Haynesville Correctional. Drugs, of course. Mom trying to get off welfare and onto her feet." He hesitated, then went off script a moment. "Funny thing is, these days people are crying about laid-off coal miners hooked on opioids. Everyone wants to get them to doctors. Back then it was the same— laid-off workers hooked on crack. But *those* poor bastards—in the eighties, everyone wanted to lock them up." He cleared his throat. "There's only one difference between then and now."

"Color of their skin," George said so melodically that Kevin nearly gave him an *Amen*. Instead, he remained quiet until George said, "So that's what brought you in."

"First I went to my recruiter."

"I thought maybe you were military."

Kevin said nothing.

"See action?"

Kevin stared across an ugly expanse of industrial sprawl along the outskirts of Sacramento. "A little."

"Afghanistan?"

He didn't bother answering that.

George said, "You've seen the world. That's good. And you got your foot in early through the black struggle."

Kevin stared at him a long moment. "It's not a black struggle. It's a human struggle."

"Sure it is," George said, frowning. "But what are humans but a bunch of special interests? That, my friend, is why we're going to win. We're an army of special interests. I'm in the antigreed struggle; you can fight for your race if you want. Someone else can fight for the whales. But in the end we all work for the same thing."

"The end of all this," said Kevin.

"'Zactly," George said as he slowed the car and pulled to the right. The exit was for Greenback Lane, a main thoroughfare lined with low houses and trees that eventually gave way to strip malls and stores: CVS, Dairy Queen, home fitness, Mexican restaurants, and a Red Robin burger joint, where George parked in the lot and killed the engine.

Kevin saw nothing but families, stuffed to the gills, limping to their cars. "I already ate," he said. "I'll wait in the car."

"We'll both wait in the car."

"For what?"

George pulled a slip of paper from his shirt pocket; it was covered in cramped numbers written in pencil. Then he took out a cell phone, the sight of which surprised Kevin. George typed out a number and put the phone to his ear.

"I love this part," he whispered, then changed his tone and said, "Mary, this is George. It's time."

4

DAVID PARKER had been through a few beers by the time he discovered Ingrid in the living room, sharing the sofa with a man somewhere in his thirties. A small crowd of Brooklyn hipsters had gathered around them.

"Where to start," the man said in answer to someone. "Corruption, maybe. I don't care what party they're with. Wall Street buys the candidates, and when they leave office they become lobbyists so they can buy their successors. Let's stop pretending it's democracy."

A few of the hipsters nodded, as if this were fresh news. Gina Ferris, with her unruly white hair and a martini glass in her bejeweled hand, stood nearby, but all David noticed was Ingrid. His wife seemed enraptured by this pretty-boy pundit who occasionally turned to Ingrid with his angelic smile, as if all this were just for her.

The man went on. "Paul Hanes—House majority whip from the great state of Virginia. He just pushed through a bill clearing the way for Blackstar to absorb its primary arms-manufacturing competition. Guess who Hanes's second-largest campaign contributor is? They're not politicians anymore; they're corporate spokespeople. Eisenhower was right on when he warned of the military-industrial complex. But no one listened."

Gina spoke up. "You're only telling part of the story, Martin. Paul Hanes is heading the Plains Capital and IfW inquiry."

Ingrid's suitor—Martin, apparently—shrugged. "Hanes says all the right words, but that's exactly how a smart guy talks just before burying an investigation." He cocked his head, reading the irritation in Gina's face. "But, okay. Even politicians have a moral center, whether or not they ever use it. Diane Trumble, also on the committee, is doing all right. If they get their way—and that's a *big* if—then for a few weeks people are going to wake up. A couple of bankers will go to jail, we'll all pat ourselves on the back, and then go back to sleep."

Martin smiled and shrugged, and that was when David realized who this guy was. Martin Fucking Bishop, "The Revolution's New Face."

David had only skimmed the *Rolling Stone* profile, but he had heard plenty about Bishop from Sam Schumer's Sunday evening news show, and standing there, seeing his wife gazing doe-eyed at a man much younger than him, a man who was arguably a terrorist—at that moment he was less concerned with the future of America than with the dreary state of his marriage and impending fatherhood.

"Piñata!"

Everyone turned to find Bill moving through the living room, herding spare children toward the backyard, where they would beat an animal until it gave them candy. It was what Bill called life training.

The disruption gave Gina a chance to escape, and as she passed David she rolled her eyes, cheeks flushed from the confrontation. David stepped up into the space she had left. "Martin, is it?"

Martin acknowledged his name with a nod. Beside him, Ingrid eyeballed her husband without expression.

David leaned close and held out a hand. "David, Ingrid's husband."

They shook, then fell back, Bishop deeper into the sofa beside Ingrid, David among the crowd. He smiled, trying unsuccessfully to hide his irritation. A few years ago, in Berlin or soon after, he could have managed the trick. But he wasn't that optimist anymore.

Ingrid seemed like someone else, too; in her cheeks, the color rose. David said, "Everyone I know seems to have another egalitarian utopia already packaged and ready to go as soon as the Revolution puts them in power. What's yours?"

Martin opened his hands. "Unlike all your friends, David, I don't presume to know. I'm not smart enough. Few people are that smart, least of all—and no insult meant—your smart friends."

"And what about the guns?"

"What about them?"

"Sam Schumer says your followers are stockpiling guns."

Martin shook his head, grinning. "Schumer is a gun advocate himself, so I've never understood him harping on about that."

"But you're not denying it?"

"Why shouldn't everyone have access to a weapon? Particularly these days. Or should a gun license come with a political test?"

"But you were more specific," David pushed, more details coming to him. "You called on people to stockpile guns for the coming revolution."

Martin raised his eyebrows. "Where did you hear that?"

"Someplace reputable."

"*Schumer Says*?" He seemed amused by the idea, but: "No, David. I'm afraid I never said that."

David hesitated. He'd heard so much over the past year about this man from so many sources. Now Martin Bishop was here, next to Ingrid, casually batting away his accusations. All the while, Ingrid just watched. David tried not to let his frustration show but knew he was failing. "The system resists change. That's what you said, right?"

"Yeah."

"Then how are you planning to make change?"

Ingrid tilted her head to look him squarely in the eye, and her voice was laced with undisguised weariness and doubt when she asked, "Are you really interested, David?"

"Of course I am," he lied.

Martin thought a moment, ignoring—or pretending to ignore—the marital strife his presence was exacerbating, then said, "The left and right give lip service to the dialectic. You talk things out, argue them, and the answers will float to the surface. Look, I'm hip to that, but it only works in a world where everyone's taking part in the conversation. In this world, in *this* America, everyone's closed off in their own ideologies. They're all talking—*everyone's* talking—but no one's listening. The dialectic has failed. What's the next step?"

"Revolution?" David suggested. "*Make* everyone listen to you?"

"Make everyone listen to each other," he said.

"And how do you do that?"

"You destroy the part of the system that allows them to ignore each other. The part that teaches them that their enemies live in the other political party, or in another demographic, when the truth is that their enemies are the people above them. Rip away the veil." Bishop scratched his ear. "What would happen if, in some basement dogfight, the pit bulls suddenly saw through it all? Not only realized they were being used, but also that their masters couldn't control them, not really? That they were free? The dogs would unite and turn on their masters. It would be a bloodbath. You just have to wake them up. Show them that their enemy is the guy holding the leash."

"You collect guns," David said. "You talk about bloodbaths." He looked to Ingrid, to see if she was putting it together.

"I'm talking about uniting right and left," Bishop said, "because we've all got the same enemy."

To Ingrid, David said, "Are you *listening* to this?"

She didn't say a word. Just stared at him blankly.

Bishop said, "Look at what's going on around you, man. People are *suffering*. And we know who's to blame. It's not a mystery."

"So you're going to decide who's guilty," David told him. "Martin Bishop—judge, jury, and executioner."

"Check out *The Propaganda Ministry*. People are making hit lists so long they'll make your eyes water."

"Hit lists. That's not terrorism?"

"It's making people accountable. Just like you are. Just like I am."

"Well," David said to Bishop, "good luck with all that." Then, to Ingrid: "You get any food?"

Quietly, she said, "I'm not hungry."

"Okay, then. Good to meet you, Martin."

Bishop got up to shake hands, but David was already turning away, heading to the kitchen for a fresh beer. It was a celebratory beer, for in his mind he had just shown Ingrid that the guy she was sitting next to was a dangerous demagogue. Hadn't he?

No, he hadn't, but it took a while for him to understand how impotent his argument had been. He and Bill were with Amy and Nasser, painters who made ends meet designing websites, a job they complained was being automated out of existence. The four of them leaned against an artfully installed boulder pocked by cigarette burns, drinking and watching the kids. The grass was littered with hard candies from the gutted piñata, but instead of shoving them into their mouths the kids raced each other, stomping the candies deeper into the professionally fertilized soil, laughing. "Look how easily they get along," Bill said.

"Give them a few years," said Amy. "Soon enough, they'll be fighting over a slice of Soylent Green."

David's mind was elsewhere. It had taken another beer, maybe three, for him to revisit his exchange with Martin Bishop and realize that he'd misunderstood the situation. No one had been interested in what he had to say. Those bearded automatons shipped in from Williamsburg hadn't listened; he was nothing to them. He remembered Ingrid's face when she'd said, coldly, *I'm not hungry.* Then the truth registered: All he'd done was humiliate himself.

"That dick in there," he said abruptly. "Martin. What a joke, thinking debate skills are a substitute for actual thought."

"You read the *Rolling Stone* piece?" Nasser asked.

"Not closely."

"You should."

"I should, should I?"

"He was in Berlin for a while."

"Same time you were," Bill said, nodding.

"You were there?" Nasser asked. "Then you really should read it. Martin Bishop fell in with some left-wing radicals."

"Which left-wing radicals?"

"Named after . . ." He started snapping his fingers.

Amy tried to help out. "You know. That old German Communist lady."

David turned sharply to eyeball them. "The Kommando Rosa Luxemburg?"

"That's the one."

"Jesus," said David. "Those are the idiots who blew themselves up. Took out the entire group. Nearly killed *me*."

"Really?" asked Amy, suddenly interested.

David felt ill, remembering. "They were planning to blow up the Hauptbahnhof—the main train station." He took a swig of beer; his expression darkened. "He's here to proselytize."

"You think Bishop's recruiting?" asked Amy.

"A guy like him is always recruiting," Nasser said.

"Recruiting Ingrid," David muttered, his voice harder now.

"Fact is," Bill said, wanting to calm his friend, "Martin Bishop is a talker. You think he's ever going to pick up a gun? He's in it for the easy access to coed sex. He's in it for the attention. He's just—"

"Look," David cut in, and all three followed his hard stare across the lawn to where Martin Bishop had paused at the top of the porch steps. He was smiling, gazing at the kids, a beer in his hand. He looked, to Bill and Amy and Nasser, at peace. David saw something else entirely. He set his beer down in the grass, straightened, and walked toward the porch.

Bill said, "Hey. Really. Don't bother."

But David wasn't listening to anyone anymore.

5

KEVIN AND George watched families, the wired and tired citizens of suburban California, arriving at and leaving Red Robin. Kevin was thinking how their lives were so completely different than his. George, he suspected, was thinking of how their cushy lives would end, and soon.

"How many have you picked up?" Kevin asked.

"Eh?"

"People like me. Deserters."

George grinned. "Deserters. I like that."

"So?"

"So I took three deserters somewhere this morning, crack of dawn. When I called you I'd just gotten back."

"We're going to the same place?"

"Nope."

"Where?"

George's smile slipped away, and for the first time Kevin felt a twinge of worry. "You'll find out. All right?"

"A man just likes to know."

In answer, George turned on the radio, releasing a blast of fuzzy speed metal, then scanned until he reached 90.9, the local NPR station. Florida representative Diane Trumble had announced five subpoenas in the Plains Capital–IfW investigation, dragnetting two CEOs, a chief operating officer, and two general managers. "Hearings are being set up for after the August recess, and Representative Hanes and I look forward to having our questions answered fully and honestly."

"Preach it, sister," George said; then both men listened as a newscaster told them of an unverified report from Nigeria, that a girls' school had been attacked by Boko Haram, the Islamic extremist group that had, only three years ago, kidnapped nearly three hundred girls from another school in Chibok.

"There she is," George said, switching off the radio and nodding at a blond woman—twenty-five, maybe, with a fat purse on her shoulder—leaving the restaurant. Jeans, a black polo, and a short black waitress's apron. A Red Robin name tag identified her in big letters as TRACEY. George got out to meet her, and Kevin watched through the windshield. She was distraught, her hands fluttering. When George whispered to her, she nodded, then shook her head vigorously and raised her voice. "I'm *not* going back in there!"

George put a hand on her shoulder; she flinched, so he removed it. After he'd said a few more words, she nodded again and opened her bag. From it she removed her phone and wallet and held them out to him. He shook his head—he didn't want to touch them. Instead, he pointed. She was going to have to do this herself. Dejected, she crossed the parking lot, back toward Red Robin, and dumped them in an outside trashcan as a sated trucker left the restaurant, picking at his mouth with a toothpick and staring at her.

George looked back through the windshield at Kevin and winked.

Tracey turned to leave, then hesitated and took off her name tag and apron and threw them away as well. George folded his seat forward so she could get in the back. She tossed her heavy purse in before her, then as she climbed in glanced at Kevin and said, "Hey."

"Hey," he answered. When she settled back into her seat, he read the words embroidered on the shoulder of her black shirt:

HONOR

INTEGRITY

SEEKING KNOWLEDGE

HAVING FUN

As George got in behind the wheel, she said, "Give a lady some warning next time, okay?"

"Gotta be this way," he answered as he started the car. "Them's the rules."

She sighed loudly and looked out the side window.

Voice bright with enthusiasm, George said, "We ready?"

"Been for fucking ever," Tracey said.

6

"HEY, *YOU*!" David called, approaching the porch.

Martin Bishop had a smile for David. A lovely, open smile of welcome. "Ingrid told me about your books, man. Looking forward to reading them."

"Tell me about the Kommando Rosa Luxemburg."

Bishop's serene face broke a little, which felt like a victory to David, so he kept pushing.

"If you're so goddam peaceful, Martin, then why were you hanging out with terrorists in Berlin?"

Bishop glanced off to the side, sniffed, and said, "They weren't terrorists."

"The German government disagrees with you. So does our government. Even the UN put them on a list. Ingrid and I were living there when their bomb exploded. I was standing across the fucking street. So don't tell us they weren't terrorists." He turned to Ingrid for backup, but she wasn't looking at him. She, like Bishop, was staring into the middle distance.

"Then you must be right," Bishop said quietly, his voice strained. "If everyone says it's true then it must be true."

David came another step closer. "You've got a great scam, Martin.

I'll give you that. But, really. Everyone's dissatisfied with their lives. It's called the human condition. You tell them it's not their fault. Blame the government. Blame big business. Find a gun and start a revolution! Instead of snake oil, you're selling slogans. What's going to happen when one of your followers actually does what you say? You already caused a riot in St. Louis, but what happens when some philosophy major shoots a dean, or a cop? You know they're coming for you, right? The First Amendment won't save you. Not anymore."

Bishop's eyes wandered, but he was paying attention. Everyone was. David hadn't bothered to keep his voice down, and behind him the other guests were gathering to witness whatever was going to happen, as if this were another of Bill's surprise party events, like the piñata.

Bishop said, "Sounds like you've got more faith than I do."

"What?"

"Faith," Bishop repeated, then shook his head. "Look, I talk to people all the time. Crowds. They applaud. Occasionally they even cheer. I'm pleased to see them filled with the revolutionary spirit. But listen, man, because this is truth: They're not ready. They look at me, they see what you see: a guy who talks a good game. What I inspire in them is not revolution but the desire to go out and talk to their friends about revolution. They're not going to step up and take action."

"You don't know this."

"I'm pretty sure about it. All I can really do is make a point, and I want the people in power to hear it, too: Armed rebellion is always an option."

"So you just talk."

"You have a better idea? I'm all ears."

David took the five steps up the porch until he was standing right in front of Bishop, who was about three inches shorter. "Sure, I have one."

"Shoot."

"Stay the fuck away from my wife."

There was, of course, a pregnant pause. It wasn't David's words but the way he delivered them—hammering a strong, self-righteous index finger into his target's chest. Physical aggression from David was a rare thing, but it was almost always preceded by a lot of alcohol.

"Your wife?" Bishop asked without much emotion. "Like, your dog? Your phone?"

"You're a manipulator," David said. "You're not dragging her into your fucked-up—"

Two things kept David from finishing his sentence. First, he didn't know how to finish it; second, his words were just to distract Bishop from the fist he was throwing.

David had been drinking, though, and the punch was slow. Bill saw the hand rise and the fingers curl. Everyone else probably did, too. But Bishop had either been drinking a lot also, or he didn't care. He took David's fist on the side of his jaw, stumbled backward, arms flailing, plastic cup flying off into the grass. He balanced on one foot for half a second then collapsed back onto the porch.

In that same instant, a large man in jeans and a leather biker's jacket bolted up the steps, grabbed David by the collar of his shirt, and tossed him without effort down the steps before squatting to help Bishop to his feet.

Bill rushed over to check on David, who was grunting and holding his ribs. "You okay?"

"Get *off* me," David said, pushing Bill away, and sat up. He watched Bishop being helped to his feet, but not only by the big guy in the biker's jacket. He was also being helped by a scarlet-cheeked Ingrid, who acted as if her husband weren't even there.

The whole party, it seemed, had gathered in the backyard to watch, and their faces were a mix of confusion and revulsion, a few struck by the dumb glee of blood sport.

"I'll let you have that one," Bishop said to David, standing between Ingrid and the large, blue-eyed man with the five-day beard. "Just get hip before our next conversation."

"Come," Bill told David.

"What did he say?" David muttered, then climbed to his feet and raised his voice. "Ingrid, I think it's time we went home."

She didn't answer. She remained at Bishop's side.

Bill said to David, "*Now.* Let's go."

David was confused; it was evident from his face and the way his hands hung like useless, twitching stumps at his sides. He didn't even have words.

Ingrid finally looked at her husband and, with a voice so cold and hard that David didn't even recognize it, said, "Go ahead, David. Just go home."

"Come on," Bill said, pulling, but David shook him off and marched away, around the side of the house. He wanted to be alone.

7

THEY RETURNED to I-80, and as they progressed Kevin watched the unraveling of civilization. After Rocklin the landscape flattened, speckled with burned yellow grass and low trees. Then the land buckled and rose and the trees grew tall and lush as they entered Tahoe National Forest. Then this, too, fell away as they reached civilization's last big holdout—Reno. That metropolis grew out of the desert and then succumbed to shrubbery and low hills. Eventually, they got off of 80, taking the two-lane US 50 south, to where humans had given up trying to control the land at all.

They had been driving for more than three hours. After some initial outbursts, Tracey had fallen silent. She was, she admitted, wound up. She'd nearly clawed out the eyes of her manager before leaving the restaurant. "A pig," she told them. "A fucking cretin. *Darlin'* this, and *sweetheart* that, while he's rubbing up against my ass in the break room. But if I'd blinded him I never would've gotten out of there."

"You kept your head," George said approvingly. "That's a valuable skill."

"But I'll be back," Tracey muttered. "Frank Ramsey will find out what happens when you fuck with an angry woman."

George winked at Kevin. "See? An army of special interests."

By the time they reached the desert, conversation had ceased completely. Tracey dozed in the back, and Kevin thought about the next steps. All he had been told was that he should shed the detritus of his old life and allow this rangy man and his GTO to deliver him safely to the Promised Land. The level of trust involved was enormous, and while he submitted to it he did so with trepidation. It wasn't just trepidation; it was also that feeling he'd had back in San Francisco: abandon. Even with the fear constricting his blood vessels, the abandon felt like an intoxicant.

They were literally in the middle of nowhere—hadn't seen another car for five miles, and that had been a shoddy pickup heading back toward Reno—when George slowed and came to a stop. He looked into the rearview, where the low sun, in its last gasp, was blinding.

"What's up?" asked Kevin. Tracey was still asleep.

"I'll tell you when I see it," George said, eyes still on the mirror. "Open the glove box, will you?"

Kevin did so. It was stuffed with papers and CDs and, in the back, a leather bag.

"Pass me that," said George.

He didn't need to open the bag to know there was a pistol inside, and as he passed it over he had a nasty thought: This was the end for him. He'd said something wrong, or some hacker in the employ of Bishop had uncovered something questionable about his past. He— and, possibly, Tracey—had been brought into the desert to be executed.

But George only took out the pistol—a Remington 1911—and laid it on his knee, eyes still glued to the rearview.

"Maybe you should tell me," Kevin suggested.

George ran his tongue over his incisors. "Saw him about twenty miles back. Ford Focus. Thing is, I saw him back at the Red Robin, too."

"Same plates?"

"Yep."

"Maybe he's one of ours."

George rocked his head. "We're all going different places. Here." He reached under the steering wheel and popped the hood. "Open it up, will you?"

Kevin hesitated. "You see him?"

"Not yet. Just go open the hood and play mechanic."

As he got out, Tracey stirred but didn't wake. George watched the mirror. When Kevin propped open the hood, he was struck by the wave of hot fumes from the engine. What was the story, really? Maybe George just wanted him outside, so the gunshot wouldn't dirty up his car. Or maybe . . .

There. He saw it: a glimmer of sun reflecting off the hood of a car a half mile back. George opened his door and climbed out, hooking the pistol into his belt at the base of his back. "Yep," he said after a moment. "That's him."

The dusty red Focus slowed when George stood in its path, his hands raised, half pleading, half surrendering. As George walked over to the driver's side window, smiling, Kevin stepped out from behind the hood and leaned until he could see past the glare of the sun—the driver was a woman.

"Excuse me," he heard George say to her. "We've got car trouble."

Unsure, the woman rolled her window down a few inches and said something. A question, it sounded like.

"Yeah," George answered. "Have you tried the reception out here? Look, if you could just call Triple-A once you get some bars, that would be great."

That was when Kevin understood. He should have understood earlier, but the heat, or the disorientation of movement, or any of a hundred other stresses on his body, had rendered him momentarily stupid.

Staring hard at the woman's windshield, he used a flat hand to draw a line across his own throat. He did it twice, three times. But he couldn't see a thing from the glare. He had no idea if she was even looking in his direction.

The door to the GTO opened, and Tracey climbed out, blinking in the bright light. "What's up?"

George reached behind himself, took out the Remington, and shot three times quickly through the gap in the woman's window. *Crack, crack, crack.* Kevin saw dark splatters on the windshield.

Tracey screamed. Kevin started to approach, his knees spongy, but George was already hurrying back to them, the gun hanging at his side. "Time to go, kids!"

"*What . . .* what?" said Tracey.

George said, "Let's get moving, right? We've got a long road ahead of us."

8

FOR ABOUT an hour Bill didn't see David or Martin Bishop or the gorilla who had tossed David off the porch. Instead, he joined half a dozen conversations, moving along whenever he started to tire. Extricating himself from conversations was a skill that had been invaluable to his career, and to parties like this. He quizzed a pair of actors who'd recently fled Miami and took note of their complaints. Gina's cousins had moved to Fort Lauderdale a couple of years before and were filling her head with dreams of white beaches and an absence of snowplows. White beaches full of white retirees drinking piña coladas served by brown waiters.

By the time he spotted Ingrid on the boulder by the miniplayground, he'd decided to have it out with Gina once everyone left. He wasn't a young man anymore, but damned if he was going to cut himself off from his people to rot in the Land of Self-Obsessed Retirees.

He brought his vodka tonic over to Ingrid, who stared at the fifteen or so kids, ranging in age from an oddly independent two-year-old girl, looking wild and dirty in only a diaper, to a twelve-year-old boy with an iPad, ignoring the smaller kids who crowded around him. Ingrid showed off a tense smile as he settled next to her on the boulder. "Thanks for dealing with David earlier," she said.

"Where is he?"

"Inside, glowering. Martin's gone, but he won't let it go. He's talking to Gina about politics. As if he knows anything about politics."

"He's just worried, you know. About you."

"He's right to be worried, but not because of Martin Bishop."

Bill let his expression ask the question.

"Do you know what it's like to live with a failure?"

"You're talking about David?"

"Don't get me wrong," she said. "I don't care if he's a success or not. If he loves his work, that's enough for me. But he doesn't. He's never loved writing. He's in love with the idea of being a novelist. Of being *seen* as a novelist. That's why he's falling apart now. His publisher turned down that last book because it was *bad*. He's only writing now because we need the money. Not because he has anything to say."

"Oh," Bill said. He'd never heard her speak so critically of David before.

"His failures are turning him sour. He's probably told you about my ultimatum?"

"I think I heard something about that."

"It's not about the money. It's because he's a misery to live with. He can't feel happy about his friends' successes, because they're just more of a reminder of his own shortcomings. He snaps at me. He disappears into the back room to drink and reread *Paris Review* interviews. I don't think he's really writing anything." She turned back to the kids, unconsciously covering her belly with her forearm. "It doesn't matter anymore."

Bill considered pressing for more, but as a lawyer he'd learned how to read intent in clients' faces. He could tell when they intended to open up and when they didn't. When they didn't, posing questions was a waste of breath. So he said, "What's your take on Martin Bishop?"

She watched the children, eyes alighting on sudden movement, on leaps and swerves. She said, "He's the first person I've met in years who actually cares."

"About what?"

"Everything. All of us. You'd think he'd be livid with David. I am. But not Martin. He told me not to hate him, because David's been twisted by consumer society so many different ways that he's no longer able to see what's real and what's not. There's truth in that."

"But Bishop advocates murder, Ingrid."

"No, he doesn't. He advocates the threat of murder. There's a difference."

"Not much."

"He knows," she explained, "that without the threat of extreme action, politicians won't listen. Anything less than that, and the only thing they'll hear is big money. We all know this—you do, I do—but Martin's the only one who sees how sick it is and is willing to say it aloud. He's the only one who hasn't forgotten how to be horrified. There's nothing cynical about him."

Bill wasn't sure how to answer this, so he essentially repeated himself. "Not just murder but terrorism. The man is advocating terrorism. That's the worst kind of cynicism."

She shook her head. "Terrorism is an attempt to terrorize the masses. Martin's only interested in terrorizing the elite by giving the power back to the masses. He wants . . ." She hesitated, looking for the words. "He wants to take the fight directly to the perpetrators. He wants people to realize how easy it is. All you need is the will."

Bill had the urge—an extremely rare thing—to slap this woman out of her adoration.

She said, "Last week I was in Newark, with a few hundred others. Maybe a thousand. We were telling the DA's office that Jerome Brown mattered. A cop kills someone, he should pay. You know the answer we got—tear gas and clubs. So I come home and try to talk to David about it, but he's just . . . I don't know, pissed off. All he can see is himself. It's something Martin told me, and it's true—back in the seventies, the progressives turned off, put down their weapons, abandoned politics, and became navel-gazers. Their excuse? They would change the world through art, get people to see themselves differently. And for the next forty years this terrible world just kept hardening. Martin gets that. Eventually, people are going to have to pull a trigger, just to be heard."

"Is this world really so terrible, Ingrid?"

"For LaTanya, Jerome's five-year-old daughter? Yes, it is." She looked at Bill with a convert's intensity. "I'm no virgin, Bill. I've known Martin's type; I know just how wrong they can be. But he's different. Really, you should spend some time with him. You'll see what I see."

When she turned back to the children, the look had slipped away, but Bill kept thinking of that expression. It was more than blind conversion to a dangerous faith; it was clarity. In Ingrid's face and in her words Bill realized that she now saw the world with a clarity that David hadn't possessed for years, if ever.

They found him inside, sitting with Gina beneath a Jackson Pollock in the lounge. A beer in his hand, eyes hollow, a slur to every fifth word. But David was too exhausted to make trouble. "Come on," said Ingrid. "Let's go."

Like the most submissive animal on earth, David got to his feet and wandered in the general direction of the front door, through a cloud of See-yas and Drive-safes. Bill and Gina shepherded them down to their car. David was straight enough to give up the keys to Ingrid, and then he gave his hosts bear hugs, on the verge of tears. "Thanks, you two." Ingrid watched from the driver's seat, as if it were a scene she saw every day. David climbed in beside her and waved, then closed his eyes. As if he were completely alone in that car. Then they were gone.

Bill and Gina stared at the lingering dust cloud of their exit. "And you wonder why I want to move south," Gina said.

They'd climbed the front steps again when a police car rolled up the drive and parked where David and Ingrid's car had been. "Goddam neighbors complaining," Bill said as he headed back to the two uniforms climbing out of their car, donning caps. Gina waited by the front door, watching along with a few others. At the far end of the front porch, an actor from Provincetown spat curses, trying to figure out what to do with his smoldering joint.

The police talked for a while to Bill, who shook his head, then spoke at length. It went on too long to be a complaint about the noise, so Gina headed down the stairs and introduced herself. That was when she learned that they were here for Martin Bishop and Benjamin Mittag—Mittag, the gorilla who had thrown David off the porch. Finally, it seemed, the two leaders of the Massive Brigade had broken the letter of the law, though the officers wouldn't tell them which law. It didn't matter, though, for Bishop and Mittag had already disappeared.

AFTER THE PARTY

SUNDAY, JUNE 18, TO
SATURDAY, JULY 8, 2017

1

AS SHE walked through the mess that a dozen caterers were working to set right again, Jersey cops questioning still-drunk financiers and stoned artists, Special Agent Rachel Proulx could see that it had been an excellent party, the kind that you can only have in this America, the America people thought of as the land of plenty. Hot dogs and veggie burgers for the kids, salmon for the ladies, steak for the fellas. Scattered bowls of nuts, chips, salsa and guacamole, and sembei of a variety of shapes and spices. Heineken and Foster's and Shiner Bock, Cuervo Gold, Bombay Sapphire, Tito's, Jim Beam, Glenfiddich, and many shades of wine. All this and seventy-five friends in a three-story Victorian on an acre of parklike land in the estate section of Montclair, New Jersey.

On another Sunday, she would have missed this entirely. Arlington was four hours away, but her mother had fallen again on Friday, and so she'd spent the weekend at the condo in Croton-on-Hudson, just over the New York border, feeding her mother soup, finding her favorite weekend TV shows, and listening to her stories about a childhood Rachel could no longer clearly remember. So when the call came in, it wasn't much to set her mother up with the remote, cross the Tappan Zee, and take the hour's drive south to Montclair.

"I'm off to bust someone famous," she'd told her mother as she gathered her keys.

"The president?" her mother asked, a twinkle in her eye.

"Martin Bishop."

"Who?"

That morning, an anonymous female had called the Bureau field office on Federal Plaza from one of the dwindling number of Manhattan pay phones, down by Stuyvesant Town. The caller had directed the FBI operator to a particular storage garage near the Jersey Shore, because "the Massive Brigade's hiding some scary shit there." When the operator asked for clarification, she hung up.

The caller—whoever she was—knew that these days all one had to do was say "Martin Bishop" or "Benjamin Mittag" or "Massive Brigade" for the Bureau to sit up and take notice. An agent was dispatched to Jersey, where the storage facility's owner unlocked unit number 394. The agent was patched through to Rachel Proulx, presently with her mother in Croton-on-Hudson. "We've got those fuckers now," he told her.

Locating Mittag and Bishop had taken a little longer—some phone calls to contacts and then a more useful, though possibly illegal, favor called in to a friend at the NSA who tracked the two men's phones to a party in New Jersey. The Montclair police were sent in to assess and take the two men into custody, but by the time they arrived the suspects were in the wind, their phones no longer visible in the cellular firmament.

By that point, Rachel was cruising down the Garden State Parkway, and while the news was disappointing she didn't slow down. If she'd learned anything during twenty years in the Bureau, it was that the key to success was neither genius nor brute force but persistence.

A mustached officer in a too-tight uniform approached and shook her hand. "Best we got is they left together, about a half hour before we arrived."

"And the hosts?"

"In the kitchen," he said, a thumb over his shoulder. As she started in that direction, he said, "What did they find?"

Rachel looked back at him.

"In the storage space. No one told us."

"An FIM-92 Stinger missile and shoulder-mounted launcher," she said.

He shook his head and whistled as her phone beeped an incoming message from Sam Schumer: "Is it true about Bishop and Mittag? Call me." She put the phone away with a sigh and went back to examining the premises.

She found more caterers in the kitchen, furiously washing soiled glasses. At the small dining table, a sweet-faced detective sat with Bill and Gina Ferris, early sixties. Introductions were made, and once Rachel began questioning the Ferrises it became apparent to the detective that he wasn't needed, so he made himself useful elsewhere.

"How did you come to know Martin Bishop?"

"We didn't come to know him at all," Gina told her. "I'm not even sure who invited him."

"Harry," said Bill. "I think Harry White invited him."

"Did he?" asked Gina. "Last time we ask him over."

Gina Ferris's comments were more pointed and direct than her husband's. With Rachel's encouragement, she recalled the political discussion that had been interrupted by the piñata. "All of us have gripes," she said. "I'll bet you do, too. But, come on. That kind of violence hasn't been in vogue since 1975."

"Are you sure about that?" asked Rachel. Over the last couple of years the country had looked to her a lot like the early seventies: polarization, weekly demonstrations, occasional ruptures of violence. The Massive Brigade was only one incarnation of the rage infecting every end of the political spectrum.

"Well," Gina said, "not among my friends."

"What about you?" Rachel turned to Bill. "You're a lawyer. You could be useful to someone like Bishop."

Bill leaned back, a man as comfortable with his newfound retirement as he was with a kitchen full of caterers. "Bishop never asked
for my representation. I don't even think I spoke to him."

"We heard there was a fight between Bishop and someone,"
Rachel said. "A David Parker."

"The novelist," Gina said as she stood up.

"I wouldn't call it a fight," said Bill. "A sucker punch. But David's
been going through some rough times. He thought Bishop was
coming on to his wife."

"That man is a mess," Gina confided.

"Really?"

They started in about David and Ingrid, and soon they had shared
more about the state of the Parkers' marriage than, Rachel suspected,
they had planned to. She scribbled it all down in a notepad with a
mechanical pencil. "And when Bishop and Mittag left, they left
together?"

Gina had seen Bishop in the living room, drinking with Harry
White. He'd answered his phone and looked concerned. That was
when he patted Harry's arm and went to Mittag. They left the room
together, but Gina couldn't say whether or not they'd gotten in the
same car.

Rachel straightened and smiled to put them at ease. But she could
tell that it didn't work—both Bill and Gina tensed visibly. "What do
you think?" she asked conversationally. "Bishop walks out of here
and . . . what? Any idea what his next step would be?"

Gina answered first. "He's going to hide away until someone like
you tracks him down."

"So you're not worried about his revolutionary talk?"

"Should I be?"

Rachel shrugged.

"He didn't move," Bill said.

Both women looked at him.

"Bishop. When David hit him. He just stood there. David swung, and Bishop didn't move. He saw it coming—we all did. But . . . he didn't care."

"What do you think that means?"

Bill thought about this, his silence a heavy thing as they waited for some wisdom, but all he said was "I suppose it means he's reckless."

Rachel spoke to a handful of guests—most had made their exits soon after the police arrived. From what she gathered, it had been like most parties, full of small cliques that were careful not to mix. She'd been to enough of them herself, Washington shindigs where she stuck close to others from her office, and the conversation inevitably turned to Hoover Building gossip. In a back room, she called Harry White, but he claimed not to have invited Bishop after all.

Had Bishop and Mittag known from the start that the police were heading toward them? Or had that phone call to Bishop alerted them that they should disappear? She had no idea. The Montclair cops promised reports from their interviews, yet she knew from their expressions that she could expect little.

2

IT WAS nearly ten when she got back to Croton-on-Hudson and found her mother dozing in front of the Food Network. Rachel poured herself a glass of rosé, changed the channel to catch the tail end of *Schumer Says,* and settled in with Sam's particular brand of American populist venom. Schumer wiped at his curly mustache and told his audience that things were about to become a lot more dangerous in America, because Martin Bishop had gone AWOL. Schumer's "inside sources" had informed him about the missile launcher and the sudden disappearing act. "Public enemy number one has just gone off the grid. And he's armed to the teeth."

Two years ago, before Sam Schumer moved his show from YouTube to Fox and dialed up the apocalyptic talk, he had been the kind of independent journalist Rachel Proulx could talk to and know that what she wanted to share with the public would make it out relatively unscathed. It was a relationship that served them both: She gained access to an audience that avoided the so-called mainstream media, and Sam Schumer could claim to have a bona fide source within the Bureau. This tit-for-tat had been approved by the then-assistant director in large part because Rachel had argued her case so eloquently, and the upper echelons grew to appreciate the gung ho patriot who always spun the story in their favor. Then Schumer moved to television, and the sudden national exposure did something to him. He still defended the Bureau, but he discovered that the loudest of his competitors, the ones who kicked up the dirt of their audiences' fears, always beat his numbers.

The shift became apparent nine months ago, when the breaking story on *Schumer Says* was called "Invasion from the South"—an exposé on the future of illegal immigration. "By 2028, the southern half of the United States will for all practical purposes be Mexico's northern states. Expect secession. Expect war."

Schumer Says became Sunday night's most-watched news program.

Given her role in bringing him on, the irony was lost on no one when, three months ago, Rachel asked to terminate the relationship with Schumer. The new assistant director, Mark Paulson, threw her old arguments right back at her as he turned her down. Now that Schumer's audience reached a half million each Sunday night in the treasured 25–54 demographic, no one in the Bureau wanted to throw away a megaphone of that size, even if Sam Schumer occasionally went off script.

Rachel wasn't going to make it easy, though, which was why, when Schumer's second text message—*On air soon. What's the scoop?*—came minutes after she left Bill and Gina's house, she'd ignored it. Schumer wanted the scoop on Martin Bishop's disappearing act, but as yet there was no scoop. But Schumer had found another source—probably the Montclair cop she'd told about the missile launcher.

He brought on a retired CIA officer who said that if they wanted to predict the Massive Brigade's next move, it would be best to look at the Berlin terrorist group Bishop had been inspired by, the Kommando Rosa Luxemburg. "They were mad bombers, and the Germans were lucky they blew themselves up. But there's no reason to think Bishop is going to be that stupid. We'll need to ramp up security at all major transit hubs."

"Americans need to stay vigilant," Schumer suggested.

His guest nodded seriously. "Everybody needs to stay vigilant."

Rachel poured herself a second glass and watched as Schumer and his guests investigated security weaknesses in America's infrastructure and spun through all the potential terrorist acts the Massive Brigade could be planning. They cherry-picked quotes from *The Propaganda Ministry* and considered which lines to fear most. By the time he signed off, Schumer was in a somber mood, telling his audience to stay strong and not hide at home—"Go out, do some shopping. Otherwise the terrorists win."

"Doing your part for the economy," Rachel said, toasting Schumer as her mother stirred. Rachel got up to help her. "Let's get you to bed. I'm going to have to leave early."

"Did you get him?"

"Who?"

"The president?"

As Rachel guided her mother through her nighttime routine, she gave her a rundown of the situation. "But you'll find them?"

"Of course I will," she said, because in that moment she believed it. It was more than the faith that all FBI agents share in the methodologies of the Bureau; it was a personal conviction. Back in 2009, she'd first watched Martin Bishop speak in San Francisco while on an extended research project, looking into the depth and breadth of the radical left and its security implications. Standing before a sparse Berkeley crowd, he hadn't been the orator he would become, but in his conviction and clear, simple logic Rachel had been able to read the promise of his future: crowds. She'd duly put him into her report as someone to watch, an assessment that many in the Bureau now considered prophetic. She'd predicted his rise; therefore, she would be the one to hasten his fall.

She was on the road by four Monday morning, and by the time she crossed into Maryland the sun had risen to bleach derelict warehouses off the highway. She parked near her Arlington apartment, showered, then hurried to the office and conferred with her colleagues. It soon became apparent that, whether or not Bishop and Mittag had been warned about the police coming to pick them up, they had been prepared to disappear, for there was no ripple in the bureaucratic waters. One moment they were there, and then, after leaving Bill and Gina's party, the two men simply vanished.

But that wasn't the worst of it. Reports were trickling in from field offices all over the country of dozens of young people also vanishing. Though they'd only had time to scratch the surface of these disappearances, the common thread became obvious as soon as they checked the young people's online activity: They were all members of the Massive Brigade.

3

EIGHT YEARS ago, she'd thought, *Someday this man will have crowds.*

He was no older than thirty, and genetics had blessed him with a permanent tan and a face too pretty to be wasted in academia. He stood at the podium under the fluorescent lights, speaking in a faintly quivering voice to the half-full auditorium. He was the next-to-last speaker of the day, smack in the middle of a five-day political colloquium hosted by the University of California, Berkeley. Given that Martin Bishop's résumé consisted solely of community work in Austin, Texas, and a "research trip" to Germany, she was surprised he had been given space in the tight schedule, so she'd decided to check him out. The crowd was a mix of American political types: aging hippies, rumpled economists, poli-sci students sporting adolescent mustaches, and punk rockers with dyed and shaved heads who chewed gum, the smacking sound carried by the perfect acoustics of the room.

Bishop said, "The classical checks on political malfeasance—the balance of government branches and free elections—have done little to fix a broken system. Politicians do as they like. So something else is needed. But what? Periodic votes of confidence? Annual independent investigations? What about actual threats to their person?

You see where I'm going here. I'm looking for ways to instill *fear* in our representatives, because American democracy is built on the most basic of human motivators: self-preservation."

Only one audience member, sitting three seats in front of her, seemed out of place: a fortysomething in suit and tie, alternately listening to Martin Bishop's critique of American democracy and checking messages on his two cell phones. This businessman, like the punks, chewed gum, but he was polite enough to keep his mouth shut.

"Because there will come a time—and we're closing in on it— when the hypocrisy and anger will reach such a fever pitch that mass revolt will seem the only option. Not just for the disenfranchised, but also for those who have been well served by the system. Even the rich, rumor has it, possess hearts."

A titter of polite laughter spread through the auditorium.

Despite the mild self-consciousness, which experience would wash away, Bishop moved as he spoke, using his hands as props, shaping the air as if caressing the faces of the downtrodden electorate he worried so much about. His voice, once he got rolling, had an actor's timbre, rich and liquid and flavored with just the right measure of emotion without risking mawkishness.

A phone hummed, but it wasn't hers; the businessman took out a *third* phone, read the number, then put it to his ear and whispered, head down. She couldn't make out the words, but the rhythm was odd, off. It was . . . it wasn't English. It was Russian.

When Martin Bishop finished his remarks and modestly thanked the crowd for its attention, he was greeted with light applause. He smiled, shuffling away from the podium. While most filed for the door, a handful approached the stage to talk with him. Rachel did neither. She pulled out a small digital camera and surreptitiously took photos of Bishop's admirers. She was surprised when the Russian businessman approached, too, and . . . *there*: in Bishop's face, an instant recognition—first surprised discomfort, then a glowing smile. The Russian leaned close and whispered into his ear, handed over something from his pocket, then left, climbing the stairs toward the exit.

Rachel got up and followed.

She kept her distance the way she'd learned to do over months of shadowing people in the Bay Area, giving her quarry plenty of leash as he wound a path through the university's bucolic grounds. The sun was uncharacteristically hot that day, but he was in no hurry, nor was she, and she watched him take and make four or five calls by the time he left the campus and reached Durant and Fulton. There, he entered an unassuming watering hole called the Beta Lounge.

She waited on the street, checking her watch and thinking, as she often did these days, of how quickly a divorce changes a life. Only hours after signing those papers in a cramped DC lawyer's office and looking Gregg in his hateful eye for the last time, this project had come to her like a divine vision. Get away, far away, to the other side of the country. Shed all the useless detritus of a decade in the DC suburbs. Devote herself to the pure acquisition of knowledge.

She put on her Sunday smile and went inside.

The Beta Lounge looked more like a lunch spot than a bar, and at the six-person tables couples drank beer and wine. Her Russian was at the minimalist counter, reading his phone, a half-full, damp martini glass in front of him with a pair of olives on a bamboo pick. He was still chewing gum. She climbed onto a stool two down from him and nodded to the bartender, a bald guy with a bar code tattooed to his neck.

"Glass of white," she said.

"What kind?"

"Cold and dry. That's the kind."

The bartender grinned as he went for a bottle. The Russian put away his phone. She cocked her head as if realizing something mildly surprising. "Wait—were we just at the same lecture?"

"I don't know," he said. "Were we?"

Even though he spoke and, with his sad, bruised eyes, looked Russian, his bland midwestern accent was entirely American. She said, "Martin Bishop."

"Then, yes." He lifted his glass, a light smile. "I guess we were."

4

ANSARI'S parents had moved from Pakistan on student visas
ears earlier—Mariam was a pediatrician, Faisal a professor of
studies at the University of Maryland. They sat with Rachel
unt Sinai waiting room done up in calming colors. Their son,
hem know, was not under arrest, but the situation was seri-
had joined a subversive organization, "and were it not for
ical condition he would be with them now, in hiding."
June 18, twenty-four-year-old Ibrahim had been struck down
ain aneurysm while riding a Greyhound from Baltimore to
ond. He'd been in a coma for six hours, snapping out of
Monday morning. Now it was Tuesday, and Rachel had
by on her way to Manhattan to confer with the field office
ral Plaza, bringing along Ted Pierce, a young agent, to act as
. Ibrahim had been taken out of the ICU and moved to a
room, his cranium wrapped in bandages to cover the piece
l that had been removed by a surgeon in order to reach his

know what you people do," Mariam said. "You've got nothing
Martin Bishop. Empty hands. So to make yourself look good
d kids who can't defend themselves, so that when Congress

The bartender returned with a bottle of Riesling and a glass, then
poured her a taste. She sipped, approved, and watched him fill it up
as she said to her Russian, "You live here?"

He shook his head. "Just a tourist today."

"Pretty lousy tourist, wasting your time with lectures. Where
are you coming from?"

He stared at his glass for a few seconds. *Ah,* she thought. She'd
overstepped. "Sorry, not my business."

He snapped out of his reverie. "No, no. Switzerland. I work for
a pharmaceutical out of Bern."

"Good for you," she said, and stuck out a hand. "Rachel Proulx."

"James Sullivan."

Now that she had a name, she could relax, and they talked about
Europe and America and travel. He was smart and charming and not
entirely unhandsome, and while he never mentioned a wife or children
she noticed the telltale white strip of flesh around the tanned ring
finger of his left hand. A man on vacation who takes off his wedding
ring when going to a bar . . . it didn't take a special agent in the FBI
to figure out what he was game for.

"And what pays your rent?" he asked.

"Writer. Well, I'm trying to be one."

"You write; therefore, you're a writer. What got you started?"

There was the story that she'd lived on for five months, which
hued close to the truth—a divorce with ample savings and a desire
to reinvent herself. But she hesitated to use that now, and she wasn't
sure why. Yet before she could come up with something new, he raised
his left hand and showed off the pale band on his finger. "This is why
I'm a shitty tourist. Three weeks."

So there it was. She relaxed. "It gets easier."

He furrowed his brow. "How long for you?"

"Eight months."

"Ah," he said, then finished his drink, waved to the bartender, and
pointed at his glass for another. Then, to Rachel: "You?"

"Why, thank you, Mr. Sullivan."

When their fresh drinks arrived—Sullivan's martinis were vodka—he asked how long she'd been married. Lying didn't even occur to her. "Six years. You?"

"Eight." He lifted the pick from his glass and slid off an olive with his teeth. "*His* fault, I assume."

"Of course."

"Affair?" He held up a hand. "Sorry, now I'm the one prying."

She surprised herself by stating the truth. "He hit me."

James dropped his pick, and his somber face looked so full of hurt that she wanted to stroke his hand and say, *It's all right,* but didn't. Finally, he spoke in a voice that had become deep and cold. "Well, I hope he only got one chance to do it."

"Of course," she lied, because the truth was an embarrassment. It had taken four of those six years, the endless naïveté, the belief that a man who expressed disappointment with his fists could magically change. Remembering the woman she'd been—and it wasn't so long ago—was humiliating.

So after another sip she turned the conversation to politics. At the start of the year, America had sworn in its first African American president, and the optimism, particularly on the left, was still high. She'd even seen it among the radicals she'd gotten to know, though their enthusiasm was always tempered by a wait-and-see attitude— no matter the color of his skin, the man was still a politician.

James wasn't derailed by the shift in subject, so she asked what he thought of Martin Bishop.

He set down his glass and rocked his head noncommittally. "Hard to tell from a single lecture."

She was disappointed that he wouldn't admit he knew Bishop. She so wanted to know: What was Martin Bishop, a budding political agitator, doing with friends in the international pharmaceutical industry?

"He *is* a compelling speaker," she pushed.

"There are a lot of compelling speakers," James said, "especially in America. We're raised to be salespeople; we sell ourselves. Guys

like Bishop—clever as he might be—a
reason to think that he's going to mov

"I got the impression you knew h

"I don't," he said, steamrolling over
a guy like him . . . he's an insect in th
corporations."

She held back her instinctual laugh.
pressed smile that broke out. He shrugge
ming. He took out one of his and rea
look crossed his face. "Ah, shit. I'm late
got off the stool.

"While on vacation?"

"There's no such thing as a vacatic
phone. "Not with these things."

"Too bad."

He said, "I'd love to meet up again,
I'm not going to have a spare minute."

"Next time."

He offered his hand, which seemed
she want? A kiss? "It's been very good to
Keep writing. You'll do well, I'm sure."

"Better than Martin Bishop?"

He grinned. "Of that I have no doul

Later, when she handed over her ph
asked Washington for a trace on James Su
ecutive based in Switzerland, it was almos
called her back to explain that there was r
for any international company registered
James Sullivan wasn't on any hotel registries
nor on any flight manifests for the night o

IBRAHIN
thirty y
politica
in a Mc
she let
ous. H
his me
O
by a bi
Richn
it early
stoppe
at Fede
witnes
private
of sku
brain.
"
on thi
you fi

asks what you've been spending tax dollars on you can list off kids in hospitals."

"Mariam," said Faisal.

"Mariam, what?" she snapped. "I've been through my son's room. He didn't even pack a bag. How was he going to vanish without a change of clothes? Tell me that, woman."

"Lauren Harrison," said Rachel. "Frank Sellers, Laura Nell, Soon-Yi Koh, Kyle Vanderbilt, Daniella Piotrowski. Those are six people, off the top of my head, who disappeared in exactly the same way. One was heading to the grocery. Two climbed out of their bedroom windows. The other three were on their way to work. None of them packed a change of clothes. They all left their phones behind."

"Are you listening to her?" Mariam asked her husband. "She tells us that they showed no signs, and then they disappeared. Now our son showed no signs, so he must have been trying to become a terrorist!" To Rachel: "You need to take a logic class."

She didn't need their consent to talk to Ibrahim. She'd known this going in, and Pierce had even suggested they skip the step. But Rachel knew how difficult it could become for the Bureau if the parents made a stink afterward, so she called them beforehand and asked for this conversation. She reached into her briefcase, took out a slender manila folder, and said, "I understand how you feel."

"You do *not*."

"Let her speak," said Faisal.

"Over the last forty-eight hours," Rachel told them, "the Bureau has been deluged with missing persons reports. All young people, between the ages of eighteen and thirty-two, and a disproportionate number of them are college students like your son. They all vanished on Sunday, the same day Bishop disappeared. Of that particular group, only two have been found."

"How many?" Mariam asked. "How many is enough for you to harass my son?"

"A hundred and twelve. From all across the country. But that number's growing every hour."

Conversation stalled as Ibrahim's parents looked at each other.

"While these people showed no signs that they were going to disappear, nearly all of them were connected to Martin Bishop's group. Emails, chat rooms, blog comments. Here." She passed the folder to Faisal. He opened it, and Mariam, after staring hard at Rachel for the better part of a minute, looked over her husband's shoulder and began to read with him.

"Where'd you get this?" Faisal asked without looking up.

"Does it matter?"

"You're damned right it does," he said, but without venom.

"NSA gave it to us."

He went back to reading, along with his wife, an analysis of Ibrahim Ansari's online activity over the last six months. Rachel saw the expression in Mariam's face shift from anger to confusion.

Pierce was standing outside Ibrahim's room, typing on his phone. He looked up at her. "Yes?"

"Let's go."

But then her phone vibrated, and she checked the screen: SCHUMER, SAM.

"You ever going to answer that?" Pierce asked.

"Not until I have to," she said, and put away the phone.

Ibrahim had been awake for twenty-four hours, but the medication still kept him fuzzy. He listened to their names, and when they showed their badges he shook his head, grinning. "My luck."

"How do you mean?" Rachel asked as she pulled up a chair to sit close to him.

"What you think? I go from free to this." He looked down his arm, where a tube supplied him with a steady drip. "And now you."

"Where were you going, Ibrahim?"

"Richmond."

"And then?"

"Just Richmond."

"Who were you going to meet?"

"A friend."

"Who?"

He sighed, then looked across to the door; through its window his mother was peering in, expressionless. He shook his head again. "You can't find them. You know that, right?"

"Can't find who?"

"There's thousands of us. Millions, probably. We're everywhere."

Rachel shook her head. "There are maybe a hundred and fifty of you, Ibrahim. Not a thousand, and certainly not a million. We know this because we're the FBI and we know a lot of things. More than you do. More than Martin Bishop knows. So don't play the ominous card with me. Just tell me who you were going to meet."

Ibrahim frowned. "Pass me that water."

Rachel took the plastic cup from the side table and watched him sip from the straw. Behind her, Pierce's phone hummed and he put it to his ear, turning to face the corner and whisper. Finally, Ibrahim said, "George. I was going to meet a guy named George at the bus station."

"And then?"

"And then I'm gone."

Once they were in the corridor again, Pierce said, "When we get to the city we might want to make a stop before Federal Plaza."

"Why?"

"David Parker's wife has disappeared."

5

IT WAS afternoon by the time they reached the tall co-op in Tribeca, and as she buzzed the intercom Pierce surveyed the crowds—tourists, mostly—inching along the sidewalk under the ever-present Manhattan scaffolding, a city in a perpetual state of repair.

"Yeah?" David Parker said through the speaker.

"Special Agent Rachel Proulx," she told him. "We spoke on the phone."

A hum, and they were inside, passing mailboxes where someone had stenciled KILL ALL PIGS. Pierce grunted at that. The graffiti inside the elevator was limited to a single word in Sharpie: MASSIVE. Though they both took a moment to reflect, neither bothered to comment on it. Instead, Pierce said, "You should read *Gray Snow*. It's his best one."

"You're a fan?"

"I've never been a fan of anyone in my life. But the novel's all right."

She noticed immediately that David Parker had been drinking. He might not have touched any alcohol that morning, but the pungent stink of gin was leaking from his pores, misting up a claustrophobic apartment that had fallen to a remarkable level of disarray, considering his wife had only walked out yesterday morning. On a table lay an old issue of *Rolling Stone*—she knew that issue, because it featured Martin Bishop. And on the screen of his open laptop, a YouTube video had been paused in the middle of one of Sam Schumer's rants.

While Pierce drove, she had followed up on the details of Parker's life, first by visiting his website with its overly detailed bio page, then by sifting through the public records. A string of bookstore and library jobs until the publication of his first novel, at which point he ran off to Berlin to live the expat life. There, he'd met Ingrid Frasier, who worked for the Starling Trust, an international philanthropic organization.

David exhaled, deflated, and settled on a stiff Bauhaus chair, hands on his knees. He told them the story of Bill and Gina's party. The way he told it, it was clear that David Parker had taken everything Martin Bishop had said and done as a personal affront. "Seduction. That's what I was worried about. But it was worse than that."

"What's worse?" asked Rachel.

"Recruitment."

"That's your theory?"

David leaned back, hands flashing open. "It's not a theory; it's a *fact*. Why else would she leave? She's pregnant. She wouldn't just take my child away. Not unless *he* convinced her the world would be better for it."

Rachel's opinion, which she formed as she watched him pace and lay out his opinions as facts, was that David Parker was utterly self-absorbed: If his wife picked up and left, it *couldn't* be the result of his behavior, that wouldn't do. David Parker could only be the victim of terrorism. She knew his type all too well.

Besides, Ingrid Parker didn't fit the profile of a Massive Brigade convert—she was forty, with (as David had just pointed out) a child on the way. She wasn't part of Martin Bishop's demographic. She'd walked out for the same reason women walk out every day: Their husbands have become unbearable.

"What happened when you got home from the party?"

He thought about that, staring down at his joined hands in his lap. He was closing himself off from them. "Well, we didn't fight. There was peace in the house."

Rachel stopped herself from correcting David, from saying that he had *wanted* peace in the house and had hoped that silence signified that he'd achieved it. In real life it rarely did.

Maybe sensing her doubt, he amended his statement. "Well, we didn't really speak at all. I put on the radio in the car, and when we got back here she went to shower and I turned on the TV. *Schumer Says*." He hesitated. "And there he was, all over again. Martin Fucking Bishop. Gone like a thief in the night. I thought about getting her out of the shower so she could see for herself what a threat he was."

"But you didn't."

He shook his head. "I made myself a drink and kept watching. Next thing I knew it was morning, and she had gone to work." He reached into his pocket and took out a folded piece of lined paper. "I found this in the kitchen."

When he handed it over, she unfolded it and saw *David* written in tight script. Then she unfolded it the rest of the way and read:

I need some time to myself. I'm staying with Brenda. Don't call, and don't come. I'll be in touch.

—Ingrid

"Who's Brenda?"

"Old friend, lives up in Pelham."

"Did you call Ingrid anyway?"

"Of course I did."

"And?"

He scratched his brow. "And she cut me off. I apologized, okay?

I've been . . . look, I haven't been the best husband. Since my last book was . . . well, it was rejected. And I've been hard to live with. But I had a new idea. I tried to explain it to her. She knows—when the work's going well, I'm great to live with."

"But that didn't convince her?"

Again, he reached for his face. He was a smorgasbord of tells. Whatever kind of woman Ingrid was, she obviously hadn't fallen for his BS. "She told me she needed a little time to clear her head."

"That sounds reasonable."

"Later I found out that she did call Brenda and ask to stay a few days," David explained. "But a few hours later she called from work to tell Brenda she'd changed her mind. Brenda thought that meant she was coming back home, but she never did."

"Other friends? Family?"

"I've called her friends. Her mother died last year. That was all the family she had."

Rachel considered the facts. It hadn't even been forty-eight hours since David had last seen his wife, and it was unlikely that a mother-to-be had decided to disappear and join the Massive Brigade. She expected that within a day or two he would hear from her, but to help him get through those hours she said, "We can watch out for her—credit cards, phone, email sign-ins. We'll find her."

"No, you won't."

His reaction surprised her. "You sure about that?"

"Ingrid doesn't do half measures," he said. "If she doesn't want to be found, she won't be. Because she commits. And when she's committed to something there's nothing else in the world for her." He pulled examples from their shared past. "First she was into yoga, and all day she'd speak that annoying lingo, and she kept rearranging the furniture to get the energies just right. Feng shui. But that wasn't for her, so she turned to the kabbala. Other than work, she refused to leave the house. After that she spent a horrible month with est . . ."

"I see."

The *Rolling Stone* caught David's eye, and he picked it up. He opened it to the Martin Bishop feature—a piece that, in Rachel's opinion, glamorized a dangerous man. "I know him," David said quietly.

"Bishop?"

"Not *know*—I'd never met him before. But I know his type. I could tell what kind of guy he was. He's dangerous."

"You're right," she admitted.

"No one else believes it," he said. "They think he's just hot air. But when I punched him, that's when I realized it. He . . ." David paused, thinking. "He was waiting for the punch. He *expected* it. As if he'd written the script beforehand, and I was just playing to it."

She remembered Bill Ferris saying something similar. When two people notice the same thing, pay attention.

"Why would he do that?" she asked.

David leaned back, throwing out his hands. "I don't know. To get sympathy? To push Ingrid farther away from me? The point is that he was willing to sacrifice himself for some little goal. Risk a broken nose or a concussion, just to make whatever point he wanted to make." He sniffed. "Talkers don't do that. Talkers pull back and save their pretty faces. Bishop is a true believer."

Earlier that morning Rachel had read the Nashville field office's interview with Bishop's parents. They painted the young Martin as a wholehearted Christian with love in his heart. His father insisted that Martin "only wants to serve God by serving others. You have to understand. Martin is not like our daughters. He was always special. For him, the value of his life is measured by how much he can help those around him."

So this is his way of helping, the local agent asked, *preaching for people to rise up against the government?*

His father shrugged. "We haven't seen him in seven, eight years."

"He'd just come back from Germany," Bishop's mother clarified.

"And what he saw during his time abroad," his father added. "I don't even know what he saw. But it taught him that people in America—the very poor, the blacks, the immigrants—are tricked into fighting each other. He said that this was backward, and that all of us are the victims. We just don't want to see it."

Rachel said, "There was some overlap between you, Ingrid, and Bishop in Berlin. Is it possible she knew him there?"

David shook his head, then frowned. "Well, she never said."

"A long shot," she admitted as she stood. "You'll call us if you hear anything?"

"Just find my wife, okay? She's not taking my kid away."

Later, as she and Pierce were getting back to their oversized Suburban, her phone rang, but it wasn't Sam Schumer. It was an analyst back in DC. "We've got an update on how many people have disappeared."

"Hit me."

"Two hundred and thirty-eight."

"Shit," she said, and closed her eyes, an uncomfortable feeling slipping over her. Despite her doubt, she said, "Let's get someone over to the Starling Trust offices here in Manhattan."

"Sure. Why?"

"To scour Ingrid Parker's work computer."

She hung up, then looked back up the street to David Parker's building, wondering why she couldn't shake her natural distaste for the man. Then she knew why: He reminded her of Gregg, her ex, he of the sanctimonious outrage and sudden fist. Narcissism made flesh. She didn't think of Gregg often these days, but when she did her thoughts inevitably slid further, to his new wife, Mackenzie. She wondered if he hit her, too, in their little house outside DC; and if he didn't, why not?

Which made her, she knew as she climbed into the Suburban, a horrible person.

6

ASSISTANT DIRECTOR Mark Paulson squinted down the length of the conference table, eyeing three of his deputies, as well as Rachel. He'd just returned from a meeting in the Oval Office, and it had taken something out of his usual swagger. Less than two months ago, Director Comey had been dismissed by the president, so any visit to Pennsylvania Avenue, alongside the new director, was fraught. "You know what the president said to us? *Your only mission is to keep the country safe, and don't let the Bureau get between you and that goal.* Not those words, but that sentiment. That's the kind of opinion he has of this organization."

A collective sigh of irritation. Lou Barnes mouthed the word "prick" as, out of the side of her mouth, Erin Lynch said, "And when he said safety was your only job, you believed him?"

"Guilty as charged, Erin," Paulson said, raising his hands. "But you know what? I don't care. I'm going to be the naïve kid in Washington. I'll be Mr. Smith. Because in the end right *will* prevail."

Lou Barnes's arms were crossed over his flabby chest—they had been glued there the entire meeting, as if there were far more important things waiting for him at the Intelligence desk. Rachel had noticed this. She'd noticed how the mood of the room had shifted as soon as Paulson entered it, having come straight from the Mountain to this pokey little conference room on the second floor of the Hoover Building, with its air conditioning that sounded like a vacuum cleaner. Once he arrived, the ripples of anxiety and discontent flattened like a thread that had suddenly been pulled taut. Word around the office was that none of these deputies had any respect for Paulson, who before his appointment had been a longtime CEO of the now-embattled Plains Capital Bank, having chosen the perfect time to step down and back a long-shot candidate on the campaign trail. Not so long ago, Paulson had simply appeared out of thin air, claiming a law enforcement expertise that had yet to be proven. But there was no sign of these administrators' contempt here. They were surprisingly good actors.

"So tell us," Barnes said. "Tell us what the Oracle requires."

"Answers," Paulson told him, tapping his ballpoint against the table, "and solutions."

Erin Lynch, again: "I thought *he* was hired to solve America's ills." Grins all around. Erin was on a roll.

But Paulson didn't grin. He didn't even look at her. He lowered his head and opened the slim folder he'd brought with him. Then he read aloud: "Martin Louis Bishop. Benjamin Thomas Mittag." He looked up at everyone, even Rachel. "Ring some bells?"

Finally rising out of his silence, Richard Kranowski from Cyber said, "Really? The president's losing sleep over Bishop? He's got to stop watching Sam Schumer."

Lynch saw her chance. "Anything to distract from the approval numbers."

This time, her joke fell flat. Though Mark Paulson had only been installed two months ago, everyone else knew that they had moved on from the warm-up shots that typified his senior meetings. Those warm-up periods had grown noticeably shorter, particularly now that the director, facing public criticism over impolitic statements about Muslims, had been shoveling more responsibility onto Paulson's shoulders.

There would be no rebuke for Lynch—that wasn't how Paulson ran his shop. Only a line of stiff mouths, and silence. Rachel watched as Erin Lynch processed this shift, leaned back in her chair, and finally made a contribution to the meeting: "Bishop is on the run. He'll float around the country until someone gives us a call. His face is out there, and two hundred grand is no small reward."

Barnes looked at his own ballpoint, clicked it open and shut. "She's right. Bishop and Mittag are stars. Of a sort. They're known. Richie's watching online activity, and we've confiscated his missile launcher—I'm not sure how much damage he can do at this point. A week has passed, and there's been nothing." Barnes hesitated, then shrugged. "But, okay. If the White House wants us to make a bigger deal of going after him, then we can do that."

As Barnes spoke, Mark Paulson's gaze moved from his deputies down the table to the far end, where, by the buffet and its dozen bottles of water, Rachel watched in silence. Now he said, "You all know Special Agent Rachel Proulx?"

Heads swiveled to look down the table. They did know her, tangentially, either from occasional reports with her name on them or as a quiet presence in meetings like this. None, however, really *knew* her. No one, if pressed, would be able to say where she had come from. Yet they all nodded.

"Rachel's a specialist. She conducted extensive research on the West Coast—you'll know her report on left-wing movements because it's the best thing we have on the subject, and she's had her eye on the Massive Brigade since before it existed. Suffice to say, when she speaks I know enough to listen. Here." From his folder he passed around copies of her ten-page memo, a brief progress report she'd emailed Paulson that morning. Suspiciously, Barnes, Lynch, and Kranowski scanned the opening lines. Paulson said, "Rachel?"

She straightened, pulled her chair closer to the table, and began.

"As you all know, we've established that a week ago, on June 18, Bishop took with him approximately four hundred followers. Based on pre–June 18 statements and communications, the reasoning for a mass disappearance has always been defensive: *When the federal gov-*

ernment comes after us, we'll have to go underground. But while we're quite sure that he's got more in mind than hiding out in perpetuity, the organization's actual plans are a question mark. And the preparations that went into this mass disappearance—the timing and techniques—were communicated through encrypted Tor clients, burners, and face-to-face. There's no way—short of trashing the Constitution—that we could have predicted it." She cleared her throat. "I was able to speak with one follower who didn't make it—a young man in Baltimore. If he's typical, then none of them were told much. Just: Go to this place and wait to be met."

"So there's nothing new," Lynch said, sighing audibly.

"Not exactly," she replied. "We followed up on the anonymous tip that sent us to Mittag's storage facility on June 18. The call was from a pay phone in Manhattan—Avenue A, between Thirteenth and Fourteenth Streets. We tracked down CCTV footage and ID'd the caller. You'll see her on the third page. Holly Rasmussen, a known associate of Benjamin Mittag."

There was movement. Nothing dramatic, but the air conditioner had taken a break, and in the dead silence any shift in posture caused a racket.

"Where is she?" asked Lynch.

"She disappeared the same day as Bishop and Mittag and the others. Our initial thought, once we had her name, was that she had turned on them. But the fact that she left her life at the same moment suggests otherwise."

"Or she was killed for her transgression," said Kranowski.

Rachel sent a nod in his direction. "Perhaps. But until we find a body we're assuming she was under orders to make the call."

"Who's 'we'?" asked Barnes.

"I," she said. "I should have said I."

"And me," said Paulson. "As well as POTUS."

Silence. Paulson looked up and down the table, waiting for his deputies to add two and two, but it was taking too long. He said,

"Bishop was playing us on June 18—everything was prepared. That's the understanding we're going with. He was drawing attention to his exit, and we assisted in the publicity. So to assume he's 'on the run' would be, let's say, idiotic. Are we agreed?"

One at a time, they nodded. Richard Kranowski placed his fingertips on one of the sheets. "Who's this on page five? James Sullivan?"

Rachel turned to page five of her report and looked again at the CCTV shot of a morose-looking man at a pay phone. When the photo had first reached her in-box, she'd lost her breath, remembering that flirtatious drink eight years ago. "Corner of Forty-First and Second, a block from UN headquarters. We don't know his name for sure, but he used James Sullivan back in 2009, at one of Bishop's early lectures. In this shot, he's calling Bishop at the party. Presumably warning him to leave the Ferrises' house."

"*What* is he?"

"We honestly don't know. A friend of Bishop's."

"Ah," Kranowski said, nodding. Everyone, in fact, nodded, even though she'd given them nothing to *ah* about.

Paulson looked at Rachel, so she continued. "You'll find in the memo a summary of conclusions we've reached based on the limited intelligence we've been able to gather. I'm afraid it's not much, but we are convinced that we haven't heard the last of Bishop. Not with four hundred soldiers at his disposal."

"Who's Ingrid Parker?" Lynch asked.

Rachel wanted to suggest Lynch read the memo for herself, but she was beginning to despair of anyone going to the trouble. "Parker met Bishop for the first time at the June 18 party. When she arrived at work the next day, she used a Tor client to talk to someone. Deleted it afterward. We don't know who she was talking to, or what she said. Whatever it was, she didn't want anyone finding out about it. She, too, is among the missing."

"What do you propose now?" Paulson asked Rachel.

"What I suggest is a more coordinated effort, nationally, to track down Bishop, Mittag, and their followers."

Morbidly, Barnes said, "You want money."

"Of course," Rachel said. "And money is another subject." Everyone looked at her. "How's he funding this?"

"We shut down his bank accounts," Kranowski said. "That was taken care of a couple of hours after he disappeared."

"Yet he's had no trouble financing the disappearance of four hundred kids. He's working with cash. Where did he get the cash? His converts would have brought in some money, but not enough to keep them going for long. Either he's going to run out in another week, or he's got a source we haven't discovered. I'm going to need some people to help me look into this."

"Erin?" said Paulson. "I believe you've got some crack accountants in Counterterrorism."

Erin Lynch admitted that she, too, was guilty as charged.

"And we have to go public," said Rachel.

"About what?" Barnes asked.

"About the four hundred kids."

Paulson raised an index finger and shook it, but Rachel wasn't done yet.

"I understand the concerns, but it's the only way we're going to get eyes on this," she explained, more to him than the others. "A group of young people show up in a town and stick to themselves, someone's going to notice. But right now they don't know to call us."

Paulson chose not to reply. Instead, he delegated by looking down the table at Kranowski, who took the hint and turned to her. "Rachel, do you know the effect it would have, telling the American people that a terrorist group captured four hundred of their children?"

"We're not talking about Boko Haram. The followers weren't captured. They went willingly."

"Brainwashed," Kranowski said. "That's how it's going to play. Kidnapped. Abducted. Whatever."

Lynch sighed aloud. "That would do a nasty job to the Bureau's public relations. And the president's?" She shook her head.

Barnes said nothing, so Paulson finally spoke. "We appreciate your point, Rachel, but that isn't the way forward. Not at this juncture. The way forward is to find them on our own. Then we present Bishop and the children to the public as a gift."

They were of a single mind about this, and nothing would sway them. Ignorance is that way. "Then we're not going to find him," she said after a moment. "We're not going to find him until he wants to be found."

Lynch came close to laughing, but not quite. "I think we've got ourselves a pessimist."

"Have some faith in your government," Barnes told her. "We march stupidly into countries we don't understand; we sit back as our cities are decimated by natural disasters; and we let our schools go quietly to shit—despite these things, one thing we're pretty good at is finding people who don't want to be found."

7

KEVIN MOORE was one of many. There were eleven people like him—twenties, college educated, full of revolutionary fervor—living in this ramshackle, two-story clapboard house near the base of Black Mountain in Wyoming. They cooked and washed dishes together, ate together and shared bedsheets. They even shared their noms de guerre—the men were all George, the women Mary. At the beginning, when they'd been told this, a single woman raised her hand. "And if we're trans?"

"Then it's up to you," said the tall, green-eyed Mary who had opened the door and welcomed Kevin and Tracey to the "fascist-free zone."

He hadn't understood the naming convention—how were they supposed to communicate when there were more than two in a room? After a couple of days, though, he got it: When talking in groups, people were forced to *look* at each other, to meet eyes and communicate. "George" was identified not by his name but by the direction the speaker was looking, whose face she or he chose to gaze at. And this brought them closer together, all these meetings of eyes.

When Kevin had imagined what would follow his call to the underground, he'd envisioned something more in line with his

military background, or the Palestinian training camps he remembered from old movies, where they marched in formation and rolled
through obstacle courses and shot at makeshift targets in the desert.
While target practice was part of their regime, it seemed almost an
afterthought to the words that filled their days.

They read books—the house was stocked with fiction, political
theory, and history—and in the afternoons they sat in circles of six
or seven or eight to discuss the ills of society. They called it the Secret
Seminar. As the murderous George with the GTO had told him,
each person had his own bone to pick. George from Ohio talked about
his older brother, who had gone from a bright young man to an un-
employed, obese, diabetes-ridden failure in the space of five years,
simply because a factory had closed down, and because society didn't
care enough about his decline. "Empathy," he said to the group.
"A civilization without empathy isn't worth holding on to."

Mary from Louisiana—this was the transgender who had asked
how she should be named—was entrenched in gender politics, finding in the very clothes of American consumer society repression and
self-sabotage. "If we don't fit in a box, we're discarded. It's such a
waste—it makes me want to cry."

Tracey felt no ambiguity about gender; she was a woman who
argued that civilization had been born with a fatal illness: patriarchy,
though she didn't call it that. She called it "men running things."

Tracey had worked all her young life for men, and could no longer take their physical and economic dominance. By the third Secret
Seminar she opened up about her first boss, at a restaurant in East
Sacramento, who had convinced her that blowjobs would help her job
prospects. Living check to check, she'd given in—and was laid off
after half a year, once he'd moved on to Santa Cruz. "I hate myself
most of all," she said, "but I hate him for making me feel this way."

Louisiana Mary rubbed her back. Tracey shrugged and said, "But
it's bigger than assholes in Sacramento. You know? Like, people say
the terrorists hate the West because of our drones and television shows
and Mohammed comic strips. Or, maybe, because of our *freedom*. But

that's not it. They hate us because of our women. It's fear. That their women will finally take revenge for history. In the eyes of angry Western women, they see the writing on the wall. They can kick Christians and Jews and Hindus out of their land, but they'll never get along without women, and at any moment those women can stick a knife in their backs. So they cover them up, slice off their clitorises, beat them down. Just the other day they kidnapped a hundred and twenty girls in Nigeria because they were getting a fucking education."

There was silence; her transition to the international sphere had been too quick, and she could see it in their eyes.

"It's an observation," she said. "I'm just saying those guys who cut off heads and stone women to death—they're as much our enemy as the American government. Only problem is, they're beyond our reach. For now. But after we've changed America we'll be exporting our revolution, and we'll go after them."

When it was his turn, Kevin spoke of being a black man in a racist society, of the unnatural deference he had to show the police, of job interviews that would, by default, go to the white man in the room. "White *man*," said Tracey, and he nodded at that, admitting it was true.

"But racism isn't about race," he went on. "It's something rich people dreamed up so their wage slaves would feel better. *Just be happy you weren't born a nigger. You angry you don't have a job? Well, don't blame me—that Mexican works for half the price.* They never say, *I only pay him half as much as I pay you.* No, it's the Mexican's fault for being desperate enough to work for peanuts." He shook his head. "Rich people, they're smart. Which is why we have to be smarter."

While they each had their own cause, Kevin noticed that they all shared a single need that life in America had not satisfied: *belonging*. All these Marys and Georges felt like aliens in their own country, disassociated from the mainstream of American belief, and so they had left their homes in search of a new, better family with whom they could finally be comfortable in their own skins. These were the misshapen pegs, the ones for whom no space was an easy fit.

One important question came up during the seminars: How many misshapen pegs were there? Not just the deserters like them, who had escaped to safe houses like this in order to avoid a government crackdown that had begun with the attempted capture of Martin Bishop and Benjamin Mittag in New Jersey—what about those who had not yet deserted? How deep into the American fabric could their group spread and grow? What percentage of Americans felt alienated from America? Five percent? Fifteen? Forty-five? Gleefully, one George pointed out that a minuscule percentage of the Russian population had been Communist when the Bolshevik Revolution took over their country.

The weapons were stored in the basement, in crates, a hodge-podge of semiautomatic and hunting rifles, slide-action pistols, and six-shooter revolvers collected from gun shows, parents' attics, and friends' locked cabinets. Every day they gathered the weapons and headed higher up the mountain, where they shot at pinecones labeled with smiley faces on Post-it notes. Sometimes ten or twenty pinecones were hung from trees, all these smiley faces, a single one among them labeled PIG—the object was to hit the cop but no one else.

"So this is the plan?" asked a George from Wisconsin. "We're all going to show up one day and shoot cops across America?"

Green-eyed Mary shook her head. "You think they're not going to shoot at you? Just learn to defend yourself, hon. I, for one, don't want to be a martyr to the cause. Not yet, at least."

Kevin, with his military training, excelled at the gun practice, and his sharpshooting gained him favorable attention. He noticed that in the afternoons they listened more closely when he spoke, as if his skills behind the trigger were a reflection of a wiser mind. When green-eyed Mary asked his opinion, all faces turned to him in anticipation.

He wasn't sure if he liked it or not.

8

UNDER DURESS, Lou Barnes had given Rachel an office, a fifteen-by-twenty-foot windowless room that, like the old conference room, became deafening when the air conditioning switched on. He'd also been ordered by Paulson to give her a more substantial budget from his discretionary fund, and while it was a pittance it was better than nothing. She was trying to remain optimistic.

Her staff had been culled from other departments. Four analysts, each assigned to one of the national regions—West, Midwest, South, and Northeast—shared three desks, while near the door was another desk for Rachel. Ashley, Erin Lynch's "crack accountant," moved in, followed by a technician pulling her computer on a cart. There wasn't any space for Doug, the loaner she'd finagled from Cyber, but he made do.

She'd flown in two SACs—special agents in charge—both of whom had been running undercover agents inside the Massive Brigade during the past year. Of the six agents who had infiltrated the community, only one, OSWALD, had been invited to move underground on June 18. Another undercover agent, who had been tracking a Massive follower named Tracey Hill, had been found in the Nevada desert shot dead in her car. While suspicion was high, there was no direct evidence that her murder was related to her work.

Janet Fordham, the SAC who had run their one success, was a diminutive fifty-year-old who looked so inconvenienced by the lack of chairs that Rachel got up and offered her own. Fordham settled down and rubbed the corner of her eye with a pinkie. "We've heard nothing from OSWALD," she said finally. "One message, then he disappeared."

"What's your assessment?" Rachel asked.

Fordham sighed. "Well, he's good. OSWALD spent a year undercover in New Orleans. He won't crack—I know that. But if he can't get word to us he's useless."

"That means something, though, doesn't it?" asked Rachel.

"Excuse me?"

"If he can't get word to you, then it means they're in lockdown. They're working toward something."

Fordham went back to her eye, rubbing. "I don't know, Rachel. I don't know what it means anymore."

Doug was a twenty-five-year-old West Virginian with a thick mountain accent that even a precocious education at Yale hadn't washed away. He'd long ago cracked the back end of *The Propaganda Ministry* and had been charting locations each time the site's administration page was accessed. This administrator, even accounting for IP masking, always visited from a different location: One day he'd be traced to Louisiana, another day Alaska. Doug's assessment was that the administration of the site was shared by an unknown number of people, each of whom checked on it once and then, perhaps, never returned.

"But how do they communicate?" Proulx asked.

A shrug. "NSA's been scouring the mobile networks—zilch. Obviously they're using phones—there's no choice in the matter—but they're sticking to burners. We've got nothing on email. We suspect they're using a hodgepodge of techniques. Burners. Shared email

accounts, communicating through draft folders. Newspaper classi-
fieds. Couriers. Mostly, though, they talk face-to-face."

"Sounds like Bishop learned his trade from us."

"Or paperback thrillers," said Doug.

"Try al Qaeda," Ashley said as she walked up and handed Doug
a white paper bag stained with oil. Each day, without fail, Ashley
walked a block to Fogo de Chão, a Brazilian steakhouse, for their
"Gaucho lunch." Rachel felt a special fondness for the post-lunch
Ashley, refueled and smelling of grilled meats.

In the afternoon, she and Doug sat down to figure out how to
divvy up the gigabytes of Martin Bishop's online correspondence,
just sent over from NSA. They looked up at a knock on the door-
jamb: a balding crewcut in a suit, early forties. He stuck out a hand
and continued over to her desk. "Ms. Proulx? Owen Jakes. Really
great to meet you. Your San Francisco report is a classic."

Unsure, Rachel shook his hand and asked where he'd come from.

"They didn't tell you?" Jakes said, then rolled his eyes. "Why am
I not surprised? I only just got into town—Lou Barnes sent me
over."

"I thought Lou believed we were wasting his money."

Jakes winked. "He's usually the last one to figure these things
out, isn't he?"

There was something about the way Jakes had moved confidently
into her office and casually mocked his boss that felt like a ham-fisted
flirtation. Rachel looked at Doug, who seemed to be reserving his
judgment. "Sit down, then," she said. "Let's find out why he's sent
you."

"Yeah," he said, then looked at Doug. "Who are you again?"

Doug stood and shook his hand, introducing himself.

"Look, man," Jakes said, "my story doesn't have anything to do
with computers. You mind?"

Doug, uncomfortable, glanced at Rachel; she nodded. He went
to join Ashley at her desk.

Rachel leaned against the desk. "Next time, Owen Jakes, I'll do the dismissing."

"Sure, sure. I get it."

"So why are you here?"

"Probably because I used to know Martin Bishop," said Jakes.

From 2005 to 2010, Jakes explained, he had worked liaison out of the Berlin embassy, sharing intel and coordinating with his opposite numbers in Germany's BfV—*Bundesamt für Verfassungsschutz*. One subject of mutual concern had been the Kommando Rosa Luxemburg, one of whose founders had been arrested in Frankfurt for hacking the Christian Democrats' main server and dumping thousands of emails onto the internet. "But the KRL didn't claim responsibility for what their member had done, and the Germans couldn't tie them to it. So other than that one arrest nothing was done about them. Then I got a call—a new face, an American, was attending the KRL meetings. We didn't have anything on Martin Bishop. So I made contact."

"Official contact?" Rachel asked.

He shook his head. "I was just a guy. A charming fellow American in Berlin. I can be very charming if I need to be." He smiled, but Rachel didn't bother to mirror him. "A few days into it, he tells me about the Kommando. Paints it like it's a discussion group."

"So he was inviting you in."

"It was a pitch. You know his history—Southern Baptist dogooder. Raise the poor so they can help themselves. Then he made himself some liberal friends and learned how to blame the rich. Not violent, no, but he was on his way. Smart—that's for sure. But gullible. And he had none of the magnetism he would later display. The Kommando was going to eat him up. So I made the decision to bring him in. Cleared it with the Germans, then took Martin to a safe house where I laid it out for him: Groups like the KRL—as you well know, Agent Proulx—are layered. Where Martin was, on the outside, it was all happy idealism. Dig deeper, you find the hackers. Still deeper: the bomb throwers who keep posters of Andreas Baader on their bed-room walls."

Rachel thought about Martin Bishop, the one she'd seen in 2009 as well as the one who swayed huge crowds, and said, "How did he react?"

Jakes shrugged. "Martin wasn't so far gone that he couldn't hear logic. That's not to say he *believed* me when I explained how danger-ous they were—he didn't—but he understood our concerns. The way he saw it, by keeping me in the loop he would help to clear their name."

It irritated Rachel that she was only hearing this now, ten days after the party and eight years after the story itself, but perhaps that was why Jakes had come personally—a charming messenger to ease the blow. "How long did this go on?"

"Four, five weeks. Then they blew themselves up."

"For some of the West Coast left," she told him, "the KRL ex-plosion is fake. A lot of people don't buy the official story."

Jakes raised his hands—he knew all about this. "The Germans blew them up? Those same idiots think the American government would fly two passenger planes into the World Trade Center." He shook his head. "I was there, Agent Proulx."

Rachel considered his story, turning it around to look at it from all sides. "I assume there's a report on this somewhere."

"You'd assume correctly," he said, a twinkle in his eye. "How-ever, it was never cleared for distribution. We don't want it get-ting out that he was on the Bureau payroll, even if we didn't actually pay him."

"That would be a mess."

"Precisely."

"Well, it would be helpful to clear me for access."

"You'll have to talk to Berlin, then."

She didn't like the sound of that, but okay: She could write up a request. "Does the report tell where Martin went afterward? There's a gap of about two months between the explosion and him reappearing stateside, making speeches."

"That's a question mark," said Jakes, exhaling loudly. "But I suspect he was pissed off at the world and sat in a hole for a while. He really believed the KRL was peaceful. It was a blow."

"You said he had no magnetism. I saw him in San Francisco later that same year. It was in front of just a handful of people, but he certainly had that magnetism there."

"September?" asked Jakes.

"Yeah."

He smiled. "We were in the same auditorium, then. I don't remember seeing you there. Remember me?"

She didn't. It had been a long time ago, and all she remembered from that day was Martin Bishop and the elusive James Sullivan who, eight years later, was the last person to call Bishop before he disappeared. She remembered the Mission District rat trap that had been her home, and the months she'd spent examining the convergence of Silicon Valley money and radical progressive action. She remembered sitting in on meetings in churches and squatters' homes and parks, and becoming friendly with anarchists and socialists and hackers convinced that anything that existed in the virtual world should be free, including other people's bank accounts. The resulting work, "Shifts in Radical Thought and Organization in the 21st Century," had made her name.

"If it's all right with you," Jakes said, "I'd like to join the team. I think my familiarity could be a benefit, and . . ." He nodded at the other desks stuffed into their cramped space. "And it looks like you could use some more hands."

9

GREEN-EYED MARY asked him to join her on a shopping trip into town—the closest town being Dayton, population 757, a half hour away. By then he'd been with them for a week and a half, and had even grown to enjoy the routine. People joined in anger were remarkably generous with one another. He mentioned this to Mary as she drove the house pickup down Highway 14.

"You've only been around a little while," she told him with a smile. "Give it time. Radicals are as catty as anyone else. Worse, probably."

"I saw that back in Frisco."

"Longer," she said, and winked.

"You've been with it a while, then?"

She didn't answer, but Kevin knew that this was her way. Mary liked to let other people fill in the blank spaces in conversation.

So he said, "I'm wondering where this is all leading." A field opened up to the left, bright under the blazing sun, full of grazing cows. "You've got these people hiding from the government. They're talking and talking and shooting in their spare time—but you've got to see it, right? They can't hit squat. Mary from Dallas and those two guys—St. Louis and Denver—they know how to aim. The rest?" He shook his head.

"You think you're the only one complaining?" Mary asked. "Every day I get an earful. Some are like you, thinking we should be running strict obedience lessons, teach everyone how to massacre at will. Others—and you probably know who they are—are horrified they have to touch a gun. They pull me aside and demand to know if we're building an army."

"You're not building an army."

"Damned right," she said. "We're building a community."

"Tell that to the George who brought me and Tracey to your place."

"What about him?"

"He killed a woman he thought was following us. Shot her in her car."

Mary went silent, chewed on her lower lip. "Why didn't you mention this before?"

Why hadn't he? "Because I thought you knew. I thought that was the way."

"I didn't get that memo," she said, then fell back into silence as the landscape unrolled around them. After a year in San Francisco's narrow streets, Kevin still found these open spaces exhilarating and terrifying.

He said, "When did you meet Martin?"

"After he came back from Berlin," she said. "Back in Austin. He was trying to figure things out."

"The Kommando Rosa Luxemburg."

"They got a raw deal," she said.

He waited for more, but she didn't look like she was going to share, so he pressed: "From what I heard, they blew themselves up."

"That's what you would hear, isn't it?" She shook her head. "False flag op, all the way. The Germans, maybe with a little help from us. The KRL had humiliated them with those email leaks, so they got them back."

Kevin looked out the window. False flag: the Twin Towers, Waco, Charlie Hebdo, Sandy Hook . . . Pearl Harbor. He'd heard all the conspiracy theories, and every time someone said "false flag" his stomach seized up, because he knew he'd entered a space where rational thought was being thrown under the bus. Thankfully, Mary wasn't interested in jumping further down that rabbit hole right now.

"Austin was fun, though. Full of possibility. We drank a *lot*." She cleared her throat. "That was in late '09, early '10—before it got serious. A lot of us were taken in by Obama, before realizing he was more of the same."

"Martin opened your eyes?"

She grinned. "My eyes were already open. Most people's are. They just don't know what to do next."

"What's next?"

"Really?" she asked. "You really need an answer?"

"What I need," he said after a moment, "is a direction to point myself. It's the way I'm built. We're not making an army, you say. We're building a community. Cool. But what's the end point?"

"Men," she said, sighing.

"What?"

"You can't just take a drive, can you? Always need a destination."

The cows had given way to sugar beets, and Mary told him about an article she'd read concerning the sharp rise of celiac disease in America, that rare gluten allergy that sent its victims to the toilet all day long. The article, she said, showed that the rise of celiac diagnoses directly paralleled the increased use of the toxic herbicide glyphosate just before wheat harvesting. The process yielded 30 percent more seeds but also left trace amounts of glyphosate in the wheat. She said, "Americans aren't falling victim to celiac disease; they're being poisoned in order to maximize profits."

When they reached Dayton she didn't slow down, not even when they passed the Corner Grocery. Once they crossed the Little Tongue River they were out of it. He said nothing, only watched the passing fields until after another ten minutes she turned down a long driveway beside a broken mailbox. The truck bounced where recent storms had dug ravines across the drive.

A part of him worried, as he had that first day, that the gig was up. Had he been marked for exclusion? Among these people, that could mean anything. He hadn't made the cut, perhaps, or they'd decided in their myopic way that he was part of the *other*—an interloper, a spy.

They reached a farmhouse, one of thousands that had been abandoned across the United States in the past decade as small farms had gone under. This one was in serious disrepair. Slanted shutters, snapped porch planks, smashed windows. Paint cracked under the blazing sun. They parked in an empty, overgrown yard. He hadn't asked a thing, and Mary hadn't bothered to tell him. She only led him up the front steps, cautioning him to watch out for loose boards, and together they entered the house, which held some abandoned pieces of mildewed furniture. She said, "You ate breakfast, right?"

"Sure."

She nodded, looking around the empty place. Was she nervous? He couldn't tell. He said, "We're waiting for someone?"

"You are," she said. "I've got groceries to buy." But she looked around the place a little more, lingering.

"Who am I meeting?" he asked.

A shrug.

"Are you picking me up after shopping?"

"I'll be told one way or the other, okay? You need a bottle of water?"

"Depends on how long I'm standing around here."

"I'll get you one."

He followed her back out to the truck, hot wind buffeting them, and accepted a Poland Spring. "Look," he said, "if I'm in the doghouse you might want to tell me."

She grinned, shaking her head. "Nothing like that. You're fine. That's why you're here." She got back into the truck and started it up. "I told them how fine you were."

"Thank you," he said.

She hesitated, then: "What happened on the road. George, and what he did. That's not what Martin is about. I know this. That George—maybe he was stressed from driving so much. Paranoia, I don't know. But that isn't the kind of people we are."

He watched her drive off, then went back inside. In the kitchen, he found a phone screwed to the wall, but it was dead. Carefully, he took the stairs to the attic floor and peered out windows, looking for signs of life: cities, houses, trailers. There was nothing, not even in the direction of Dayton, which meant that there was no place to go.

The warmth inside the house was worse than in the open field, so he went outside again and drank half the water, then took a leak around the back of the house. The day came and went, and by the time the sun first brushed the horizon he heard the engine. It came from the north, an SUV bouncing through difficult, untended terrain as it headed toward him. He considered going back inside but didn't see the point. So he stood in front of the house, his hands loosely held together like a man considering prayer but not yet committed to the act.

When the dusty SUV pulled up, two men climbed out. One—a wiry Hispanic—he didn't know, but the other one—big, with a wheat-colored beard and blue eyes—he recognized as Benjamin Mittag. Neither was smiling. Without introducing himself, Mittag walked past Kevin and entered the house. The other man approached Kevin and said, "Get inside."

He didn't like the sound of that, but there was nothing else for him, so he went back into the house to find Mittag sitting on the old coffee table. Beside him lay a Springfield 1911 semiautomatic pistol. The other man entered behind Kevin and closed the door.

"Tell me," Mittag said.

"What?"

"Who you're working for."

Kevin didn't answer immediately. He took a breath. "No one."

Mittag laid the Springfield on his knee. "Look, Kevin Moore.

We know you're working for someone. FBI? Homeland Security? Fucking CIA?"

Kevin put some effort into controlling his expression but had zero idea how he really looked. "How do you know this?"

"Because we're Massive. Because we've got an army of hackers on our side. There are no secrets anymore. Not from us. So let's start with who you work for."

"I don't work for anyone," Kevin said.

Mittag stood and raised the pistol so that it was two feet from Kevin's forehead. Kevin closed his eyes, exhaled, then looked again at Mittag. He said, "Pull the trigger."

"Is that what you want?"

Kevin frowned, shook his head. "You don't trust me? Then pull the fucking trigger. But don't waste my time with accusations."

Benjamin Mittag didn't move. He just stared into Kevin's eyes over the barrel of the pistol. Then he lowered it and smiled. "All right, then." He stepped forward, clapped a hand on Kevin's shoulder, and said, "Let's go fight the good fight."

Then he and his partner were gone. Kevin took a moment, fighting an onrush of nausea, wrestling with his bladder. He inhaled and exhaled, then followed them outside.

10

SHE HAD successfully avoided Sam Schumer for nearly two weeks when Assistant Director Paulson called. Schumer, it seemed, had gone above her head. "You may not like him, Rachel, but you're in bed with the guy. Cut him off completely and he'll invent worse stories than what's actually going on."

"He does that already, sir."

"As bad as things seem, they can always get worse."

Which was how she ended up having coffee with Schumer at the Politics and Prose bookstore on a gray, drizzly morning, twelve days after the party. She was as congenial as she could manage, and he was as self-aggrandizing as she remembered. He rubbed his bald scalp, fooled with the ends of his mustache, and asked if it was true that dissident elements of the FBI had assisted in Martin Bishop's escape on June 18. "Are you really asking me that?" she countered, and he shrugged, telling her that there were a lot of stories going around, and that was one of the more believable ones.

Then he took a sip of his coffee and said, "Look, Rachel. Politically, you and I are on the opposite ends of the spectrum. I know it. You know it. But I'm just here to get at the truth, and I know you are, too."

"No, Sam. No one in the FBI helped Martin Bishop escape."

He leaned closer. "What happened? We used to get along so nicely. Have I ever stuck it to the Bureau? You guys are my goddam heroes!"

"If we're your heroes, Sam, then try emulating us. Verify your facts before you share them with millions of Americans."

Schumer frowned, leaning back again. "This is about that North Mexico story, isn't it? That was based on a respected study—"

"By a right-wing foundation that had been accused of race-baiting by the Southern Poverty Law Center."

"Their numbers add up, Rachel."

"Not according to *The Washington Post,* to *New York Times,* CNN—"

"Not according to the corporate liberal media. What a surprise! If this is the kind of head-in-the-sand thinking that runs the Bureau these days, then I'm not sure I'm such a fan anymore."

They both let that sit a moment. She was experiencing the same uncomfortable feeling that, days before, Kevin had felt at the mention of "false flag." If two people could not agree on the validity of *numbers,* then what hope was there for the future?

But she had a job to do, and that trumped numbers and her feelings of disgust. "I'm told you have a question for me, and I don't think you've asked it yet."

"Yeah," he said, and licked his lips. "There are a lot of reports of young people—teens, twenties—going missing on June 18, when Bishop and Mittag disappeared. Parents on Facebook are noticing each other. They're starting groups looking for their kids. Is this connected to the Massive Brigade?"

"Not that we know of," she lied. "But thanks for the information. We'll look into it."

That afternoon, she gave Paulson's deputies an update that consisted of potential leads that had not yet borne fruit. Barnes asked pointedly what the president was thinking now—was he still afraid of shadows? Lynch cracked a few jokes. Kranowski equivocated.

There was a collective sigh of exasperation when she reported on Sam Schumer's question about the missing kids. "If we don't get ahead of this now," she warned them, "we'll never control the message." But they would not budge.

Back in the office, she spoke openly about her frustration, and Ashley and Doug shared her dismay, while Owen Jakes, leaning against the wall with his hands behind his back, disagreed. "That might have mattered a decade ago, Schumer breaking out an exposé on lost children, but do you think that really matters these days?"

The three of them looked at him.

"It's not a matter of what's being said," he explained, "but what's accepted as truth. Schumer says something, all we have to do is say the opposite, and convincingly."

"And the truth?" asked Ashley.

Owen grinned. "We misplaced that back in 2001."

"I thought you were tracking down leads from the tip line," Rachel said, irritated.

"I was, and then we intercepted this." He took his hands out from behind his back to reveal an envelope in a plastic sleeve. He handed it over and watched as Rachel slid it out and saw the name on the outside: It was addressed to David Parker. "I'd love to be the one to take that to him," said Owen. "See how he reacts."

Rachel took out the single page, examined it for a moment, then showed it to Doug and Ashley, who made appropriate expressions. She folded it back into the envelope and said, "Thanks, Owen. I'll take care of this myself."

Which was why she showed up in Tribeca at noon the following day, took the stairs this time, and asked David Parker how he was holding up. The question was rhetorical, for she'd had her answer as soon as she saw him standing hungover in the middle of his living room surrounded by open cardboard boxes. He was dressed, but she imagined that if she hadn't called ahead he would have been stumbling around in a pair of briefs.

He said, "I'm still on my feet."

She nodded at the boxes. "Moving?"

"Ingrid's stuff."

"Given up already?"

"Why? You know where she is?"

She shook her head. "But it's only been two weeks."

"Long enough to figure out that I don't give a shit anymore."

They both knew that was a lie. She'd seen it before: The biggest surprise for men who'd been abandoned was that they were no good at being alone. The apartment, like his body, was going to pot, and he no longer maintained the pretense of controlling his drinking. He'd become a homeless person with a roof over his head, and the only thing that had changed was his wife's absence. Without Ingrid, his work and daily routines were collapsing. The discovery of this dependency, for most men, was heartbreaking.

"What are you going to do with the boxes?" she asked.

He rubbed his face, unsure, then sat down.

"When I last talked to you," Rachel said, "you told me that we'd never find Ingrid because she's *committed*."

"Yeah. I remember."

"How'd she get that way?"

He scratched at his neck, then shrugged. "Her father was a union organizer, back in Flint. I never met him, but I heard a lot about him. Staunch Communist, very old school. Bitter. He hated that Stalin had ruined the one chance for Communism to thrive in the world. Somehow, he took it as a personal slight. His disappointment—it was so big that his friends used it to explain away his cruelty." David hesitated, maybe wondering if he should go on; Ingrid wasn't around to establish boundaries for him. "Ingrid's mom, she was a regular at the local free clinic. Cracked ribs, swollen jaws, black eyes. This was Ingrid's childhood. Then when she was sixteen she went at the bastard with a shovel, and that's what finally convinced her mother to leave him. Two years later, during a bad winter, her father drank himself to death on the banks of the Kearsley Reservoir."

Rachel knew, because she read such things, that the UN estimated that one in three women in the world experiences physical or sexual violence in her lifetime, usually from an intimate partner, and this was a statistic that she had never been able to shake. In her world, that ratio was even higher, and not only because she was a victim herself. It was because violence begets more violence, and the women who'd lucked out tended not to end up under her microscope.

"Do you think that helps explain her actions?" she asked.

"I don't know, Special Agent. What do you think?"

She didn't answer, only took her briefcase from beside the chair and opened it. "Well, we haven't found her," she said, "but we do have something." She removed the envelope Owen had given her and held it out.

David recognized the handwriting immediately, which was probably why he had so much trouble taking out the single sheet of paper even though it had already been opened, scanned, and tested for fingerprints and DNA. He stared hard at the page. He turned it around, as if he thought it was upside down; then his eyes caught the single sentence Ingrid had scribbled across the bottom corner. He looked up at her. "You intercepted this?"

"Yesterday," Rachel said. "It's postmarked Idaho Falls, Idaho."

"*Idaho?* What the fuck is she doing in Idaho?"

"It's not surprising," she explained. "Large, open spaces. Not necessarily a good tactical choice, but it gives fugitives the illusion of being far away, out of our reach."

"Fugitive?" he said, but it was a whisper, a thought that had slipped out unawares. She knew it was a word that hadn't occurred to him, and probably hadn't occurred to the families and friends of the other four hundred. But that's what they were: fugitives. They were grains of chaos thrown to the winds of America, spreading through the beautiful and frightening heartland. Public enemies. His mouth worked the air a few seconds; then he shook his head to get rid of the cobwebs. "So you're closing in. Yes?"

Rachel tilted her head. "If they know what they're doing, they'll have couriers to mail letters from other towns. I doubt she's there. But our people are looking."

"Idaho. You've got a state to look at," David said. "Cordon it off."

She didn't bother to explain how difficult it was to cordon off anything in those wide, open spaces.

David looked again at the ultrasound in his hands. The fuzzy black-and-white smear of pre-child, the printed numbers and measurements running down the right side, and at the bottom corner, in ballpoint: *I'm going to call her Clare.*

"You'll be all right?" Rachel asked.

David didn't answer. He folded the sheet and held it between his fingers. His eyes were wet.

11

IT WAS an M-40 just like the one he'd trained with on Black Mountain, but with a new Schmidt and Bender day scope with a Horus reticle. Beyond the lines and dots and numbers were people. Hundreds. So many little lives buried behind that grid, filling the street, ready to celebrate the Fourth of July.

When he blinked, he remembered that windshield in the Nevada desert. Spots of blood appearing like magic.

Kevin had a decision to make, but didn't know if he could.

He'd spent three days trapped in a Toyota with Benjamin Mittag, and it had been a relief to finally arrive in Florida and emerge from that claustrophobic car, even though by then he knew why he'd been brought there.

"Where's Martin?" Kevin asked between towns in Missouri, mountains in the distance.

"Couldn't say."

"Meaning, you don't know?"

Mittag rocked his head, staring hard at the road. "This is a big country, man. And when you're not using the internet you can't direct people from one spot. Martin's got his half of the country, I've got mine. He's east, I'm west."

"But we're driving to the East Coast."

"Yep," Mittag said, as if there were no contradiction.

"So how do you talk?"

"We don't. Not often."

Kevin wondered how anything could get done if the two leaders couldn't sit down on a regular basis and strategize. And, really, what *were* they supposed to be getting done? Were they really just hiding out to avoid detection, as some said? Or was there a master plan that Kevin had now become a part of?

"How do you know what to do, then? If you can't talk to him."

A flash of anger crossed Mittag's face. "How does he know what to do if *he* can't talk to *me*? That man does the talking because that's what he's good at. But without me, there would never be any action."

Kevin let that sit a moment, then: "I heard you used to lecture, back in the beginning. What I *heard* was that you took the paint off the walls."

The compliment relaxed Mittag, just a little. "Yeah, I didn't mince words. But if I'd kept it up I'd have been thrown back inside long ago."

"Inciting violence."

"Inciting action."

If everyone was his own special interest, Mittag was unique, for he seemed to hate every part of society. He'd spent much of his youth incarcerated and felt that this gave him a more realistic view of the world than the college-educated kids he now found himself allied with. The cops who'd put him away, the wardens, the politicians who made the laws, the shop owners he stole from, the mothers and fathers who twisted their kids into kleptomaniacs in the first place, the teachers who tried to mold children into good little consumers, and even the thieves like the one he'd been—everyone was lined up for ridicule. They would all be standing at the wall come the Revolution.

Unlike Bishop, who spoke as if hope were his engine, Mittag was motivated by the angry conviction that he had always been looked down on, and it was time to make America pay for its contempt. But this kind of motivation, Kevin reflected, is volatile. The desire to get back at the elites who scorned him could easily change if his comrades started to piss him off—what was to stop him from turning on his own people?

"Where'd you grow up?" Kevin asked somewhere in Tennessee.

"One of Pennsylvania's many assholes."

"And Martin? Why hook up with him?"

Mittag gave him a sidelong glance. "I saw an opportunity."

"For what?"

"For change," Mittag said, but the way he said it Kevin wasn't sure if he meant change for the world or change for himself, for Benjamin Thomas Mittag—he suspected the latter. "And you're the first step."

"Me?"

"You, brother. But you won't be alone. Don't worry. You'll never be alone anymore."

That, perhaps, was the most frightening thing Benjamin Mittag said the entire drive.

Kevin sniffed, drawing his sight across the crowd, then raised it to the platform at the intersection of Crandon and Harbor, festooned with the colors of the flag and full of local dignitaries. Through speakers, Miley Cyrus sang "Party in the U.S.A." Though blocks away, the music rose to his open window on the seventh floor of a condo building. He measured distances. He estimated wind resistance. The platform was partially obscured by palm trees, and when he turned slightly the oppressive sun flared across his lens. But he'd done this in worse conditions.

In small-town Georgia, Mittag used a pay phone while Kevin waited in the car. When he returned he was jubilant. "Six!"

"Six what?"

Mittag started the car, grinning. "Six fists into the face of the country. Six drops of blood to feed the vampire."

A windshield under the glare—six spots scatter across it.

Time to go, kids!

So there were six of him. Six Kevins across the United States, sweating, clutching rifles or wiring explosives or poisoning meals—or any of the numerous ways there are to kill a person. Six operations, simultaneously.

Of course, knowing this made none of it easier. It did him no good. When they reached Liberty City, Holly was waiting for them. She took custody of Kevin and brought him to a suburban house with no phone line. A safe house for two. She was a pretty girl—twenty-two, sun-dappled blond. And she didn't let Kevin out of her sight.

She had already drawn up the plans, which she unrolled on the dining room table. There was his building. That was the street. Here was the platform where the target would speak. A single road across the Bear Cut Bridge would take them to the place of assassination; a boat would take them away. Holly knew it all, knew how to get in and how to get out, and she would have been happy to pull the trigger herself. But like the Revolution itself she knew her limits.

What had happened? After two weeks among comrades whose primary concern was staying out of sight of the law—two weeks in the position of defense—Mittag had dragged him into the epicenter of an offense that he'd never even caught a whiff of. Whatever he'd thought he knew about the Massive Brigade, it turned out, hadn't been much more than conjecture. And while green-eyed Mary hadn't gotten the memo that killing people was part of the Brigade's MO, she was still a gatekeeper—*I told them how fine you were.* Now, because of government-trained skills and dumb luck, he'd ended up at the sharp end of the revolutionary bayonet.

The music ended abruptly, followed by cheers and hoots and applause, and the mayor approached the mic, or someone who looked like a mayor. Kevin wasn't sure. There was only one face he needed to watch out for, and she'd been sitting at the far edge of the stage, chatting and laughing with one of her aides. Now she was on her feet, still smiling, brushing her long skirt straight.

The mayor thanked everybody for coming out on this beautiful day, and thanked, with a wink, Miley Cyrus.

Hoots. Hollers.

Sun-dappled Holly had driven him across the bridge and into the key. She'd parked a block over from the condos, and as he started to get out, shouldering his bag, she'd told him to slow down. Take it easy. She walked with him the whole way; they were part of a growing crowd, enjoying the clean ocean air. Holly gave him the condo key and told him that she would be waiting for him right there once it was over. He told her to stay safe, and in reply she opened her light jacket. She was carrying a little Walther PPK "in case these Florida boys decide to get fresh," she said, then kissed his cheek. "Good luck."

There was no one in the lobby, just an empty desk. There was a phone in the seventh-floor apartment, but it had been disconnected. Stale furniture—he wondered how long Bishop, or Mittag, had held on to this place, waiting for today, and for someone like him. Then he walked to the window and unzipped his bag.

The mayor said her name, and she heard it. One last brush of the skirt, plaster on that smile, and step confidently forward into the bright sunlight, arm raised, waving. A congresswoman ready for the public. A shining example of modern democracy working so damned well.

He remembered: *Crack, crack, crack.*

The lines and dots and numbers lined up on her face. They added up. Everything was balanced.

Let's get moving, right? We've got a long road ahead of us.

He had a decision to make, but wasn't sure he could make it.

12

DESPITE HIS earnestness the previous week, pulling into her office and offering his historical perspective on Martin Bishop, then sitting in a corner to read through all available files, Owen Jakes soon made himself scarce. Rachel had verified with Lou Barnes that his Berlin story was legit, but not even Barnes knew much about him. Jakes had dutifully gone through the messages sent to the FBI's tip line—since they hadn't released a statement about the four hundred missing followers, and Schumer hadn't yet broken his story about them, the leads were only a handful of unconfirmed sightings of Martin Bishop himself. When he called to update her, Jakes admitted that nothing had come of the tips. "But I'm running down old contacts."

"For what?"

"Too soon to say."

That irritated her—who was working for whom here? "Why don't you tell me anyway?"

There was a brief silence on the line before he said, "With the internet, everything's international. I'm working my European contacts. Arguably, that's where Massive was born, and there's a growing number of fans on the Continent. You should see the spray paint in Berlin."

Given that they had four hundred people to track down, his brilliant idea sounded like busywork. But on the other hand, it would keep Owen Jakes out of the way. "Okay, then," she said. "Keep me posted."

She kept an open line to SAC Janet Fordham in New Orleans, who promised to keep Rachel in the loop if anything came back from her undercover agent. Fordham, though, wasn't full of hope. "I've known OSWALD since he first went undercover in 2010. Twenty-two years old, fresh from Quantico. We chose him because he'd come from the streets. Funny thing—a year at the academy had made him softer. Cleaner. And five weeks later, when he showed up in the hospital with a knife stuck in his right lung, I tried to pull him out. But he wouldn't have it. He asked me what I thought would happen if he suddenly disappeared. Shonda, the woman he'd used to infiltrate the gang, would be accused of working with him. She'd be mutilated, or killed. So he went back. Two years later we took down the whole operation, primarily as a result of his work."

The story, to Rachel's ears, was a testament to OSWALD's formidable skills and level of devotion, but Fordham had been trying to say something else. "He cares too much, and that's his weakness. New Orleans was beginner's luck. Now he's dropped off the face of the earth, and for two weeks we've heard nothing. I'm too old to believe that luck holds."

She was thinking about that conversation on the morning of July 4, her first day off since the disappearances. She was drinking coffee in her mother's living room in Croton-on-Hudson, reading the paperback of *Gray Snow* that Pierce had given her. It was better than she would have thought having met David Parker; in fact, she was hooked. One character, Irina, a starving concentration-camp survivor, had just been robbed of her tiny morsel of food after starving for three days straight. What the hell was going to become of Irina?

"Why don't you go back to bed?" asked her mother, using a walker to move from the doorway to the comfy chair, her puffy green robe looking too big for her meager body. "You got in so late."

That was true. Rachel had flown into Westchester Airport on a red-eye from Tennessee after a difficult reconnaissance with Hank Abernathy, who ran the regional office in Memphis. "I slept enough."

"Don't fight it, honey. Or you'll end up like me."

"Lack of sleep leads to arthritis?"

"Could be," her mother said as she lowered herself into the chair. "Where's the remote?"

Rachel found it between the sofa cushions and turned on the TV. She raised the volume so her mother could better hear the Food Network, then went to the kitchen to open up her laptop and go over the notes from Tennessee.

"Two whole weeks," Abernathy had reminded her in his humid conference room. "You fly down here from DC like you got the light of God on your shoulder. You really think we've been sitting on our hands down here? Five kids vanished from Memphis, another nine from Nashville. Not a one of them has called his folks. Every single one left his phone and credit cards behind. Look, it *means* something when a young person abandons his computer these days. Leaves his phone behind. You know?"

Rachel knew, but Abernathy was trying to make another point that lay just beyond her. From the moment she'd entered his office, he'd been trying to make points. It wasn't the first time she'd faced this kind of reception: Jackson and Detroit were high on her shit list. "So you have a working theory," she said.

"Yes I do," he said, then took a sip of his coffee, drawing it out, waiting for her mouth to water in anticipation. She decided not to oblige. He said, "They're dead. All four hundred of them."

Her first thought was instinctual: *This is how you clear your work-load; you kill it off.* She said, "You're telling me that Martin Bishop gathered four hundred people from around the country to have them . . . what? Drink poisoned Kool-Aid?"

He leaned forward, hands open. "Look, these kids—they aban-doned the things they love most. Two whole weeks, none of their folks have heard from them. They've *vanished.* How's that possible?

How does one kid *not* give a call home, just to say he's still alive? Here's how: They're not."

"Why would Bishop do that?"

Abernathy dropped back in his chair and shrugged. "Who's to say what Bishop is thinking? Maybe he wants a bunch of martyrs. I mean, that man's insane. He's running his own cult. Wouldn't be the first time."

"Have you read any of his writings?"

"Should I?"

The agent who drove her back to the airport was sympathetic. "Memory," he told her as Memphis International, adorned in red-white-and-blue posters celebrating the holiday, came into view. "If it's not exploding in front of him, Abernathy's going to forget it exists. Then he comes up with theories to justify what he doesn't remember."

Tragedy plus time isn't comedy, thought Rachel. *It's amnesia.* She'd seen the same thing in the report Philly had sent to her on Benjamin Mittag's mother, Jenny, a trailer-park queen living on the outskirts of Waynesboro. "Yeah, he was trouble," Jenny had said. "But all boys are. He had beliefs, though. You know he tried to become one of you?"

Me? asked the interviewer.

"A federal agent. Applied and everything. If you'd accepted him, everything would have been different."

A note mentioned that the agent had verified the mother's claim before arriving: Benjamin Mittag's 2008 application had been swiftly rejected and filed away. The decision had been justified by Mittag's spotty juvenile record.

"But he did try to convince his mom," Jenny went on. "What I'm telling you. He had beliefs. Year or so later this guy comes to speak to him. They go off to have a beer. Ben comes back, he tells me that the FBI changed its mind. They want him."

A note here stated that her claim could not be verified, and the agent explained this to Jenny: *We have no record of that, ma'am.*

"You think I'm an idiot?" she demanded. "Yes, I believed it at first. I'm a mother, for God's sake. I should've remembered, but I chose not to. He was always a good liar, the best. He went south and I didn't hear anything from him until his name came up with the Massive Brigade. A liar."

"Ray!" she heard from the other room. Rachel found her mother holding her phone, which was lit up bright, vibrating. Doug was calling on his day off.

"You watching this?" he asked her.

"What?"

"Turn on your television."

On the screen, a woman was instructing her mother on how to make turkey stuffing. "Yes, and?"

"The news, Rachel. Put on the news."

13

KEVIN WAS shaking when he reached the lobby and pushed through to the sidewalk, kicking a discarded plastic cup, and found Holly leaning against a Lamborghini. Christ, it was bright out here; his eyes hurt. From the other side of the palm trees they could hear screams, shouts. Sirens.

Holly said nothing, only met his eye, smiled nervously, and started walking; Kevin followed. The parade crowd was breaking up in a panic, families rushing from the main route, Crandon, into the side streets. Holly stayed a couple of paces ahead, and he sometimes had to push through wild-eyed people to stay close. Once he knocked down a woman. In a panic himself, he stopped and helped her up, apologizing. The woman was yelling something at him, but he couldn't hear; everything was buzzing. He turned away and realized he'd lost track of Holly. He hurried forward until, finally, he saw that she'd stopped at the next corner and was watching him. The smile was long gone. Fear, perhaps, or something else. He didn't know. He hurried on.

Another block, and they were in the car. He tried to ignore the pandemonium he'd caused. He thought of the woman he'd knocked down, and imagined how many other women, children, and men had tripped or been pushed aside, and then trampled. Humans did that. They lost their minds. Their feet became weapons against the weak.

She drove south, staying off Crandon until she had no other options, but they were far enough away to be outside the melee. They entered Bill Baggs Cape Park, the narrow road bordered by thick foliage. Before reaching the entrance, where a park guard would be waiting, she pulled off the road.

"You okay?" she asked.

"What?"

"Are you all right?"

"Yeah. Sure. Let's go."

They got out and worked their way slowly through the low, wind-stunted shrubbery to reach the shore. His face and hands were scratched. In the distance, they saw it: a small motorboat heading toward them. Holly stepped into the water, then looked back at him.

"How do you feel?" she asked.

"Good."

"Don't lie."

How did he feel? Not good, no. He'd realized, as soon as the bullet left the barrel, that it was all wrong. That distance, estimating at wind resistance and trying to calculate the arc of the bullet—why did he think he could do it? Who was he trying to impress? Did he want to hear stories, later on, about his shooting prowess? *Incredible— he only nicked her from that distance!* In his state of mind, that was as good an explanation as any, and now a politician was bleeding out.

"Come on," said Holly, and she waded out into the water toward the motorboat.

14

DURING THE first year that he lived with Ingrid in Berlin, David would walk the three blocks from their coffin-sized Prenzlauer Berg apartment, laptop in hand, to the Communist-themed Bar '56. He'd take a corner table under the mural of Khrushchev and sip Americanos as he worked. After three or four hours, once he'd finished a day's writing, he would order gin tonics and chat with the bartender, Elli, the tattooed singer of a band called Unterwelt, or Underworld. She had huge eyes and an attractive sort of heroin chic about her, and she quizzed him intensely about "ridiculous" and "criminal" American politics while he in turn questioned her about growing up in Leipzig, in the old East.

He quickly began to look forward to these mildly flirtatious conversations, and began ordering his first drink earlier—fifteen minutes, a half hour, an hour—until eventually he found himself writing only an hour or so before catching her eye and finding a question to ask.

This went on for weeks, drinking and chatting until four in the afternoon, at which point he would pour a double espresso down his throat and rush home to greet Ingrid, just back from work. Sometimes she noted his tipsiness, and he'd lie, telling her he was exhausted from too many hours of writing.

What was it about Elli? Was it the way she wore her cutoff T-shirts so that the sleeves of her tattoos were on full display? Was it the way she opened up so easily about the various little traumas of a childhood in the depressed post-Communist East? Or maybe it was simply that a young, hipper-than-thou Berliner found this frumpy, thirty-five-year-old American interesting enough to spend her time with. She validated his high opinion of himself, and thoughts of her followed him all day and to bed, even as his wife dozed beside him.

Ingrid had just gotten a promotion at the Starling Trust, and part of her new duties included attending April meetings at their global headquarters in New York. He helped her pack a bag for the four-day trip, and once her taxi disappeared around the corner from their apartment he walked directly to Bar '56 and asked Elli what she was up to that evening.

Later, he wouldn't recall having a specific plan. Infidelity wasn't foremost in his mind. Ingrid was so distracted by her job that when she came home she had little interest in asking about the book; Elli, on the other hand, was fascinated by his creative process, which he could talk about for hours. So when he went to her that day he was merely seeking a receptive audience. Or so he told himself.

Whatever the motivation, Elli told him that Unterwelt was playing a gig that evening in a squat apartment block in Friedrichshain, just south of Prenzlauer Berg.

It took him a while in the crisp, chilly darkness to find the building, but once he reached it he paid his cover to a multiply pierced, chain-smoking bouncer and was pointed to a crumbling courtyard illuminated by fifty oil lamps. On one side was a cash bar stocked with beer, and on the other the four-piece Unterwelt setting up to play. Elli, tuning her rhythm guitar, gave him one of her gorgeous smiles and thanked him for coming as the crowd, dressed like down-market Brooklynites, streamed in.

Throughout the evening he tried, largely in vain, to find the melodies in Unterwelt's songs, an odd mix of acid rock and Kraft-werk. Still, he admired Elli's voice and how she stalked the audi-ence hungrily. She needed open spaces to express herself, not the narrow confines of a bartender's domain. She was, in front of the crowd, someone quite different, but no less intriguing.

Because of the neighbors, they shut down at nine, and he waited for her to finish packing up. He lied magnificently, pointing out the songs that he admired most, and sharing his surprise at her electric performance. He wasn't sure if she believed him or not, but she let him carry her guitar case and walk her home to another bleak-looking squat nearby. "I'd invite you in, but my roommates are assholes," she told him. Then she kissed him on the lips, a long, lingering kiss that tasted of the beer she'd sipped between songs. "See you tomorrow?"

"Man's got to work," he said, and she laughed, because even she had noticed that he was no longer getting any work done.

Turning away, David told himself that he hadn't planned a thing, and this marked the beginning of an eight-year self-delusion. What, really, had he done? He'd come to listen to a band he'd heard so much about. Supporting a friend—then *she'd* kissed *him*. David Parker had done nothing wrong.

He pulled his jacket tighter as he walked, light-footed, down the cracked sidewalk. Kids in leather were smoking hash. Up ahead a guy was on a phone; across the street, two girls were laughing. From a window, someone was playing the Velvet Underground's "All To-morrow's Parties," and he'd just been kissed by the lead singer of a Berlin rock band. Pretty fucking cool.

Then his eardrums shuddered at the huge bass *thump* as—there, ahead, above the laughing girls—the top floor of a dilapidated apart-ment building exploded in concrete and fire. The girls screamed and ran. The man on the phone stepped back and lowered his phone. David's bladder, bubbling from too much beer, released itself.

Eight years later, he told this story to Bill, who had called him—out of pity, he knew, but he didn't care—to celebrate Independence Day with him and Gina in Montclair. Bill served him drinks and nachos, CNN playing in the background, while Gina spent most of the time in the kitchen gabbing with Francine, her cousin in Fort Lauderdale. It turned out that she had finally convinced Bill to give Florida a try, and they were in the middle of arranging their plans for a seasonal move.

"What happened with Elli?" Bill asked, swirling the whiskey in his glass.

"Don't know."

"What do you mean, you don't know?"

"I never stepped foot in that bar again."

Bill cocked his head, maybe wondering what kind of friend he really had.

David sipped his beer. "That was the Kommando Rosa Luxemburg. Martin Bishop's gang. That's the kind of guy Ingrid has gone off to join."

"She's smarter than you give her credit for. Probably smarter than you. I'm guessing that once she sees his operation up close—if he even *has* an operation, which I doubt—she'll leave."

David thought that two weeks was plenty of time to see an operation close-up, and was going to comment on this, when he noticed that Bill was staring at the television. He turned, too, and saw that something had happened. Bill raised the volume.

They listened closely to a serene CNN newscaster reveal the details of a shooting: Arlington, Virginia, House Republican Paul Hanes, at the annual Barcroft Fourth of July Parade. Already, the studio in Atlanta was lifting amateur phone-camera footage from YouTube and Facebook: wobbly, sun-bleached shots of Hanes with his wife and two boys on a porch of some kind—place of honor—laughing in the midst of local families. Then Hanes tipped his head back (more accurately, his head was tipped back by a single bullet that marked a black spot in his forehead), and he dropped, disappearing behind others. Because of the noise of the crowd, the gunshot was unheard, and there was an instant—a second or so—when no one realized he was gone. His wife continued to smile, and his boys, in unison, held their cupped hands to the sides of their mouths and shouted at someone unseen. Then the wife turned, perhaps to say something to her husband, maybe remind him to smile, and realized he was no longer there. She looked down, then shouted as she, too, dropped out of the frame.

"Well, shit," David said.

"Gina!" Bill called, but she was still on the phone, making plans.

It was too early for the police spokesman to share details, and too early for CNN to put cameras in front of their experts to speculate on who, what, and why. A specialist in international security, the only one they happened to have in the studio, suggested that this was not al Qaeda, simply because the target was a House member who had no record of anti-Muslim comments. An ISIL devotee would have targeted a large number of people. Conversation veered in the direction of mental illness, though David noticed that, as usual, no one pointed out that the mentally ill are almost never violent toward others. The bulk of murders in America are committed by the healthy.

Bill took his glass and headed toward the kitchen to share the news with Gina. Then the newscaster said, "This just in—we have reports of another shooting, in Miami. At the . . . yes. At the Key Biscayne Fourth of July Parade."

Bill halted, the empty glass in his hand, and returned to the couch.

There was no useful amateur footage from Miami, not yet, but the news came in quickly: Representative Diane Trumble, a Democrat, had been shot. Her condition was unknown. Up north in Arlington, the police spokesman verified that Paul Hanes had indeed been killed by a single gunshot to the head. Down south, Diane Trumble was wheeled into an ambulance. That was when the newscaster, losing the script a moment, turned to someone off-screen and just stared, dumbfounded. A full three seconds of silence—an eon on television. Then she cleared her throat, turned to the camera, and muttered, "Breaking news. Again. Republican Senator Joseph Wallace has

been killed in an explosion in Little Rock, Arkansas. Excuse me—
no, his death has *not* been verified, but he was reportedly inside the
car with his driver, and as it left his driveway in the neighborhood of
Pleasant Valley, it exploded."

"*Gina!*" Bill called.

She appeared in the doorway, phone in her hand. "I'm not deaf,
Bill."

By five o'clock, there had been four attacks. A few minutes before
the hour, in Helena, Montana, Representative Gary Heller, Democrat, was shot dead in his own backyard, on the way to his in-ground
pool. Three dead men and one lone woman, Diane Trumble, on life
support in Jackson Memorial Hospital.

The now-exhausted newscaster touched her ear, nodded, and
said, "This just in."

David gasped, expecting a fifth assassination, but this was news
that had been taken from the internet, because the event had occurred
on *The Propaganda Ministry,* the blog Martin Bishop had let go fal-
low for the previous two weeks, ever since he disappeared. It had
then spread like wildfire through Twitter, Facebook, Tumblr, Google+,
Reddit, and any number of other social websites. Notified by their
own alerts, CNN staff shared its message with the rest of the country:

America!

This is the first day of the first situation that will give rise to
further situations leading to the liberation of you, each of you,
each one.

Do not be confused or frightened—there's no need.

Those who do not move do not notice their chains.

The time for analysis is over.

Let's move.

"Where there is power, there is resistance."

The Massive Brigade has opened its membership to include the entire country. You are one of us now.

The Massive Brigade is resistance. You are resistance.

What we have done anyone can do.

Go. Do.

                        —The Massive Brigade

"Oh, shit," said Bill.

Gina, unsurprised, said, "Of course."

David said nothing. He was remembering that explosion in Berlin, stumbling home in his piss-stained jeans, climbing the stairs to his apartment. Pausing to answer his ringing phone. Ingrid, in New York, had just heard about the explosion and wanted to know if he was all right.

"Of course I'm all right," he'd lied.

15

THOUGH SHE could have gloated, she didn't. Rachel was simply grateful that once four members of Congress had been attacked and the federal government went into lockdown, the purse strings finally loosened, and her team was moved to a set of three interconnected offices on the fifth floor of the Hoover. Each regional analyst got his own desk, as did Doug and Ashley, and Rachel got her own room.

She slowly filled the third room with agents who could do the legwork that was beginning to run her into the ground. By July 5, seven of the twelve desks were already in use by agents focused on the tidal wave of leads being called into the FBI's hotline.

They had reports of unknown men of suspicious character, sketchy vans passing through new-car suburbs, neighbors reporting on neighbors. There were politically minded citizens reporting on newscasters who seemed under the sway of the Massive Brigade. Students reported on classmates who'd once professed a distaste for the federal government. And foreigners, so many foreigners. What they got, really, was a cross-section of American paranoia, of hidden prejudices rising to the surface. Whatever diverged from the mainstream was suspect.

That first full day, Owen Jakes invited her to join him on a conference call with Fay Levinson, a rosy-cheeked legal attaché officer in Berlin. When the video connected, Levinson cheerily said, "Hi, Owen!"

Jakes whispered to Rachel, "I got her her job."

Levinson updated them on the cooperation they were receiving from German intelligence, which had spent the past twenty-four hours tracking the web of Martin Bishop's European connections.

"Do the Germans really have time for this?" Rachel asked.

"Yesterday," Levinson told her, "the Reichstag watched three American politicians die, a fourth on life support, and they know Bishop was inspired by a local group; they're terrified they're next. The BfV is kicking in doors all over Berlin. Don't think the Bureau's going through this alone. The moment they find anything useful, they'll be on the horn to me, and I'll get it to you and Owen."

"Thanks," Rachel said. "And how about getting me clearance for Owen's KRL report from 2009?"

Levinson hesitated, head cocked, then nodded. "I'll see what I can do on that front, okay?"

After they hung up, Jakes said, "Isn't she great?"

Even though the conversation hadn't been materially useful—and Rachel held out little hope of getting the 2009 report—learning that the Germans were just as worried was reassuring, and in the face of four hundred people doing a remarkable job keeping themselves hidden, it was almost as good as a lead.

Still, there was uneasiness, and she struggled with basic questions. "It doesn't match," she told Jakes. "*Why* kill these people? Bishop's writings never advocated direct, targeted attacks. He mentioned them, yes, but as a threat to hold over elected officials. He never actually advocated murder. And now, right out of the gate, he goes for the most extreme action? What changed?"

"As you well know," he countered, "the world doesn't run on airtight logic."

"But he's smart enough to know that he's shooting himself in the foot."

Jakes shrugged and got up to go. "The real question is: Why does it matter why? That's not going to help us put Martin Bishop behind bars."

The next afternoon, Ashley dropped off a bundle of pages that smelled of Fogo de Chão's grilled lamb. "Magellan Holdings," she said.

Rachel had just gotten off a dismal call with the Albuquerque office. "This better be good news, Ash."

Ashley took a chair with a grand flourish and smiled. "Magellan Holdings LLC is the source of Massive's funding, pre–June 18."

"And they are?"

"A shell company. Well, the end of a line of five shell companies scattered around the world. Magellan's incorporated in the Bahamas. The only listed officer is one Laura Anderson—we looked her up. Australian, seventy-eight years old. Resides at a nursing home in Brisbane."

Rachel leaned back, trying to picture this. "Does that make any sense to you?"

"It sure does," said Ashley. "It means someone really doesn't want to be found."

In the outside world, the press was knocking on the Bureau's door. Sam Schumer had come out quoting a confidential source saying that on June 18, nearly four hundred people with connections to the Massive Brigade had disappeared. He rubbed his endless forehead, tugged at his mustache, and spoke to his audience with the faux desperation of a shyster. "This is the question, fellow citizens: *Where are our children?*" Rachel got an angry call from Assistant Director Paulson, who demanded to know if she had been Schumer's source. When she denied it, he told her to reconnect with Schumer, ASAP, "because if we're not driving the story someone else will gladly do it for us."

16

THIS WAS what it was like to never be alone.

There was Holly, and the pimply-faced George who took their sopping wet selves around the key to Cutler Channel, where a Latina Mary waited at the end of Paradise Point Drive in a Range Rover stocked with snacks, blankets, towels, and a change of clothes. He lay with Holly in the cargo space as Mary drove them nonstop up the chicken leg of Florida, higher, playing the radio loud so they could all listen to what they had wrought.

Holly pulled the blanket over their heads when they stopped to fill the tank, and in the humid darkness she whispered that he was a hero of the Revolution, and that one day his name would be in the history books. He didn't ask if he would be there as a villain or a hero, because he wasn't sure he could form the words. As Mary pulled onto the highway again, Holly kissed his forehead and ran her fingers down his chest to his groin, and he closed his eyes. He had submitted to everything else; why not this?

Afterward, he slept.

It was long after midnight, and they'd been on the road thirteen hours straight when they arrived at a large, rambling house in the swamplands of Louisiana, deep in the kudzu empire. Both he and

Holly walked weak-kneed into the embrace of eighteen Georges and Marys, all excited and terrified by what had occurred, but however they felt about the act they were uniformly in awe of Kevin, one of the Revolution's bloody hands. They served him and Holly homemade gumbo, watching every bite he took. He felt as if the eyes of God, everpresent, had suddenly become flesh. That wasn't all he felt.

He felt as if, by virtue of one little trigger, he'd aged considerably. It wasn't the first time—there had been Afghanistan, after all—but the intimacy of him, a sniper's rifle, and a woman on a stage was something entirely different. Like someone opened a door in his head, ignoring the sign that said, "Don't open until midlife crisis." Like he'd walked through that door and gotten cozy with a new kind of mortality.

The adoration only made him more claustrophobic, made him want to kick them out of the house and tell them not to come back until they'd found a fucking cell phone so that he could call his mother, but not even those who blow the first trumpet of the Revolution are allowed such things. A room of honor on the top floor, yes. And Holly, who stared down any Mary who showed signs of interest. But no phone.

He didn't sleep—how could he? Holly made sure he didn't, and even without her he knew he wouldn't have been able to. So he tried out her Pall Malls, holding down coughs as he smoked by the window and watched the sky brighten into morning. He felt so lost.

A day passed. A day of leftover gumbo and cans of Miller Lite and eager looks and Holly, midday, bringing him back up to their room. By then everyone knew that Diane Trumble would likely survive the bullet in her neck, but that didn't undermine their awe and appreciation. A man could live like this, he thought, but only as long as the ruse lasted; only until they realized that he wasn't the hero they'd made him out to be.

It was nine the second morning when Benjamin Mittag pulled up to the safe house in a pickup truck driven by a young woman.

Kevin saw them approach from his window. Both Mittag and the woman were in rough farmer's clothes; Mittag wore a fake mustache and mirrored cop glasses, a small bag on his shoulder.

The Georges and Marys watched as, in the living room, Mittag gave him a bear hug, then turned around and raised a fist in the air. They raised theirs, a field of floating knuckles. He said, "This is one of the first heroes of the Revolution. In the future, children will know his name."

Kevin tried to control his bowels.

Mittag said, "Come on, motherfucker," and pulled him upstairs. When they entered the bedroom, Mittag closed the door and sat on Kevin's stained sheets. He rubbed his hands through his hair. "You got her in the neck, but weren't you aiming for the chest? Was there trouble with the shot?"

He'd had plenty of time to prepare his answer. "I heard— well, I *thought* I heard—someone in the building. Outside the room. Coughing."

"Did you see anyone?"

He shook his head.

Mittag frowned. "And that threw your shot?"

"I don't know, but it's the only thing I can think of. Just as I was pulling the trigger. Aim. Cough. Fire."

Mittag leaned back. "Yeah, that might do it."

"Or maybe I'm not as good a shot as I think."

"You are, man." A grin. "Look, you and me, we're going on another trip."

"Where?"

"Boss man wants a meeting."

"Bishop?"

"Daddy's pissed off. But we've been quiet long enough."

Kevin had no idea what that meant.

"We leave in a couple of hours," Mittag said, then sniffed the air. "Does it smell like pussy in here?"

His good-bye to Holly was easy; she'd always treated him as if he were leaving. To the others, he just nodded. After a late lunch, he and Mittag were driving a car with Texas plates through the swamps, and north. They didn't speak, which was a relief. Though nearly two days had passed, Kevin still felt the residual echo of his shock and feared that if he started speaking he might not stop, blabbing his entire life, from birth all the way to now.

When, the following morning, they stopped at a backwoods gas station near Marshall, Texas, Kevin went in search of a toilet. The fat woman behind the counter directed him around the side of the building, but when he got there the bathroom door was locked. He was turning back to ask for the key when he heard a toilet flush.

The door opened, and a skinny black teen opened the door. His eyes were shy, embarrassed, and Kevin felt an inexplicable urge to hug him, to tell him everything was fine. Instead, he said, "Hey, brother."

"Hey."

Though his scrambled brain felt a few degrees west of crazy, he controlled his voice, keeping it steady. "Can you do me a solid?"

The boy just looked at him.

"My cell died. I gotta get word to my mom. Tell her I'm gonna be late for dinner."

The boy looked him up and down, shrugged, then shoved a hand deep into the pocket of his low-hanging jeans. He pulled out a cell phone. "You ain't calling another country?"

Kevin laughed, then cut it short because he didn't know how it sounded. "No, man. She's in San Antonio."

The boy watched as Kevin, hands trembling, dialed the number he'd been holding on to for months, the one he had last sent a text message to on June 18.

After two rings he heard a woman's voice. "Yes?"

"Mom, it's Kevin."

Janet Fordham, who had only days before told Rachel Proulx that she had given up hope of ever hearing from her agent, almost shouted. She got control of herself, but when she spoke she was choked up. "So good to hear from you, son."

Kevin started to cry.

"Shit," said the boy, turning away to give him privacy.

17

RACHEL SAT in Mark Paulson's office, the aroma of Ashley's lunch still lingering in her nose, waiting for him to reach the end of the memo she'd quickly thrown together after her call with Janet Fordham. "This is the beginning," she said, impatient for him to finish reading. "This is how we close it down."

She wasn't sure Paulson had heard her, but there was no point saying it again. The information spoke for itself.

Finally, he said, "Where's Butte La Rose?"

"Louisiana. In the Atchafalaya Basin." In answer to Paulson's blank stare, she said, "The bayou."

That was enough for him. "And how old is this intel?"

"Three hours."

He nodded. "We could have a team there in twenty-four."

"Bishop isn't there. Mittag isn't either."

"But eighteen members are right there, waiting to be rounded up," said Paulson. "Those other houses—they might be empty now. This is an assured capture."

She'd worried about this before handing him the report. Paulson's background in banking left him, on occasion, surprisingly ignorant. Which was why she didn't share OSWALD's role in the shooting of

Diane Trumble. She tried to make it simple for him. "If we sweep in now, it's bound to expose OSWALD."

Paulson sighed.

She knew what was on his mind—the press. Now that Sam Schumer had revealed to the world the four hundred missing followers, grieved family members were shouting to the press about FBI secrecy. That afternoon, a *Wall Street Journal* editorial had castigated the FBI as symptomatic of a bloated federal system that was as fat as it was ineffectual. The Massive Brigade, the paper argued, was too nimble to be caught by bureaucrats. Paulson could feel the hot breath of his critics on the back of his neck and was waiting in terror for the president to call his direct line. So she threw him a bone. "Look at the third page."

He turned to it, scanning the other safe houses Kevin had identified for them. She said, "I've asked our field offices to surveil them. We'll have choices. We can pick off an earlier one. It won't expose OSWALD, but it will show the press we're not sitting around doing nothing."

Paulson returned to the first page and sighed. "OSWALD's still in contact?"

"He's going to try for daily reports, but no promises. It's not easy getting away."

Paulson rubbed an eye with his pinkie, and finally nodded. "Let's go put the fear of God into them, then, shall we?"

By five thirty, the Denver field office had struck gold—at least a dozen Massive followers were still living in the safe house near the base of Black Mountain in Wyoming. She told them to fly a SWAT team up there. Before heading out to Ronald Reagan Airport, she stopped by Paulson's office to give him the news. The man seemed positively giddy.

A Bureau jet flew her five hours to Sheridan County Airport, and, upon landing, a local agent picked her up in a black Suburban and drove her through the redbrick center of Sheridan. The bars were closing, and a few tall men in cowboy hats wandered down the

sidewalks, wobbly from drink. Independence Day signs, already starting to fade, advertised steer roping and bronc riding.

"They're in position?" she asked the agent.

He checked the time on the dash: 12:42 A.M. "Should be."

On their way up I-90, north of town, her phone buzzed. It was
Owen Jakes. "It's all ready?" he asked.

"Just about. What's up?"

"Can't sleep. Wish I'd come along."

"There'll be plenty of raids soon enough."

"May I suggest something?" he asked.

"Sure."

"Keep your finger on the trigger tonight. These people are
psychopaths."

The next call was from Commander Stephen Reyes, and she told
him she would be there in twenty.

"There are some lights on," he replied.

She knew what he was getting at; all evening he'd sounded
nervous. "They can't all be asleep, can they?"

"Are you sure about your plan?"

Given the armaments inside that house, she'd decided that
instead of surprising them, she would announce herself from a safe
distance. Give them a moment to think through their options and
consider surrender. A sudden attack would result in a confused gun-
fight and a lot of blood. Reyes disagreed—an announcement, he con-
tended, would only give them time to arm themselves and draw out
the fight. He'd been in Waco for the disastrous Branch Davidian raid,
and he didn't want a repeat performance.

But these weren't members of a religious cult. They were young
people who, no matter what they thought of the government, didn't
want to die. There was nothing waiting for them on the other side.

"We'll talk when I get there," she said, and hung up.

"He wants to be a hero," the agent said as he drove through blackness under a white moon.

"What?"

"Reyes. He wants to do it himself. With stealth. Doesn't want any bureaucrats standing in his way."

"I don't see any bureaucrats in this car."

He laughed. "Just keep telling yourself that, Agent Proulx."

They cut the lights and rolled at half speed until they reached the outer edge of the property, then pulled into a ditch. She took a bullhorn from the trunk and walked to meet Reyes farther up the road. Because of his black outfit, she didn't see him until he was right next to her. He shook her hand, then led her through spindly trees to where the land sloped; in the middle of an open field lay the large ranch house. A couple of lamps glowed in windows along the wrap-around porch. As they walked, he reported in whispered tones that earlier that evening a woman had left the property, and his men had tracked her all the way to a previously unknown safe house south of Nephi, Utah.

"Great work," she said. "That'll be our next one."

He pointed across the field. "There's twenty-seven of us scattered out there. We can be at the front door in sixty seconds." He touched his ear, listening. "A female is in the kitchen. Making coffee."

Moonlight lit up the craggy path between Rachel and the house. She'd gone over maps to figure her best approach, but here, actually preparing to approach the house, her plan to stand at a safe distance and shout to them through the bullhorn . . . it felt wrong. How would a group of paranoid kids react to the sound of an amplified voice telling them to lay down their weapons and surrender?

Alternately, what would they do when black-clad agents smashed through their doors with battering rams?

"Take this," she said to Reyes, and handed him the bullhorn. "There's been a change of plan."

It was nearly two o'clock when she walked up the long gravel driveway, then stepped onto the cracked stones that led to the porch. She walked steadily, careful not to hurry, but also making no effort to be quiet. By the time she reached the steps she'd noticed curtains parting. She was surprised she even had to knock on the door, and more surprised that it took them a full minute to open it.

A young woman cracked open the door and showed her face. "It's kinda late, lady," she said.

"Sorry," Rachel said, "but we need to take care of this before dawn."

18

THEY HAD just passed through McAlester, Oklahoma, and were heading through the predawn gloom of big-sky country when on KLCU, 90.3, National Public Radio told them about the bust in Sheridan, Wyoming. Kevin looked over at Benjamin, waiting for the inevitable explosion, but it didn't come. Ben looked out over grassy farmland as, on the radio, FBI Assistant Director Mark Paulson said, "The so-called Massive Brigade is on the run. Special Agent Rachel Proulx led the raid that resulted in thirteen arrests."

"Who the fuck is Rachel Proulx?" Ben asked.

"Hell if I know," Kevin said, because he had no idea.

Paulson told reporters that the public should expect more arrests in the coming days. "The Bureau, in partnership with Homeland Security, is closing in." Then he made an appeal to those among the four hundred who were having second thoughts. "Turn yourself in to local authorities. Our fight is not with you, but with Martin Bishop and Benjamin Mittag."

"You got that right," said Mittag, grinning.

"You're not worried?" asked Kevin.

"Do I look it?" He shrugged. "What you have to understand is that the Massive Brigade leads by example. What we did on

July 4—what *you* did—that was unprecedented. It was *massive*. We showed everyone that everything is possible, as long as you're determined. You have to want it."

"Sure."

"Fidelity, bravery, integrity," Ben said to the road. "Know what that is?"

Kevin did, but it felt like a trick question. "Three abstract nouns in a row?"

"It's the FBI motto. Might as well be ours, too."

Though he'd planned to, he hadn't stolen the teenager's phone in Marshall. As he'd hung up with Janet Fordham, he'd clocked the teen's physique and quickly laid out a plan to knock him unconscious and hide him in the bathroom. He knew his plan was wildly reckless, but a phone that Fordham could track . . . that was gold. Then he and the boy turned at the crunch of gravel, and the fat woman from inside said, "Trey, Stacy's looking for you," and his opportunity passed. He thanked Trey for the phone and went back out front to join Mittag.

Had the Bureau gotten a lock on his call in time to track their car via satellite? Even if they had, there was no guarantee that they would get the satellite coverage—more often than not, the satellite they wanted had already been booked by one of the other sixteen security agencies. Until he found another phone, he had to assume he was alone.

"It's all hype anyway," Mittag said after another mile. "The FBI's gonna play up any little success as a big deal, even if it's peanuts. They're gonna say we're on the run."

"You don't want to refute them?"

He shook his head. "Massive plays it cool. Drop some politicians and a manifesto. Then let the others chatter all they want. We're not going to become part of a discussion where *they* make the ground rules. When we speak, they'll know because they'll be hurting."

"But when we're silent, they control the narrative," Kevin protested. "*They're* the ones who are defining you to the people."

"Let 'em. They could paint us as pedophiles. What's important is the message we, as a movement, send out when we do choose to talk."

Nearly a thousand miles from Butte La Rose, they reached Lebanon, Kansas, by early afternoon and parked on Main Street in front of the American Legion Hall. Next door was Ladow's Market, where they ordered plates of meatloaf with parsley potatoes and green beans as around them farmers laughed and gossiped and tried not to stare at the two strangers in their midst.

"We should've gotten this to go," Kevin whispered.

Mittag looked boldly around at the men and women of Lebanon, then shook his head. "As long as we don't have Martin's face, we're copacetic."

He was right. No one said a word to them, or showed any sign of alarm. The only alarm was Kevin's when he noticed cell phones on neighboring tables, lying beside coffee cups and soiled plates. So close that it hurt.

Though the pineapple cobbler intrigued them both, they decided against dessert and paid for their meals (four dollars each, plus tip) and when they got to the car noted a policeman across the street talking with a local. The cop glanced in their direction—they were strangers, after all—then returned to his conversation without missing a beat.

The meeting point was just a little outside town, a plot of grass and trees where the American and Kansas flags rose over a stone pedestal beside a bench. A few yards away, a gazebo had been set up with picnic tables, and beside it was a shed-sized building labeled U.S. CENTER CHAPEL. A wooden sign said WELCOME TO THE GEOGRAPHICAL CENTER OF THE 48 STATES.

Benjamin took a zip-lock bag from his pocket, and from it removed the pieces of an old Nokia with a black-and-white screen and Chiclet buttons. He inserted the battery, snapped it together, then powered it up.

Kevin checked his watch—it was nearly three. "How long we here?"

"About a half hour to go," Benjamin said; then as if on cue a synthetic *bleep* sounded. The Nokia lit up with a message. Benjamin read it and said, "I take that back," as he turned to look down the gray road that led straight to the blue-and-cloud horizon. Dust rose from a red pickup truck heading toward them. "Come on."

Kevin followed him to the gazebo, where they sat and waited, protected from the hot sun. The truck was farther away than it looked, and eventually it looped around the rear of the site and parked behind their car. The first person to get out was a woman, dark hair and sunglasses, jeans and a light blouse. She looked up each direction of the crossroads, then across the grass to where they waited in the gazebo. Then she looked back to Martin Bishop getting out from the driver's side and taking off his sunglasses. He wore a mustache and beard, a flannel shirt and jeans, and a weathered red cap that said MAKE AMERICA GREAT AGAIN.

"So that's her," Benjamin said, standing.

"Who?"

"The bitch who's been fucking with his head." He spat in the dirt. "Ingrid Parker."

19

THE GIRL—the one who'd opened the safe-house door—was crying. She'd entered the interview room erect and strong, but once they settled at the table and Rachel asked her name and age, the tears began, and fifteen minutes later they were still flowing.

She had expected tears, of course, but not so quickly. As they'd filed out of the house they'd all worn a similar kind of shell-shocked expression, as if the world outside their walls were an indecipherable puzzle. In one moment, they'd been safely cocooned in a universe where their ideologies had become flesh; in the next they were being led out into the cool, predawn gloom by armed men in black who shouted at them to lie facedown in the grass.

So, yes, she'd expected tears eventually. But before that she expected denial and anger and deal making, and was surprised to find so little of it. It was, she reflected, as if they'd been waiting for someone, anyone, to drag them out of that house.

"I didn't know. None of us knew. I mean—what could we *do?*"

"Why did you leave?"

The girl showed her confusion with an expression that looked, with her wet cheeks, more like agonizing pain.

"Leave home," Rachel said. "On June 18, you left everything behind and ran."

"But . . . we *had* to."

"Why did you have to?"

"Because you were coming. People like you. The government."

By her own accounting, the girl was twenty-four, and her name was Mary. Rachel might have believed her, but this was the sixth Mary she'd spoken to in the crowded corridors of the Sheridan County Sheriff's Office, and they all gave the same reason for June 18. Rachel leaned closer and said, "Listen to me, Mary. Are you listening?"

Her eyes were wet, but she nodded.

"No one was coming to get you. That's a lie."

Mary shook her head. "You came after Martin. You came after Ben. We were next."

It wasn't worth arguing the point, so she went on. "What did you expect to happen after you disappeared?"

"I expected a safe space."

"Safe?"

"Where we could speak openly, without fear."

"Is that what you got?"

Mary frowned, unwilling to judge what she had gotten.

"So you arrived here," Rachel said. "You met up with your comrades. But you had a plan. And it wasn't to sit around and talk forever. What was your plan?"

"Well, it *wasn't* to shoot people!"

"Then why did we find a dozen rifles and handguns in the house?"

"We had to defend ourselves."

Rachel tried not to let her irritation show, but after listening to these kids, each of who seemed to have had an entirely different idea of what going underground really meant, she'd come to the conclusion that the only thing they really shared was the conviction—misplaced, as it turned out—that Martin Bishop would show them the way. What happened, though, was that Bishop had never shown up at this particular outpost, and so they were left to stew in their paranoia and dream up plans for the overthrow of everything.

"We were gonna spread the word," Mary told her.

"Word?"

"We were gonna disappear and then come back with the word."

"You're not making any sense, Mary."

She sniffed, and Rachel offered her a tissue. Waited as she blew her nose. Mary shook her head. "It's what I wanted, at least. We would figure it out on our own and then come back. And we were going to share what we had learned. We were going to educate ourselves and then educate our families."

"Really?" Rachel couldn't quite swallow this as a workable plan, but then again she hadn't been trapped in a house in the country-side, suffering from a myopia that made every plan, no matter how pie-in-the-sky, seem workable.

Mary hesitated. "We had to make our own way, because no one was telling us what to do. But then they killed those politicians and . . ." She shook her head, still so confused.

Mary, who Rachel would later learn was actually named Louise Barker, was much like the others in that house. Though details changed, they were all variations on a theme. They had gathered in the week following June 18, and in lieu of specific orders they had focused on learning how to protect themselves while engaging in revolutionary conversation.

Later, Rachel asked one of the Georges about the shootings, and unlike Louise Barker, he didn't recoil. He just shrugged. "Sometimes you have to let go of plans. Others, they freaked out. Thought every-thing must be falling apart. But, look: You have to be able to adjust based on the present situation. If Martin thought that killing those suits was necessary, then it probably was."

"So you had no trouble with it."

"I could deal."

When her phone rang, she was taking a nap in a back room the sheriff had cleared out for her. It was David Parker; he sounded out of breath. "Tell me—is she there?"

"Is who where?"

"Ingrid. My *wife*. Is she one of the people you arrested?"

"No, David. She's not. I'm sorry."

Silence, as the hope David had felt faded away. "Well, you're a star now. *Special Agent Rachel Proulx led the raid, approaching the house at great danger to herself.*"

"Who said that?"

"Sam Schumer."

Rachel closed her eyes. Paulson had chosen to put her name in the press release; she wished he hadn't. Then David said, "Oh, shit."

"What, David?"

"Shit!" His volume rose. "Why didn't you tell me?"

"What are you talking about?"

"Why didn't you tell me he was dead?"

"Who?"

Though David told her, she didn't believe it until she hung up and used her phone to reach the *Schumer Says* website. And there it was, a flashing red EXCLUSIVE BREAKING NEWS banner: "Martin Bishop, leader of the terrorist group Massive Brigade, shot dead by his partner-in-crime Benjamin Mittag."

Even then, she couldn't believe it, because it didn't seem possible. On the day she'd made her first arrests, the leader of the Brigade was suddenly dead in a field outside Lebanon, Kansas? She called the Kansas City field office, which patched her through to agents still heading to the scene, and over speakerphone they gave her a run-down of what they knew: Forty-five minutes ago, there had been an anonymous call to the Lebanon police department, claiming that four people had been spotted at the intersection of 130 and Aa Road—three men and one woman, with two vehicles. As he drove past, the caller recognized one person as Benjamin Mittag, which was why he had called. By the time the police made it out there, they found one vehicle and one dead male, shot through the head. Maybe Bishop, but they couldn't be sure. Then they called the Bureau.

"I don't know what I'm going to find out there," the agent told her, "but if what we've heard is legit, then I'm getting drunk tonight."

"Not alone," said his partner.

"You haven't even verified it yet," Rachel said. "Who leaked it to Sam Schumer?"

"Hell if I know."

She was literally on the edge of her seat, the rest of the sheriff's station a flurry of activity on the other side of her closed door, when the agents reached the intersection of 130 and Aa, found the body, and squatted to check its fingerprints. There was silence on the line.

"So?" Rachel said, trying not to shout. "Who is it?"

20

A LIGHT breeze came up, whisking away some of the heat as they left Kevin sitting in the gazebo to argue in front of the chapel. He watched, thinking that Martin Bishop, for all that was said and written about him, looked, more than anything, tired. He waved his hands and made shapes in the air, but unlike the man in the videos inspiring crowds, he just seemed to be going through the motions as he angrily laid into Benjamin, who didn't look like he was having any of it. Ingrid Parker, by Bishop's side, was no less furious. Kevin couldn't make out much, but sometimes the wind shifted, and he caught phrases and words:

Martin: "What the hell were you *thinking*? You've ruined—"

Ingrid: "Wait! Calm—"

Ben: ". . . just the start! There's no other way . . ."

Martin: "The start of *what*?"

Ingrid to Ben: ". . . political neophyte!"

Ben shoved Martin and shouted: "Fucking snowflake! Are you in or are you *out*?"

Eventually, they calmed down, huddling close and talking, and from that point he could hear nothing. Kevin got up and walked in their direction. When he got too close, Ingrid glared at him, and he withdrew again. Defeated, he returned to Benjamin's car, where he rifled through the glove compartment, finding chewing gum but little else, so he popped a piece into his mouth and went back to the gazebo. By then they'd taken a break, and Benjamin joined him while Martin and Ingrid remained in front of the chapel and spoke.

"What's going on?" Kevin asked.

Benjamin shook his head, visibly upset. "He doesn't get what has to be done; he never has."

"Then why have you stayed with him so long?"

Benjamin furrowed his brow and looked suspiciously at Kevin. "Because how else is it gonna get done? You think I've got the money to run all this?"

Kevin looked past him, to where Ingrid was shaking her head at Martin. She then walked ten feet away, staring down at the grass. Martin turned to look back at them in the gazebo. Kevin met his eye, and in Martin's bearded face saw the passage of mixed emotions. What was he thinking? *What* was the big disagreement?

Then Martin jerked, and the left side of his head exploded, splattering red across the white chapel door.

Seeing the look on Kevin's face, Ben turned, but Ingrid didn't look back until the delayed *pop* of the gunshot arrived from out in the fields. Her scream was automatic, and she ran toward his body. Then, before registering what he was doing, Kevin ran toward her, shouting, "Go, go, go!"

Finally, Ben moved, shouting, "To the car! Now!" as he bolted toward it himself.

Kevin found Ingrid on her knees by what was left of Martin's head, her hands wet from his blood. She wouldn't move, so he grabbed her by the waist and lifted her even as she kicked and screamed at him. But he wasn't going to let her go. He half-carried her around to where their vehicles were parked safely behind the chapel. He let her drop into the grass, her face red and teary. She was in no state to move, so he said, "I'm going to pick you up again. Please don't kick me anymore."

He leaned down and reached out, but she slapped his hands away and, suddenly very calm, said, "I've got it." He watched her climb to her feet, and while her knees were clearly weak, she made it to the car and climbed into the passenger seat as Kevin threw himself into the rear. Ben, sitting as low as possible behind the wheel, was already stomping on the gas pedal.

"Keep your heads down," he said with a voice wobbly from adrenaline and fear as they sped out from behind the trees, now exposed, kicking up dust and gravel. They turned onto 130 and headed west.

Carefully, Kevin raised his head to look out the rear windshield, and far away he saw the glimmer of sun against what looked like a white pickup truck, all alone, in the middle of a field of wheat. Then it started to move.

21

WHO HAD killed Martin Bishop? What did this mean for the Brigade? And how had Sam Schumer learned it before Rachel had? She was preparing to call him when her phone started ringing. Paulson wanted to know what the hell was going on. "Bishop dead? Are we looking at the light at the end of the tunnel?"

"We're looking at something," she admitted, but didn't want to be more specific.

"You sound worried, Rachel."

With the adrenaline coursing through her, she didn't know what she felt. Then she did. "I'm feeling apprehensive, sir."

"Tell me."

She took a breath, but the cigarette stink of that back room in the sheriff's office left a bad taste on her tongue. "I've spent the last several hours talking to these followers, and what I'm hearing doesn't make sense. July 4 wasn't what they were expecting, and in a way it wasn't what I was expecting. Bishop's spent the last eight years maintaining a balancing act. Talking about violence while never actually encouraging it. He's been so careful . . . and now this?"

"People don't make sense," said Paulson. "Try spending an hour talking to my daughter."

"That's not it, sir," she said, wanting to make herself clear. "By doing this, by killing politicians, Massive delegitimized itself. It's the kind of act that either triggers spontaneous revolution, or it buries everything you've spent your life working toward. And look outside. There's no revolution in the street."

"They fucked up—I agree. What we have to do now is capitalize on it."

It was, in Paulson's opinion, a moment to celebrate while pushing forward with renewed vigor. She felt the same, but there were still too many questions to answer, and it hurt to know that she would never be able to put those questions to Bishop himself. The only person who could answer them was Mittag, and she didn't know where he was.

She spent an hour videoconferencing with Ashley and Doug; Owen was in Chicago, checking on a source who claimed to have set up Bishop with five foreclosed houses. At the same time, interrogation reports from the second raid in Nephi were starting to come in, as were preliminary forensics from the murder site. Bishop had been killed with a 7.62 millimeter shot from a rifle. Long range. Sam Schumer's story was that Mittag had committed the murder, but if he had he had used a sniper. "How do we think Schumer got his intelligence?" she asked Doug and Ashley.

"I don't think you realize how popular Sam Schumer is," Doug said. "He could start his own revolutionary organization in about two tweets."

True enough, and the only way to get any further on it was to talk directly to the man. She stretched out on the sheriff's leather sofa, one of many items the sheriff had pointed out proudly when she arrived, saying, "Asset forfeiture," and made the call.

Schumer picked up quickly, and before she could speak he said, "You finally going to confirm a few things, Rachel?"

"I've called to find out how you talk to the Massive Brigade."

A laugh from his side. "You think those guys speak to me?"

"How else did you learn about Martin Bishop's murder before we did?"

"Rachel," he said, turning to the professor's voice that he sometimes used on his show, signifying that it was time to dumb things down. "I learned long ago not to tie myself to a single source in any government department. Particularly when my one source doesn't like me anymore."

"What makes you think I don't like you, Sam?"

"I like you, too. But who do you think told me, back in March, that Martin Bishop's merry band was preparing for terrorist action?"

She remembered Schumer's anxious "exposé" on Bishop, which she'd always taken for a business move—his ratings had been on a downward slide. "I assumed you'd made that up."

"I'm a journalist, Rachel. You don't have to agree with my conclusions, but I don't make these things up. And since you don't talk to me anymore, I've had to lean on my ace in the hole."

"Who is . . . ?"

"Who is confidential. You know that."

The conversation stalled because they both knew what they wanted but neither had come with anything to offer. When she hung up, it was dark outside, and the asset-forfeiture sofa was feeling extremely comfortable. She closed her eyes and didn't open them when the phone rang again. She just brought it to her ear, saying, "Proulx."

"He called," said Janet Fordham.

Rachel's eyes snapped open, and she sat up. "Does he know how Bishop died?"

Janet sounded flustered a moment. "A sniper. He doesn't know if it was Mittag's doing. But listen—"

"How does he not know?"

"Forget that," Fordham snapped. "It's not important. What's important is that we know where Mittag is. And we have enough time to get him."

22

THEY HADN'T seen the white pickup since fleeing Lebanon, and as far as they knew it hadn't followed them. Ben, at the wheel, was scared, and then angry—he was unsteady enough that Kevin nearly offered to drive before thinking better of it. After a half hour, Bishop's friend, Ingrid, started talking and crying. She was pregnant, it turned out, and this wasn't how she'd imagined her child's future. Kevin remained quiet; he had no idea what had occurred back in Lebanon, and he knew he didn't have enough information to figure it out. All he could do was hold on tight and listen.

Ben eventually calmed, processing what had happened, while Ingrid used fast-food napkins to wipe Martin's blood off her hands. It was clear to Ben that the FBI had done it. One safe house had been closed down, and while they were driving they heard about a second bust in Nephi, Utah. "The Bureau's closing in," he said in a rare moment of naked fear. "They're wiping us all out."

Kevin didn't believe that, if not for moral reasons then for logistical ones—when he'd called Janet Fordham from East Texas he'd had no idea where they were heading, and he doubted she could have gotten satellite coverage so quickly. Still, he had no other theories to present, so he just agreed with Ben. And Ingrid said nothing. She kept turning to look at Kevin, as if measuring him with her eyes, until they topped off the tank in St. Paul, Nebraska. Ben went around the back of the station to have a piss while Kevin filled up. Ingrid leaned against the car and said, "How far away were you?"

"What?" Kevin asked.

"From Diane Trumble. When you shot her."

"I don't know," he said, checking the scrolling numbers on the gauge to hide his expression. "Half mile?"

"Pretty precise," she said, then turned away as Ben emerged from around the corner of the building, hiking up his pants. She said nothing more, and neither did Kevin. But it had been a loaded question, and the asking of it added a fresh tension to the car that Ben never noticed until, about a half hour beyond the South Dakota border, Ingrid reached into her jacket and placed a Smith & Wesson revolver on her lap. "Going hunting?" he asked.

"Asking a question, and I want to be sure I'm heard."

From the backseat, Kevin saw Benjamin's eyes flash at him in the rearview. "Shoot," said Benjamin. "So to speak."

She turned to place her knees against the back of her seat, so she was facing both men, wedged against the door. Gun in hand. To Benjamin: "Did you do it?"

"What?"

"Martin. Did you kill him?"

"*What?* Are you crazy?"

She waved the gun at Kevin. "You've got a sharpshooter right there. You've got others, too. The FBI's not magical; they're not omniscient—if they were we would've been caught weeks ago. The simplest solution is usually the right one."

Benjamin stayed cool, driving steadily, but Kevin didn't like the sight of the gun in this small space. Shooting either of them would deafen them all, for one thing. He saw a fiery crash in their future. So he said, "That might be simple, but it makes no sense. As soon as everyone finds out Martin's dead the Brigade's going to splinter. You know it. Ben knows it. This is the end of us."

But Ingrid had already considered that. "You know what Martin told me when we heard about those assassinations you guys pulled off? He said, *It's over.* Everything he'd worked for, it died the moment you pulled the trigger. And it's his fault," she said, swinging the barrel toward Benjamin. "What do you think we were fighting about back there? The fact that you assholes have turned the Massive Brigade into a terrorist organization. Now tell me again that Ben had no reason to kill Martin."

Kevin leaned back in the seat and closed his eyes, remembering that moment in the window, above Key Biscayne, squeezing the trigger, hoping without hope that he would maim but not kill the congresswoman. All that, to find out that it hadn't even been endorsed by Martin Bishop? It was hard to control the rage bubbling inside his chest. "Answer the woman, motherfucker. Did you kill him?"

"Hell, no! Of course not. I about shit my pants back there."

Kevin felt very warm. The car seemed to close in on him, and the only way out of it was for him to say, *"Fuck,"* and slap the side of Benjamin's head.

The car swerved, Benjamin said, "Ow! Shit!" and Ingrid held on to her seat to avoid tumbling. Kevin looked out the window. He didn't want any more of any of this. He didn't even give a damn when Benjamin once again blamed the Federal Bureau of Investigation for Martin Bishop's murder. Kevin no longer gave a shit.

By the time they reached the farmhouse outside Watertown, South Dakota, they had gone back over it all, Ingrid directing the conversation, and Kevin learned that violence had been a point of disagreement from the very start of the Massive Brigade. Benjamin, unsurprisingly, had insisted that revolution was by necessity violent, and to think otherwise was liberal weakness. Martin agreed that the threat of violence was necessary, but actual violence would undermine their support among the masses. "Our disappearance was an act of self-preservation, but Martin knew we could turn it into a statement," Ingrid said. "And when we returned, however we returned, all of us would carry with us the threat of vanishing again. Fear would surround us as we organized in our hometowns, preparing to shut things down. *That* was where we were heading. We were going to bring the country to a standstill. And it would've worked, until you," she said to Benjamin, "fucked it all up."

Benjamin said nothing; his cheeks were scarlet.

At the Watertown safe house, amid fields of soybeans glowing in the sunset, the news of Martin's death had just dropped, and while Sam Schumer was pushing the story that Benjamin had killed him, the local radio station was less adamant, and so, by now, was Ingrid. When they gathered with the other nine followers in the kitchen, Kevin noticed that there was a telephone on the wall with its number writ large in Sharpie on the handle. But there was no way he was going to be able to use it without being seen.

"We need to take a few days," Ingrid said after she and Benjamin had told them the story of Lebanon. "We have to reassess and figure out what the best way forward is. Mistakes have been made, and Martin is dead, but we aren't. We know enough to do whatever we want; we just have to agree on what that is."

"What does that even *mean*?" asked a Korean guy on the verge of tears.

"It means that we stay smart," said Ben, but over the course of the drive his voice had lost much of its natural authority. So Ingrid clarified:

"It means we act. We don't react."

A few people cleared out so Benjamin could get his own room upstairs. No matter his mistakes, he was a founder. Kevin sat on the bed, watching him unload his pockets, filling a bare set of shelves with car keys, wallet, and the zip-lock with his phone and battery. Ben was even starting to sound contrite. "What do you think, man? Do you think it was the wrong way to go?"

"You want the truth?"

"Always."

"First of all, you're an asshole for making me think Florida was the accepted plan." Ben didn't reply, so he continued. "But yeah. I think it was too early. The people aren't ready for bloodshed yet."

"When will they be ready?"

"Maybe they need more education. Maybe they won't be ready until we're dead and gone."

"You're a ray of fucking sunshine," Benjamin said, and grinned. "Use my bed if you like. I'm going to go do some team building. I might get drunk, too."

"Do it," Kevin said, and watched him leave. He waited five full minutes, listening to people moving around in the hallway, then grabbed the zip-lock, stuffed it into his jacket pocket, and left the room.

Downstairs, he ran into two housemates, Michael and Keira. "Where you going?" asked Keira.

"Fresh air. Back in twenty."

Michael perked up. "Company?"

Kevin raised his hands. "Need some alone time."

"I feel ya."

He paused just outside the door, looking up the gravel driveway that stretched into the dusky fields, and took a breath. There were no houses for as far as his eye could see, just a blue barn to the east and small islands of trees here and there. He was, finally, alone. He walked, consciously meandering since he knew someone would be watching from the house, and worked his way in the gathering darkness toward a copse of ash trees carefully planted for privacy. Once he was among them, he looked back across the field. No one was following. He took out the zip-lock and assembled the Nokia quickly. He powered it up. He dialed.

"Mother?"

This time he didn't cry, though he did feel the urge. He told her that Mittag was with him, but he didn't know how long he would stay. Janet Fordham told him to sit tight. She told him they would be on their way, but he knew all that. He didn't need to be told. What he needed was something else:

"Did we do it? Did we kill Bishop?"

"No," she told him. "Of course not."

Leaves crunched, and he turned to find Ingrid standing ten yards away, just visible in the shadows. He hung up and dropped the phone into the zip-lock. He was about to tell her the story he'd prepared, that after the whole experience he'd called his mother out of weakness, but he saw the look on her face, and he knew that she had heard too much of the conversation.

He was already hurtling toward her when she turned and ran toward the house. She only made it ten steps before he tackled her into the leaves. She hit hard, the wind gasping out of her. He turned her over, holding her wrists together with one hand, the other hand gripping her mouth. Her eyes, wide and bloodshot, swiveled in their sockets.

"Listen," he said. "I'm going to save your life. Do you understand?"

She made no reaction.

"Do you understand?"

She nodded.

"Very soon," he said, "everyone in the house is going to be taken away. There's nothing to do about that. You have no control over it. What you do have control of is yourself, and your baby. You stay, you're giving birth to that child in a federal penitentiary, and then your kid'll be taken from you. You don't want that. So you're going to leave."

She knitted her brows, as if she wanted to question that, so he said, "I'm going to take my hand off. Scream, and I break your neck."

Carefully, he took his hand off her mouth. She bit on her lips, trying to get blood back into them.

"It's simple," he went on. "You walk in that direction." He pointed west. "And I go back to the house. You have money?"

She nodded.

"You just go."

After a brief moment, she said, "Why?"

Why, indeed? "Maybe I like you, Ingrid. Maybe I don't want to have to kill you."

"When are they coming?"

"In less than fifteen minutes, the first ones will surround the place," he said, though he had no idea how long it would take them to get there. He just needed to get her moving. "Which is why you have to go now. You wait, and they'll pick you up before you can reach the next house."

The argument was playing out in her head; he could see that.

"You said it yourself," he told her. "This isn't what you imagined for your child."

That seemed to register. He stepped back and helped her up. She pulled her hair back out of her face and gave him a look. "Did you really shoot that congresswoman?"

He nodded.

"Maybe you're more of a believer than you think," she said, and walked westward without looking back. He waited until she had crossed the field and was out of sight. Then he turned back to the house.

23

SINCE HER plane had been recalled to Headquarters, Rachel waited at the county airport for Denver to send a Cessna six-seater. She checked in with Ashley, who had asked the consulate in Sydney to check on Laura Anderson at her nursing home in Brisbane, and the report had just come in. Though Anderson's signature on various company documents had been authenticated, she had never heard of Magellan Holdings, nor, in fact, Martin Bishop. "They used her," Ashley said.

"But who is they?"

"Exactly. Sydney's checking on family connections, but she's spent all her life Down Under. Worked her last fifteen years, until 2004, for the UN in New South Wales. Other than that, there's nothing raising any red flags."

"The United Nations?" Rachel asked, remembering James Sullivan, the man she'd met in 2009 in San Francisco, the same man who had warned Bishop to flee that party in Montclair, calling from the corner of Forty-First and Second, a block from the UN headquarters.

"Coincidence," Ashley said, reading her mind. "The UN doesn't have the funding to waste on American politics. Do you know how broke they are?"

Rachel didn't, but she also didn't put much faith in coincidence these days. "Forward me whatever they sent you," she said.

Before disconnecting, Ashley hesitantly asked, "So this is it? You're really going to close down the Brigade tonight?"

"Let's wait and see," she said, because she wasn't allowing herself to feel excitement. She'd dug in, prepared for a long war, and it was unimaginable that, in the end, she would face only a couple of skirmishes.

Over the three hours she spent in the air, she conferred with the team already on the ground in Watertown, which had eyes on Mittag's new safe house. "We've verified three males, two women," said Luis Gonzales, the SWAT commander, "but there are more."

"Anyone leaves, pick them up quietly, out of sight of the house. I'll be touching down in . . ." She checked her watch. "Two hours."

The pilot pushed the old jet to its limit, and by twelve thirty she'd landed at Watertown Regional, where a Bureau Suburban was already waiting. The driver, Special Agent Lawrence Young, was a heavyset black man who asked excited questions that were all variations on Ashley's: *You're really going to close down the Brigade tonight?* "All I know is that we've got a long night ahead of us."

He drove her through flat farmland and past signs for Lake Kampeska. Trees lined one side of the road, while the other side extended into the nighttime darkness, and she found herself thinking not of the forthcoming arrest but of the hours and days that would follow. She had questions that only Benjamin Mittag could answer. Who killed Martin Bishop, and why? Who had been funding the Massive Brigade through Magellan Holdings? What was the next step in Massive's grand plan? That last one nagged at her. The followers they'd picked up in Sheridan and Nephi were aimless and, more often than not, confused. What did their leaders imagine they were going to do?

Eventually, they headed up a driveway where the Bureau had commandeered a house owned by an elderly couple who tended ten acres of soybeans. Outside, a dozen men and women, some in flak

ackets and the rest in FBI windbreakers, talked on phones and conferred over tablet screens. Gonzales met the Suburban as they parked.
He was younger than the commander in Sheridan, a leather-skinned
crewcut with a pencil mustache. He pumped her hand, then pointed
westward. "The target is one klick in that direction, and I've got
twenty-three men with M-4s lying in the fields around it. No one
has entered or exited the premises."

"Any more sighted?"

"We're up to nine, ma'am—three women, six men."

"Let's not waste any time, then."

He took her into the house, and on the way said, "Serge
Phillips is with your man at the vantage point, a half klick away

She stopped. "My man?"

"Owen Jakes, from Headquarters. He *does* work for you,

She tried to hide her surprise. "Of course. I just didn't
him to land so soon."

In the claustrophobic living room, the farmer couple s
with cups of coffee, and she took a moment to thank ther
assistance. The husband stood on shaky legs and gave
salute. "I went to Vietnam for this country. This is the le

Gonzales introduced her to the rest of the team in
where a map of the area had been laid out on the din
rounded by five rugged laptops with reinforced shells.
through the plans, and she tried to foresee disaster; g
rain in this part of the country, everything looked b
nothing else to do. Unlike in Sheridan, she wasn't
and knock on the door. She wanted to be alive to

Then Owen Jakes entered the kitchen, and al
He was rubbing his hands together when he no
Proulx. Good to see you."

"Can we have a word, Owen?"

She walked him out the kitchen door
the cool, clear night, but before she could s
"Rachel, I'm not stepping on anything h

Chicago when Paulson called me, and I lucked out wit[h] new Gulfstreams that fly like the wind."

His line caught her off guard. "When did Paulson cal[l]

"Just after you talked to him, I guess. He wants to be sur[e] plenty of Bureau presence—which, now that I'm here, I totall[y] They showed me the terrain, and it's going to be tricky."

The kitchen door opened, and Gonzales poked his head out "Looks like fresh activity in the house—a bunch of them ran upstairs. It's now or never."

"Then I guess it's now," she said, and followed Gonzales inside. Once Jakes passed the threshold, she told everyone, "Agent Jakes will remain here. We don't need a crowd out there."

The insult flashed across Jakes's face, but he recovered quickly.

"Of course, ma'am."

On the drive, she called Paulson and talked him through the plan. He shared her concern about the lack of natural cover, but he was eager to put an end to this. "It has to be done quickly," he said. "No standoffs. Hit them hard. I don't need a Waco on my watch."

"Agreed," she said, and glanced at Gonzales in the seat beside her, who was thumbing through messages on his phone. She lowered her voice. "Sir, why did you send Owen Jakes?"

"Is he making trouble?"

"No, it was just a surprise. It would've been nice to know be[-]forehand."

Silence, then: "He'd gotten in touch about some other matters, [an]d so I told him he'd be more useful in South Dakota."

"He said you called him."

"He would, wouldn't he?" Paulson said, then sighed. "You're [righ]t, I should have informed you."

She appreciated the apology. "Thank you, sir."

"Now let's do what we do best."

Their approach was concealed by a blue barn flaking paint, [t]hey joined another Suburban parked behind it. Gonzales intro-her to the local sheriff, Carl Donegal, who adjusted his flat

cap and led them through the barn, past a foldout table where a technician kept check on two monitors, and on to an open window on the other side, which looked across a wide soybean field toward the house.

"Where's that old boy?" Donegal asked as he handed her a pair of binoculars.

"Excuse me?"

"Jakes. He said he was coming back."

"He's not," Rachel said, staring across the field. Two lights were on in the second floor of the farmhouse, but she couldn't make anything out. "Think he's a good old boy?"

"He's from Kentucky. Least that's what he told me."

"Put him out of your mind." She handed back the binoculars and headed to the table with the monitors. On display was infrared footage from cameras attached to two SWAT members' helmets. From their positions, lying among the plants in the deep darkness, she saw two rocking chairs on the porch, which struck her as undeniably quaint. To Gonzales, she said, "Is everyone in place?"

"Yes, ma'am."

"Okay, then." She checked her watch. "It's one thirty-six, and we're a go."

24

KEVIN HAD been sitting at the kitchen table with Michael and Keira, drinking beer, and in the quiet of the house the sound of the phone on the wall was deafening. Keira said, "Who has that number?"

"Just us," said Michael.

Others entered—two young women, and Ben. Everyone stared at the phone.

"Someone should get it," said Keira, rising. "It could only be one of us."

"Or a telemarketer," Kevin suggested. "In which case I wouldn't—"

But by then Ben had stepped forward and snatched it.

He put it to his ear and said nothing. From the table, Kevin heard the tinny sound of a woman's voice, but not the words. Ben's expression changed. He said, "Where *are* you?" Then he listened, and as the tinny sound continued, worry took over his face, and the beginnings of anger. Nausea was already sinking into Kevin's stomach when Ben turned and settled his gaze on him. That was when he knew. He stood slowly, so as not to attract attention, but it made no difference. Ben shot out a finger and said, "Don't let him leave!"

Confused, Michael and Keira converged on Kevin as Ben spoke

quietly into the phone. Then he hung up and said, "Please escort Mr. Moore up to my room."

But these people hadn't known Ben long, and when they joined the Massive Brigade it was Martin they had looked up to. They needed more. "Why?" asked Michael.

Ben sighed and shook his head. "Because he's a fucking federal agent."

That was enough for them. Kevin felt hands on his shoulders and arms, and they pushed him along. He felt a fist strike the back of his head, another his lower back—that one hurt. There were five people shoving him up the stairs, and another four in the living room, watching, hatred in their faces. As Kevin reached the second floor he heard Ben say, "Pack up your shit, everyone. We're getting the fuck out of here."

But by then, Kevin knew, it was too late for them. He just didn't know if it was too late for him as well.

When they pushed him into Benjamin's room, he stumbled and fell to the floor, and that seemed to light a spark in his captors. Someone—he didn't know who—kicked him in the ribs. Then another kick struck his kidney. He instinctively curled up into a fetal position as the blows fell on him. *Fucking traitor! House nigger! Motherfucker!* It went on until Benjamin arrived and said, "Enough, okay? Leave him."

As they withdrew, Kevin tasted blood. Ben's Springfield semi-automatic hung from his fist as he looked down at Kevin.

"Leave me with him. Go pack."

Again, they hesitated, watching as Benjamin walked up to Kevin, who had gotten to his knees. He threw a hard fist. Knuckles like four stones hit Kevin's temple and threw him back onto the floor. Benjamin turned around, gave everyone a nod, urging them out, then shut the door in their faces.

Kevin's head throbbed as he pushed himself up again. There was blood on the floor, but he didn't know which part of his body it had come from. Ben dragged his wooden chair across the room and set it in front of Kevin. He sat down, knees open. He said, "What the fuck is your problem?"

"You really believe her?" Kevin asked.

Benjamin just watched him.

"She disappears, just like that, then calls in order to turn me in? Why didn't she do it while she was here?" He pressed his fingers into his forehead, fighting the urge to puke. "Looks to me like she was trying to throw the scent off of herself."

"Where's my phone?" Benjamin asked.

"How the hell should I know?"

Benjamin got up and went to the shelf, where he took down the zip-lock bag with the two parts of the Nokia. He held the bag up to the light, then set it down. He said, "She told me about this. She told me about the phone and the bag and the battery. I never showed it to her. She never saw it until she saw you outside with it."

"That's a stretch," Kevin said, though he knew it wasn't. Ingrid had told Benjamin just enough to prove her story. Christ, he was stupid. He'd entirely misjudged Ingrid Parker. For the gift of empathy he'd been given a death certificate.

Benjamin returned to the chair and spoke quietly. "Now that that's out of the way, tell me who. FBI, right? Who's running you? That Rachel Proulx woman?"

Kevin didn't answer.

"Christ," Benjamin said, shaking his head. "Just tell me what the plan is, okay? Let's not end this with me putting a bullet in your head."

Though he didn't want to, Kevin said, "You're going to put a bullet in my head anyway."

Benjamin stared, as if offended by the notion; then he smiled. "Man, you've really got it all wrong, don't you? We're on the same side."

"What?"

"Or, we used to be."

The lights went out suddenly, and in the darkness they heard the *boom* of a collision somewhere downstairs. Then the *crack crack* of gunfire. "Mother*fucker*!" Benjamin shouted as he shot to his feet, just visible in the moonlight, the Springfield up by his shoulder, and headed for the door. Before opening it, he turned back to Kevin and said, "This is *your* fault." Then he ripped open the door and ran out.

Confused, Kevin did the only thing he could think of as screams and gunfire sounded throughout the house. He lay facedown on the old, musty carpet and spread his arms out straight. And waited.

25

ON THE other side of the soybean field, the smell of dust in her nostrils, she watched the two monitors that lit up the foul-smelling barn. She watched the silent approach in infrared, soft footsteps up to the doors and windows, the placing of small charges, the 3-2-1 countdown, and then chaos.

Flashes of people, bright lights, shouts, and commands.

Screams.

Women, men.

Shouted commands.

Furniture crashing.

The barrels of those M-4s swinging left, right, up, down.

Then a single shot—*crack*.

More screaming.

A voice: "That's a grenade!"

Crack, crack, crack.

Screams. Stairs—up up up . . .

"Where is he?"

"Gun!"

Crack, crack, crack, crack.

"Down, down, down!"

"It's him!"

Crack, crack, crack, crack, crack, crack, crack.

Silence. Distant wailing.

Rachel looked at Commander Gonzales, who was breathing heavily, his finger glued to the communicator in his ear. "What the hell just happened?" she demanded.

But he was only listening to his men. "It's clear now," he finally told her. "Two survivors. Benjamin Mittag—he didn't make it." His face was so pale. "It's over."

"What the fuck was that?" she shouted at Gonzales, who raised his hands, turning away.

Sheriff Donegal, just behind her, said, "They was just following your orders."

"What?"

"What that old boy told them."

She turned on Donegal, saw that he'd popped a cigarette in his mouth and was trying without success to get a flame from his lighter; his hand shook too much. "What did Jakes say?"

He eyeballed her a moment, then took the unlit cigarette out of his mouth. "Gave them a pep talk. Reminded everyone that these people had killed congressfolk. Enough of due process, right? Intel said the house was wired for explosives—don't take no chances."

Rachel didn't say another word to the sheriff, and Gonzales had already headed out across the field to join his men. She wasn't in the mood to look at what they'd done. Not yet. She told Young to take her back to base. She wasn't going to call ahead, wasn't going to give him a chance to run or weave some elaborate lie. Which was why, when she burst in and stood over him, she found Jakes sitting in the kitchen, talking on his phone to Paulson.

"Just a sec," he whispered to her, and raised a finger for patience.

That was when it took her over. The way he raised his index finger, condescending, then turned in the chair so that he could have a little privacy. Everything stopped, yet at the same time it moved too quickly. There, on the table, was the map covered in pencil markings, and the five sturdy laptops. And right in front of her was the soft white bald spot on the back of his head. She picked up the closest computer. She took aim.

THE AGE OF NO

EIGHT MONTHS LATER

TUESDAY, MARCH 13, TO
TUESDAY, MARCH 20, 2018

1

LATELY, RACHEL had been snapping awake early, a tickle in her unconscious alerting her to . . . to what? Her cramped studio was no different. No intruders. No sign of attempted entry. Her alarm system hummed along without warning. Yet, often before four, she'd wake in a sweat. She'd sit on the edge of the bed, massaging the Y-shaped scar that had been branded onto her aching thigh, searching for the answer to an urgent question she couldn't even put into words.

Was it a question, though? Probably not. It was a statement, or a phrase—some medical term. Whatever doctors said to mean mild, ever-present paranoia. The kind of perpetual disquiet that chopped her nightly sleep into unsatisfactory fragments. There was something familiar about this disquiet, an unsettled state of being that she had known so well when she and Gregg were still married. But Gregg was long gone, and this feeling was borne of other things.

Next came 40 mg of dihydrocodeine washed down with a bottle of Poland Spring. Then she pulled the dime-store cane from under her bed and used it to reach the bathroom. This was all she allowed herself; after that first hour of assistance she slipped the cane back into its place and lived the rest of the day as if she'd never broken down and bought one.

On these early days, when it was still too dark to see Elliott Bay from her window, she'd bring a coffee to her desk, open her laptop, and study the old files, perusing interviews and refreshing her memory with newspaper articles and influential blog posts from last year. The breathless accounts of terrified civilians, the stuffed-shirt punditry, the follow-up investigative reports that led to industrial wastelands and college campuses that had been the breeding ground for the Massive Brigade. She had a folder of posts from *The Propaganda Ministry* that she'd collected before the site was shut down on July 5. Another folder was devoted to videos and opinion pieces by Sam Schumer, most of them hyperbolic rants with wordy headlines, like THE MASSIVE BRIGADE IS COMMUNISM'S FINAL ASSAULT ON THE AMERICAN DREAM. Then the later ones—his mysterious inside line on Bishop's murder, and afterward: LEAD AGENT ON MASSIVE INVESTIGATION RESIGNS AFTER BREAKDOWN.

Resigned? Stripped of badge and service weapon. Told by Paulson to get the fuck out of his office.

She'd done it to herself, of course. She'd grabbed that computer and smashed Owen Jakes right on his skull. Then, taken over by a sense of purpose that she hadn't felt in a long while, she'd gone back out to the Suburban and told Agent Young to take her to the Massive safe house, which had in the space of minutes become a mausoleum. OSWALD, aka Kevin Moore, was in the back of an ambulance, his shoulder bandaged where a stray bullet had found him on the floor of an upstairs bedroom. She wanted to know everything, but the drugs had made him groggy and wired at the same time, dragging him from dumb silence to manic bursts.

Yes, Bishop had been killed by a sniper; no, he didn't know who was behind it.

Who was the woman who'd been with them outside Lebanon? Ingrid Parker. Rachel pressed—is she in the house, one of the dead? He shook his head, and told her that Ingrid walked off before they ever got to Watertown.

What were they doing in Lebanon? Fighting. Bishop and Mittag, fighting.

Why? A shake of the head.

Who in the Brigade was communicating with Sam Schumer? Kevin had no idea what she was talking about, and though she wanted to press further she was interrupted by Agent Young. "Ma'am, this way, please."

"I'll be there in a minute."

"This is urgent, ma'am."

So she'd followed him back to his car, where he told her that he'd been ordered to drive her to the airport immediately.

"Ordered by whom?"

"By Headquarters."

"I'll go after my interview's done."

"I was told," he said, hesitant, "that you will interview no one."

"By whom?"

"The assistant director."

She'd turned around and started back toward the ambulance when two more agents materialized from the darkness, stepping into her path. From behind, Young said, "Agent Proulx, I'd really prefer not to get into a fight about this."

The Cessna was already on the tarmac, and the two nameless agents had come along to make sure she didn't lose her way. As the plane was waiting to take off, she brought herself down a notch, reassessing, and realized that the anger she'd let loose back at the farmhouse had changed everything. She was now in a race against time. She checked emails that were coming in—names of the deceased, a preliminary inventory of the house, assorted updates from her people back at Headquarters—and began to write, because her only defense lay in her story. She first typed her version of Watertown, down to the smallest detail, and then utilized all her notes from the last weeks to write everything else, because this night, taken out of context, was no defense at all. Everything was context.

Two more agents were waiting at Ronald Reagan, and they drove her directly to Paulson's office. But Paulson wasn't interested in her story. He was only interested in her final act, involving a laptop and Jakes's head. He was fucking furious. Everyone was furious, it seemed. Everyone except preternaturally cheerful Owen Jakes, smiling even from his hospital bed. *She'd gone through a lot. It was a tough night.*

Had Jakes not played the magnanimous role, she'd have ended up on her ass, out of the Bureau, and possibly behind bars.

At morning therapy the nurse told her, "Slow down. Take it easy." To spite her, Rachel leaned at a deeper angle on the treadmill, drenched, each pounding step shooting thick cables of pain through her reconstructed femur. On the wall in front of her hung a television and the twenty-four-hour news channel she chased every other day.

This morning, she ran toward but never reached an update on the protests that had been simmering in more than twenty cities across the country, growing as the weather heated up for another record-breaking year. Global warming, the late-night comics joked, was the opposition's best friend. The crowds were coming out in Charlotte and Houston, in Santa Cruz and St. Louis, and of course here in Seattle. They were even marching in Anchorage, two thousand strong. It had become, someone had said, the Age of No.

Despite what everyone, including Rachel, had thought last year, the brief, bright life of the Massive Brigade had made the opposition nimbler. It had learned a lesson from Martin Bishop and Benjamin Mittag: All power lies in crowds. Five thousand people decide to do one thing, and it is done. Now, within hours, a single news story, amplified by social media, could trigger a million people and bring cities to a standstill.

But the crowds filling her therapist's screen—now in Manhattan, now in Los Angeles—hadn't appeared overnight. They'd been building for months, as reporters dug into the sketchy details of the Massive Brigade's bloody end in Watertown, South Dakota. The White House had done itself no favors by denying minor facts that turned out to be easily verifiable, and after noting these little lies the reporters dutifully returned to their beats and dug more. There was a lot of talk of smoke and fire. The cover-up, they said, was more damning than the crime, even if the crime itself was still unclear.

It all came down to a single question: Why did so many people have to die in Watertown?

In those first weeks, there had been little outcry, because the story made sense: The Massive Brigade had proved itself to be on a murderous rampage, and when it was cornered in Watertown it kept to its violent MO and came at the Bureau's officers with guns blazing. The FBI had put itself in harm's way to protect American citizens.

Then the steady drip of revelations began. Conversations with rehabilitated Massive followers, photos unearthed from raided safe houses, and, most damning, anonymous leaks by Bureau agents troubled by their own recollections of Watertown. The director stonewalled the press, the president lashed out on Twitter, and surrogates denied every accusation with a counteraccusation against the media.

From the start, journalists and activists had asked for one thing: the Bureau's internal report on the Massive Brigade. A growing chorus demanded that it be declassified and made available to the public, while the counterargument—steadfastly elucidated even by Sam Schumer—was that releasing it would endanger agents and operations still in play, and reveal the Bureau's secret methodologies at a time when the Bureau was working to keep a lid on the country's simmering civil unrest.

A BREAKING NEWS logo flashed across the screen, and she was surprised to see a familiar face: Assistant Director Mark Paulson, among a gaggle of congressmen. The Bureau, he announced, was in the process of declassifying the Massive Brigade report, and it would be released as early as next week. "Now I hope some of these people disrupting our streets will go home."

It meant something that she was learning this from television rather than a phone call from Headquarters, or from Paulson himself.

It meant that she was no longer at the center of the storm. A slap in the face, yes, but also a kind of relief. Months of therapy had taught her that what happened outside her little world wasn't her responsibility. What happened inside her world most definitely was.

2

BECAUSE OF demonstrations cutting off the streets around City Hall, it took over an hour to drive from the clinic to the FBI field office in the Vance Building on Third Avenue, and on the way NPR talked to Representative Diane Trumble, who had recently returned to Congress after recuperating from last summer's gunshot. While grateful for the standing ovation she'd received upon entering the chambers, she made no secret of her anger that the Plains Capital–IfW investigation had been closed down only a few weeks after Paul Hanes, its chair, had been killed, and she had been laid up in the hospital. Legislators had abandoned it to join the new, constituent-pleasing investigation into the FBI's handling of the Massive Brigade. "This is a cynical move by colleagues who get their funding from Wall Street," she said, real bitterness in her voice. "Terrorists might disrupt our daily lives, but they should not disrupt the path of justice. Let's not allow international tax dodgers to benefit from the tragedy of July 4, 2017."

"Amen, sister," said Rachel, once again thinking about the irony of July 4—not only had the Massive Brigade delegitimized itself, but it had undermined one of the few government investigations that aimed to make corrupt bankers pay for their crimes.

There were eyes on her as she limped to her fifth-floor cubicle. The pain had returned, a sharp rebuke from the morning's therapy, but just as she'd learned to master her anger over the last half year she'd learned to master her face; other than a little twitch around the eyes, no one would have noticed her agony. Max, their Special Agent in Charge, was chatting with two visitors in his glassed-in office. Paula and Chuck stood with coffee cups, their conversation dying as she passed. Up ahead, rising from his own cubicle, Henry said, "Well, that's some shit, isn't it? Releasing the report?"

Henry had spent the last four months trying to become her friend, but friends weren't what you found in the Bureau. "We finally gave in," she said.

"Or maybe we've got them right where we want them," he joked.

"Rachel?" she heard, and turned to see Max's unhealthily gray face sticking out of his office. "Come in here a minute?"

She turned to cross the floor again, still working to master her face. While the pain would eventually fade, she could do nothing about the limp, and her doctor had assured her that she shouldn't try. It would be with her the rest of her life.

The visitors stood when she entered, and Max introduced them as Sarah Vale and Lyle Johnson, both from Headquarters. They shook hands. Johnson, a military stiff, had a salt-and-pepper mustache that made her think of how few men she knew wore mustaches, while Vale was a Latina who smiled a lot, her method of encouragement. Johnson clearly found that kind of forced friendliness a waste of effort.

Stating the obvious, Johnson said, "We're here about the Massive Brigade report."

As Rachel took a free chair, she spoke to cover her pain. "This is part of the declassification?"

"You could say that," said Vale. "A lot of people have been burned over these past months, and we don't need more collateral damage after it's released."

She understood their point. Two senior Bureau officials had stepped down from their posts after being caught in too many on-camera lies, and with the constant patter of press leaks the first order of business at the Hoover Building would be job security. "You might have tried not bullshitting the public for the last half year. That's why we're in this situation."

"Woulda, shoulda," said Vale, smiling. "Let's not drag history through the coals."

"If we wanted to do that," Johnson said, "we might start by asking about your own contact with reporters."

Rachel gave him a sharp look. "Are you accusing me of something?"

"No, he's not," said Vale.

"I'm just making a point," Johnson said, then shrugged. "Mistakes are always made. What matters is how you deal with them afterward."

Rachel's thigh, which after reconstruction had begun to act as a bullshit detector, throbbed. It would have been a lie, though, to say she wasn't interested in knowing what they were selling. Besides, when *wasn't* there some level of bullshit when dealing with Headquarters? "Who sent you to me?"

"No one," Vale told her. "We've just been asked to make sure that what the Bureau shows the world is as perfectly aligned with the facts as possible. You were at the center of this."

"But you report to someone."

Vale looked at Johnson, who, almost embarrassed, said, "Owen Jakes." They knew about her history with him. Everyone knew. "But this," he went on, "is a request from higher up."

Rachel gazed at these two emissaries from DC. They looked young to her—but once you've been shot, everyone seems young. She turned to Max, who'd been so uncharacteristically silent all this time. "What's going on, Max? Are you part of this?"

Her SAC rose to his feet and headed to the door. "I think I'm going to get a coffee. Anyone?"

Both Vale and Johnson shook their heads.

"Okay then," Max said, and left. Rachel watched him head not to the kitchenette but to the exit.

Johnson said, "I thought he'd never leave," and for the first time he cracked a smile.

Vale turned to Rachel. "Have you read the final draft of the report?"

"I was never put on the distribution list."

Vale arched a brow. She really liked showing off her feelings. "Does that seem odd?"

It did, of course. That the final report on a case that had absorbed her for months and had culminated in nine deaths in Watertown— that *that* report wouldn't be accessible to her was certainly odd. Then again . . . "Well, I did crack Jakes's skull with a laptop."

There—in Vale's face, a twitch of the lip. She was trying to hold down her smile.

Johnson wasn't amused. "Six stitches," he said.

Vale leaned closer. "How much of your own report had you written before you, uh, went on leave?"

Rachel remembered the wild rush, the bleary-eyed hours in that Cessna, trying to get it all down before going to the office to face the ax. "Fifteen thousand words? Something like that."

Johnson said, "The final report is three times that length, but only about three thousand words are attributed to you."

This was news to her. "Well, it's not all that surprising. Jakes and I would have come to different conclusions."

"Which is why we're here," Johnson said. "We want your version."

"You don't have my fifteen thousand words?"

"Missing," Vale said, sadness filling her face.

Rachel almost told them she had a copy if they wanted to see it, but by keeping that classified document on her personal laptop she'd broken a few federal laws that, in today's climate, might not be so easily brushed aside. So she said, "Give me the report, and I'll happily mark it up for you."

They were quiet a moment; then Johnson cleared his throat. "Like you said, you're not on the distribution list."

3

INTERVIEW ROOM 2 was a fluorescent box, typical with its two-way mirror and heavy door. Reinforced-concrete walls, ubiquitous gray table, three aluminum chairs. She took her place across from Vale and Johnson, who leaned a fashionable briefcase against the leg of his chair but didn't open it. "Where is this going?" she asked.

Johnson looked confused. Vale said, "How so?"

"Paulson's releasing this next week," she told them. "Now that he's said the words aloud, and the director has backed him up, Congress isn't going to let us walk it back. Are you going to include our talk in an amended version? Will I get my own appendix?"

"Let's just see what we get first," said Johnson.

"Maybe you'll turn the whole thing on its head," Vale said as she placed her phone on the table. "Mind if we record this?"

"Thanks for asking," Rachel said.

Vale pressed the red button and spoke. "It's March 13, 2018, and we're at the Seattle field office with Special Agent Rachel Proulx. The time is . . ." Though the time was right there on her phone, Vale made a show of looking at the slender gold watch on her wrist. "Ten oh eight in the morning."

Their initial questions were scene-setting and verification. Had she worked on the Massive Brigade case during the summer of 2017? She had. How long before the July 4 action had she begun her investigation? Two months. What had triggered the investigation?

"The pressure came from outside," Rachel said, thinking back. "You remember. People were claiming, without evidence, that the Massive Brigade was a terrorist organization."

"People?"

"People like Sam Schumer. The talk shows. We'd never listed Massive as a threat—something to keep an eye on, yes, but not a threat. But then constituents began calling their representatives, who in turn asked the director why we weren't closing down the group. People didn't feel safe. So I was asked to look into it."

"You were the expert," said Johnson.

"I was knowledgeable."

Vale said, "Your study on radical movements is required reading."

"That old thing?" she asked. "I'm surprised it's still around."

Johnson and Vale smiled, and she realized that both of them were fans. Had they known how slapdash those months on the West Coast had been, or how she'd been suckered by a Russian-speaking enigma named James Sullivan, then maybe they'd be less impressed. But wasn't that the way with all great works? The composition is never as glorious as the result.

She straightened herself, concealing her pride. "I may have been qualified, but now, looking back, I can see that I went into the Massive Brigade investigation prejudiced."

This seemed to interest them both. "How so?" asked Johnson.

"I'd been sucked into the hysteria like everyone else. Two thousand seventeen was a year of absolutes. The new president, the marches that were just starting—Women's, Science, Immigration, the Tax March. Jerome Brown—that was big. You were either a sympathizer or a fear merchant. There was no in-between. There was no gray in 2017."

Johnson snorted. "But July 4—that validated labeling the Brigade terrorist."

"Did it?" she asked.

"Three politicians dead, one injured."

"I suppose so," she said, as if she'd never really thought about it before, though of course she had. She'd thought of little else over the last eight months. "But before July 4 they were labeled based on fear rather than direct evidence. You remember. A kind of psychosis took hold. Didn't you feel that?"

"That's the question," Johnson countered. "Did we *feel* it, or was there evidence of this psychosis?"

It was a good point, and Rachel gave it to him. But she would not be swayed on the issue, for it had troubled her a very long time.

"Can we move on?" Vale asked. Not impatient, just practical.

"How much do you want to know?"

"Well, we don't really know how much of your work was left out of the final report."

"So, you want to know everything."

"We've got unrest in the streets," Johnson said. "We're worried about some nutcase taking his marching orders from whatever's left of the Massive Brigade. We're worried that if we don't release this report the right way we're going to have blood on the sidewalks. So, yeah, Rachel. Everything."

"Everything" lasted until the end of business. Seven hours of questions that prodded, sometimes painfully, at Rachel's formidable memory. They weren't memories she would have chosen to spend the afternoon with, but she could tell they were of interest to Johnson and Vale, and perhaps even helpful.

After asking permission, Vale powered up a clumsy-looking e-cigarette that, in place of an ember, had a pale green light on the end that glowed stronger when she inhaled. Her exhales smelled faintly of sandalwood. She asked about June 18, the day Martin Bishop went underground, which led to a discussion of Bill and Gina Ferris's party and, inevitably, David and Ingrid Parker. Everyone knew about David Parker—published excerpts from his forthcoming novel rehashed his experiences—but his estranged wife, Ingrid, was still missing.

"You have no idea where Ingrid is?" Sarah Vale asked, as if this question were very important.

"It's a big country," Rachel replied. "She could be anywhere."

"Well, it would be really helpful if we could find her."

"Why?"

Vale rocked her head from side to side. "From what we've gathered, she was closest to Bishop at the end. We expected her to show up when the amnesty was announced, but she never raised her head."

Rachel, too, had wondered about Ingrid's disappearance. "Then why isn't her picture on the wanted lists? I haven't seen it."

Johnson leaned forward. "Honestly? We don't want some local cops going Rambo on her—she's got a baby. We just want to bring her in and have a conversation."

By the time she'd worked her way through the events of July 4, their Thai lunches had arrived, and as they cracked open polystyrene boxes, releasing fragrant steam into the little room, Rachel took the opportunity to turn the conversation around. She asked if her story thus far jibed with the report Jakes had filed, and their replies were noncommittal. She asked if the congressional investigation into Watertown was causing anxiety in the halls of the Hoover Building—was Jakes worried about keeping his job? Paulson? Neither wanted to answer that, but Vale said, "Sometimes the idea of being here in Seattle, on the edge of the continent, feels like a smart career move."

That answer said a lot without admitting a thing, just like Johnson's reply when she asked if Owen Jakes knew they were meeting with her: "Let's try not to bother him with details."

She liked them both.

4

"IT'S ODD." she admitted once their trash had been taken by an assistant whose name, after four months, Rachel still couldn't remember. "You keep referring to my 'report'—it was hardly that. A collection of notes. An attempt at a narrative. There's no way what I wrote could be considered a report."

"Why not?" Vale asked, pressing RECORD again.

"My information was too fragmented. I obviously never got the chance to speak to Bishop or Mittag, and I was only able to get a few minutes with OSWALD—Kevin Moore. I made mistakes, certainly, but I never imagined that I wouldn't be able to sit down with Bishop and ask all the questions that needed to be answered. The Massive investigation ended with more questions than it had begun with."

"Such as?" Johnson asked.

"Such as, why shoot those politicians? Where did the Brigade get its funding? We tracked it to Magellan Holdings but ran into a dead end. Has that led any further?"

She gave them a moment to answer her question, but they just stared back at her, waiting.

"But maybe the most important question is: Who was sharing information with Sam Schumer?"

"Schumer?" Vale asked, now that Rachel had broached a subject she was authorized to engage with. "Is this about him finding out about Bishop's murder before us?"

"Exactly."

Johnson nodded slowly, as if she'd brought up a very important point. Vale vaped, that green ember pulsing. But neither wanted to follow up on her important point, so Rachel said, "Bishop was killed in an empty field, outside of a tiny town in the literal center of the country. *We* only learned about it because a passerby noticed Mittag and some others standing around. We hadn't even verified his death by the time Schumer posted the news."

Vale nodded, as if she agreed that it was a mystery, then said, "Schumer has a hotline for calling in tips. Whoever called the Lebanon police could have called him. Or one of the officers might've called. He's got quite a following out there."

"The anonymous caller didn't mention a murder, just Mittag and three others, talking. And we asked the police officers—they didn't call Schumer."

"But it was news in the station, certainly."

Rachel didn't want to argue the point so long after the fact, but Johnson and Vale really wanted her opinion. "I didn't think that was what happened. The only thing that made sense to me was that Schumer had a source within Massive. That he was communicating with the group. Which meant that he was privy to information we didn't have access to, and maybe he had been all along."

"So you went to Sam Schumer," Johnson said as he rubbed his face. Exhaustion seemed to be settling in.

Rachel didn't check the time, and there were no windows to gauge the hour, but she guessed they had been talking six hours by then. Vale puffed on her e-cigarette, and Rachel told them about her phone call with Schumer, remembering the cigarette stink of that back room in the sheriff's office as, over the phone, Schumer told her about his "ace in the hole."

"His other source was FBI?" Vale asked. "Is that what you're saying?"

She shook her head. "I'm saying that Sam Schumer had a source in Massive but wasn't about to admit it. So he lied. It's second nature to him."

"You're sure about that?"

"No," Rachel said. "I'm not a hundred percent about anything. I just know the alternative is unthinkable."

Johnson woke up a little. "How so?"

"Because if Schumer's source really was FBI, then the timing damns us. How else could we have known he was dead? It would mean that *we* killed Martin Bishop, not his own people. And if that's true, those crowds out there, who already suspect this, are going to set fire to this country."

That earned a moment of silence. Vale turned the e-cigarette in her fingers like a baton while Johnson stared at Rachel, chewing his lip. Finally, he said, "We might as well move on to Watertown."

"Yes," Vale said quietly.

Rachel stared at the pulsing green light, then shrugged. "OSWALD had given Janet Fordham the location of Benjamin Mittag, so there was nothing to do but fly straight to South Dakota."

Johnson scratched the corner of his mouth. "Was that the only information OSWALD shared?"

She shook her head. "Fordham said he was upset. *He* asked if we had killed Bishop. Later, he told me about the long-range rifle shot, from a white pickup truck."

Johnson and Vale exchanged looks, as if each wanted the other to speak first.

"What?" said Rachel.

Johnson finally succumbed, stretching in his chair. "Weird thing. The Bureau's worried that if that detail—the white pickup—goes into the final report it's going to open a can of worms. Martin Bishop dead from infighting—that story makes sense. It's something you can hang your hat on. But this, a deus ex machina bullet coming from the cornfields to—"

"Wheat," Vale cut in.

"What?"

"Wheat fields, not cornfields."

Johnson, irritated, shook his head. "Whatever. A magic bullet suddenly gets rid of public enemy number one. How's that going to look? It's going to be the seed of a thousand conspiracy theories. You said it yourself—it would be unthinkable."

Rachel finally understood what was going on here. "What does it say in the report?"

"It doesn't," said Johnson. "It's concluded that Mittag killed Bishop. The report doesn't mess with details. And you can see why, right?"

Rachel didn't bother answering. She had a feeling that this was why they'd flown across the country to spend all day with her in this room. To get her to this point in the story.

"Who killed him?" she asked.

"We don't know," Johnson said. "Whoever it was, though, did us quite a solid."

"It's not like we're not investigating," Vale said. "We've got a team puzzling through it as we speak. But for now, for the public, it would be dangerous to present questions we can't answer."

"Yes," Rachel said.

Vale leaned closer, smiling. "Yes?"

"Yes, I can see that."

"So you're on board?"

"On board?"

Vale's smile faded; she looked at Johnson, who said, "Can we depend on you to not go telling the press about that big, glaring hole in the report?"

Ah. There it was. Rachel lowered her head to give them a good, strong look. "Like I said before, I don't talk to the press. Not anymore."

5

"HAD TO be a letdown," Johnson said after a moment.

She looked at him.

"There you are, working months—years, really—tracking these people. And then suddenly Bishop's dead."

She thought about that—*had* it been a letdown? Had she been so driven by ego that this unexpected turn of events troubled her in that way? Yes, actually. She remembered listening to those giddy field agents—*we're getting drunk tonight*—and the deflation that followed. The sudden emptiness. And then . . .

"And then there was Watertown," she said heavily.

Vale sucked on her nicotine, released a cloud. "Sounds to me like you did everything right, though."

"Maybe," Rachel said. "But just because you do something right doesn't guarantee that anything's going to turn out right."

"No matter how it turned out," said Johnson, "the fact is that, after the night of July 8, the Massive Brigade was no longer a threat to American security."

Vale agreed. "It always sucks to see how the sausage is made, but people just keep ordering sausage."

Rachel looked at them both, thinking that it was easy to talk about the pros and cons of unnecessary deaths when you weren't present for them. It was like a flat-footed twenty-year-old joining a war rally, or a male politician expounding on abortion legislation. She hadn't been there either, though. She'd been on the other side of a soybean field, watching two monitors that lit up a foul-smelling barn. She'd seen the silent approach, soft footsteps up to the doors and windows, the placing of small charges, the 3-2-1 countdown, and then chaos.

And then that sheriff. She said, "Donegal made it clear that Owen was responsible for what had happened."

Johnson exhaled, long and hard. "And you believed Sheriff Donegal?"

"Why would he lie?"

"I don't know, Rachel. Why would anyone lie? But they do. Every day, and in every way. People lie. It's what makes our jobs so goddam hard."

Rachel leaned back, rubbing her leg—it was screaming. "Look, I'm not proud of what I did. But Owen's little unauthorized pep talk killed nine people. I'm not sorry I did it, and I never will be. I'm only sorry that it made him into a victim, and that as a result he's got himself a new office and now lords it over good agents like yourself."

Vale reached over and paused the recording. "Don't worry. I can erase that last bit."

"Don't," she said. "If he ever listens to this, then I want him to know exactly what I think of his sorry ass."

That earned a lengthy silence and, eventually, a grin from Vale, who started recording again. "There were two survivors, yes?"

"A girl from Portland, Oregon, and OSWALD."

"OSWALD," said Johnson. "Now, his debrief we do have. How much time did you get with him, before . . ."

"Not long. Twenty minutes, maybe, before I was shipped back home. All I had left was my story, which I wrote on the flight back."

She could have said more, but neither of her interrogators cared about the fury she'd felt as she banged at the keyboard, making very clear how Owen Jakes had, with malice, undermined her operation.

No, that wasn't their mission. Blame was beyond their purview. *Just the facts, ma'am.*

"How long," Vale asked, "before you were shot?"

Instinctively, she rubbed her leg again. "Ten days. I was on leave, waiting for my hearing. And, yes, I'd been drinking."

"Alone?" asked Johnson.

"Alone," she admitted. "What's frustrating is that I'd had too much; my vision was bad. I was on the sidewalk, heading home. Late. Empty street. Then a man appeared at the next corner. Had I been sober, I would've realized what was happening. But I didn't." She took a deep breath, feeling that spot in her thigh, remembering the blinding pain. "He just stood there, as if he were waiting for me. Or waiting until he could ID me. I stopped. Then he fired once—a .357 caliber—and disappeared."

"Did you ID him?" Johnson asked.

"I gave a description—Caucasian, forties, a little gray—but it wasn't enough for a match. And whoever he was, he knew how to avoid street cameras."

"It's still an open case," Vale pointed out.

"Half open," Rachel said, and when they looked confused she shrugged. "Come on. Paulson put me in the press release—my name was out there. For anyone who worshipped the martyrs Bishop and Mittag, I was the devil. You should've seen the threats on my Face-book page before I closed it down." Neither seemed impressed by what she was saying, so she spelled it out for them. "We'll probably never know who shot me, but we damned well know that he was a follower of the Massive Brigade."

"Yes," Johnson said, agreeing finally. Vale nodded as well.

What Rachel didn't tell them, and wouldn't—it wasn't their business—was that she'd felt no fear when she was shot, just confusion. The only time she felt actual fear was the next evening, when she woke in the hospital, after the operation, to find Gregg sitting in a chair, eyes on her. She even jerked, wanting to get away from those hands of his, but her leg was in no shape to help her escape. *It was in the paper,* he said by way of explanation, and when he nodded at the bouquet of lilies he'd brought—*Mackenzie's idea*—and leaned in close to kiss her forehead she thought she might vomit. It had been a very long time since she'd been able to trust kindness from Gregg Wills, because she knew how quickly it could turn to acid.

"You know," she said, wanting to purge any thoughts of her ex, "getting shot probably helped me. It was harder for them to can an agent who'd just taken one for the team."

That earned her more silence; then Johnson checked his watch. Rachel checked her own—it was nearly four thirty. They'd spent the entire day in this miserable little room. "Are we done?" she asked.

Again, these two emissaries from DC conferred with a glance. "Almost," said Vale. Johnson reached down and finally lifted the briefcase that had been next to his feet all day. Popped it open, took out a manila folder, and passed it to her. Vale said, "Given the sensitivity of the investigation, and the way public opinion is so volatile right now, it would be really helpful if you signed this."

Rachel opened the folder and found three pages, stapled. There was her name and address, and below it a series of paragraphs and subsections that led to a final page with space for her signature. She read the opening lines, verifying what she had suspected from the moment he pulled out the folder. "It's a nondisclosure agreement."

"Yes," said Vale.

She furrowed her brow. "This isn't necessary. Everything I've done for the Bureau is classified. And I already told you, I'm not speaking to the press."

"Then just consider it a lawyerly formality," Vale suggested.

Rachel returned to the contract, reaching a section called "Penalties." It said, among other things, that if she were to speak to anyone—not just the press, but anyone—about events related to the investigation and apprehension of the Massive Brigade, not only would she be prosecuted with life in prison and forfeit her government pension, but she would automatically relinquish her United States passport. She looked up at them. "Have you *read* this?"

"Of course," said Johnson.

She pushed it back across the table. "I'm not signing."

"Rachel," said Vale, a pleading note to her voice. "*We* believe that you have no plans to approach anyone, but, hey, we're all adults here. You have well-documented anger issues, and you blame Owen Jakes for what happened in Watertown. You've said it yourself. Put those two together, and when the report comes out next week and you read it and get angry about something you don't agree with . . . what *will* you do?"

"Why don't you show me the report now, so I can tell you?"

Vale leaned back, and Johnson leaned forward. "We're not joking around. Do you think the report is going to describe the Watertown raid the way you just did? People's jobs depend on the story—and it's true, by the way—that the occupants had guns and explosives. You throw a wrench in that? Good people lose their careers, and assholes in the streets will start smashing private property."

Rachel stood up, and her leg, immobile for so long, tingled and barked in pain. She really didn't want to listen to this. "You two seem like decent agents, and you probably believe a lot of what you're saying. But, no. Take those pages back to Jakes and tell him to smoke them, okay?"

Vale shook her head. "Don't be stupid, Rachel . . ."

"Have a nice flight home," she said, and limped past them to the door. She opened it, stepped through, and once the door closed behind her she grimaced and rubbed her thigh. Christ, but it hurt. Then she looked up to see Paula, Chuck, and Henry staring at her from their desks. Awkward smiles. She hobbled over to her desk and grabbed her things. Henry hovered around her. "Everything cool?"

"Tell Max I've gone home, will you?"

He turned to look back to where Lyle Johnson and Sarah Vale were exiting the interview room. Johnson was on his cell. As Rachel turned to leave, Vale looked in her direction and, sadly, smiled. The poor woman looked like she was about to cry.

6

SHE ATE at a dependable vegan restaurant around the corner from her apartment, and while waiting for the mock duck she ran through messages, then called her mother and listened to her day. A pharmacy visit, a minor scuffle with her insurer over medication preapproval, and lunch with Derek, the widower who had been courting her for years now. It was good to listen to her mother's life. It helped distract her from what her own life had become—rising early, chasing that television for therapy, hiding her pain in the office. Back in DC, before attacking Owen Jakes, and before the stranger with the .357, her days had been unpredictable. Upon waking she couldn't be sure in which city she would sleep that night, and the hours in between carried an urgency that she hadn't known since.

And now she'd spent the day being reminded of that other life. She'd been asked to spill all of it and then promise to never speak it aloud again. Had she been wrong to blow up at them? Wrong to deny them their little signature? Maybe, but she wasn't in the mood to judge herself just yet. Tomorrow, or the next day, she would go through it again and, most likely, call Headquarters to ask Johnson or Vale to please send that form for her to sign. She wanted to be as free of this as the Bureau did.

What troubled her more, though, was that a life reexamined is a source of mystery. She'd been tossed off the case without answers, and by voicing the questions today, they felt more pressing than they'd felt in eight months. Who had funded Martin Bishop before his magical disappearing act? Who killed him with that long-range sniper's rifle? Why had Jakes pushed for deadly force in the end? And what, really, had Martin Bishop wanted to do with his band of followers?

Though the questions nagged at her, she knew from experience that every case ended with blank spaces. The Bureau was never all-knowing, and answers were never complete. What you did was paper over holes with a grand theory, finding ways to divert the eye from the flaws. That was what the report would do when it came out next week—decorate and deflect. Nothing new, yet the questions still wouldn't leave her.

From her purse, she took out her bottle and popped another dihydrocodeine, then tipped the dreadlocked waiter generously. But instead of getting up to leave she went through her contacts and paused on FORDHAM, JANET. She hadn't thought much about her until today, remembering her breathless updates on OSWALD. The last time they'd spoken over drinks they'd had a good rapport, both decompressing from the fiasco. *Kevin's had enough,* Janet had said. *He's retired to the mountains outside Boulder. He wants to be a lumberjack.*

She sometimes thought about Kevin Moore's surrender to nature and wondered if she should've chosen a similar life, somewhere in upstate New York to be near her mother. But that wasn't her, never had been. She'd worked too hard for too many years to give it up.

She scrolled on, passing names that brought on more memories, some good and some not, then paused on one that in this shrine to veganism brought on welcome carnivorous memories. She pressed CALL, and Ashley answered on the third ring. "Rachel? You in town?"

"Seattle. Just thinking about you. Got a minute?"

"I've got hours. DC traffic is no better than when you were here, and the protests aren't helping. Don't know when I'll get home."

"Still giving all your money to Fogo de Chão?"

"What else would I spend it on? The poor?"

She'd forgotten Ashley's dry humor. "Mind if we talk work?"

"Have we ever talked about anything else, Rachel?"

It was a slight, but a fair one. She'd never really gotten to know Ashley, or any of her colleagues, during the Massive investigation. "How far did you ever get on Magellan Holdings?"

She heard the distant sound of honking; then Ashley said, "Beyond Laura Anderson? Not far. We followed the family tree, thinking she'd been chosen by a relative. No kids, only a few living relatives. There was a nephew we were looking at, but he didn't fit our profiles."

"So, nothing."

"You worried about the report?" Ashley asked.

"It's not mine to worry about anymore. Seattle, remember?"

Ashley laughed. "Can I join you?"

Rachel had a thought. "What about co-workers?"

"What?"

"Didn't you say that Anderson worked for the UN for . . . what? Fifteen years?"

"Yeah, but . . ." Another car horn—it sounded like Ashley's. "But why would the UN want to fund some US radicals? Has the West Coast turned you into a conspiracy head?"

"Just thinking aloud."

"Well, I don't think that's the direction to go. But it sounds like you're having trouble leaving it be."

Rachel remembered those monitors in that chilly barn. *Crack, crack, crack.* "You're not?"

"Erin Lynch keeps me busy. Drug lords. Want to shoot myself."

"Take care of yourself, then."

"You, too, Rachel. Keep fighting the good fight."

7

DESPITE HER creaky leg, she managed to get out of the restaurant without stumbling. A brisk chill had settled in, and the streetlamps made puddles of light between black sidewalk. Light, dark, light, dark. In her foyer the mailbox presented her with bills, and the elevator clanked and banged on the way up to the ninth floor. The building's owner had promised a repairman by the weekend, but none of her neighbors were holding their breaths.

It wasn't until she'd entered her apartment that she realized something was wrong. The alarm, which she dependably set every morning, was disarmed. That thought barely had time to cross her mind before she felt, against the back of her neck, the movement of air. Instinctively, she dropped to the floor and felt a scratch against the rear of her skull as she kicked backward with her good leg, digging her heel into something—a shin. She rolled against the carpet, finally catching sight of her attacker: a hand holding a syringe; sneakers covered in clear plastic protectors; a green windbreaker; a black balaclava.

The man was stumbling back, one leg up to keep balance, and without thinking Rachel grabbed his other leg and jerked with all her strength. His arms flailed, leg kicking out, and when he crashed onto his back she plunged a sharp, hard elbow into his groin. A choked gasp of pain. She was up on her good knee by then and dropped herself on top of him, all her weight behind an elbow aimed at his solar plexus. The little air still in his lungs escaped him in a tiny explosion, and he lay stunned, gasping, arms splayed out, the syringe rolling across the hardwood floor. Just enough time for her to scramble up his body and shove her forearm into his throat while her other hand snatched the syringe. She slid it into his carotid artery. His eyes popped open. His mouth opened, too, but he didn't have enough breath to speak.

"I'm going to squeeze the plunger if you don't tell me," she said. Since she couldn't read the expression in his masked face, she jiggled the needle; he winced. "Let's start with who," she said.

He managed two syllables. "Don't . . . know."

"What's in the syringe?"

The man blinked, eyes now bloodshot. "Et—or—phine."

Now Rachel blinked. A drop of pure etorphine would kill her, but diluted it would knock her out instantly, and deeply. Which version was she holding? His strength was returning; she wouldn't be able to hold him down much longer. She squeezed the syringe. Once he realized what was happening it was too late. He tried to yell but fell unconscious, his body relaxing before the sound escaped him.

Her leg hurt like hell.

She closed her eyes. Counted to twenty. Then checked his pulse.

He was alive.

She tugged the balaclava off his sleeping face. Forties, Caucasian, thick eyebrows and a flabby jawline. Gray hair. She tried to steady her breathing, but it was hard, because this was him: early August 2017. An Arlington street corner. A .357 Magnum.

Though her impulse was to call the police, she changed her mind after searching his body and finding that he carried nothing at all, not even keys, and that the labels had been cut out of his clothes. No—not like an aggrieved Massive Brigade follower coming for revenge. Not that, but . . .

Thoughts ran fast and slow in her head, crashing into each other. She closed her eyes, trying to focus on one: *Who?*

He said he didn't know, and she believed it. He was just a hired hand who'd failed back in August and had been sent back to finish the job.

Why?

She had nothing. Without one she couldn't know the other. *Who* would explain *why,* and vice versa. But she had neither.

In her steamy bathroom, she discovered that the tub had been prepared with hot water and a straight razor.

Oh.

She threw up in the toilet and cleaned herself off in the sink, trying not to look at the razor.

When she came out, patting her face with a hand towel, she noticed that her desk was clean, her laptop gone. Slowly, she walked through the studio, saw where this nameless man had rifled through shelves and opened up books. On the kitchen counter, she saw an open tin of Quaker Oats, and her heart sank. She hurried over and discovered that the Browning pistol she hid there was missing.

The gun and laptop were nowhere to be found, which meant that either they had been taken by an accomplice or her visitor had put them in his car, still parked someplace nearby . . .

But he had no keys on him. Therefore . . .

She pounded her forehead three times with her fist.

Therefore, someone was waiting downstairs for him to return.

She went back to the man, who was still out cold, and slapped his face. "Hey. Wake up." But his skin felt cool, and she noticed, looking down, that his pants were wet from a bladder that had relaxed completely. Hesitantly, she placed two fingers under his jaw and waited.

Tried again.

Again.

"Shit."

Though only five minutes had passed, it felt like a half hour had trickled by before she pocketed her cash and left the building, wearing the dead man's windbreaker, hood up. Rain had begun to fall, black puddles reflecting the lights above. She walked quickly, half-hobble, still trying to get her thoughts straight. Light, dark, light, dark. She watched for waiting cars—accomplices, perhaps, or maybe, she thought, the killer's car took a fingerprint instead of a key—when a parked van ahead of her started up, lights flashing on, then going dark. It pulled out into the steady drizzle and drove slowly past her. As it passed, in the shadowy cabin she caught sight of the green, glowing tip of an e-cigarette, balanced between a woman's fingers. Then it was gone. She walked faster. From behind, she heard the van stop. She looked back to see red brake lights. Then the white lights of reversal.

She ran.

8

THERE WERE police barricades at the intersection of Fifteenth and Spruce. Beyond the wooden barriers, contained by concrete façades, women and men and children clutched signs as they shuffled toward City Hall, shouting words Rachel couldn't make out. As she'd driven into Boulder, radio commentators had estimated fifteen thousand; real numbers, they admitted, were hard to come by. On the sidelines, actually witnessing the thoroughfare packed from edge to edge, she knew their estimate was conservative. Slogans bounced in the cool, crisp air:

TRANSPARENCY NOW!

OPEN UP THE FILES

REMEMBER WATERTOWN!

THE TIME FOR ANALYSIS IS OVER

It had taken two very long days of driving, crossing Washington, Oregon, Idaho, and Wyoming, to reach Colorado, and each mile she'd been plagued by the feeling that Johnson and Vale were in the car right behind her, or were in some control center full of monitors and blinking lights, spying on her through traffic cams she'd somehow missed when plotting her escape. She'd slept once during her journey, five hours of shut-eye parked behind a billboard for Vicodin outside Buhl, Idaho, and for the rest of the journey had sustained herself on convenience-store provisions: energy drinks, microwaveable meats, bagged chips.

Now, she stood on the tranquil side of the barricades, among locals who, like her, wanted to check the pulse of the city. Whether these spectators were sympathizers or critics, they, and she, hadn't made the leap to participant. Not yet.

She backtracked and found a Starbucks identical to the ones she frequented in Seattle, and like those it was packed. On their phones, customers watched live coverage of the march a block away. When she finally reached the counter, she ordered a double espresso from a plump, fuchsia-haired teenager who, as she gave Rachel change, said, "You marching?"

"I'm just passing through town."

"Well, that's no excuse—is it? If I didn't have this stupid job I'd be out there screaming with them."

"Why?"

The girl looked as if the question made no sense. "I mean, look around. Is this really the world you want?"

Though she didn't reply, Rachel could have, for she'd had two days to wrestle with some of these big questions. She could have said that we're born into the world; we don't shape it. We can adjust it and add to it, but thousands of years of history and patriarchy can't be erased in a single lifetime, not even by a million people in the street; it can only be built upon. Everything is built on the past.

The same, she guessed, was true of this girl. After sixteen or seventeen years of felt history, her mind wasn't going to be changed by a stranger on the other side of this counter. So Rachel only thanked her for the coffee and took it outside to the pedestrian street, where she could keep an eye on the car she'd stolen from a long-term lot near the Seattle airport. It had been easier than she'd imagined, waiting for the attendant to step out of his box for a bathroom break and grabbing a fob that led her to a white Chevy Impala. By the time the owner returned from his trip and discovered his car was gone, Rachel would be far away. At least, she hoped so. While she'd cringed at the idea of theft, there had been no other options. She'd only been able to withdraw a thousand dollars, split between two ATMs, before hitting her daily limit. Until she figured out what was going on, her cards were useless to her. As was her phone—her first precaution had been to shut it off and remove the SIM card.

While waiting for the parking attendant to leave, she'd struggled to get some kind of clarity. Had she misread the situation? Was she jumping out of her skin like the anxious, wild woman her colleagues saw in her? Really—in a city of six hundred thousand, did she really believe Sarah Vale was the only woman who smoked green-tipped electronic cigarettes?

In that moment, though, the *who* had felt less important than the *what*: a man with the labels cut from his clothes—the same one who'd failed to kill her seven months ago; the bathtub scene; the fact that her laptop had already been removed—the laptop that held the fifteen thousand words of her original report, the report that she had just been asked to regurgitate. These were the cornerstones, and she could only build on these facts, which was what she'd done endlessly over the past two days.

Whatever the truth, in those initial moments she'd known only one thing: to stay still was suicide; she had to move. First on foot, her hobbled run through wet alleyways, then a taxi out to Bellevue, suburb extraordinaire. Two ATMs, then an airport-bound bus in the other direction. Evasive maneuvers in a camera-ridden city like Seattle were nearly useless, though. So now in Boulder she just waited, watching the Impala, filthy from a thousand miles of American dirt. She waited for someone—anyone—to approach it.

In 2009, while working on her hallowed report on the left, she'd listened to a drug-addled Marxist lay out his evidence for the murderousness of the ruling classes. He cited stories ripped from the web that chronicled chilling deaths that had followed Hillary Clinton from her time as first lady through the beginning of her tenure as secretary of state—men and women who had served the Clintons and either had turned against them or were rumored to be in possession of damning evidence of one kind or another. Despite the drugs, he was a convincing orator, able to lay on questionable rumors at a rate that left the listener lost in a conspiratorial web. She tried attacking him with logic—despite multiple investigations costing millions, not a single charge had come close to being proven—but that only shored up his opinion: It pointed to a cover-up. The original proposition—that the first lady, New York senator, and secretary of state was a murderess—had morphed from a wild accusation in need of facts to a fact that was a litmus test for any documented evidence Rachel might bring up.

Was she doing the same thing? Was she beginning with a ridiculous proposition—that two Bureau agents had arrived in town to question and then kill her—and looking only at the evidence that might bolster the proposition?

But what else made sense? The only people who cut the tags from their clothes were professionals, not aggrieved radicals.

No—with her life on the line, she didn't need proof. Suspicion was enough. *Possibility* led to radical moves: a stolen car, a disassembled phone, and disappearing from her life.

And now, Boulder.

She was like one of the deserters who'd gone off to join Martin Bishop. But she wasn't joining anyone. She was down to $632, alone, standing outside of Starbucks with a now-cold double espresso, staring at her stolen car, waiting for her pursuers to show themselves.

But after an hour no one did, so after pouring the caffeine down her throat she tossed the cup and walked through the growing crowds back to the car. On the way she saw a young woman in a pink pussyhat, carrying a sign to the demonstration: THE FUTURE IS FEMALE.

9

IT TOOK an hour to reach the mountains, and twice she stopped on empty roads deep in the forests to wait five, ten minutes for shadows who never appeared. Eventually, she pulled up in front of a tidy little cabin made of planks and sheet metal. A narrow coal chimney stuck up like a damp cigar. She parked next to a filthy pickup truck with Virginia plates and got out, stepping onto the moist carpet of dead leaves. There were three loose steps leading up to the screen door, and when she rapped on it the doorframe shivered as if ready to fall off.

"Hey!" she heard, but from behind, and turned to find Kevin Moore, in heavy boots and flannel, climbing out of the woods, a shotgun hanging from a strap over his shoulder. Just like she'd imagined. There had been three Kevin Moores in the Boulder-area telephone directory, and this had been the only one living outside the city limits.

She raised her hands in surrender, coming down to meet him. "Remember me?"

"I remember," he said without breaking stride.

"How long have you been up here?"

He took the shotgun off his shoulder and carried it in both hands as he passed her and approached the steps. "Five months, about."

"Neighbors?"

"There's a nice couple up the road. We share recipes."

"You're kidding."

"No, Agent Proulx. I'm not."

"So you're not a hermit."

He shrugged, not caring what she thought of him. "Want to come inside?"

He'd gained some weight since they'd spoken in Watertown. Back then, he'd had the thin and wiry frame of someone who'd spent weeks on the road, and when he'd answered her questions in the ambulance he'd spoken in short, clipped phrases. He'd been in shock, of course, but his answers had been lucid and detailed, with a manic undercurrent, as if he hadn't quite come down from the contact high you get from touching the Revolution. Since then he'd gone cold turkey, and eight months later his body was returning to its equilibrium. Perhaps to replace that high, he'd taken up smoking, and his little cabin in the woods reeked of the Marlboro Golds he took from a carton marked with a persuasive color photo of open-heart surgery. He offered her one, but she declined.

They sat in his kitchen and drank bitter tea he prepared from Lipton bags. He was, he told her, on extended leave.

"You mean you're out of the Bureau?" she asked.

"My paperwork's still in order."

"What does that mean?"

"It means I'm still meditating on it."

It was an answer of sorts. "Still in touch with Janet Fordham?"

"Keeping my distance." He grinned. "The news these days doesn't help. The idea that very soon the whole world will have access to a report with you in it is a little disconcerting."

"Your name will be redacted."

"But I'll be a subject of speculation. Pressure will be applied. Someone along the way will slip up, or more likely leak, and then there'll be a caravan of television vans leading up to this place. I'll probably have to leave the country," he said, nodding toward the back of the cabin. "Got my passport and a change of clothes all ready."

"Aren't you a ray of sunshine," she said.

He looked at her a moment, frowning, as if she'd said something inappropriate. Then he took a drag. "The rules of conduct have been broken for a long time. You've been in town, right?"

"The marchers."

"Three days straight. Just to force the government to release a single FBI report a few days sooner than planned. You'd think there'd been a massacre or something. Nine people were killed in Watertown. You know how many people were killed on the streets of Chicago last week? I don't see anyone marching for them."

"The report," she said. "Have you seen it?"

He shook his head. "I told them what I knew, then I got the hell out of there. Is it damning?"

"I wasn't on the distribution list."

He raised a brow, curious.

"I wasn't in a position to argue the point."

A look of understanding passed across his face. Though he'd been lying in an ambulance when she attacked Jakes, he had to know about the incident. He said, "Well, we'll both be able to read it soon enough. PDF download."

She looked at the brown liquid in her cup, muddy at the bottom.

"So?" he said. "What's this about?"

"Can't I make a nostalgic visit?"

He smiled. "You know what I remember about you? That short time we sat together in the ambulance, talking through everything, you had your phone in your hand. Every couple of minutes your eyes would move over to it, checking for messages. You'd even pick it up and look at it while I was speaking. It was pretty rude."

"Sorry," she said.

"You've been here a half hour now, and you haven't taken it out once."

"I'm trying to break my addictions."

"No, you're not. People like you never do."

She wanted to ask what that meant, people like her, but more important she wanted to know why he didn't seem surprised by her appearance. He showed no worry that she was sitting in his cabin, the place he'd come to hide away—from many things, but the Bureau in particular. Or was he simply a terrific actor who, on the inside, was frantically running through his options, all the gradations of fight-or-flight?

He got up and threw the dregs of his tea into the sink, then re-filled the electric kettle and switched it on; it hummed. He turned to look down at her, hands behind himself against the edge of the counter. "So? Why don't you tell me, Rachel. Tell me what you've come here to find out."

I'm here because the Bureau is trying to kill me, she wanted to say, but she didn't know Kevin Moore, not really, and she didn't know where he stood in this. She didn't know where anyone stood.

"Everything," she told him. "I've come to find out everything."

He said nothing, just stared at her, the gears in his head working away. What was he thinking? Had he already sent a signal to Johnson and Vale while she wasn't looking? Maybe he'd sent it from the woods, after he'd seen her but before he'd said "Hey." Or was he merely what he seemed to be, a mildly disillusioned undercover agent who wanted to be left alone?

He straightened and took her teacup away, poured it into the sink, opened a cabinet, and brought out a bottle of Knob Creek bourbon. He put a splash into her cup and poured more for himself. He brought the drinks to the table and sat across from her again. He had made up his mind.

"Thank you," she said, then took a sip; the taste of smoke filled her mouth.

10

UNLIKE THE Kevin Moore she'd met in Watertown, this one was matter-of-fact, telling her without embellishment of his departure from San Francisco, his entry into the underground of the Massive Brigade, and the arrival of Benjamin Mittag. The first time she noticed a crack in his serene exterior was when he reached Key Biscayne and looked down the scope of his M-40 and made the decision that, he could admit, he would never be able to defend to himself, much less to a court of law.

"You would've lost everything if you hadn't," she reassured him. "There was no other choice."

"There's always another choice," he said, then sipped his drink. "You just have to know how to find it."

He brushed over his brief respite in sultry Louisiana, then focused on the second cross-country drive with Mittag. "It was clear by then that there was tension at the top. Ben wanted to run it his way—that was why he'd collected me and the others, the people who knew how to kill. Martin saw it differently. I didn't really understand until I saw them arguing in Lebanon, and after."

"You got in touch with Janet Fordham before Lebanon, right? From a gas station."

"In Marshall, Texas. Yeah."

"And then in Lebanon you saw Bishop and a woman named Ingrid Parker."

He said nothing, just stared, and she realized he was holding back. Why? She thought back over everything she knew about Ingrid, which wasn't much—the slanted descriptions her husband had given, the suspicious Tor-encrypted conversation from work and subsequent flight, appearing next to Bishop in Kansas before disappearing again. And Johnson and Vale—*It would be really helpful if we could find her.*

Rachel said, "Tell me about Ingrid."

He hesitated, then rocked his head. "Not much to tell. She was traveling with Bishop, and she was there when he was killed. It was hard on her. She was pregnant. We drove off together."

It was starting to come back to her, the interview eight months ago in the back of that ambulance. "But she didn't make it to Watertown, correct?"

"We dropped her off somewhere in Nebraska. St. Paul. Left her at a gas station. It was too much for her."

She leaned back and crossed her arms over her stomach. He was very convincing, which must have served him so well, even as he followed through on Mittag's orders and shot a congresswoman in Florida, carefully shifting his sights in order to maim but not kill. Briefly, she closed her eyes and remembered Agent Young driving her to the airport, and her reading the emails that were flying in the wake of nine deaths. She said, "That night in Watertown, when they were patching you up, I got a preliminary inventory from the house. Know what they found in the upstairs bathroom?"

"I do not."

"A bottle of prenatal vitamins." He didn't answer, so she pushed further. "None of the women in that house were pregnant."

"Of course not," Kevin said dryly, "because they were dead."

She watched as he took another sip of whiskey and placed his cup on the table.

"She's gone now," Rachel said. "No one's going to find her. So, please. Just tell me the real story. Okay? There's more riding on this than Ingrid Parker's safety." He didn't seem moved, so she said, "I'm not the only one wondering what happened to her."

He shook his head, then surprised her by saying, "You guys don't give up, do you?"

"What?"

"I already told him."

"Told who what?"

"That I don't know where she is."

"What are you talking about?"

He sighed, and from the way he spoke it was clear he wasn't buying her ignorance. "Ingrid Parker got in over her head. Those others, the kids—they're young, their time with the Brigade is a blip on their résumés. It's street cred. Otherwise, it makes no difference. But by now Ingrid's made a life with her daughter, and the last thing she needs is you or me coming in to fuck it up."

Rachel took a moment to absorb this, then said, "Who already asked about her?"

Instead of answering, he said, "Why do you care about Ingrid?"

Why, indeed? Because Johnson and Vale cared about her, that was why. "I'd like to speak to her."

"Why?"

"Because I never talked to anyone who really knew Martin Bishop. You didn't spend time with him. Ben Mittag is dead. People only talked to Bishop for minutes at a time. They worshipped him, but no one actually knew him."

"And you think she knew him?"

"Why else would he bring her along to Kansas to meet with you and Mittag?"

Kevin looked into his cup and, seeing that it was empty, pushed it, scratching, to the center of the table.

Again, Rachel said, "Who already asked about her?"

Kevin nodded at the window, to the trees beyond. "A week ago,

Owen Jakes comes right up that muddy road with a couple of suits, wanting to know where she is."

"He came personally?"

Kevin looked at her, not bothering to answer.

"Why does *he* care about Ingrid Parker?" Rachel asked.

"Same reason you do, I suspect."

"Is that what he said? That Ingrid knew the most about Bishop?"

Kevin got up and took the Knob Creek from the counter, then turned around, the bottle in both hands, and said, "They were running through the report, prepping it for dissemination. Crossing their t's and dotting their i's. He knew there would be questions about her, since her husband's publishing stories about her. So what could I add? I told him to look at my debrief, because I already told them everything I knew."

"And that was it?" she asked. "He came out to the middle of nowhere for that?"

Kevin returned to the table with the whiskey bottle and sat down. "We talked a few hours, Jakes and me. Right here. The two suits he'd brought sat in the living room over there, reading magazines. They were cool customers." Kevin aimed the bottle at her. "We talked about you, too."

"Me?"

"He told me about your breakdown. I knew what had happened, of course, but he said it was more than just anger. The Bureau shrink worried you were unstable. Maybe bipolar."

"Well, my therapist never mentioned that to me," Rachel said, a queasiness growing in her stomach.

"He asked how you were when you interviewed me that night. How you took my words. Did you seem upset by how things had gone down? Suspicious? Did you believe me?" Kevin shrugged. "I told him I didn't know what was in your head. I told him you were professional."

"Thanks," she said, but it came out as a whisper because she didn't have much air. Bipolar? Christ, whatever was happening to her had been going on for weeks.

Kevin didn't seem to notice. "He wanted to know if *you* had spoken to Ingrid Parker. I told him I seriously doubted it."

Rachel stared for what felt like a long time, and she knew that her gaze was uncomfortable for him, though he showed no sign. He, too, was professional, even now.

She said, "The suits who came with Jakes. You remember their names?"

The question seemed to confuse him. He thought a moment. "The man . . . Lyle Johnson. And the woman—"

"Sarah Vale," she said.

Just as she often woke to an anxiety of indeterminate origin, Rachel had fled Seattle plagued by a fear that hadn't come into focus. Of death, yes, but she hadn't quite swallowed the idea that her employer was trying to kill her. It was just too much. Now, the chain was undeniable: a contract killer, Vale, Johnson, and Owen Jakes, and she was the through-line connecting them. The terror that she had wrestled with for two days had gotten to its feet, shaken itself off, and raised two sturdy fists.

Her feelings must have been all over her face, for Kevin uncorked the Knob Creek and splashed plenty more in both their cups.

11

RACHEL COULDN'T help but remember Janet Fordham's critique of Kevin Moore, that he cared too much. There had been that woman in New Orleans he'd risked his life to protect—she wondered if he was doing that now with Ingrid Parker. She said, "When you and Mittag went to Kansas to meet Bishop, were you afraid?"

"I was fucking terrified."

"But you'd proven yourself to them. You'd proven yourself better than nearly anyone else."

Kevin considered this as he lifted his cup. Then, reconsidering, he set the cup down. "You've worked undercover?"

"A little."

"Then you know. From the moment you go under, the fear starts, and it never leaves. Not even after you get out." He finally took a sip of whiskey. "It's here, now, in this room."

She knew what he meant; she knew fear better than he could imagine. She said, "And Ingrid was there, in Lebanon."

He nodded. "I'd never met her before, never heard of her. But Ben had. He said, 'So that's her. The bitch who's been fucking with his head.'" Kevin tilted his head. "You should know that I never told them this."

Rachel frowned. "The Bureau?"

"She wasn't their business."

"Then why are you telling me now?"

He looked her straight in the eyes for five full seconds. A thin smile. "Because I don't think you're bipolar."

"Thank you," Rachel said. It was one of the stranger compliments she had received, but she took it, and by accepting it she felt as if she and he had become closer, that they were beginning to build a little room of shared secrets. She felt an urge to push it further, to deepen their connection by telling him what had happened in Seattle, but she didn't know how far he was willing to go. Would that ever-present fear raise its head again and convince him to report her to Jakes, if only to save his own skin? Her life was too valuable a thing to risk on the unknown.

She thought back again to the interview she'd conducted with him in the ambulance, when—apparently—she wouldn't let her phone be. "You told me that Bishop went directly at Mittag. That he was angry."

"Yes."

"And you couldn't hear what they were saying because you were too far away."

"And it was windy."

"Right. Was *that* the truth?"

This time he stared at her longer, blinking. Maybe now, she thought, was the time to tell him about Seattle. Maybe he was waiting for her to offer up something in return, and as he stared he was making his own risk assessment, deciding whether or not to stonewall her until she left. Then he said, "It was a partial truth."

"How so?"

"Because Ingrid took part in their argument."

She inhaled deeply. "I can see why you skipped that."

"Do you?"

She hesitated to say it aloud, but: "If Ingrid was important enough to be an equal in that argument, then that means the Brigade hasn't been wiped out." He didn't bother replying to that, so she went on. "Which may be why they're looking for her."

"But they're wrong," he said.

She thought on this, her mind inevitably drawn back to the image of Owen Jakes sitting in this crummy little cabin, quizzing Kevin. "But if you never told the Bureau these things about Ingrid, then why is Jakes looking for her? Why doesn't he think of her as just another follower who's vanished?"

He closed his eyes, then opened them. "That, Rachel, is a question I don't have an answer for. They certainly never heard it from me, and I check this place twice a week—no one's listening to us now."

Of course he'd taken precautions. That's the kind of person Kevin Moore still was, even out here. She sipped her whiskey and decided to let go of the enigma of Owen Jakes for the moment. "The pickup truck. The one in the field. It didn't follow you?"

He shook his head. "Didn't see it again. Ben floored it, heading west and then north, but he stuck to country roads. The highway was a no-go."

"And what did Ben and Ingrid think had happened?"

"They didn't know what to think. Not at first. It was pretty emotional. Ben was scared, and then angry—all over the place. Ingrid was crying. But after a few hours they started processing it all. Ben was the first—it was clear to him that the Bureau had done it. One safe house had been closed down, and while we were driving we heard about the second bust in Utah. He said the Bureau was closing in and wiping us all out."

She thought back to what she'd said to Johnson and Vale—the unthinkable alternative, that the Bureau had killed Bishop. "Did that strike you as a possibility?"

"I considered it," he said after a moment. "When I called Janet the day before, I didn't know where we were headed, and I didn't think anyone would be able to track me. But maybe I was wrong. Maybe they *had* gotten access to a satellite and tracked us from Marshall, all the way to Lebanon."

"*They* was me, and we never did track your car."

He shrugged. "The Bureau's a big place. We both know that. Lots of moving parts that don't always meet." He shook his head. "But it still wouldn't work. Track us to Lebanon and *then* send in a sniper in . . . what? An hour, max? I couldn't see it. But in the car, all I could do was go along with Ben. Ingrid, though—it wasn't until after we topped off the tank in St. Paul that she accused Ben. He'd used snipers like me to take over the Brigade."

"She really believed that?"

"It's what made sense to her. I would've thought the same thing in her shoes."

"And now?"

"Maybe he did it. Maybe not. Maybe the report will clear everything up." He took a sip, then licked his lips. "Maybe it'll muddy the waters even more."

12

AGAIN, RACHEL considered opening up. She might have cornered him here, but they both knew that she didn't have any kind of authority. He didn't have to tell her anything. Yet he was telling her a lot. Everything? She couldn't say, but he was trusting her in a way she was unable to reciprocate. Perhaps his openness was a kind of trap, something to seduce secrets out of her. Who was to say this place wasn't wired, after all?

"What does all this mean?" she asked finally. "If the Bureau didn't kill Martin, then who? Ben? A rival faction in the Brigade?"

"Far as I could tell, there were only two factions: Martin and Ben."

"And Ingrid," said Rachel, but he didn't weigh in on that. "So you lean toward her theory, that Ben got rid of him."

Kevin downed the last of his whiskey. "I live in the middle of nowhere, Rachel. I've made a new career of not leaning toward any theory."

She watched him get up to look in the refrigerator. He took out two bottles of Poland Spring and set one in front of her.

"The tap water up here tastes like sulfur," he said by way of explanation as he unscrewed his own bottle and drank.

She let hers be. "Tell me what happened when you got to Watertown."

He did, and as he had in that ambulance he told the story with concision, but this time he told more, explaining how Ingrid discovered what he was. "You just let her go," she said.

"Like I told you, she'd had enough. That's why I kept her out of my report."

She shook her head, stunned by the stupidity of what he'd done. "She could have ruined the whole thing. All she had to do was walk back inside and tell everyone about you."

"What would you have done, Rachel? Strangle her?"

"You could have tied her up."

"I didn't have any rope."

She hesitated, trying to picture the moment from his perspective. What *would* she have done? Would she have killed Ingrid?

"Look," he said, "I did what seemed like my only play. I wasn't going to murder her—I didn't have that in me. So I had to commit to something. And it seemed to work. I sent her away and went back inside. They asked where Ingrid was, of course; I said she was taking some time to clear her head. They had no reason to doubt this."

Kevin drank more water, then wiped his mouth. Rachel noticed that his fingernails were chewed down to the quick, the skin on the fingertips dry and peeling.

"All I had to do was wait for the cavalry. People started going to bed. I imagined how easy it would be, everyone asleep when the SWAT guys showed up. And then the landline rang. Ingrid had found a pay phone."

"Shit," Rachel said.

"Yes. Shit."

He told her about being dragged upstairs, and the few words Mittag said to him in the bedroom before the lights went out and the SWAT team poured in, guns blazing.

Man, you've really got it all wrong, don't you? We're on the same side . . . Or, we used to be.

"What did that mean?" Rachel asked, puzzled.

Kevin shrugged. "I thought maybe you'd have some idea."

There was something in his tone, and the way he stared coolly at her, waiting. Was he trying to turn this interview around on her? "I don't," she said. "Was he trying to say he worked for the Bureau? He did put in an application long ago. But he was turned down immediately."

Kevin rocked his head, but she couldn't tell if this was news or not.

"Why didn't you tell me about this when I interviewed you before? When we were in the ambulance. It had only just happened."

"I didn't know you, Rachel. A man with a gun tells me we're on the same side right before being shot, then a woman I've never met bangs against my stretcher and starts asking me questions . . . I didn't know what to think."

"And now?"

"I'm testing you, Rachel. Can't you tell?"

She wasn't insulted, though she might have been. "And what about the official debrief?"

"I kept Ingrid out of it, but Ben's last words?" He shrugged. "I told them, and they didn't like it at all. Told me how the common people would suspect the worst. They wanted my assurance that I would stay quiet. Gave me something to sign, so I signed it. I bet you did, too."

She shook her head. "I didn't sign it."

"Oh?" he said, surprised, and she knew then that this had been her great mistake in Seattle, not signing that nondisclosure agreement. If anything had put a mark on her head, it had been that. Christ, what was her problem? Why couldn't she just let things go? Hadn't she learned over the past eight months that what happened outside her little world wasn't her responsibility?

She tried to focus. "You really don't know where Ingrid Parker is?"

"I really don't," he said. "And I don't want to know."

"How much money did she have?"

"She'd been carrying Martin's stash—twenty, thirty grand. Enough to get her started."

"So she could be anywhere."

"That's what I'm saying."

"Any thoughts on how Massive got hands on all that money?"

"Money was just there."

"Did anyone mention a company called Magellan Holdings?"

He shook his head. "No one told me anything about any of that."

Whether or not she believed him didn't matter; this was all she was going to get. The problem was that the only way for her to know what to do, and who she could trust, was to get clarity on what had happened last year. Ingrid Parker, it seemed, was the only one who might give her that clarity—why else would Owen come all the way out here with Johnson and Vale, looking for her?

Through his kitchen window the sun was low. She said, "What do you think of Watertown now?"

Kevin sucked on his lip. "Do I agree with all those protesters in the middle of town? Is that what you're asking? Do I think it was an unnecessary massacre?"

"Yeah. That's what I'm asking."

He snorted. "Of course it was."

"And now you're out here, thinking about leaving the Bureau."

Kevin leaned back, closing his eyes, as if ready for a nap. He said, "Anyone who tells you there's a single reason that they're leaving the only job they've ever known is a liar." He opened his eyes and got up, then grabbed the bottle of Knob Creek. "There's never a single reason for anything a human does."

He refilled their cups, and while they talked for another half hour Rachel still did not tell him about Seattle. By then she trusted him well enough, but she read in his laconic behavior a clear message: *I do not want to be involved.* He was out, and that was where he wanted to stay, communing with nature and sharing recipes with neighbors. It was what you did when you resurfaced after a year undercover: You hooked your wagon to the repetitions of domesticity. You kept things as simple as possible and tried to reconnect with whoever you originally were before you spent a year being someone else.

There was a chance she was misreading his message, but those who take no sides in a fight are pawns for both sides. Tomorrow, Johnson and Vale could show up and ask questions and quickly deduce her next stop—a stop that the bourbon haze had suddenly helped her see with clarity. But she needed a little time, and she didn't need Kevin Moore giving her away.

As she got up finally and pulled on her jacket, she posed the question that had begun to nag at her above all others. "The Bureau killed Mittag. For the sake of argument, let's say we killed Bishop, too. The question is: Why? Why risk martyrs? Why open the door to demonstrators shouting conspiracy theories in the street?"

Kevin thought about that. "The same reason I probably should have killed Ingrid. To shut them up."

"About what?"

He had no answer.

As she drove back down his hill in the Impala, the late-afternoon sun twinkling through branches, she looked out for rental cars, or oversized Suburbans that were the hallmark of unexpected Bureau visits. All she saw was a rust-speckled pickup, not unlike Kevin's, driven by a pretty brunette wearing a bandana on her head. The neighbor, she guessed, who shared recipes with Kevin. No wonder he didn't want to leave his mountain. It was the American dream, circa 1880.

That was when she realized that she'd forgotten something in Seattle: her cane. For nearly three days she'd survived without its support and hadn't even noticed.

led that other auditorium on the other coast, in 2009. Martin Bishop, now dead, but back then so full of dire optimism.

It had been three days and eighteen hundred miles since Boulder, and Rachel had crossed the New Jersey line in a 1985 Ford Escort she'd picked up in little Paxton, Nebraska, for $400. Neither the air conditioning nor the heating worked, and if she left her foot off the gas at a light it died, but the car had brought her all the way to High Bridge station, at the end of the Raritan Valley Line. She'd parked and taken the train to Penn Station before continuing on foot—she wanted to avoid the subways—down to NYU.

Halfway through her long journey, while dozing in an Illinois rest stop, she'd sunk into a vivid dream about James Sullivan, and while looking over the bright young faces of David's students the dream came back to her. She and Sullivan were drinking martinis in a coastal bar, maybe Florida or California, and he wore a Che Guevara beret. He told her, "The Third World is just around the corner." Then the bar rose and fell, as if an earthquake had struck, drinks spilling and customers tumbling, but Sullivan held her upright as their stools spun. The last thing she remembered was a huge wave smashing through the windows, filling the bar with salt water.

As the hour was wrapping up, Rachel moved down to the front, and Parker caught sight of her, stumbling over his final lines. Then he turned back to the students. "Next week, then, okay?" The auditorium was suddenly noisy with the sounds of packing up. Rachel approached the podium and told David, "Josie Woods."

The name seemed to confuse him briefly; then he recognized it. "Okay," he said.

She turned away and pushed through the students, and by the time she reached the street she'd pulled on the hood of her new jacket, picked up from a roadside Target. She continued to the corner of Waverly and Mercer and took the stairs down into the Josie Woods Pub, a brick-walled underground sports bar. Today, though, instead of sports, CNN played on the screens. She stared for a long time at the face of Mark Paulson, who explained to a newscaster why it was

13

"IN THE shift from a fragmented world of powerful nat
the emphasis on cooperation and a dual-power structure
war world—the West and East in a perpetual standoff
fiction found its ideal soil for growth."

There were maybe two hundred undergraduates fillin
auditorium, and at the front David Parker, in obligatory
galed them with his expertise on the world of spy
expertise Rachel never would have suspected. From th
she reflected that the man she'd seen at his lowest had re
self. As chapters from his new novel appeared in the rags,
and now he could preach to an army of aspiring write
like a born actor, on the attention it brought him.

Sitting in on History of the Espionage Novel had
her best bet, since Parker's home would certainly be ur
lance, so she stayed for the full hour and listened to Park
of the two major strains of spy fiction—the fantastic (J
Jason Bourne) and the realistic (George Smiley, Paul Ch

The students were a healthy bunch, fresh faced ar
ately cynical, which reminded her of the mishmash that h

taking so long to declassify a report for public consumption. "Have you looked at the streets recently, Mr. Paulson?" asked the newscaster. "People are getting impatient."

It was true. On her long walk to NYU she'd seen protesters heading to competing demonstrations around City Hall and Trump Tower. Painted faces and signs and effigies of both the president and the Bureau's long-suffering director. She remembered Lou Barnes and Erin Lynch and morose Richard Kranowski making fun of the White House's fear of the Massive Brigade. How did they feel now? The president's poll numbers were tanking even worse than usual, which meant that theirs were, too.

"What the fuck are you doing here?" she heard, and looked up to see David Parker heading toward her, laptop bag banging against his hip.

"Nice to see you, too, David."

He sat down, agitated. "They warned me I might hear from you."

She stiffened. "Who?"

"I don't know their names. Couple days ago, these two stiffs told me to call if I heard from you."

It wasn't a surprise, not really. If Jakes had made a house call to speak with Kevin Moore, then someone certainly would have visited David. "What else did they tell you?"

He hesitated, as if worried about bruising her feelings, then plowed on. "That you've gone off the deep end. They said that having this shit in the news again, it's dredged up a bunch of demons in your psyche. They said that inevitably you'd come to me."

"Demons?"

"They said you'd be looking for Ingrid."

"Let me guess. Lyle Johnson and Sarah Vale," she said, stifling a yawn. It wasn't boredom, though; the exhaustion of crossing the continent was catching up to her.

He made no sign to suggest she was right or wrong. Her detective work meant nothing to him. "They said you're dangerous."

She smiled to help him see that she wasn't dangerous, but from the look on his face she could tell it wasn't working. "I'm just trying to find out what's going on," she said.

"What do you mean, what's going on?"

"They were right about one thing. I do need to talk to Ingrid."

His head bobbed. "Well, I'd like to talk to her, too, but I don't know where she is. And I keep telling you guys that."

"Who's been asking?"

"Couple weeks after Watertown, this asshole shows up at my apartment. Bandage on his head. Says he's one of yours."

"Owen Jakes." She shook her head. "By then I was out, under investigation. He wasn't one of mine anymore."

He nodded—maybe he knew the story, maybe he didn't. "Well, that's what he told me."

"Go on," she said.

David scratched his chin and explained that, at first, it had been friendly. Owen Jakes showed his badge and said that Rachel had asked him to check up on David. Jakes carried a file, and he referenced it while asking questions about Ingrid. Where were her relatives? She had none. What were her political leanings? To the left of left, usually. Then: "When was the last time you talked to her?"

"June 19," David told him. "The day she disappeared." Then he brought out the ultrasound, which he'd protected in a plastic sleeve and kept on a high shelf. "And you guys saw this already."

"But you've spoken to her since," Jakes said, a statement more than a question.

"No, I haven't."

"Maybe not by voice, but emails. Texts. A woman doesn't send this," he said, referencing the ultrasound, "and simply go silent. That's not done."

"Well, that's how Ingrid does it."

That was when the friendliness abruptly ended. Jakes stood and thrust a finger at him. "Cut the bullshit, okay? Ingrid wasn't just another one of Martin's followers—she was traveling *with* him."

"What?"

"They were lovers. Are you really going to stand there and protect her when she went on a sex spree with Martin Bishop across the
fucking nation? Tell me, David. Tell me where Ingrid's hiding, or I
swear to God I'm going to drag your ass into federal detention and
throw away the key."

Now, months later, David's cheeks flushed from the memory.
Why had Jakes gone after Ingrid Parker with such venom? Rachel
didn't know, but the story only reinforced her conviction that if there
was an answer to be found it lay with Ingrid, and only with her. She
pursed her lips. "So? Any ideas?"

"I didn't know where she was back then. And I still don't."

"Really?"

He nodded, averting his gaze angrily, and she knew then that
she was out of options. She covered her face with her hands, rubbed
her eyes. Had she really thought she could track down Ingrid without the Bureau backing her up? Hubris. Maybe she should just turn
herself in. Sign away her rights, just like Kevin Moore had. Was it
too late for that?

Six nights ago, a man had come to kill her. He'd stripped himself of anything identifiable. He'd prepared her bath to stage a suicide, then come at her with a needle rather than a gun. That was the
definition of too late.

Maybe it was exhaustion, or the realization that there was nothing
left to fight for, but Rachel began to cry. It wasn't obvious, just the
dampening of her eyes, the blinking, and when she wiped at her left
lid a single tear traced a line down her cheek. In that moment she was
more terrified of breaking down in front of David Parker than she was
of Johnson and Vale. She sniffed, pulling herself together, and stood.

"Okay, David. Thanks."

He frowned up at her, brows knitted. "You all right?"

"Yeah—I'm fine. I just . . . ." She just what? "Take care of yourself, okay?"

He looked confused.

"And so you know, David: There was never any suggestion that Ingrid and Martin Bishop were lovers."

By the time she was out on the street the tears had returned, and knowing she was alone—or, hoping she was alone—she let them flow.

14

SHE SERIOUSLY considered taking the train north to Croton-on-Hudson. Though they talked regularly, she hadn't laid eyes on her mother in months, and it would have been good to get the visual evidence that she was in decent shape. But to go to her mother, to even call her, would be to direct her would-be murderers to Croton, which could not end well.

In a Cuban dive in Chelsea, she ate *boliche*—beef roast stuffed with chorizo and potatoes—which brought her down to just a few dozen dollars. She tried to get her head around things. It was hard, because all she had was a handful of notable facts and too few lines of connection. Were there connections, or was her Bureau mind merely desperate to create an intricate web when in fact she was looking at parallel lines of inquiry that would never meet?

There was July 4, and the assassinations that Kevin had taken part in. This had always troubled her, for it was incredibly shortsighted. This one act of revolution could only ruin the image of the group and push its agenda back a decade. With that act—instigated, apparently, by Benjamin Mittag—they had ruined everything, even targeting some politicians who were relatively sympathetic; Hanes and Trumble had been prepared to face off with Plains Capital and

IfW for helping international billionaires commit tax fraud. How did their murders make sense, even to a hothead like Mittag?

Then there was the Brigade itself, and its funding, which had led to Laura Anderson, an old woman in an Australian nursing home. She was obviously a cutout for someone else, but whom? Her old employer, the United Nations? Down that path lay unhinged conspiracies—next thing, she'd be marching across town to bang on the door of its headquarters. Besides, the UN survived on a shoe-string budget, every penny meticulously accounted for, and funding a movement to undermine its largest contributor made little sense.

What about James Sullivan, her mysterious person of interest from nine years ago? An American who spoke perfect-sounding Russian and pretended—or maybe he wasn't pretending?—to work for a pharmaceutical in Switzerland. Was he the financial through-line between his employers and Martin Bishop, using Laura Anderson?

And then the murder of Martin Bishop. *Had* the Bureau done it? As Kevin had pointed out, that was logistically impossible. There was simply no time between his call to Fordham and the shooting for even the Federal Bureau of Investigation to pull it off. Ben Mittag was the more believable culprit, but what was he aiming to achieve? To take over an organization that was synonymous with Bishop's name?

And what about Sam Schumer? That purveyor of self-promotion masked as objective news had learned of Bishop's murder before the Bureau had. Maybe Vale was right—maybe a witness had decided to call Schumer's hotline but not inform anyone else. But Sarah Vale had smoked her green e-cigarette and waited for news of Rachel's murder, so anything she said was in doubt.

Rachel got up and paid, thinking that this was too much for her to deal with alone. She needed help, but help was something she couldn't depend on. Kevin wanted nothing to do with it, while David was a man motivated by fear. Her colleagues at the office were loyal to the Bureau, and she didn't know how she stood with her employer. Maybe Ashley would be willing to look into something; maybe not.

When she returned to Penn Station, rush hour was under way, and she joined the cattle-car press of warm bodies trying to get home. If she was going to be on the run, she didn't want to be trapped on the island of Manhattan.

She boarded the train, looking over her shoulder but finding only strangers' eyes, then settled next to a sad-looking woman with a Macy's bag. Where, she wondered, could she hope to find answers?

In the final report, perhaps. The timing was too perfect—they had asked for her version of the Massive Brigade story, then asked her to give up her right to ever speak of it again. Her refusal had signed her death warrant, which could only mean that she had contradicted their version of events. In what way, they hadn't told her. Certainly Watertown would look different, but was protecting Owen's job enough to justify murder? If so, then she was living in an even darker world than she'd imagined.

Of course it was about more than just Owen's job, because this hadn't been their first attempt on her life; her sore leg attested to that. As early as last year, they believed that she knew something, or could find out something, that would make trouble for them. That they'd left her alone for so long suggested that they assumed the attack in Arlington had knocked the fight out of her. In many ways, they had been right.

They, she thought with dismay. That all-encompassing *they,* that evil shadow behind all conspiracy theories. She'd become the kind of person she despised.

By the time the train left a station called Lebanon, two stops from the end of the line, most of the car had cleared out and she was plotting the near future: picking up her car and driving upstate and crossing over to the vast farmlands of New Hampshire, where she could find a small town and lie low for a while. Money was an issue, but that was tomorrow's problem. She was thinking in terms of hours, not weeks or even days, and this left her in a state of anxiety that she knew would exhaust her sooner rather than later.

As the train stopped, released its passengers, then continued on, she thought that what she really needed, more than anything, was a drink.

And as if on cue, Kevin Moore sat down in the seat across from her. She straightened, shocked.

"Where you headed?" he asked.

She didn't know if she should reply. Maybe—and this was only a passing thought—she'd dreamed him up as a kind of salvation. No. He was here, and he was asking her a question. "End of the line," she said.

He shook his head and stood slowly. "No, you're getting off at Annandale. It's the next stop. My truck's parked there."

"Am I?"

He shrugged, looking down at her. "Your choice, Rachel. But I'd take this chance if I were you."

15

IT TOOK an hour for Kevin to drive her to Montclair under cover of darkness, but he refused to answer her questions. He parked on a side street near the center of town, and from there they went on foot, following sidewalks past lit-up homes squeezed together in tight rows. Despite his infuriating silence, when Rachel said, "You lied to me, didn't you?" he said, "Once or twice."

"Had a change of heart?"

Kevin smiled at her. "Did you really *cry* in front of David?"

She rubbed her face, blushing.

She knew where they were headed, and remembered how, in the summer, the street outside the house had been full of cars. Now, there were no cars lining the street, and the driveway was empty. The house itself was dark.

"Where are the Ferrises?" she asked.

"Florida," Kevin told her as he jangled a key ring in his hand. "And, no—they don't know."

He stuck the key in the front door, unlocked the deadbolt, and pushed it open. He let her in first; then, once he closed the door, he turned on the light.

The entryway windows, she could now see, had been covered with cardboard. The doors to the other rooms were closed, and when he opened the pocket doors leading to the living room, she was faced with the enormous space she remembered from last summer, lit up, the high windows covered in more cardboard. David Parker stood by the fireplace, looking nervous, while on the sofa Ingrid Parker, her hair chopped short and a soft layer of mother's fat filling out her cheeks, was breastfeeding a chubby baby girl, who, Rachel calculated, was about three months old. Then she remembered, and said the name aloud: "Clare."

But the mention of her daughter's name did nothing to soften Ingrid. She looked at Kevin. "This is a mistake."

"It might be," Kevin admitted.

"It's not like things are getting better here," David cut in. "And going to the cops isn't an option."

"You're so fucking impatient," Ingrid said. "You always were."

"You want to raise our daughter in a boarded-up house? Hidden away from everyone? That's *crazy*. She might be able to help us out of this."

Though they were arguing about her, they were arguing as if Rachel weren't standing right there, hearing everything.

"Cool it," Kevin said to them both. "This is the situation now. All right?" David and Ingrid acquiesced, falling silent. To Rachel, Kevin said, "Come on, have a seat."

Slowly, so as not to startle anyone, Rachel took a comfy chair that faced the fireplace and sofa. Clare's cheeks were pink, eyes closed in milk-sucking bliss. "Is she healthy?" Rachel asked.

"Gassy," Ingrid told her, almost defensive. "But otherwise, yeah."

"You have a pediatrician?"

Ingrid hesitated. "She has her shots."

"Good," Rachel said, then tried to look at David and Kevin, but her gaze was continually drawn back to the baby, as if Clare contained her own gravitational force.

Visibly irritated, Ingrid said, "What I *need,* more than a pediatrician, is an internet connection."

"Yeah, right," said David. "So you can rally whatever's left of
your troops."

"So I can Google advice on her health."

Kevin sat next to Ingrid, breaking into the domestic dispute.
"Rachel? I know you're tired, but you're gonna have to start. You
know that. We don't say a thing until you tell us the truth. Why are
you driving across the country looking for Ingrid?"

"I told you—"

"You didn't tell me shit."

David headed to a spare chair. All eyes were on Rachel, in particular Ingrid's. She had that new-mother fatigue, but there was
also the fierceness of a mother's perpetual adrenaline, the kind that
could take down a lion. Her gaze was so intense that, were Rachel
clear-headed enough to fear anyone in that room, she would have
feared Ingrid.

"A week ago, an attempt was made on my life back in Seattle.
I think it was the Bureau."

Kevin leaned back, not taking his eyes off her, and both David
and Ingrid looked to him for some kind of confirmation. He leaned
forward again, elbows on his knees. "Okay. We'll dig into that later.
How does that lead to here?"

"Vale and Johnson, those agents who came with Jakes to visit
you," she said, then turned to David. "The same two who told you
I was off my rocker. They spent seven hours that same day debriefing me about last summer. The whole thing."

Kevin shook his head. "But didn't you write a report on that?"

"Not much of my report ended up in the final draft. Or so they
told me."

Silence descended again as Kevin thought through what all of
this might mean. When he finally shook his head, disbelieving, she
said, "I know, me, too. But it's true."

"But why come looking for me?" Ingrid asked.

"Because that was one of their most urgent questions. Where is Ingrid Parker? They wanted to know why you didn't come in when the amnesty was announced. They said they wanted to talk to you about Bishop."

Ingrid had developed a defiant streak after months on the lam, but even that couldn't hide the fear that bled into her features. She looked at David, who nodded. He told her, "You called it."

"Martin called it," Ingrid corrected, then turned to Rachel. "He told me that the Bureau would be after me, once they knew we'd spent so much time together. He said that once they knew what I knew, they might even try to kill me." She shook her head, using her free hand to rub her forehead. "And look at me now. In a room with two FBI agents. How stupid am I?"

Kevin, overcome by nervous energy, stood again and walked to the cardboard-covered windows. He squeezed his eyes shut and thought a moment, then turned back to Ingrid. "You need to tell her."

Ingrid didn't like the sound of that. "I don't need to *do* anything, Kevin. You said it yourself—there's no proof. And until there's proof it's dangerous to spread my story around."

"I said it's self-defeating. I said if you post it online it'll just be another conspiracy." He nodded toward Rachel. "But there obviously *is* proof."

"Proof of what?" Rachel asked.

Kevin ignored her and crossed back to Ingrid. "They'd only try to kill her if there was proof."

They argued a little longer, and Rachel tried to decipher the detail-free points everyone was making. "Look," she said finally. "It sounds to me like we need each other. But I can't help you if I don't know what's happening. So can you please tell me your story?"

Ingrid held Clare tighter, working her way through a decision. Rachel understood the anxiety: Ingrid wasn't simply putting her life at risk; she was putting her baby's life at risk. But something had to be done, so Ingrid turned to face her squarely and said, "Remember Jerome Brown?"

Rachel did. The young father in Newark. He'd been all over the news back then. "What about him?"

"He's as good a place to start as any."

16

DO YOU know why I pulled you over?

No, sir.

Registration's out of date.

Ingrid had watched the video fifteen times, and more—from her desk at the Starling Trust, on her phone in the subway, at home in the kitchen while David sat with a drink, watching B-grade TV.

Anything in the car I should know about?

A gun. But I got a license.

Don't—

Bang. Pause. *Bang.*

The few times she'd brought up Jerome Brown and that New Jersey cop, David had shown little interest, quickly pointing out that, hey, the guy *was* reaching for a gun, right? Then he'd find a way to redirect the conversation back to his long-suffering novel.

Jerome? You kill my boyfriend? Wake up, Jerome! Did you kill my boyfriend?

So she let it be, creating a secret space in her life that held Jerome Brown, his girlfriend, Moira, and LaTanya, the five-year-old in the backseat who'd filmed her father's execution.

This wasn't the first time she'd heard this kind of story. Not the first time she'd seen handheld video of uniformed cops and young black men and heard the two-strike thumps of a trigger being pulled. Cities as catchphrases for institutional racism: Ferguson, St. Paul, Baton Rouge, Los Angeles, Montgomery, Raleigh, Charleston, Staten Island, Baltimore. She commiserated with friends at work; together, they shook their heads and lamented the state of the country—white supremacists marching in Charlottesville, after all! And knowing that even if they weren't part of the solution at least they recognized there was a problem. They weren't coldhearted.

How could she *not* watch it, along with five million others? How could she not read the *Times* for its hourly updates and listen to the talking heads who commented on all the sticky topics that surrounded the murder of black men in America? Ingrid's head filled up with incessant partisan chatter: race and gun control and insufficient police training and fatherless childhoods and the medieval state of America's criminal justice system. Then all that was swept away by the final moments of the video: a five-year-old crying off-camera as she tried to hold the phone still, just as she'd been told to, her mother telling her it'll all be fine, telling her to not shatter completely.

Baby. Baby, it's all right. Mama's here.

When on Facebook she saw the call to gather in the center of Newark to protest the genocide of African Americans by the police, how could she not go? Back in college, she would have joined the struggle without a second thought, but she was a different person now. She'd grown addicted to comfort and quiet, while around her the world had deteriorated and the ruling class had consolidated its enormous power. She and her peers had slept for too long; it was time to do more than simply recognize a problem.

On Friday afternoon she left work early and took the Montclair Line to Newark's Broad Street station, then hailed an Uber to take her to police headquarters, but the driver had to let her out a block away because the protesters had spilled into the road all around the building. She paid with her phone and got out and approached a crowd that seemed to have no end. Young and old, black and white, a kaleidoscope of ornate religions. Children on the shoulders of chanting fathers and grandfathers, teenagers waving signs and fists, watched over by police in riot gear, faces hidden by Plexiglas helmets. At first, she was overcome by weakness and a sharp terror—*What are you doing, Ingrid?*—wanting to turn around and hurry back to Tribeca and watch all of it through the safety of her television. But she'd made a decision, and so she moved beyond the police and into the crowd, through the sparse periphery—deeper, to where the night grew humid from the press of bodies and warm words. It was so loud, the shouts—*Black lives matter! Hey hey, ho ho—these racist cops have got to go! Off the sidewalks, into the streets! Why are you in riot gear; we don't see no riot here!*

And then it came out of her, too. She couldn't help it. Her mouth opened of its own accord and shouted: *The people united will never be defeated!*

On another day, in another place, sipping from a glass of rioja with her smart friends, she'd have laughed at clever jokes about these kinds of slogans. But now . . . now she stood with them. She spoke with them. Her voice had a thousand mouths. Her fist was in the air, punching the evening sky. Not just her fist but hundreds of them, punching holes in the clouds. If this went on, she thought with a hint of giddiness, the sky was going to crack and fall.

Speakers climbed on crates and shouted through bullhorns. A well-dressed local alderman, scores of fevered citizens, and a zealous preacher who asked, "What do we want?"

"Justice!" she called back.

"When do we want it?"

"Now!"

"Praise the Lord."

She'd grown. She had a thousand hands and feet; she was as big as a city block. Her voice could be heard for miles.

She was so entranced by the expanse of her body, the sheer power of all her limbs, that the brief shout, and then the scream, didn't register. When a fat woman to her left looked over, past her, and said, "Oh, *damn,*" Ingrid looked, too. There was a fight breaking out. She jumped to see better, and at the apex of her leap she saw the shining Plexiglas helmets and the white smoke of tear gas. Everyone saw it now. The shouts erupted, mouths no longer in sync. Voices dislodged from the great beast, each voice betraying only panic. Someone shouted, "Hold your ground!" A few people did, pulling up shirts to cover their noses and mouths, but T-shirts and blouses aren't made to repel tear gas. A gunshot—she didn't know from where—and the panic took over. *Run.*

It was a mess now, her massive body breaking apart into smaller pieces that stumbled and shouted and fled. The cops mingled with the crowd, sticks high, grabbing shirts, pulling and dragging to waiting vans. The young fought back, throwing rocks and swinging backpacks, but were soon overwhelmed. Truncheons rose and fell. She saw an old man trampled. The flash of a Plexiglas shield. Another gunshot. A dazed boy with blood on his head. Sirens. Ingrid's body was scattering, tumbling down side streets into the city.

Then she, too, was gone. Alone again in the streets of Newark. She didn't know where she was anymore.

17

"YOU REMEMBER when I got home?" Ingrid asked David nine months later, and he didn't reply; his embarrassed expression was enough. To Rachel, she said, "He saw blood on me, and when he found out where it was from he lost his shit. It was all about Clare. I was out there risking our baby for some people I didn't even know."

"I didn't use those words."

"Don't lie, okay?" She turned to Rachel. "I'm telling you all this because by the time I got to Bill and Gina's party, I was ready for a change."

Rachel looked over to Kevin, but he was standing by the window again, eyes closed, listening to a story he'd probably heard many times already. She said, "You don't need to make excuses."

"No," Ingrid snapped, shaking her head. "These aren't excuses. They're explanations. Don't think at any point that I'm apologizing for my decisions. I might be stuck in this house worried about my baby's safety, but this isn't the result of bad decisions. It's the result of the hypocrisy that feeds this selfish country."

Rachel leaned back, feeling an instant revulsion but trying to hide it. Hypocrisy was just another word for reality, but not to someone like Ingrid. She lived in a world of absolutes that, history taught, led to blood in the streets.

"Seventeen people were injured at that demonstration. A couple of days later, an old man died from injuries there. Why? Because the police were paid to get rid of what the ruling class fears most: angry people who are ready to smash banks and businesses in the face of injustice."

"Enough, Ingrid," Kevin said, sounding annoyed.

She looked at him. "What?"

"There's no soapbox here. The only thing that's going to help is if you tell her what happened."

Ingrid locked eyes with him, and Rachel felt there was a lot unsaid going on between them. But of course there would be—Kevin had saved her from arrest and, more likely, death in Watertown, and she had repaid him by turning him in, guessing that Ben Mittag would kill him before the Bureau's team arrived. Yet here Kevin was, protecting her from everyone, even Rachel. She'd seen no sign of affection between them; this wasn't a love affair. So why was he risking himself for the sake of an ungrateful revolutionary? She was beginning to finally understand Fordham's critiques of Kevin.

"Fair enough," Ingrid eventually said, then turned to Rachel. "Look, I get carried away. And I'm not saying anything original; I know that. I just want you to understand me. And you should know that when I met Martin at the party here, I knew him—I knew his type. My father was a Communist, and that was both good and bad."

She paused, looking down at Clare, who was dozing, little bubbles forming on her pursed lips. Rachel remembered the details David had shared about Ingrid's father, the ones Ingrid was choosing to keep locked away: the abuse, going after him with a shovel, him drinking himself to death beside the Kearsley Reservoir. As Kevin had told her, anyone who tells you there's one reason for what they do is a liar.

Ingrid said, "I fell in with the radicals at U Mich. This was pre-Twitter, but we spray-painted Twitter-length manifestos all over the buildings. I got into the language of the left, and soon I was an expert on the Red Army Faction and Weather Underground, Black Panthers, Action Directe—all those guys. So when I met Martin, I was back on familiar ground. And after the police attacked our protest in Newark, I needed to get involved again."

"Did you start the conversation?" Rachel asked.

She shook her head. "I'd wandered around the party, looking for someone, anyone, who wanted to talk about Jerome Brown. No one did. Like the subject embarrassed them. Then this guy sits next to me on the sofa and says, 'So what do you think about what went down in Newark?' He had me from his opening line."

18

HE LOOKED different from his photo in *Rolling Stone,* and as he talked Ingrid was surprised, in a way, by his ignorance. "All I know is there's something wrong," he said. After days of well-spoken and well-educated pundits filling the airwaves, the famous Martin Bishop, radical provocateur, was underwhelming.

She said, "I thought you and your people had contingencies for all this. Didn't you say in some article that you supported rioting as a way of fighting back?"

He rocked his head, noncommittal. "What I support is an honest expression of emotion. I support voices being heard."

"And smashing store windows?"

"Depends."

"On?"

"On how pure the emotion is."

She laughed. "Do you even know what you're saying?"

He smiled. "Want me to grab you a drink?"

Ingrid hesitated, for some reason not wanting to admit that she was pregnant, and only said, "Get me a water, will you?"

By the time he'd returned with a beer and a glass of tap, she'd recalled more of the *Rolling Stone* piece, and as they spoke of Newark she reassessed him. It wasn't ignorance. He was just open to being wrong, a trait she hadn't seen in a very long time. Which wasn't to say he didn't believe in anything—his beliefs were hardwired—but his beliefs were built on a foundation of self-criticism that was unfamiliar to most everyone she knew.

Ingrid shared far more than she thought she would, simply because Martin asked. She began with her employer, the Starling Trust. Founded in 1972 by the hippie child of a hotel magnate, its mission was to spread freedom of thought to the darkest corners of the world and bring about a new age of wisdom. But over the decades, Ingrid confessed, it had gone from idealism to pragmatism, and by the time she came on board in the early aughts, the foundation had fallen prey to the conviction that only under a stable government could free thought flourish. Which meant that they, and Ingrid, spent as much time helping regimes stay in power as they did engaged in their original mission.

"Time rots," Bishop told her, but his tone was sympathetic, not cynical. "The most beautiful things are like a proper punk band—a blast of energy that quickly self-destructs."

A couple of hipsters squatted around them and started a discussion about the dysfunction of democracy in America. Eventually Gina arrived and joined in, then David, and Ingrid watched how Martin dealt with resistance, drawing back into the realm of what was provable. "Unlike all your friends, David, I don't presume to know. I'm not smart enough. Few people are that smart, least of all—and no insult meant—your smart friends." Ingrid kept thinking about how David had reacted to Jerome Brown's murder: *Hey, the guy was reaching for a gun, right?* Now he was acting as if he had put a lot of thought into social justice. It was excruciating to watch.

After David left, Martin confided that before finding himself in the service of political justice he had barely been living. "I clocked in and clocked out every day. I drank myself to sleep. All my friendships were surface. The problem was that it was always about me. I, I, I.

They say I'm converting people. Not true. I'm the convert. Everyone out there—the miserable and wretched and oppressed—they converted me." He smiled, gentle. "Know what I mean?"

"Yeah." She told him about her college obsession—the West German Red Army Faction, or Baader-Meinhof Gang. To prove her knowledge, she rattled off the names of its major members, its acts of arson, robbery, kidnapping, and murder, and then quoted at length from its manifesto, "The Urban Guerrilla Concept."

"Wow," he said, impressed. "I never would have guessed."

"Of course you wouldn't have," she said. "Why would you?"

He shook his head, as if he were going to dispute this, but instead he came out with his own quote from "The Urban Guerrilla Concept," which was in fact a quote Baader-Meinhof had borrowed from Eldridge Cleaver, minister of information for the Black Panther Party. He said, "'Either you're part of the problem or you're part of the solution. There is nothing in between. This shit has been examined and analyzed for decades and generations from every angle. My opinion is that most of what happens in this country does not need to be analyzed any further.'"

They shared a warm moment of mutual recognition, and he talked about the Plains Capital–IfW scandal, and how he wanted to be optimistic but knew from history that the investigation would lead to nothing. "They'll find a way to shut it down. They always do."

Then Ingrid remembered something from the *Rolling Stone* article. "We were in Berlin at the same time."

A look crossed his face, his smile quickly disintegrating, and he said, "What?"

"I lived there for ten years. Prenzlauer Berg. I miss it. Where were you?"

"Friedrichshain," he said, almost reluctantly. "Left in '09."

"Oh-nine . . ." It was coming back to her. "That group— Kommando Rosa Luxemburg. Did you know they were going to bomb the train station?"

Martin opened his mouth, then closed it. As if he couldn't find any air. Then: "The Kommando wasn't going to bomb anything. They weren't violent."

"I read in the—"

"The newspapers were wrong," he said with finality, and she felt stupid, as if by having bought the line of the mainstream media she had lost all the credibility she'd spent their conversation building up. But he showed no sign of contempt, only smiled and shook his head. "They always get it wrong. This is the world we live in. Listen," he said, reaching into his pocket. He took out a notepad and a short pencil, the kind that littered IKEA stores, and wrote down four numbers separated by periods—an IP address. He handed it to her. "If you ever want to talk more. Here's a way to do it without anyone listening."

Then they walked out to the patio, and David marched up through the grass and said, "Hey, *you!*"

19

THE NEXT day, when Ingrid thought back to the hours that followed Bill and Gina's party, she would be surprised to find that they were mostly a blur. Which was troubling, because once she'd followed through on her radical solutions to her marital troubles she would need to justify herself. She would need to say, *When David did* this *I knew it had gone too far.* If not to her friends, then, one day, to her unborn child. And whatever "this" was had to be so horrendous and unbelievable that her reaction, no matter how extreme, could be justified. But her memory would work against her in this project, as if it didn't give a damn about right and wrong.

The things that came to her, in fact, had little to do with David. She remembered the silence of the drive home, and the continued silence in the apartment, her shower, then waking in the middle of the night to find David asleep on the couch while the television played desolation: A factory had leached mercury into a midwestern town's water supply. A baby in a hospital bed, fighting for its life. A weeping, overweight mother. She turned it off and lay in bed, thinking of babies and the diets of the poor and the great, rich expanse of the United States that lay between its coasts.

It wasn't until her alarm woke her in the morning that she heard from NPR that Martin Bishop and his associate Benjamin Mittag were being sought for questioning in connection to a missile launcher discovered in a New Jersey storage space. "Authorities are asking for the public's help tracking down the pair."

David was still passed out in front of the television, and when she looked at him she thought less of the embarrassment he'd caused yesterday than she did about the past months, the past year, and the past decade of their lives together. She wasn't thinking of social justice or proletarian revolution but about a marriage that had been based on a premise that, she now realized, had been proven false. The premise was that she and David saw the world similarly, that they both held the same basic values. That was why they could do something as dangerous as raise a child together. She'd known this was wrong, probably from the beginning, but out of comfort or laziness or some other sin she'd chosen to ignore it. David looked inward, while she looked outward. All the meaning in David's life was built on a craftman's pride in the books he wrote, whereas Ingrid found meaning primarily in her effect on others.

Did this mean that David was self-centered, and she was a paragon of philanthropy? No. It only meant that they had and would forever engage the world in different ways, and therein lay the source of their conflicts. They were simply not made for each other.

So with the clarity that followed her coffee she wrote a note telling him that she would spend the night with her friend Brenda up north in Pelham. She wasn't sure Brenda would be open to her staying there, but she would make do. She wasn't leaving David, not yet at least, but without a few days' separation she would never be able to think through the enormity of what she'd just discovered.

On the way to the subway she called Brenda, who seemed happy to have a visitor, even if it was because of a collapsing marriage.

Then she was at her desk on the twenty-fourth floor of the Starling Trust headquarters in Midtown, reading the most recent report from their local office in Abuja, Nigeria. Boko Haram fighters had descended on an all-girls' school in the northeastern district of Borno, slaughtered the administration, and kidnapped 120 children. The girls were gone, and the local police held out little hope of finding them. This was the second time Boko Haram had stolen Nigeria's daughters. Across the region families were weeping, and that sadness was beginning to morph into anger at a government that had been unable to perform its most basic role: protecting the lives of its citizens. The Starling report spent six full pages speculating on the potential for destabilization in that corner of the country, based on political trends, and the ramifications in the capital. Nigeria was one of Africa's success stories, and the report lamented how the weakening of the government would lead to pressure from neighboring countries, which would lead to further destabilization.

But Ingrid wasn't thinking about the repercussions. She wasn't thinking of stability. She only thought about 120 girls in chains, their crisp white uniforms filthy, full of terror. One moment learning how to diagram sentences in a clean classroom, the next dragged across the desert by men who would, sooner rather than later, rape them, and either sell them on to traffickers to fund their war, or execute them on camera, to be uploaded for the world to see. There would be two or three weeks of international outrage before the public eye moved on to other atrocities, and the girls would be left to their dismal fate. Yet all the Starling Trust worried about was whether or not this act of terror would undermine the ruling party. Ingrid didn't give a shit about the ruling party.

This is the world we live in.

She'd already walked out on her husband. The first step was done, and it had been so easy. Much simpler than she'd ever imagined, because the buildup is always worse than the act. So she took out the slip of paper Martin Bishop had given her and typed in the IP address. A blank page with a single link to download and install a Tor client. She did so, and the program told her what to do, what settings to change. Then a single cursor blinked in a small black window, waiting for her to speak. She typed, *This is Ingrid Parker. We met at the party yesterday.*

Return.

Wait.

She looked around at her colleagues with their coffee mugs and TV-show conversations. From the kitchenette, a burst of laughter. A hundred and twenty girls gone, and the small talk rolled on. Her cell phone rang. She almost didn't answer it, but she didn't want to feel like she was hiding.

"Hi, David."

"Well?" he said.

"I'm at work. And I asked you not to call."

"How am I supposed to not call?"

"I'll call you tonight, okay?"

"Look. I'm hammering out a new book. It'll . . . I'll be easier to live with."

Did he really think that a book could cure a marriage? "And then you'll finish that book and go back to how you are right now."

"We can fix this. You know that, right?"

"I just have to clear my head. Sometimes we all need to clear our heads."

When she hung up, her computer said, *Hi Ingrid. It's Martin. I'm really glad to hear from you.*

Her hands were cold as she typed, *Where are you?*

You know I can't tell you that.

Of course he couldn't. He was a wanted man. She wasn't sure what to write back, but he knew:

Would you like to visit us?

So easy.

20

THEY REACHED Chicago under cover of darkness, and she soon lost track of their direction along the ribbons of asphalt. What was the shape of the city? A ring road? A cross of highway like a sniper's view of the world? She had no idea, and asking Mary—the tired Vietnamese med student who had picked her up outside the Pelham train station, and with whom she'd shared a room in a motor lodge outside Youngstown, Ohio—seemed pointless, so she just waited. She decided to trust. It was a decision she'd made time and again since yesterday morning.

During those first hours, as they had gradually escaped the congestion of Westchester County and crossed through New Jersey headed west, Mary had been chatty. She was an intern at Montefiore in the Bronx, a person used to the sight of damaged humanity. "And blood," Mary told her. "Not at first—when I first observed an operation I seriously considered changing my major to gender studies." But her parents had forced her to stay on track, and by now she was over being resentful—she was proud of what she did.

"So why this?" Ingrid asked.

"I'm proud of what I do, not proud of how this country and the drug companies run my profession. And without good doctors, the Revolution will burn out before it's gotten started."

"Revolution?"

"Well, right now we're just trying not to get arrested."

"I see."

"What about you?"

"Me?"

"Why this?" Mary asked.

Ingrid mulled over that, because though later she would be able to describe the cause and effect that had led her to this car, so soon after her escape the only answer she had was "Because this is the only thing that makes sense to me."

"Foreclosure Lane," Mary said now as they cruised down an unlit, pockmarked Chicago street lined with dilapidated, abandoned row houses half obscured by overgrown postage-stamp yards. The toddler-high grass and boards over the doors brought to mind postapocalyptic movies, Nature coming back to consume the works of Man. And it was hot, the city heat settling into her even with the windows down. Mary pulled up to one of the rougher-looking houses and killed the engine. Unlike the others, this door was unblocked, and there was dim light coming from deep inside, glinting off the jagged edges of a broken window.

"You can go in," Mary said.

"You're not coming?"

"Each of us has a role," Mary told her. "Right now mine is to go from point A—here—to point B."

"Where is point B?"

"Your role is to enter that house. What you do from there? It's not up to Martin. Not up to me. Not up to anyone, just you. Remember that."

Ingrid exhaled, only now in the silence hearing that music was coming from the house—short stabs of punk rock, a female voice shouting accusations.

Mary started the engine, and Ingrid got out. She wanted to say something else, to thank Mary for the ride, maybe, anything to keep their connection alive a little longer—but the car was already pulling away, heading to another stop where another naïve American would be waiting to vanish from his or her life.

Then she was alone.

She took a moment to breathe in the faint smell of exhaust and burned tires, then walked through the chain-link gate, through the high weeds, and up a few spongy steps to an aluminum screen door. She didn't know if she should knock or just enter. Then she spotted a rusty doorbell. She pressed it and heard, through the faint thrashing of guitars and wild horns, a happy three-tone melody. After ten agonizing seconds, the door jerked open, and she was faced with a shirtless, finely muscled black man, shiny with sweat, eyes bloodshot.

"You Ingrid?" he asked, though it sounded like an accusation.

She nodded.

He looked out past her to the dark, empty street, then pushed open the squeaky screen door. "C'mon, then."

She, too, glanced at the street, hesitant, before stepping inside. The light and music came from a back room. These two front rooms were barren, the old wallpaper scratched and marred by patches of water damage.

"I'm Reggie, by the way." He was smiling and sticking out his hand, so she took it. His handshake was strong and quick. He led her to the back room, where, illuminated by a single floor lamp beside the kind of old boom box she hadn't seen since the nineties, Martin Bishop set aside a laptop and rose from a foldout chair, smiling at her.

"Oh, Christ," she said without thinking. "It's good to see you."

She was surprised but relieved by the way he embraced her. After her long journey the hug felt right. "You made it," he said into her ear. Then they separated, and he offered her a chair. Was she hungry? They had pizza in the kitchen. He asked about her journey, and she praised Mary in the way you praise an employee to her boss.

"And . . . David?"

"Let's not talk about him."

She couldn't tell if Martin approved or not. Then she caught herself—why would it matter either way? *Not up to anyone, just you,* as Mary had said.

"And you're sure about this?" he asked. When she gave him a look, he raised his hands. "It's just that you're going to be living rough. At this point, all you've done is take a break from your life, and you can step right back into it. Once you stay, you've made a commitment. That's how the Feds will see it. You stay, and you're on their lists."

"How about you tell me what the plan is?"

He bit his lip, hesitant.

"If you don't think you can trust me, then okay. Then I'm leaving. Because by showing up, I'm trusting you, and I'm too old to go into an unrequited relationship."

He smiled and rubbed his face. "There is no plan, not really. We had to get all our people out of harm's way. It's not like we wanted to disappear."

She was surprised. "I thought that was part of the master plan."

His smile grew, and he shook his head. "It's what *Ben* wanted. He's been pushing for us to move underground for months. He set up the whole communication structure, the safe houses, the triggers. But using that—actually performing our vanishing act—that was a defensive move. But Ben's happy. He's been vindicated."

It was something to wrap her head around, and with this knowledge her own escape lost some of its luster. It wasn't a sprint *to* something but a panicked flight. She said, "How many are there?"

"A few hundred."

"Hundreds?" she asked. "Just vanished, like me?"

He nodded. "That missile launcher they found? It's not ours. The Feds planted it in order to arrest me and Ben. We were lucky—a friend called to warn me. First arrest us, then everyone. I don't know if you've noticed, but this country's been turning into a police state for years."

"That's it?" she asked. "You get hundreds of people to drop out of their lives, but you're not going to use them for anything?"

"We've got some ideas."

"Such as blowing up buildings?"

"There are more poetic ways of making a point."

What could he be thinking of? "Mass strikes?"

"Sure. Or maybe it's as simple as disappearing and then, all at once, reappearing."

She thought about that. Hundreds of people vanishing for weeks or months and then, one day, showing up again. "It would depend on what they said when they returned."

"And what if they said nothing?"

"What?" she said. "That's ridiculous."

"Maybe it is, but then again maybe it's not."

Reggie, eating cold pizza in the kitchen, said, "Martin?"

"You think on it," he said, then left to join Reggie at the counter, where they huddled over a large map. Beside the map lay a revolver.

She turned to the windows that gave way to blackness, thinking of hundreds of vanished people reappearing, mute . . . and then what?

On a doorframe she saw pencil lines notated with dates that had marked the growth of a child up to about four feet. Standing there, it didn't occur to her that maybe the family had moved to another, better neighborhood; she could only imagine that the family had been evicted. Children weren't only suffering in Nigeria, she thought. They were suffering all over.

21

"**DIDN'T THAT** strike you as weird?" Rachel asked.

"What?"

"That Martin didn't have a plan. He'd gathered four hundred people and squirreled them away around the country. Yet he didn't know what to do with them."

"Yeah," Ingrid said, lightly stroking Clare's head. "But their first responsibility was to save everyone. For months they'd heard the rhetoric on television. All those accusations. They were being labeled terrorists. It was just a matter of time before you guys started rounding them up."

Rachel shook her head. "Sure, the media was blowing up, but the Bureau wasn't. We weren't going to move against the Massive Brigade until we believed they were going to do something. Once we found the missile launcher we knew we had to move."

"It wasn't their missile launcher."

"Well, Ingrid, it was somebody's. And, no—we didn't plant it. Do you know who called to tell us to look in that storage space? Her name was Holly Rasmussen, and she was a friend of Mittag's."

Kevin shifted, and Ingrid glared at Rachel. "Okay," she said, but her face became more reflective, as if the Holly Rasmussen news meant something.

Rachel went on. "So don't tell me there was no plan in the works. The missile launcher was part of the plan, and even if not everybody was on board, July 4 was, too." She turned to Kevin. "Is this really the story you wanted me to hear?"

Kevin shrugged. "Maybe you want to let her finish."

Rachel's leg was acting up again, and immobility wasn't helping. So she limped over to a wall and stretched the leg out. The pain rose and then subsided. She nodded at Ingrid. "Okay, then. Go on. What more did Martin Bishop tell you?"

Ingrid seemed amused by Rachel's irritation. She said, "Nothing, yet. He had to go somewhere, and Reggie drove me west, to Montana. It took two days, but we didn't stop. Drove in shifts."

"You just handed yourself over to this stranger."

"That's what trust is, Special Agent."

Rachel didn't reply.

"Lolo, Montana, a stone's throw from the Idaho border. A log cabin in the mountains. Sixteen people, young people, and they went by the names George and Mary. Most of them were scared, you could tell. They didn't know what to do next, so they stuck to a schedule. Chores, firing practice, group talk sessions. Most of them *were* peaceful, though there were some exceptions. George from Albuquerque, an economics grad student. Albuquerque George wanted to ride into Lolo and take over the town by force, establish a beachhead. 'One city at a time,' he liked to say."

"And how did the others react to that idea?" Rachel asked.

"They didn't. All ideas were on the table. Though I did point out to him that Martin wouldn't be on board, and Reggie agreed. He and I were the only ones who had spoken with Martin. To the others, he was a face on a screen or words on a web page."

"He was an idea," David said, his first words in a while.

"Yeah," she said, looking back at him. "He was an idea."

22

DESPITE ALBUQUERQUE George's obvious disapproval, Ingrid left her Smith & Wesson in the truck. "It should never leave your side," he said.

"This doctor's an ally, right?"

"Yes, but who knows about the people around her?"

"There's a time and place for everything," she told him as she got out. "One day you'll be old enough to understand that."

During the hour's drive from the safe house to the little clinic in the middle of nowhere, he'd played country music and, instead of asking why she needed to see a doctor, lectured her on the difference between Keynesian economics and the Stockholm School, and how both were doomed to fail. "Once we've dealt the big blow to the system, someone's going to have to come up with something else."

"The big blow?" she asked.

"When we crush it."

Ingrid wondered how George thought their little band of outcasts would bring down a two-hundred-year-old system that had been bought into by 320 million Americans. That was a future discussion. As Waylon Jennings sang about some good ol' boys never meanin' no harm, they parked in front of a little block of building with a weathered sign that said WOMEN'S CLINIC. When she opened the door he said, "Don't forget your gun."

The sight of Dr. Hernandez—a bald woman with huge brown eyes and a lab coat, tattoos emerging from under her sleeves, no older than thirty—filled her with anxiety. The ultrasound was already set up in the back room. "You're nervous," said Dr. Hernandez. "Don't be. Women have been doing this a very long time." Then she showed off the most beautiful smile Ingrid had ever seen.

She'd spent four days with strangers like George whose time was filled with intellectual adrenaline, self-righteous anger, and little splatters of utopian hope, everything seasoned with the fear of capture. The safe house was rich with emotion, but only the strident emotions of radical debate and sudden paranoia. It was refreshing to simply fall in love with a smiling face.

"See that?" Dr. Hernandez asked, and Ingrid looked at the fuzzy screen. Nothing but static. The doctor adjusted the probe, pushing it through a puddle of clear gel on Ingrid's belly. "There," she said, now touching the monitor, and Ingrid really could see it, just barely. Oblong head, curved back, fragile extremities . . .

"Oh," she said.

"Would you like to know the sex?"

Ingrid nodded.

"You're sure?"

"Why wouldn't I?"

The doctor hesitated. "Well, your life is different now, isn't it?"

"You could say that."

"You'll be moving around a lot. I don't know what you'll be doing each time you reach a place—I don't *want* to know—but I'm guessing it could be strenuous." Dr. Hernandez was a sympathizer, but not even sympathizers wanted to know the secrets and methodologies.

"What's your point?"

Dr. Hernandez settled her hands in her lap. "Do you want to keep the baby? If you don't, I won't tell you anything else, and I'll take care of it right here, right now. It's your choice."

An hour later, clutching a paper bag with a printout of the inside of her belly and a big bottle of pills, Ingrid climbed down from the pickup truck and thanked George for the ride. In reply, he opened the glove compartment and handed over her pistol.

As he drove around the back to where they kept the cars under a shelter of leafy trees and green tarp, she approached the ruggedly beautiful cabin that overlooked Lolo Creek Road. In the distance, higher up in the mountains, she could hear her housemates shooting at their targets, playing army. She'd been up there herself, learning to use the Smith & Wesson M&P 9mm that she'd been presented on Day 2 by Mary—real name Yelena—the unofficial house mother.

Reggie had moved on to other parts of America, and she hadn't seen Martin since Chicago and the boom box that had been playing, she learned, a band called the Downtown Boys. Though her new companions were welcoming, Lolo Creek didn't feel like a destination. It felt like a pit stop on the way to somewhere—both metaphorically and literally. They shot guns and made vague and sometimes outrageous plans to export the Revolution outside their cabin. It reminded her of the conversations at Bill and Gina's parties. But the devil was in the difference. At Lolo Creek, they were all fugitives, and because of that their conversations, no matter how outlandish, had the ring of possibility.

She was in the kitchen boiling a pot of twenty eggs when Albuquerque George returned. "You never told me how it went with the doctor."

"Well," she said.

"What are those drugs she gave you?"

"Prenatal vitamins."

"Oh," he said, then blinked. "Oh, *shit*."

He was the first person she'd told, and the flash of worry in his face reminded her of Dr. Hernandez's concern. She was bringing a baby into a world where fugitives shot at trees, and eventually their talk of revolt might actually turn into action. George's face said what the doctor had been too polite to ask: *Are you fucking crazy?*

Maybe, yes.

23

SHE'D LIVED at the house for six days when Martin came on June 27. The others fell over themselves trying to get an audience with him, but Ingrid could see that what they really wanted was reassurance. They wanted to know what they were supposed to be doing. Martin was trying out his disappearance-and-reappearance idea, and he asked what they thought would happen if all of them returned to their homes on the same day and said nothing.

"Say *nothing*?" Albuquerque George demanded. "Then what do you think's gonna happen? Nothing! This is *bullshit*."

Martin didn't defend his idea, just looked around for more reactions. Mary from South Carolina shook her head. "Well, first of all, it would be a media sensation. Every local station would carry it, and the national media. Then they'd ask us questions: Where were you? More importantly: What are you planning?"

"But no one says a thing," Ingrid said.

Mary nodded. "What will they think? They'll think we *are* planning something."

George shook his head. "And you know what they'll do? They'll arrest us all. Which is why we disappeared in the first place!"

"Will they?" Mary asked.

"They can't," Ingrid said. "None of us have broken the law." She turned to Martin, who was watching them hash it out. "They'll be terrified."

Mary nodded. "And there'll be nothing they can do but live with their fear."

Ingrid was finally able to see it, that by returning and saying nothing they would be able to create a kind of terror that the elite had never felt before. Because unlike demonstrations that filled the streets of American cities, this threat would be invisible, something that could not be monitored, because it remained locked away in these young people's heads. And the media would be Massive's ally, whipping up a fury of breaking news excitement that would set the country on edge.

So simple.

Martin turned to Albuquerque George, who was still frowning. "What do you think?"

He scratched at his eye, shaking his head. "It's just not how I imagined it."

Mary grinned. "You imagined soldiers shooting cops in Lolo. That's a lack of imagination."

"No it's not," Martin said. "It's an expression of frustration. That's all any of this is, an expression of anger. But we've always known that the only way for the ruling class to serve us is for them to fear us. I'm just trying to find a way to accomplish that without getting anyone killed."

"So is that the plan?" George asked. "Is it settled?"

"This isn't an autocracy," Martin said. "I'm going around and collecting opinions. And even if we do it, we want to wait long enough for everyone's absence to be noted. It's not in the news yet."

"They'll arrest *you*," said another Mary, from Toledo. "There's a warrant out for you."

Martin shrugged. "I can spend some time behind bars. I'll be in good company. But even if they can't arrest you, you should know that there will be resistance. You'll be harassed; some will be beaten. Maybe killed. In some ways, this would be harder than heading into town with machine guns."

"But then what happens?" George asked. "We're there, we're silent. Eventually the news will find other shiny things to look at."

"That," Martin said, "is another reason I'm bringing this to everyone. What do you think?"

They spent the rest of the evening discussing possible next actions, and the ideas ranged from violence to hackers leaking state secrets to another mass disappearance, but larger this time. By the time they'd finished dinner, Ingrid had tired of the conversation and went out to the porch, where she tried to identify constellations in the clear night sky. The Big Dipper, curiously enough, eluded her. Eventually, the door opened, and Martin came out with a beer in his hand. He sat down beside her and said, "How many months?"

By then, everyone in the house knew that she was pregnant, and now Martin did as well. "Four and a half. If I wasn't wearing this sweatshirt, you'd be able to tell."

"Taking care of yourself?"

"Yep."

He sipped at his beer. "You don't have to stay with us, you know. No one knows what's around the corner. We make our plans, but all it takes is one gun-happy Fed to ruin your day."

"Stop worrying about me, okay?"

He grinned. "Listen, tomorrow morning I'm heading out. For the next few weeks I'll be visiting safe houses, and we'll have this same conversation. Would you like to come?"

"Me?"

"A grand tour of the Resistance."

She looked up and found the Big Dipper immediately. It had been there all along. "Why me? You think you can protect the pregnant lady only if you're next to her?"

He rocked his head. "I've got thousands of miles ahead of me, and the most important thing I need is good conversation."

She thought a moment, then nodded. "But first I need to mail something to my husband."

24

"OVER THE next five days, we visited six houses," Ingrid said.

"How many safe houses were there in total?" Rachel asked.

She shook her head. "In total? I don't know. But he was going off of a list he kept in his wallet. Must've been twenty or more there. In each house, it was the same thing, these young people wanting reassurance from him. Wanting a plan. Over time, the basic idea gathered details. For example, a Mary in West Virginia suggested that after we returned, we release a steady drip of leaks, suggesting a date—maybe New Year's—when something would happen. So rather than media attention fizzling out, it would build steadily toward that date. It would require an actual event, and no one could agree on what that was. But the leaks became part of the plan. And it was up to each person to find ways to connect to each other once they returned home. And bring in newcomers. So that by the prearranged date we could send out a message—just a single word—to trigger thousands to act at once."

"A single word?"

Ingrid opened her hands. "Something known but not commonly used. Martin suggested 'inscrutable.' I pushed for 'circumnavigation.' It didn't matter what the word was, as long as everyone knew it."

"Tell her about Berlin," said Kevin.

Rachel raised her head, curious.

"Yeah, right," Ingrid said. "He told me about the Kommando Rosa Luxemburg. They had been his friends, those people who were killed in the explosion. He was still upset when he spoke about them. One of them, a woman named Anika, was his lover."

Rachel blinked. "I didn't know that."

"Well, she died. And after the explosion he left, went south to Spain."

"Did he tell you what he did in Spain?"

She shook her head. "Not really. But he did say he met someone important there. Without this person—a man—he never would have been able to do what he'd done."

"Financially?" Rachel asked, then saw the question in Kevin's face. "We followed his money back to the shell company I asked you about: Magellan Holdings. But we weren't able to ID the owners."

Kevin took this in, interested, and Ingrid said, "He never told me why this guy was important. Maybe it was inspiration. Or, yes, maybe money. But he said he was international, that he knew an un-believable number of languages. Martin spent a week with this guy in Spain, and they drank vodka martinis and discussed the future of Western society."

"Vodka martinis?" Rachel asked, remembering her Russian who was not a Russian, James Sullivan who was not James Sullivan. The only thing she really knew about him was that he drank vodka martinis. "Anything else about him?"

She shook her head. "We didn't dwell on him. Martin didn't tell me more until everything went to hell. After July 4."

"The day of the assassinations."

"We were at a house in Indiana—near Lexington—when the news came on the radio. At first, and like everybody else, we thought it was al Qaeda, or ISIS."

"Everyone except Martin," Rachel said.

"Everyone *including* Martin. You don't get it, do you? He never ordered those killings. He had nothing to do with it. We wanted to frighten the politicians, but actually kill them? All that would do was turn people against us. When that message came out on *The Propaganda Ministry* we were all stunned. But Martin—he was fucking furious. I'd never seen him like that. I was scared."

To be sure Rachel understood, Kevin said, "The assassinations were a rogue operation, run entirely by Benjamin Mittag."

"And with that one action," Ingrid said, "Ben ruined absolutely everything. Martin was laying out a plan for everyone to return home. How did that look now? Massive was officially a terrorist organization. Each one of us was now a criminal, and we'd be thrown in jail as soon as we showed our faces. Everything had been for nothing."

David got up and went to the kitchen. He looked as if he'd heard this story too many times already.

"But . . . *why*?" Rachel asked. "Why would Mittag do that?"

Ingrid turned her attention to Clare, and when she finally spoke it was directed, softly, toward her daughter. "Because he wanted war. On both ends of the political spectrum live people like him, who see bloodshed as the only way to real change. They're inspired by the French Revolution, the Russian Revolution—"

"The Red Army Faction," Rachel cut in.

"Exactly."

David returned with an uncorked bottle of red and three glasses. He placed them on the table and, as everyone watched, filled the glasses, then took one back to his seat. Rachel took one as well. With the first sip she knew she needed it.

"How did Martin get word to Benjamin to meet?" she asked.

"He had a phone," Ingrid said. "He kept it disassembled, but once a day he'd drive out somewhere, put it together, and check for messages. Once Ben's manifesto made the news, he got in the car and drove off to send a message. By the time he returned he had calmed down, and we discussed other options. It was looking like surrender was all we had. But he didn't want to make any decisions until he'd faced Ben. I told him I was coming with him. He didn't like that—

he wanted to go alone—but I wasn't going to be denied. I remembered Ben from the party. I remembered how easily he'd tossed David off the porch."

"So you were worried Mittag might do something to him."

"After what he'd done to those politicians? I was sure of it."

25

ON THE long drive, Martin filled a lot of hours complaining about Benjamin, whom he had saved from a life of petty crime and penitentiaries of increasing levels of security. "I taught him every word he used in that manifesto," Martin said, gradually leaning toward self-recrimination. "I should have seen it, back at the party. When my friend called to warn us that the cops were on their way, I told Ben that we had to split. That it was time for everyone to disappear. You know what he said? 'Already done, boss.' I took that as a figure of speech, but later I talked to people, found out when they'd gotten the word to leave. He wasn't lying—people had been leaving from early that morning."

"How did he know so early?" Ingrid asked.

Martin glared at the road ahead of them. "Because he set the whole fucking thing up. He put the missile launcher there. He called in the anonymous tip."

"Jesus."

"I'm going to kill him."

By the time they were halfway across Missouri, heading to Kansas, his murderous impulse had faded. He'd regained the composure that had attracted her and four hundred others. But they both knew the situation was dire.

He said, "I need to tell you about Berlin."

"Why?"

"Because someone other than me should know about it."

Berlin, he told her, was supposed to be an education. He was a young man who'd soaked up progressive thought in America but was increasingly drawn to European movements. "In America, we're already co-opted by capitalism. Private property, the authority of the employer, the profit motive—these are American progressives' starting points. But Europe has been through horrors, and nothing is taken for granted. Everything is up for debate."

He made contacts at rallies and left-wing watering holes, trying to learn *in the field* about the ways in which citizens could influence the path of government. At BAIZ, a Marxist bar in Berlin-Mitte, he became involved with a group of bookish Berliners who were so well versed in radical history that they named themselves after Rosa Luxemburg, the fiery revolutionary socialist who was killed by government-sponsored paramilitaries during the Spartacist Uprising after World War I, her body tossed into the Landwehr Canal. The KRL had come together as a political study group at the Free University, and after graduation they simply kept meeting, growing slowly, though they never had more than twenty-five members at a time.

What separated the KRL from other discussion groups was the fact that, a year before, a hacker had sliced his way into a government email server and released the entire trove online. The emails dominated the news for months, and three of Angela Merkel's Christian Democrats were forced to step down due to impolitic messages that had come to light. A month after that, the BfV, Germany's domestic intelligence agency, arrested a twenty-two-year-old who had been one of the KRL's founding members. "But he acted independently," Martin told Ingrid. "They could never pin it on the group as a whole, and it frustrated them. Their efforts only succeeded in giving the Kommando fifteen minutes of fame—in Germany, at least. By the time I arrived, that was all part of their history. Some of them had talked to the press, and one had gotten a book deal, but they were essentially back to what they had been—a study group focused on political theory. Though I was trying to learn German, they usually switched to English for me. It was wonderful. Back home, my friends would only get so far in a debate before stopping themselves. They self-censored. These people didn't. They let the conversation go as far as it possibly could, the assumption being that even the impossible could inspire something possible. So no one blinked an eye when we talked about mass suicides or murder, mandatory gender reassignments, or shipping city dwellers, Mao style, into the countryside to rediscover their connection to the land."

"Mandatory gender reassignments?" she asked as Missouri unfolded around them.

"That's what you do in a study group. You brainstorm and spitball, and sometimes you stumble upon wonderful ideas. Personally, I found it exhilarating. And then, a few weeks after I started going to their meetings, an American struck up a conversation with me in a bar. Eventually he admitted he was FBI. He told me that the Bureau, and the German government, were worried about the Kommando Rosa Luxemburg. I told him they were wrong. The KRL were talkers. No one needed to be scared of them. Maybe one of them had hacked some government servers, but that had been more embarrassing than threatening. They weren't terrorists. Our most pressing real-world concern, I told him, was that the television in the apartment we used for meetings had died."

The story Martin told Ingrid, which Ingrid related eight months later, matched the version Owen Jakes had told to Rachel. Up to a point. Where Jakes had skipped from Martin "keeping me in the loop" to "they blew themselves up," Martin filled in that space.

"He and I met twice a week—not at the bar, though. We used a safe house in the center, a crummy little apartment where he would mix instant coffee and I'd give him a rundown of the latest conversations. I did this—I *cooperated*—in order to prove to him that the KRL wasn't a threat to anyone. To show him that, if anything, they were guilty of wasting time they could have spent helping out in community centers—that, by then, was a critique I'd started to bring up. But he told me that the Germans were picking up information that I wasn't privy to. He told me to keep digging. When I asked what kind of information the Germans had, he said I didn't have clearance for it, but he could vouch that they were planning something serious."

As he drove, Martin checked the rearview, tracking cars and trucks. She noticed how he occasionally pulled into the right lane and slowed down, letting cars pass them, before climbing again to sixty. "Did you ever find anything?" she asked him.

He shook his head. "Nothing. Then one day, as I was getting ready to go to Friedrichshain for another meeting, I got a message from this guy. He wanted to meet me at the safe house. By then I was sick of his paranoia, and I was sick of trying to convince him. I was even thinking about telling everyone about him. Certainly Anika, who I'd been dating a month by then. I was in a bind, though—by telling them about the FBI, I'd be admitting my own collusion. But that didn't mean I had to make life easy for him. I told him we could meet the next day. He said it was important, that he had new information. But I'd had enough. I told him to fuck off."

"Was this the night?" she asked.

He didn't answer, just watched the road. "Anika—she had put together contributions and ordered a new television for the apartment. It had been delivered a couple of hours before I arrived, and we set it up in the living room, where we usually talked. Ulrich—it was his apartment—turned it on, but the reception was messed up. The only channel that worked was playing these cartoons—sixties, faded color, Italian. The others had grown up watching them, so we left it on with the sound off, opened some bottles of wine, and got to talking."

He paused again, looking off into the fields. "I remember the subject—nationalizing health industries. It wasn't a particularly lively discussion; sometimes we were just there to drink. Anika sat with me, and eventually she got bored and told me that we should go back to her place. I told her, 'Let's give it a half hour,' because I was hoping for something fresh to come up." He grinned, but there was no happiness in the expression. "My phone rang. I took it out and realized it was Mr. FBI. I was worried someone would hear, so I gave Anika a kiss and hurried downstairs to the street. I told him that I wasn't going to meet him, and he asked where I was. I told him, and he said, 'Outside or inside?' I said, 'Outside.' He said something I couldn't understand because music was playing loudly through some window—'All Tomorrow's Parties,' Velvet Underground. So I said, 'What?' And then, right in front of me, Ulrich's apartment exploded."

26

THE SILENCE in the living room was complete; then Clare stirred, crying a little as she woke. "She's hungry," Ingrid said, and turned her attention to the baby, shifting the little body around. She pulled out her breast and began feeding.

Kevin sighed loudly. "He never told her the name of this FBI guy."

Ingrid kissed Clare's forehead.

"It was Owen Jakes," said Rachel.

Kevin turned to her, eyes big. "You're kidding."

"He told me his version of that same story, but there was no mention of a phone call or a television." She looked at Ingrid. "That was it, wasn't it? The television."

"It's what Martin thought."

"Hold on," said Kevin, hands up. "You're telling me that Jakes planted a bomb in that apartment in order to frame some German lefties? To make them look like terrorists?"

No one bothered to answer him.

"Martin was supposed to meet Jakes the next day," Rachel said to Ingrid. "Did he go?"

"What do you think? He got the hell out of Germany. He'd met people from other groups—sister organizations in Poland, Italy, Spain. He tried Spain."

"And in Spain," Rachel said, "Martin met his new benefactor, who set up a company to funnel money to him."

"Protector."

"What?"

"He called the guy his protector," Ingrid said, then turned. "David?"

Only now did Rachel realize that David had fallen asleep in his chair. He blinked, coming to.

"Can you cook up some formula?" Ingrid asked. "My boobs are running on fumes."

He pushed himself to his feet and wandered off. Soon they heard a radio playing in the kitchen—NPR morning news. Rachel knew without being able to see outside that the sun was rising. She turned to Ingrid. "So you arrived in Lebanon, Kansas. And Martin was killed."

"Yes," she said, raising Clare to her shoulder and patting her back. "At the time, I wasn't thinking about Berlin or Spain. All I could see was Ben, the fucking idiot who had ruined everything, and how he would benefit from Martin's death. The whole movement would be his. He'd be the one giving orders. He could burn everything down as he saw fit. I was blinded by rage. It wasn't until we'd gotten to Watertown that I remembered Martin's story about this FBI guy— Jakes, I guess. He'd killed eighteen people in Berlin, and Martin knew all about it."

Rachel rubbed her sore thigh, remembering what Jakes had done in Watertown. "So you thought the FBI killed him. Specifically, Owen Jakes."

"Yes."

Kevin stood and paced, swinging his arms to shake off the anxiety. "But eight years had passed since Berlin," he said. "You think Jakes couldn't have taken him out plenty of times before then? Like, before he became a star?"

It was a valid point. "Maybe," Rachel said, "Bishop really did
have a protector." She thought of James Sullivan, watching over Martin
Bishop for eight long years, even calling to warn him to flee this
very house . . . until, in the middle of a wheat field, his protection
finally failed. She still didn't know how Jakes could have placed a
sniper in that Kansas field on such short notice. And she didn't know
who James Sullivan was, or what had happened between him and
Bishop in Spain. There was so much she didn't know. She rubbed
her forehead and asked, "What did you do then, in Watertown?"

When she began speaking, Ingrid switched to bouncing Clare
on her thigh. "I went to the bathroom to take my vitamins, and that's
when I started to feel the walls closing in. I rushed out, ran across
the field, and sat under a tree. Had myself a good cry. Look, it wasn't
just Martin. It was everything. I'd thrown away my life to join something that, in no time at all, had unraveled. I had to deal with that
alone. Then I heard this guy," she said, nodding at Kevin, "tramping
through the leaves. I stayed where I was. I heard him make that call.
Mother, he called her. 'Benjamin Mittag is here.' And then: 'Did we
do it? Did we kill Bishop?' And I knew. This guy with a cell phone
and a zip-lock bag, he was a Fed. *He* was responsible for everything.
So, yes, once he sent me off, I tried hard and remembered the phone
number from the kitchen. I found a pay phone and gave him up to
Ben. It didn't matter that I hated Ben by that point, that he'd done
more damage to the Brigade than Kevin ever had. I wanted to make
life hard on the people who had killed Martin and those eighteen
kids in Berlin."

When she looked at Kevin, that old hatred had returned to her
face, and with the baby in her arms it was an incongruous sight.
Rachel wanted to say something, to mediate between them in some
way, but that wasn't her role. She wasn't here to comfort them but to
learn as much as she could.

"Where did you go afterward?"

"East, back to Flint. I hadn't been since high school. I still had
cash from Martin's bundle, and that lasted me a couple of months

while I looked for a job. Enough to keep me in bottled water—I wasn't going to drink Michigan lead. I found a restaurant that wouldn't hassle me about Social Security numbers, and I thought I was doing a good job. I visited Planned Parenthood for checkups. No one knew where I was. And then—this was in late November, I was about ready to burst—my landlord called me at work and told me that two FBI agents had shown up looking for me." She looked at Rachel. "You've heard of Sarah Vale and Lyle Johnson?"

Almost a whisper, Rachel said, "Yes."

Ingrid nodded, as if she'd expected this answer. "I went back to Montana and found Dr. Hernandez. She took me through the rest of my term." She looked down at Clare, who was starting to fuss. "David," Ingrid called. "The formula about ready?"

"Almost!"

"So once she was born," Rachel speculated, "you went back to David?"

She shook her head. "Kevin showed up."

Both women looked at him, and he shrugged. "I knew she hadn't gone home, even after the amnesty was announced. So I asked Fordham for a peek at the debriefs. This one guy from Albuquerque talked about driving Ingrid to a clinic in Montana. I followed the clues." He looked over at Ingrid, and there was warmth in the look. "She wouldn't be safe staying with me. That's why we contacted David, and it turned out the Ferrises had left him their keys when they moved to Florida."

"We know it can't last," Ingrid said. "Bill and Gina will come back eventually. But we were waiting for something to change. We thought that once the report was released the story might come out on its own."

Kevin cleared his throat. "Then you showed up. Turned out you were the change."

Rachel didn't like the way both of them looked at her, as if by entering their lives she had brought solutions. She hadn't. She'd simply been trying to stay alive and had been sucked into a world of conspiracy theories that, true or not, were still not verifiable. What *could* be done next? What could be done to save Rachel's life, to keep Ingrid and her baby safe, and, ideally, expose the truth behind the story she'd just heard? Was that even doable? Or was it better for them all to try to relocate beyond the reach of Owen Jakes and his two smiling minions?

Christ, how had she ended up here?

She'd opened her mouth, ready to speculate on their options, when David returned from the kitchen, a towel over his forearm but no baby bottle in sight. His lips trembled from nerves, or maybe just fatigue. "The FBI just released the report on Massive."

Rachel looked at Kevin, and Kevin said, "Looks like there's change all over the place."

THE END OF ANALYSIS

THURSDAY, MARCH 22, TO
MONDAY, MARCH 26, 2018

1

AFTER LANDING at Berlin Tegel early Thursday morning and showing his passport to a nonplussed German officer, Kevin used cash to
buy a prepaid credit card and a throwaway phone with data service
from the airport gift shop. He stepped outside to smoke and set up
the phone, pulling up a Russian hosting site he'd already used to
create an email account with fake information in the account's NAME
and FROM lines. Then he typed up a friendly but brief email, signed
it with Owen Jakes's name, and sent it to the address for Fay Levinson of the embassy's FBI legal attaché office.

From there it was a matter of slowing down, shuffling in the line
leading up to the Hertz counter, then meandering through Berlin's
midmorning traffic to the center of town. He was struck, like most
first-timers in Europe, by how narrow the road was, girded by busi-
nesspeople on bicycles who rode beneath a slate-gray sky. He checked
the time—forty minutes had passed since he'd sent the spoofed email,
which was just about enough time to be sure she'd read the message.
He parked in front of a DM drugstore and dialed the number he'd
found online.

An embassy operator picked up, and he asked to be connected

to Fay Levinson's line. Who was calling? He gave his name, and after three rings he heard a lilting voice say, "Levinson."

"Hi, Fay—listen, I don't know if you got Owen's email—"

"Was just reading it. Kevin Moore?"

"That's me. Just need five minutes of your time."

"Are you in town?"

"Just landed," he said. "Are you free in, say, a half hour? Or is that pushing it?"

"I can set aside five minutes for Owen."

"Terrific."

"See you soon, then," she said, and hung up.

Christ, but that had been easy. Too easy, perhaps, and maybe before he got there she would call and wake up Jakes—it was three thirty in the morning back home—and the whole ruse would fall apart, ending with the embassy marines shackling him in some basement room.

He'd already been taken aback by his good luck at JFK, where despite the tension in his chest he'd gotten through the chaotic security without incident, and no one had cornered him at the gate before boarding. He eventually realized that, unlike Rachel, he'd signed away his right to free speech, and there was no reason to think anyone from the Hoover was tracking his movements.

The flight had given him time to think, and time to ask himself if he really knew what he was doing. The truth was that he usually acted from instinct. Back in November, when he'd searched in vain through the detainee lists for Ingrid Parker, he'd been moved by an unnamed instinct. Had he fallen for a woman he'd only known for a handful of hours, a woman who had tried to kill him?

He remembered Shonda Jardoin in New Orleans, the youngest of three Creole sisters who'd fallen deep into the heroin underworld out of desperation—five years earlier Hurricane Katrina had left the family penniless. So she, like her sisters, had done what was necessary to survive and even thrive—a character trait he knew well from his own single mother, who had worked herself sick to raise him right.

Later, in the hospital, after a rival shoved a knife into his lung, Janet Fordham told him to close down the operation, and he refused, explaining that if he didn't return Shonda would end up dead. Fordham accused him of being in love. "No," he told her between painful breaths. "Empathy, not love." Which was how he felt about Ingrid.

Fordham, though, hadn't been convinced. "Don't fool yourself, Kevin. Empathy is just another word for love."

What about Representative Diane Trumble? What had motivated him to follow through with the shooting? Months later, he would run through it all again, finding avenues of escape: sabotaging the car Holly used to drive him to the site; feigning sickness; simply missing entirely. But at the time those ideas had seemed risky, or simply hadn't occurred to him.

And now he had been presented with other choices that, eventually, had put him on a plane to Germany. Each step of the way he'd had so many options but had, more often than not, taken the least reasonable-sounding one. What was wrong with him?

He walked with crowds to reach Pariser Platz, a huge open square full of tourists taking selfies with their backs to the Brandenburg Gate. As he approached the embassy, which a German newspaper had rightly called "ugly but safe," a uniformed guard asked him his business. Kevin flashed his patented I'm-not-a-threat smile along with his passport. "I've got an appointment." The guard waved him on.

He made it through security without a problem, leaving his burner in a box, then crossed the circular lobby to reach the front desk, which was staffed by a preternaturally calm woman whose accent sounded suspiciously Canadian. He asked if she could call up to the FBI's legat office, but as she picked up the phone he heard "Mr. Moore?" and turned to see a white woman with very pink cheeks approaching in a navy blue pantsuit, hand outstretched. "Welcome to Berlin, then."

As Fay Levinson walked him to the elevators, they passed a framed Sol LeWitt and a Jasper Johns. He was impressed. "I'm imagining the most ridiculous art heist in history."

Levinson grinned. "Don't think you're the first."

Her windowless third-floor office sat opposite a long room of cubicles that overlooked the Memorial to the Murdered Jews of Europe, a field of concrete slabs behind the embassy. "You move up in administration," she said, "and they steal the natural light from you. Come on."

As he took a seat opposite her desk, she closed the door and said, "How are things back home? I heard the protests are winding down now that they can read for themselves that the Bureau isn't a monster."

"It's only been two days," he said, reaching again for that guileless smile.

She matched it. "So Owen's working on a secondary report?"

He nodded. "Focusing on Bishop's history. Berlin, 2009."

"You mean the Kommando Rosa Luxemburg."

"That's it."

Levinson sighed and rocked her head. "Well. If Owen Jakes wants me to dig back into that, then you know I'll do it."

"He'd appreciate it," Kevin lied.

"How is he?"

"Busy."

"I bet," she said, then started typing on her computer, pulling up the old files.

Kevin said, "What we're interested in is *after* the Kommando blew themselves up. What was the effect here in the embassy? Where did Martin Bishop go? What did he do?"

She leaned back and put on reading glasses, squinting at her screen. Kevin could see the reflection in her lenses. "Well, first you have to know how it was *before* the explosion. Relations with the Schröder administration had been rough sailing, but Merkel came in looking for a new way. Despite some awkward shoulder massages, she and W. made friendly, and we were all hoping for a lot of goodwill from the German intelligence agencies. What we didn't account for was the power of the bureaucracy to override the chancellor's wishes."

Kevin shifted in his seat. "I'm afraid I'm unfamiliar with this part."

"Ask Owen; he knows. He suffered through it longer than I did. The real problem was an old Cold Warrior named Erika Schwartz who had taken over foreign intelligence, the BND. She was one of the most virulently anti-American Germans I've ever had the displeasure of meeting."

"Was?"

"Oh, she died a few years ago. Drank like a fish. Certainly didn't watch her weight." Levinson shrugged. "But in 2009 she was still going strong and was busy cutting us out of the intelligence pool. We registered our disappointment, but Schwartz had by then convinced Merkel that we weren't to be trusted any more than we had to be. That bigotry also permeated domestic intelligence—the BfV—and we even lost the right to engage in joint antiterror operations on German soil. It was unbelievable. But then, the Kommando Rosa Luxemburg blew themselves up. That was the Germans' come-to-Jesus moment. We had been warning them—*Owen* had been warning them. But Erika Schwartz said otherwise. After the bomb, the BfV finally came back to us."

"So you felt the difference."

She snorted, a half-laugh. "The difference between their cooperation before and after the bomb was night and day. Everything changed for the better. Owen asked them for something, he got it. We all got what we wanted after that."

"I'll bet that was good for everyone's career."

"You could say that." Levinson pursed her lips. "More importantly, it was good for our joint security." She went back to the computer. "But nothing's ever storybook, is it? In 2013, they discovered we were listening to Merkel's phone calls, and it all shut down again. They canceled our intelligence-sharing agreement, sent the Agency's station chief home, compared the NSA to the Stasi, and told us to go fuck ourselves. As if they hadn't known all along." She shook her head, then looked at Kevin over the rim of her glasses. "Owen knows it all. I'm still not sure why you had to cross an ocean for this."

"I was already coming on other business," he said, then leaned closer. "Confidentially? Jakes is worried. In DC there's a leak culture the likes of which we've never seen. If it gets out that he's preparing a secondary report, then he'll be forced into releasing it. At this point, he doesn't know what he's going to find."

"You're telling me he doesn't trust anyone in his own office?"

"I suppose he trusts me, but if I access everything from HQ, there's no way to keep it a secret."

"Still," she said, "it's a radical move."

"Well, you know Owen."

Levinson smiled. The story wouldn't survive a call to Jakes's office, but if she hadn't called yet, she wouldn't until DC woke up. That was all that mattered. She looked at her screen again. "You wanted to know what Bishop did after the explosion."

"Yes."

"Well, I'm afraid we don't have much. This is who he went to," she said as she turned the monitor so he could see what she was looking at: a file on a thin-faced woman, blond dreads: ELLI UHRIG. Quickly, he scanned the screen, catching important details: Uhrig's last known address on Lückhoffstraße, and her phone number. He committed them to memory as Fay explained, "Uhrig wasn't a KRL member, but she was part of their circle. Lived just down the street from their meeting place. You know that Bishop was outside the apartment when it exploded, yes? Well, he went directly to her."

"Any reason other than convenience? That she was nearby?"

She blinked, as if surprised by what he'd said. "Uhrig," she said. "Anika Urhig, Bishop's lover, was her sister."

"Right," he said. "Of course."

Levinson turned the screen back to herself. "We interviewed her. So did the Germans. She was a bartender. Budding singer. She didn't know Martin that well, but she gave him some cash so he could leave town."

"And go where?"

She held up her hands, palms exposed. "I told you we didn't have much. Sorry you wasted a trip."

Kevin leaned back, hands on his knees, and sighed. "Grist for the mill."

"Want me to send the paperwork on to Owen?"

"Can you send it to my address?"

She cocked her head, squinting, finally showing signs of apprehension. "This is all sort of sudden. I'd rather shoot it to him."

"Sure, I get it."

"Everything?"

Kevin didn't want her to send anything to Owen Jakes. He wanted to leave Levinson's office and never be spoken of again, but he knew that was beyond the realm of possibility. It was too late, anyway. He knew from that brief squint that as soon as nine, or maybe seven, eastern time rolled around she would be putting in a call to Jakes. There was only one thing to say if he wanted to get out of this building in one piece. "Absolutely. He'll want everything."

2

FROM ACROSS the street, Rachel watched the lunch crowd of government employees entering and exiting Fogo de Chão, the Brazilian steakhouse only a block away from the Hoover Building. There were cameras, she knew, which was why she'd gone for a light disguise of sunglasses and a scarf she picked up during the four-hour drive from Montclair. She looked like an old woman.

She had hoped that the report released by Headquarters would shed new light on their situation, but after hours in Bill and Gina's house, all of them scouring each line, it became clear that the report was a careful construction built to support a particular narrative by choosing certain facts and ignoring lines of inquiry. There was no mention of the Brigade's funding sources, and no established reasoning for the assassinations of July 4. The death of Bishop was firmly blamed on Ben Mittag, a move to take over the Brigade, while the deaths of Mittag and his Watertown comrades were blamed on gun-happy followers who gave the Bureau SWAT team no choice but to return fire. That this was patently untrue was something only Rachel and a handful of others knew, and she suspected those others had signed away their rights to speak. Perhaps some of them, like her, had refused to sign the draconian nondisclosure agreement; perhaps they, too, were running for their lives.

It was just after one when Ashley arrived for lunch, a bounce in her step, but she wasn't alone. A young man, probably from Erin Lynch's department, walked with her, and they were holding hands. That surprised her—but what, really, did she know about Ashley? She'd never invested in a friendship with the accountant, and as a result she didn't even know where she lived; too bad, because a meeting at her apartment would have been far safer than this.

When they entered, Rachel deliberated, wondering if Ashley's lover would be the type to report her presence later. Was Lynch's department even aware that Owen Jakes was looking for her? Was anybody? Though she'd visited internet cafés and scoured the Seattle newspapers, there had been no mention of the dead man in her apartment with his anonymous clothes. Johnson and Vale, or someone who specialized in it, had cleaned the place up.

She finally crossed the road and stepped into the restaurant that smelled of post-lunch Ashley. A rough-cheeked maître d' asked if she had a reservation. She scanned the crowd and, finding no one familiar, removed her scarf and told him she was meeting a friend. With a smile she pushed on, through the assortment of tables and diners' backs, past the huge food bar, and toward the rear, where Ashley, back toward her, sat with her young man drinking bottled water.

"Ash?" she said, and the man looked up first, big eyes and crew cut. Ashley turned, looking up, and gaped.

"Rachel? What are you *doing* here?" Then, to her date: "Tom, this is—"

"Rachel Proulx," he said, sticking out a hand and half rising. "I recognized you from your photo."

"Photo?"

"In the paper. Some write-up this morning in the *Post*. About the report."

She suddenly felt very exposed; she'd had no idea her face was out there again. Who had approved it? Jakes? Of course—a famous face is hard to hide. But she gave them a smile. "I hope it was flattering."

"Sit down," Tom said, looking around. "Let me find you a chair."

"No, thanks. I can't stay." She touched Ashley's shoulder. "Can I borrow this one a moment?"

Tom gave no sign of resistance, so Ashley got up and followed Rachel to the front of the restaurant, whispering, "Where have you *been*? They've been asking me about you."

"Who?"

"Erin, Lou Barnes. Jakes. What are you doing off the grid? You can take off those sunglasses, you know."

Knowing now that her picture had been disseminated in the city's largest paper, taking off her glasses didn't feel like an option. "Did you read the report?"

Ashley's expression flatlined, but she arched a significant brow. They both knew it was a whitewash. "What do you need?" Ashley asked.

Rachel took a Post-it note from her purse. On it was a phone number with a Wisconsin area code. This had been Kevin's idea, and he'd called Janet Fordham to ask for the number he'd called her from last summer. Rachel said, "This is the number of the phone Mittag was using during his last days. Can you get records?"

Ashley frowned at the number, then at Rachel. "How much trouble are you in?"

"Hard to say. But if you could make sure Tom . . . "

"He won't say a word," Ashley assured her, raising a pinkie. "He's firmly wrapped around this."

"Thanks."

Then Ashley brightened. "Wait—you remember Magellan Holdings?"

"Tell me."

"When you asked me about it the other day, I started thinking about a different approach. I'd been focused on the direct route, not the indirect one."

"What are you saying?"

"I went back to Magellan's original paperwork. Though it was registered in the Bahamas, the paperwork was faxed in from a number in Bilbao, Spain."

"Spain?" said Rachel, not wanting to admit what she already knew about Spain. Because the next question would be: Who told you that? "Great work," she said.

"You think that's good?" said Ashley. "How much would you like to know the name of the lawyer who filed the papers?"

Rachel returned her smile. "Very. That's how much."

3

IT WAS nearly one in the afternoon when he drove slowly down Lückhoffstraße, a tree-lined, cobblestoned street in a neighborhood called Nikolassee. He passed ivy-plagued houses that looked old enough to have survived Allied bombs. There was a chill in the air because he was near Wannsee, a large lake to the west of Berlin, off the road to Potsdam. Clean Mercedes-Benzes sat in the driveways of overgrown yards.

Because the weather was so mild, he parked at a corner and walked the rest of the way, but soon felt conspicuous—a black American walking through the white German suburbs was something to remember. The feeling only intensified when he knocked on the door of number 54, a flat-faced stuccoed monstrosity, and faced a very pregnant woman whose face was full of undisguised surprise. "Elli Uhrig?" he asked.

"Ja."

"Sorry, I don't know German. Do you mind—"

"What do you want?" she asked in a clotted accent.

Unlike in her years-old photograph, her cheeks were full and healthy looking, and her once-dreaded hair had been parted down the middle and tied tightly back. He took out his FBI ID and said, "Do you mind if I ask a few questions about Martin Bishop?"

He saw it in her face, how with the mention of that name she closed down, doors slamming shut. But the physical door between them remained open.

"Please," he said. "There are questions we need answers to."

"Does any of this have to do with David Parker?" she asked.

He wasn't sure what to say. How did she know David? Yes, he was semifamous these days, making hay of his connection, via Ingrid, to the Massive Brigade—but why would Elli Uhrig start with him? He said, "David's a friend of mine, in fact. He and his wife, Ingrid." She tilted her head, seeming to soften, so he added, "Actually, they're the ones I'm trying to help. That's why I need to ask about Bishop and the Kommando Rosa Luxemburg."

Her smile went away, as if she didn't know quite what to think of all this. Then: "Do you know what my life became after my sister blew herself up? The police, the Verfassungsschutz, the press?" She shook her head. "Why do you think I ran away to . . . to *here*?"

Following her gaze, he looked up the street and saw an old man walking a dog. The man gave a "Hallo" to Elli before noticing Kevin and falling suspiciously quiet.

"Just come in, okay?" she said.

In the entryway he was surprised to find a painting of Jesus Christ on the wall, an amateur work, maybe by Elli herself.

"Take off your shoes."

He did so, then followed her across a jigsaw of rugs to a claustrophobic sitting room with large glass doors looking onto a tree-filled backyard.

She said, "I'm not going to offer you anything to drink."

"That's okay."

"Because you're not staying long."

"I have no plans to," he assured her as he sat on the old striped couch. She took an upholstered chair on the opposite side of the coffee table and put her hands between her knees. She was waiting, so he said, "Your sister, Anika. She was a member of the KRL, correct?"

"For a year, maybe two. Then she fell in love with this American boy—that was Martin Bishop."

"And you? Were you . . . involved with the KRL?"

She shook her head. "I wasn't educated enough for them. I *knew* things, but if you didn't speak the right language they couldn't hear you. At first I'd visit them with Anika, but it wasn't my scene. I had my music. I met Martin, of course. He was nicer than most of them."

"Why did you mention David Parker?"

A curious smile broke her features. "We were friendly for a while."

She didn't seem to want to say more, or maybe she was trying to provoke him into more questions. But that wasn't why he'd come. He said, "After the explosion, Martin came to you. Is that right?"

"I lived on the same street. He said he wanted to make sure I was okay, but he was in shock. He didn't know what to do. Me, too," she said, picking at the hem of her shirt. "But we both knew that the bomb hadn't been theirs."

"You were sure of that."

"I *was*. Now . . ." She hesitated, then pushed a tear out of her eye and smiled pitifully. "Now I'm not sure. You know how many articles have been written about that night? I've read them all. They all agree that the KRL did it to themselves. How can so many journalists get it wrong?"

"Did Martin have a theory?"

"Not at first. First, we both cried and watched the cops and fire trucks from my window. We were so confused. He slept on my floor and woke early. He was . . . agitated? Yes. He told me they'd gotten a new television. He said that must have been it. A bomb in the television." As she spoke, her fingers found loose threads in her shirtsleeve and unwound them. She kept licking her lips.

"Who did he blame?"

She let go of her sleeve. "He blamed the FBI. He blamed you."

Kevin tried not to react to the accusation. "And what happened afterward?"

"Well, the story came out the next day, that they had been planning a terror attack on the Hauptbahnhof. Martin knew he had to leave. He called this Spanish guy Anika had introduced him to. Part of some radical group in Bilbao. This man had seen the news already, of course, and he was excited that he'd been asked to help."

"Can I get his name?" Kevin asked.

She shook her head. "I don't want to get him in trouble."

"You won't," he assured her. "If I can talk to him, he might be able to help me . . . and David."

"What is it," she asked, "that you want to do?"

He thought about that a moment. "I want to bring the facts to light."

She furrowed her brow. "Does this have to do with that report on the Massive Brigade?"

He nodded.

"I thought that was cleared up."

"I wish," he said.

4

AFTER THAT second sleepless night, poring over the FBI's report and listening to the others put together a puzzle that was still missing too many pieces, David had returned to his apartment overcome by the feeling that nothing around him was real. It was all simulation, a false surface covering a world that was too horrifying to be looked at directly, and as he forced himself to stay awake, making his way to his Thursday afternoon class, he thought that this was why fiction existed, as a way to look at the world without being broken by it. The thought was intriguing enough for him to squeeze it into his lecture.

As he spoke, though, a part of his exhausted mind disconnected from the words, and that part surveyed the auditorium, all those rapt pairs of eyes on him, the hands taking notes on his precious words. That part of him, the part that needed adoration to survive, was the same part that had years ago decided that it wasn't enough to write good books in semiobscurity; what mattered was the trappings of fame. That part had convinced him to take Ingrid out of Berlin and bring her to Manhattan; to attend cocktail parties and sit on panels; to pay close attention to the reading trends of Average Americans and try to turn their eyes toward him. The irony was that all the effort he'd put into building himself up into a "brand" had done nothing for him. In fact, it had cost him his productivity, whatever style he'd once had, and it had destroyed his family. It had been a five-year exercise in self-immolation.

Yet here he was, at the head of a class that had filled within hours of registration; when prepublication chapters from his forthcoming book came out in *People* magazine, they were subjects of discussion in the papers of middle America, where the Average American lived. The irony was that he hadn't found fame; fame had found him through Martin Bishop and the Massive Brigade. If Bishop hadn't talked to Ingrid, and Ingrid hadn't walked out on him, then his life would be where it had been at the beginning of last summer—a miserable marriage and a book that would never get done. Instead, he spoke on television to interested journalists—he'd once been on CNN as an "expert" on the Massive Brigade—the magazines asked for his words, and his agent had negotiated a wildly unrealistic advance for his book. His sex life had improved considerably.

Even with the constant attention, an enormous part of his life had gone into lockdown the moment that he'd returned home in December to find a black man waiting in his living room with a notepad, on which he'd written *I don't know if anyone's listening, so stay quiet. Ingrid and your daughter need your help.*

Before heading to Florida, Bill had entrusted him with the keys to the house, and now he visited weekly with groceries and baby supplies bought with cash. He didn't know how Ingrid could survive during those seven-day stretches, but she'd returned a different person than the one he'd known and loved. She was harder, and there was no ambiguity in her opinions. She was also a survivor.

And then there was Clare. Had it not been for that child, he doubted he would have risked his new life with any of this. Clare's beautiful fragility was mind-numbing, and for the first time—even he could admit this to himself—he'd discovered something more important than David Parker.

He was packing up his notes, giving quick replies to some eager students, looking forward to getting home and crashing, when he noticed two familiar faces, the FBI agents who had questioned him about Ingrid and Rachel. Lyle Johnson stood with his hands crossed over his groin, staring at him, while Sarah Vale, hands on her lower back, stretched and eyeballed the students heading off to find their next classes. Eventually, David's students dissipated, and Johnson and Vale approached the podium.

"Quite a crowd," said Vale.

"Five o'clock class, an easy A," he said, then slipped on his shoulder bag. Johnson, though, stood in his way.

"You look tired, David."

"I'm too old for the college lifestyle."

Johnson smiled as Vale swiped at her phone and held it up to display a studio portrait of Kevin Moore, a flag in the background, staring back at him. "You know this guy?" she asked.

David shook his head.

"Thing is," she said, "he flew out of JFK yesterday and walked into our Berlin embassy earlier today."

"Is that weird?" he asked.

"Well, he lives in Colorado. Wasn't even supposed to be on the East Coast."

David looked at each of them, unsure where to take this. Finally, he said, "Who is he?"

"One of us," said Johnson. "FBI."

"He knew Ingrid," Vale added.

David nodded, taking this in. "Do you think he would come to me?"

"Maybe," said Vale.

"Why?"

Johnson opened his mouth, then closed it. He said, "We don't know. But maybe that's why he was in New York."

"How about Rachel Proulx?" Vale asked. "Any sign of her?"

"No. Nothing." He shrugged, trying to come across as nonchalant, but he felt as if all he was doing was throwing tells at them. And he was so fucking tired. There was sweat under his collar, but he resisted the urge to wipe at it. "Does this mean you're closer to finding Ingrid?" he asked.

Neither answered. They just stared, as if waiting for him to break. He thought about how good that would feel, to just break. They were FBI, after all. What if all this paranoia was wrong? What if Rachel and Kevin and Ingrid had misjudged everything?

"Afraid not," Vale finally said. "Sorry."

Johnson handed over his card. "In case you lost it."

"Thanks."

"You'll let us know if you hear anything."

"Sure," David said, then added, "And I hope you'll let me know if you hear anything."

"Of course," said Johnson, scratching at his cheek.

He watched them until they had exited the auditorium and he was alone. A sudden queasiness latched on to him until he left the building and walked east to the Astor Place Theatre, where, he knew, he could find a pay phone. His stomach settled down as he pulled out a quarter and tried to remember the phone number Rachel had given him.

5

RACHEL GOT back from DC a little after five with a new, unfamiliar feeling. It wasn't quite optimism, but something like it, and it was buoyed by the sense that things were finally in motion. Ashley was going to find out what numbers Benjamin Mittag had called before he died. Kevin was tracking Bishop's European connections, now armed with the name Alexandra Primakov, the lawyer who had worked for Magellan Holdings. She'd put that name into a draft email in their shared Hushmail account, and in that same unsent message Kevin had given her the name of Bishop's Spanish contact in Bilbao, 2009: Sebastián Vivas. Things *were* moving—but to where?

She found Ingrid curled up on the couch, watching television with the volume low.

"Clare asleep?"

Ingrid nodded.

Rachel smelled coffee, so she poured herself a cup, then sat with Ingrid. Bill and Gina had turned off the cable, so they were stuck with over-the-air stations. A local newscaster cut to demonstrators at a town hall protesting cuts in education funding. Angry mothers shouted at a red-faced councilman, leaping from chairs and shaking their fingers.

"I should've been that kind of mom," Ingrid said.

"What?"

"Grassroots. One issue at a time. Writing letters and knocking on doors. Instead, I jumped directly into taking on every injustice at once." She pointed at the screen. "That's how sisters get things done."

"Once this is over, you can do just that."

"Over? What does 'over' mean?"

Rachel wasn't sure. Whatever they were doing, they could only see to the next step. Right now, they were simply trying to understand the parameters of the situation. Making the world safe for Ingrid and her baby, or for Rachel, seemed very far away, a destination shrouded in fog. She had no idea what resolution looked like. "Getting back to a normal life," she said.

"I just want to be able to see the sun again."

"Well, *I* wouldn't mind a normal life."

"When was the last time your life was normal?"

Rachel thought about that. These last eight months? No. The time she spent investigating Massive? Further back. She said, "Probably the half year I spent in San Francisco on a research project, investigating fringe thinkers."

"Fringe thinkers, huh?"

"I heard Martin speak for the first time. I had a drink with a man who might have been the one he met in Spain."

"That doesn't sound normal."

It didn't, but it had felt normal, living alone and taking short trips up and down the coast, pretending to be someone she wasn't. It meant something, she supposed, that she was more comfortable being someone else.

"Is that a phone?" Ingrid asked.

Rachel heard it—the *buzz-buzz* of a vibrating phone. She went to the door, where her coat hung, and took out her burner. It was a number she didn't recognize. A 212 Manhattan number. Her instinct was to not answer it. Johnson and Vale could be fishing, checking a number they'd triangulated to Bill and Gina's. Or it might be something else entirely.

She answered but said nothing. Hiss on the line, horns blaring in the background. Then David said, "It's me. Your two friends just questioned me."

"And so you're calling me?"

"It's okay. I'm at a pay phone."

She closed her eyes, thinking how she would have done it if she were them. Rile up a suspect, then watch everything he does. "You're on the street?" she asked.

"Yeah. Why?"

"Shit."

"What?"

She didn't want to explain it to him, but if she simply hung up he would panic, and even if she didn't like David, even if he reminded her of her abusive ex-husband, he actually had skin in this game—an estranged wife and a child. So she spelled it out, telling him that even if he couldn't see Johnson and Vale they could see him, and the moment he dialed her number they had traced it to Bill and Gina's house.

"But I don't see them," he insisted.

"Because they're on their way here."

"Oh, shit," he said. "Where are you going now?"

"That's not something I'm going to tell you, David. Good-bye."

Ingrid saw the look on Rachel's face and snapped awake. "What?"

"We have to go. Get Clare, and I'll pack."

Ingrid was on her feet, heading for the stairs. "How much time do we have?"

"Half hour," Rachel said. "If we're lucky."

6

IT WAS after 11:00 P.M. when Kevin landed at London's Stansted Airport, and he took a black cab into town. His Jamaican driver pretended not to notice that Kevin had no bags with him, and instead quizzed him about life in America. "You got riots, I hear. Bad time to be American, innit?"

"Not so bad," Kevin told him.

"Well, black American."

"That's always bad." He leaned forward, so he could look at the road ahead of them. "You know a place a guy can get a bed for the night without a lot of paperwork?"

The driver looked at him in the rearview. "You got some problems, brother?"

"Who doesn't have problems?"

He brought Kevin to a small street in Croydon, south of the city center, where he introduced him to Mattie, an old woman from the Turks and Caicos who ran an off-the-books bed-and-breakfast. She was round, with rough gray hair in a bun, and after looking Kevin up and down she said to the driver, "He'll do, Elijah."

Kevin slept hard and woke after eight to the smell of baking. His room was a Spartan affair—a mattress and two boxes that served as dressers—but the window was covered in sheer fabric that diffused the light from the morning sun. Downstairs, Mattie served him a plate of coconut flour pancakes and watched him eat. "What you doing here?" she asked suddenly. "How come you not at the DoubleTree?"

He took a bite, chewing thoughtfully. "I'm here to see some-one."

"You runnin' away from a wife? That why you stay with Mattie?"

He shook his head. "Nothing like that. I need to go to Black-friars Road. Number 203."

"That's Southwark. You take the Tube to London Bridge, walk over to Blackfriars."

"You got the whole city in your head?"

She smiled, her eyes twinkling as she got up. "You're a charmer, sir."

He bought a ticket, and after a half-hour subway ride he found himself right in the center of everything, the full congestion of the city. He smoked a cigarette as he walked westward, parallel to the Thames, all the way to Blackfriars Road. At number 203, he found a glass-fronted building that looked like it was from the fifties. Above the entry was a green logo, like a broken infinity symbol, for the ODI, Overseas Development Institute.

Inside, a pretty desk clerk smiled up at him. He tried to look as if he'd been here before.

"Good morning," she said.

"Hello. I'm looking for Alexandra Primakov. I've just gotten in from New York."

"Certainly," she said, setting up her fingers over her keyboard. "Which office, please?"

All Rachel had given him was a name—Alexandra Primakov—and the slimmest of bios: "lawyer, formerly with Berg & DeBurgh, she also came up as a former UNHCR adviser—don't know her connec-tion to refugees. Keeps a desk at the London office of the Overseas Development Institute, a policy think tank."

"I'm not sure exactly," he told the clerk. "My assistant set up this meeting, and he . . ." Kevin rocked his head. "Let's just say he's *new.*"

She smiled, then began to type. "Well, I should be able to . . ." She frowned at the screen, then nodded. "Yes. There we are." She reached for her desk phone. "Who may I say is calling?"

"Martin Bishop," he said.

Unfazed, the clerk called and explained who was here to see Ms. Primakov. She hesitated, glancing up at Kevin, then lowered her voice and talked more. He'd considered using his real name, but depending on how busy Alexandra Primakov was she might not come down. He didn't want to sit waiting in that lobby all day.

Finally, the clerk hung up and pointed to the corridor. "Elevator's at the end. Third floor. She's waiting for you."

The elevator was slow, and it gave him just enough time to put on his game face. Then the doors opened to reveal a striking white woman, forty maybe, in high heels. Her arms were crossed, and her dark, bruised eyes glared at him so forcefully that he considered staying in place until the doors closed again. Instead, he took two steps forward and held out his hand. "Ms. Primakov."

With just a hint of a Russian accent she said, "Kevin Moore," and he felt the blood drain from him as she turned and walked off with long strides. Eventually, he followed.

Her office reminded him of Mattie's rooms—just the essentials. There was nothing personal here, no photos, no life-affirming mottos on the wall. Just a desk and a couple of chairs and a closed laptop that he guessed she packed with her to take home each evening. She took her chair behind the desk and nodded for him to sit, too.

"How do you know my name?" he asked, since it was the question he was expected to ask.

She opened her computer. "It doesn't matter. The question that matters is: Why are you here?"

She was wrong—his question *did* matter—but he wasn't in a position to push the issue. "In 2009, you filed the paperwork for a company called Magellan Holdings LLC. That company proceeded to funnel money to Martin Bishop and the Massive Brigade. It's likely that you did this for one or both of two people: James Sullivan and Sebastián Vivas."

Her computer was awake by then, and she typed a line, then looked up. "The Massive Brigade is history."

"Then I guess I'm a historian."

"And I never discuss the details of my clients' business."

"But in this case, your clients funded a recognized terrorist organization. Look, you're not in trouble, but—"

"Oh, I know I'm not in trouble," she cut in. "You, though." She squinted at the screen. "The Americans and the Germans are seeking you for questioning. Did you know that?"

He didn't. Fay Levinson had obviously gotten through to Jakes, and he was lucky to have flown out of Berlin as early as he had. "Good thing I'm in England," he said.

"Brexit hasn't happened yet," Primakov told him. "The borders are open, and extradition treaties are still in force. I make one phone call, and there'll be a lot of boys with guns waiting for you outside."

She could have been making all that up, but it didn't matter: He was dead in the water. "I'm just trying to find out what happened," he said. "I worked undercover for months against the Massive Brigade. It ended with a lot of unanswered questions."

She took a moment to look at him, and he thought he saw her features soften, but that might have been a mirage. She said, "Have you read the report the FBI released?"

"Yes."

"And that doesn't answer your questions?"

"Did it answer all of your questions?" he asked.

She leaned back, non committal.

He looked around the barren room. "I'm a little confused. What does someone working in the Overseas Development Institute's worst office space have to do with underground political movements in the United States? Is that what you call overseas development? Funding agitators and terrorists?"

"I rent this space," she told him quietly. "The ODI has nothing to do with me."

"Can't you just help me out?" he asked, opening his hands. "Who do you work for?"

"I'm sorry," she said, shaking her head. "My client list is confidential, and unless you come with a warrant issued by the British government, then I can't help you."

He closed his eyes, knowing that she wouldn't budge. Then he stood to leave.

"And you?" she asked. "Who do you work for?"

He just looked at her.

"Owen Jakes? Yes?"

"No."

"How about Rachel Proulx?"

He said nothing, but his expression said it all.

"She disappeared a week ago. Is she all right?"

"Who *are* you?"

She stared a few seconds, as if she might answer, but instead lifted her cell phone. "Go on, Mr. Moore. I don't want to have to make the call."

7

"WHERE THE hell are we?" Ingrid asked as the midnight street lamps of suburbia passed them by. On the drive from Montclair, taking the long but less conspicuous route through Lancaster, they'd stopped at a gas station, where Ingrid fed and burped Clare, and by now the baby was dozing in her lap again, barely visible under folds of blanket.

"Waldorf, Maryland," Rachel said, driving slowly and watching for parked cars.

"How can you tell?" Ingrid groaned.

By now Rachel had grown to appreciate Ingrid's cynicism, cultivated by months on the run. Bitterness had been given enough time to take root and grow so wild that it had turned on itself, morphing into ironic humor.

"We should be able to stay here a few days," Rachel said as they passed number 6301, the mud-colored bi-level with the pristine front yard lit up by in-ground lighting. But she didn't stop. She kept driving and watched for cars parked on the street, or vans in driveways—any signs that the house was under surveillance. It was doubtful—the Bureau was quite familiar with the nasty details of her past, and knew

how she avoided it—but you only had to be wrong once for everything to fall apart.

She made a U-turn as Ingrid looked down at Clare and said,
"Friends?"

"Maybe."

They parked in front of a house three down from 6301, and Rachel told Ingrid to get into the driver's seat and wait. On the off chance
that she'd miscalculated, Ingrid would know pretty quickly—the sudden appearance of flashlights and men, or even gunfire. In that case,
she should floor it and disappear into the country again. Possibly even
make her way south to Florida, to Bill and Gina.

Rachel walked along the sidewalk as sprinklers in neighboring
yards misted the air. The place made her think of David Lynch movies. Immaculate shrubs, barbeque parties, children's soccer and slum-
ber parties all serving as cover for the perversions and brutality that
bubble just beneath the surface.

Or maybe she was just thinking of 6301.

She reached the front door and hesitated. Looked back at Ingrid's
silhouette in the car. She pressed the doorbell and heard it ring faintly
from inside, and then footsteps. A pause at the eyehole. Then the door
opened and the ever-beautiful Mackenzie stood there, radiant and
irreproachable in a plush white robe.

"Rachel," she said, surprised. Not pleased.

"Hi, Mackenzie. Is Gregg in?"

She opened her mouth, then closed it. "It's pretty late, Rachel."

"Sorry. But it's kind of important."

They'd spoken for long enough that Gregg had pried himself from
his glass of wine, or whatever late-night sitcom they religiously
watched in the suburbs these days, and he approached from behind
his wife, placing his big, hard hands on her slender shoulders. He'd
aged, but she could tell from the tendons behind his thumbs that age
hadn't weakened him. "Rachel. What's up?"

She tried not to show any of the weakness that had defined their relationship for so long. "A huge favor. From you both. I've got a woman with a baby who needs to stay somewhere safe for a few days."

"And you thought of us?" Gregg asked, perhaps irritated, perhaps surprised, perhaps gearing up for a fight.

Mackenzie, though, softened at the mention of a baby. "Who is this woman?"

"A mother who needs protection."

"From whom?" Gregg asked.

Rachel had considered cover stories—the Mob, foreign agents, the press—but she wasn't dealing with neophytes. Gregg's lobbying work had brought him in contact with all levels of the federal government, and Mackenzie's background was international business law, though she was taking some time off. "By not telling you," she said, "I'm protecting you."

They both understood what that meant, and it visibly disturbed Gregg. He took a step back, deeper into the shadows. To Rachel, Mackenzie said, "She needs our help?"

"Yes."

"Okay, then," she said, then turned back to Gregg. "Right?"

Gregg shrugged. "Sure. Of course."

Rachel liked that, seeing the perfect wife putting Gregg Wills in his place. Maybe the brute she'd known had only needed the right kind of tamer.

8

KEVIN WAS almost at the London Bridge station, having fled the ODI headquarters, when he hesitated. Was he really giving up on Alexandra Primakov so quickly? Had she scared him off? Maybe. Not the warning that she would call the police—that, he now suspected, had been an empty threat, because she wouldn't want them to ask her any questions either. What scared him was that she knew his name, knew about Rachel and Owen Jakes. Who the hell *was* she? A lawyer who had helped fund the Massive Brigade, who knew about the inner workings of the FBI with a precision that most inside the Bureau didn't possess. Yes, *that* scared him. Anyone who knew that much was to be feared.

He was in a strange city where he didn't know the rules, dealing with a woman who was miles ahead of him, but to flee when others—Rachel, Ingrid, Clare—depended on him . . . what was that? Was it rational self-preservation, holding on to his freedom long enough to take the next step in his investigation? Or was he running away from something that would prove crucial to protecting these women? Ben's last words came to him: "This is *your* fault." Back then, his decisions had led to a house full of corpses. What would a mistake cost him now? What was the correct course of action?

When he abruptly turned around on the sidewalk and headed west again, he wasn't entirely sure what he was going to do. Was he going to march back into her office and demand answers? Or was he going to lurk outside like a stalker? Would he accost her when she left the building? Or could he manage to track her across this unfamiliar city? San Fran or New Orleans—those were cities in which he could surveil without a problem. But the tangled, crowded streets of London?

He was almost at the crossing for Blackfriars when he looked up and saw her on the other side of the street. Yes—Alexandra Primakov, phone to her ear, walking in the direction he had just come from. He turned on his heel again, bumped into a Pakistani couple, and hurried to keep up. He hung back when she went through the turnstile at London Bridge, then ran so that he wouldn't lose her. On the steep escalator, he was twenty people behind, and when he leaped onto the car behind hers he wasn't even sure which direction they were going. By then she'd pocketed her phone and had taken out a second one, on which she typed messages.

It wasn't until they disembarked at East Croydon that the feeling of unease came over him. Ahead, her light skin stood out among the brown faces all around her, and then they were out on the street and . . . there: She turned down the little lane he had first visited last night when a Jamaican driver named Elijah brought him here. She stopped in front of Mattie's door and checked the number with something on her phone. She was getting ready to press the buzzer.

"Ms. Primakov!" he called, jogging up to her.

She looked back, gave him a double take, then cracked a smile. "Mr. Moore. How'd you get behind me?"

"How do you think?"

She raised a brow, then nodded toward the main thoroughfare. "Want to take a stroll?"

Before he could answer, she was walking, and he had to jog. By the time she joined the noisy lunchtime crowd, he had caught up. "Are you going to talk now?" he asked.

"No," she said. "It's not my place to tell you anything."

"Okay . . ."

"I need to you to verify something first."

"Shoot."

She glanced at him again, a wry smile. "You are working with Rachel Proulx, correct?"

He wasn't sure he should answer, but if he didn't talk she wouldn't either. She'd already made that clear. "Yes."

"She's not here, though, is she? Back in America?"

This time, he nodded, not wanting to put voice to what he was starting to feel was a failure on his part to hold any cards.

"Right. Tell her that she's wasting her time worrying about ancient history."

"What does that mean?"

"It means that whatever papers I wrote up in 2009 are of no importance. Tell her to look at July 4 of last year. Tell her to ask who benefited the most."

Her coyness was beginning to irritate him. "How about this, Alexandra: How about you tell me who benefited?"

She shook her head. "That would be telling you what I know, which would lead to you asking how I know it. I don't like those kinds of questions."

They walked on, past a rack of sneakers presided over by another woman from the islands. "How do I know you're not trying to divert us from the real story?" he asked.

"Good," she said, smiling. "Now you're getting the hang of this."

9

RACHEL DROVE to Arlington holding down yawns and trying to focus her vision. An awkward night sitting up with Gregg and Mackenzie, then in the guest room with Ingrid and Clare, wasn't conducive to any kind of rest, and only after Gregg left for the city in the morning was she able to catch a couple of hours' sleep. When she came downstairs at nine, she found Mackenzie and Ingrid sitting with coffees, talking like old friends. Mackenzie was explaining that she had left her job when she married, so she could focus on the dream her own mother had had for her—raising a family. But after years of failing to conceive—and Mackenzie was the first to admit it—she'd developed a horror of returning to a nine-to-five life. She'd tried out some online businesses, but nothing had taken yet. Rachel poured herself a coffee and listened to the two of them speak as if nothing were strange in the world, as if both of them shared the same preoccupation with finding a satisfying career. Ingrid seemed to have shed her dogmatism, at least for now, and said nothing about wage slaves or the machinations of the ruling classes.

"I should be back in a few hours," she told them.

"Something?" Ingrid asked.

"We'll see."

She stuck for as long as possible to the Beltway simply because it skirted the edges of DC. As if taking that highway meant Johnson and Vale would have no idea how to find her—which, given the state of surveillance technology, was ridiculous. Still, it made her feel a little better. Within a half hour she was parking among cute houses on Stuart Street and walking south to take the escalator down into the Orange Line's Ballston-MU Station. This was Ashley's station, five blocks from her rental duplex.

Once she'd descended into the cavernous space, the Metro's famous grid arching overhead, Rachel wandered to the inbound platform. Along the edges of the station a concrete barricade rose to waist height, and she dragged her fingers along the back of it as she slowly made her way to the end of the platform. About halfway down, just past the dot-matrix sign telling her that the next train would arrive in nine minutes, her fingers ran into a stuffed envelope that had been glued against the back of the wall. She ripped it off and kept moving, her hand not leaving the wall. When she reached the far end, she turned back, slipping the bundle into her jacket pocket, and headed back to the exit as, ahead, commuters hurried down the escalator to catch the incoming train.

She didn't look at the envelope until she had reached Stuart Street and was safely behind the wheel again. The outside was blank, torn where she'd ripped it off the wall, and inside were five sheets of printout, folded tightly to fit. It was a spreadsheet listing calls made to and from Benjamin Mittag's phone, beginning June 18, 2017, the day Bishop and Mittag disappeared, and continuing until July 8, the day Bishop and then Mittag were killed. The calls were made to a total of three numbers, one of them—Janet Fordham's, presumably—only once, on July 8. She concentrated on the coordinates of the other two numbers—longitudes and latitudes to the fourth decimal point. One of the two numbers bounced around the country, coordinates changing constantly. 30° to 50° N and 70° to 120° W. Martin Bishop, certainly, always in motion. Then there was the third number.

What she noticed was that this final number, with the exception of one call, remained around a single place—38° N and 77° W. While she only had an entry-level familiarity with map coordinates, she recognized this set: the DC area.

It took ten minutes to find an internet café in the rear of a tiny grocery, and in the darkened space she typed in the full DC coordinates: 38°53'40.7976", -077°01'30.0468".

Was she surprised by the result? No, not entirely, but it still hurt a little when she found herself looking at 935 Pennsylvania Avenue, NW, the Hoover Building. She sniffed, feeling a cold coming on, then checked the dates. There: July 8, a couple of hours after Bishop was killed. She typed in the coordinates of Mittag's phone and found herself staring, bird's-eye view, at a gas station around St. Paul, Nebraska.

Benjamin Mittag had made that call, but the other number wasn't in or around the Hoover this time—the coordinates were completely different. She typed them in and found herself in central Chicago. She rubbed her temple, something nagging at her.

Yes: *Rachel, I'm not stepping on anything here, don't worry. I was in Chicago when Paulson called me, and I lucked out with one of those new Gulfstreams that fly like the wind.*

On the same day he would later be killed, Mittag called Owen Jakes in Chicago.

She closed her eyes, pressed the bridge of her nose, and tried to work through it slowly. Tried to remember that last conversation Kevin had had with Benjamin in Watertown. After punching him and closing the bedroom door, Mittag had said, *FBI, right? Who's running you?*

And then:

Man, you've really got it all wrong, don't you? We're on the same side. Or, we used to be.

Then she remembered more.

10

KEVIN LANDED at Aeropuerto de Bilbao—in Basque, Bilboko aireportua—at five in the afternoon, and when they touched down he looked across the tarmac at the wedge, like a wave, that rose from the roof of the terminal. It was a small airport, but its glass-and-steel modernism gave it a magnificent feel. He joined the other passengers on a bus that brought them from the plane to the old customs counter. In some months, the separation of Britain from the European Union would ensure that staff waited behind the counter, but for now there was no one to listen even if he'd wanted to declare something.

He joined a queue leading to a line of white taxis marked by red stripes on the doors. On the short flight he'd decided to take it one step at a time. He'd used the Hushmail account to pass on Alexandra Primakov's message, and until Rachel replied he was an independent agent. He would head to the city center, check into a room, and then find out if the paperwork for Magellan Holdings had been filed with the local government offices. While finding new names on the paperwork Primakov had drafted was a long shot, it was a place to start before diving into the more daunting task of looking for Sebastián Vivas, about whom he still knew almost nothing.

The taxi was a bubble-shaped economy car, and the driver played

Basque music full of flutes and drums as they drove south toward town. The music was loud enough that at first neither of them heard the siren. When the driver noticed, he frowned into the rearview but kept driving at full speed. It wasn't until the police car was right behind him, blinking its lights, that he finally got the message and slowed down, then pulled to the side of the road, muttering, *"Arraioa!"*

Kevin didn't bother asking any questions. He only looked over his shoulder as the driver kept cursing, and watched a tall, dark-skinned man exit the passenger side of the police car while a uniformed policeman behind the wheel stayed where he was. That didn't look right at all, but they were on the side of a highway with bright, open fields all around, and no matter how fast he ran Kevin wasn't getting away.

When the man approached the driver's side window and conversed in Basque a moment, Kevin noticed that the driver relaxed, his tone lightening, and he looked in the mirror at Kevin and raised his hands from the wheel, international sign language for *Take him if you want.* The man turned to look at Kevin through the window. He had a pencil mustache, a wandering right eye, and excellent English. "Mr. Kevin Moore? Please come with me." Kevin followed his instructions, getting out of the taxi and walking with him toward the police car.

"Who are you?"

"I work for the Centro Nacional de Inteligencia."

"You're an intelligence officer."

"Just so."

"Do you have a name?"

"Indeed," he said. "I am Sebastián Vivas."

He briefly wondered if this could be a coincidence—was it a common name? Then Vivas said in a friendly tone, "These idiots let you leave the airport. We're usually more professional."

"Why pick me up?"

"Because you've come here to find me, and I'd like to know why."

It was the kindest abduction Kevin had ever experienced.

Vivas joined him in the backseat as the mute police officer—had he been reprimanded for his ineptitude?—sped farther down the road and used an access road to cross the median and take them back toward the airport.

"So," said Vivas. "You have flown from London to Bilbao in search of myself. Am I correct?"

"Have you always worked for the same employer?"

He smiled. "Right to it! Well, yes. For a long time."

"In 2009?"

"Why do you ask?"

Kevin looked at the dry fields passing them by. "That's when you helped Martin Bishop, who had just come from Berlin."

"Did I?"

Kevin couldn't tell if it was innocence or playfulness, so he just kept going. "At the time, you were part of an underground group connected to the Kommando Rosa Luxemburg. Or were you a plant?"

"Like you and the Massive Brigade?"

Kevin sized him up a moment. Unlike many in their line of work, Sebastián Vivas wasn't being smug. He was merely establishing what he knew so that Kevin wouldn't waste time dancing around the facts. "Alexandra Primakov called you?"

Vivas's smile broadened, but he wasn't going to verify that. Whoever these people were, this network of individuals in London and Bilbao and perhaps Berlin—they were knowledgeable as hell.

"Nine years ago you were a revolutionary," Kevin said.

Vivas looked like he might laugh. "Spain was a fascist country until the seventies."

"I've heard."

"Well, revolutionary is not a bad word in Spain."

It was a kind of answer. "Were you one of the officers in Magellan Holdings?"

Vivas shook his head. "I was not."

"How about James Sullivan?"

Kevin's words seemed to please the Spaniard. He rubbed his scalp and brushed at his mustache and shook his head, a quiet gasp of laughter escaping him. "I haven't heard *that* name in a long time."

"Well?" Kevin asked.

"Perhaps he was."

"So his name is on the company charter."

"There is no charter for Magellan Holdings, not anymore. The company was dissolved months ago."

"After Martin Bishop was killed?"

"Perhaps."

"There's no paperwork left?"

He rocked his head. "Sadly, there was a fire."

"A fire?"

"Just so."

The cop at the wheel took a turnoff for the airport. Kevin had no idea what awaited him once they arrived, so this might be his last chance to ask questions. "Can you draw the connection for me? Who is James Sullivan?"

"Just a name."

"A name for whom?"

"That's all you want? Someone's name?"

"I could start with that."

"Okay, Mr. Moore. But once I tell you, you have to promise to leave my country, and myself, alone. Can you do that?"

It was a big ask, but Kevin had nothing on his side but a credit card nearing its limit and a change of clothes that were by now dirty. "Yes, I can do that."

"Good," said Sebastián Vivas. "Now, have you ever heard of the CIA's Department of Tourism?"

11

RACHEL COULDN'T get that call out of her head. Just a few hours after the shooting of Martin Bishop, Ben Mittag had called Owen Jakes from a gas station in Nebraska. It hadn't been their only conversation—no, Ben and Owen talked regularly, Owen usually inside and around the Hoover Building. In fact, there had been a call on July 6, two days earlier—the same day Ben Mittag told Kevin that they were going on a drive together: *Boss man wants a meeting.* The connection, now, was undeniable: Mittag knew that Bishop would be outside Lebanon, Kansas, when he called Owen on July 6. That gave Owen two full days to pull in a sniper and set him up in that field of wheat. A cinch.

Yet it still didn't compute. Benjamin Mittag, a petty criminal who, by all accounts, despised everyone. What had he to gain from working with the FBI, or with Owen Jakes?

Were that the only mystery to solve, then her course would be clear. She would push and push on that one question until a crack formed in the wall of her ignorance. But there was more: Why did Owen wait until Bishop was underground to kill him? It would have been so much simpler and less risky to get rid of him at any other point during the previous eight years. And then there was the message from

Alexandra Primakov, which she'd read in her and Kevin's Hushmail drafts folder: *She says we should be focused on who benefited on July 4. She says everything else is distraction. I don't know—we have no idea who she's representing, so everything she tells us has to be taken with a grain of salt.*

Kevin was right, of course. Nothing given to them could be taken at face value, particularly anything handed over by Alexandra Primakov, who with her unknown friends had spent years supporting Bishop and Mittag's brand of anticapitalist rabble-rousing.

As for who benefited on July 4, they both knew the answer, because only a week ago Representative Diane Trumble, in her anger, had spelled it out: *Let's not allow international tax dodgers to benefit from the tragedy of July 4, 2017.* Plains Capital and IfW, and the super-rich protecting their secret systems of money laundering—they were the ones who benefited.

What had Martin Bishop said to Ingrid at the party in Montclair about the congressional investigation? Yes: *They'll find a way to shut it down. They always do.*

But wasn't this more of that diseased logic that convinced her Marxist friend, nine years ago, that the Clintons were serial killers? She didn't know.

It was late afternoon when she reached Waynesboro, Pennsylvania, near the Maryland border. She'd traveled miles along curving mountain roads that cut through the Appalachians, following the lines on a state atlas she'd picked up in Gettysburg. She was still behind on sleep, and despaired of ever catching up.

She found the Stayfair Trailer Park by using the phone directory at a Shell station, and once she reached the community she rolled down her window to ask a skinny teenager where Jenny Mittag's trailer was. He pointed deeper into the park and said, "Lot twenty."

The road that wound through the place had been covered in gravel, and the mobile homes sat in plots of overgrown grass, spotted with puddles from recent storms. The rusty shell at number 20 sat on cinder blocks and was decorated with a pink flamingo leaning at a dangerous angle. She got out and took a circuitous route to the screen door to save her shoes. While she rapped on the door, a couple with a yapping Chihuahua stared suspiciously as they passed. Then the inner door opened, and a haggard-looking blonde stared back at her, looking just as suspicious as the couple had been.

"Who're you?"

She took out her badge and held it close to the screen. "Special Agent Rachel Proulx. I need to have a word with you about Benjamin."

"I already talked to you people."

"I know. I read that report. This is a follow-up."

Her face tightened. "He's been dead for a while."

"May I come in?"

Jenny looked back into her home, made another face. "I haven't cleaned up. We can talk outside."

"Sure," Rachel said, and stepped back.

Jenny disappeared, then reappeared with a pack of menthols. She pushed through the screen door, let it slam shut, then sat on her stoop and lit up.

"You told our investigator that Benjamin wanted to join the FBI. That he actually applied but was turned down."

"Yeah."

"Then, some months later, someone showed up. Do you remember his name?"

Jenny shook her head.

"But Benjamin told you that the man was from the Bureau, and that he had been accepted."

"My Ben was a hell of a liar. But mothers always believe, right?"

Rachel had no idea but nodded agreeably.

Jenny took a drag. "Next week, he packed his bag and left. But what kind of choice did he have? Stay here, he ends up a coal miner or working checkout at Walmart. I don't blame him for lying to me."

"When did you realize he'd lied?"

"Not for a long time. That *Rolling Stone* thing. Shock, I can tell you."

As Rachel nodded, Jenny's gaze flashed off to the side, at another passing couple watching them.

"Motherfuckers," she said.

"What?"

"They all hate me. After the Fourth of July, my son was a terrorist. I'm the one who raised a terrorist."

Rachel watched the couple disappear, then turned back. "Do you have a computer?"

Jenny frowned at her. "I'm poor, but I'm not a savage."

"Some people like to stay disconnected."

"Well, not me." She crushed her cigarette and stood. "You wanna use it?"

"Can I?"

Jenny opened the screen door, and Rachel followed her inside. It was a cramped but tidy space, the kitchenette smelling faintly of mold, and in the living area Jenny opened a cabinet and took out an old, chunky Dell laptop. She placed it on the coffee table and powered it up. "I've been wanting to get a new one," she said, almost defensive.

"I just need to get online."

"I got the Hendersons' password."

Once she'd connected to her neighbor's Wi-Fi, Jenny turned the computer around for her guest to use. Rachel pulled up a browser and searched for images of "Owen Jakes." A few hundred images came up, most of them random men spread across the United States. She added "FBI" and immediately found an official photo, Jakes standing in front of a blue curtain with an American flag off to the side.

When she turned the computer around, Jenny pulled a pair of reading glasses out from between the couch cushions and slipped them on. She squinted at the screen, then nodded slowly. "Yep. That's him. That's the guy who told Ben he was getting into the FBI." She saw the search bar above his face. "Owen Jakes?"

"Yes."

Jenny hesitated, eyes back to the photo, to the American flag. "Wait. Are you telling me he *was* FBI?"

"Yes," Rachel said quietly.

"Oh shit," Jenny said. She stood. "Oh shit, shit, shit." She took off her glasses and wiped at tears. "What does that mean?"

Rachel closed her eyes, this final confirmation pulling her back in time, back through her memories and all the reports, connections sparking all around her. In the face of mounting evidence she'd kept pushing the truth away, but now there was no rejecting it. It was all there, right in front of her face, and she felt as if her whole life had been stolen from her. It was a horrible feeling.

"You all right?" Jenny asked.

Rachel reached out and gripped Jenny's hand. "Thank you," she said. "Can I use your computer for one more thing?"

She signed into a VoIP account and made two phone calls. The first was to Ashley. It was foolishness to dial her directly, but she didn't know when she might have the chance to get in touch again. Rachel gave her the phone number Owen had used while communicating with Mittag and asked her to run the same trace on it that she'd done with Mittag's phone—calls made and their locations. Ashley, hearing the hoarseness in Rachel's voice, knew this was important. "I'll go back in tonight."

"What about Tom?" she asked, remembering her date.

"Tom's spending the weekend with his wife," Ashley said without a hint of embarrassment.

She made a second call, and by the time she left Jenny's trailer darkness had fallen and a chill had settled in. Just beyond some nearby trailers, someone was having a party, blaring hip-hop throughout the park. She'd left things ambiguous with Jenny, explaining that whatever her son had been doing with the Massive Brigade, it wasn't quite as it appeared. "You'll know more soon enough," she said. "Everyone will."

She got in her car and thought about the route ahead of her, south, to the suburbs of Chevy Chase in Maryland. Shut-eye would have to wait a little longer.

She drove slowly, crunching gravel in the darkness, worried

some spare children might jump out in front of her. Through her open window she smelled burned pork, and then she saw the party itself—barbecue pit, twelve-packs of Bud, and fifteen or so middle-aged revelers, most of them already drunk, grinding to the boom box. Around the next curve, she came to a stop: A Lincoln Town Car was parked in the middle of the lane, lights off.

She was considering getting out when she noticed movement to her left, a figure emerging from the darkness. A tall man who, she knew before she could make out his features, was Lyle Johnson. Twenty feet away, he said, "Where you headed, Rachel?" with a smile in his voice. "We've been looking all over for you."

Ahead, Sarah Vale walked into her headlight beams.

Rachel closed her window.

"Why are you meeting with Jenny Mittag?" Johnson asked, now approaching very slowly. "What would someone like you have to say to someone like that?"

Vale had reached the passenger side, one hand reaching beneath her overcoat, toward the small of her back.

"You know," Johnson said, stepping up to her door, "we found a dead guy in your apartment. Someone had injected the poor bastard with etorphine. Know anything about it?"

Rachel checked the rearview, then threw the car into reverse. Vale jumped back and took out a pistol.

A gun magically appeared in Johnson's hand as well, but he yelled, "Don't!" at Vale. Or maybe he was yelling at Rachel not to move. Either way, Rachel ducked her head as she switched to drive and hit the gas, throwing gravel and dirt in her wake as she skidded around the Town Car and smashed through a pink Big Wheel in someone's crabgrass yard. As she swung back onto the gravel on the far side of the Town Car, she caught a glimpse of Johnson running and Vale getting into shooting position. But with the next curve she was out of sight, and she did not slow down until she reached Chevy Chase, Maryland.

12

GREGG AND Mackenzie had given Ingrid an attic room, away from the center of the house, but what they didn't realize was that the central air also funneled the sounds upstairs, so when they fought Ingrid could hear every word. Which was why it took forever to get Clare to sleep.

Not only their words, but the nuances of their words, the thump of an angry fist hitting a wall, the sound that Mackenzie's voice made when she didn't want to cry. At first Ingrid thought she was the reason for their fight, she and Clare, but she soon realized she was unimportant. The reason for the fight was Rachel, and that Mackenzie had taken them in. Gregg, apparently, would have sent them packing.

It was educational, this eavesdropping. She learned that Gregg was Rachel's ex-husband, and however they'd ended it there was still a lot of baggage between them.

She didn't begrudge them their fights, because the upstairs room she and Clare had been given was also an office, with a foldout couch and a computer connected to the internet. After months hidden away from the online world, she was finally back, reading about the demonstrations that had persisted despite the release of the FBI report. Analysts had been picking it apart since its release Tuesday morning, boiling it down for the masses. "You can't fight violence with kid gloves," said a conservative commentator, while someone from the other side of the political spectrum said, "In its rush for a 'quick win,' the FBI demonstrated the sin of impatience, which is how people get killed."

She read an interview with Assistant Director Mark Paulson, who had been directly involved in the hunt for the Massive Brigade, and was impressed by his calm, measured tone. "The fact is that no one in the Bureau wanted this kind of a win, certainly not Special Agent Rachel Proulx, who spearheaded the case. What happened was tragic, but had we not moved against them when we did there's no telling how many more acts of violence they would have committed." Impressive, too, was the way he smoothly inserted Rachel into conversations, so she would be the one to take fire.

When she heard the front door slam and the quiet sound of crying, Ingrid crept down to the second floor, where she tracked the noise to the closed bathroom door. "Mackenzie?" she said. "You all right?"

The crying ceased; there was a loud sniff. "Hey, yeah. I'm fine."

She wasn't, of course, and Ingrid didn't want to leave it at that. After reading about the demonstrations, seeing with her own eyes that people were no longer content to wallow on their sofas and let the world go to shit on its own, she'd been filled with optimism. While she couldn't join the crowds just yet, she could at least help the one person she had access to. She leaned against the door and said, "Look, we'll leave tonight."

"No."

"I'm not getting between you and your husband."

Mackenzie pulled the door open, and her face was splotchy, her eyes bloodshot. "Really," she said, her voice choked. "You and Clare should stay."

There was something in her face, something Ingrid couldn't put her finger on. But it was familiar. It reminded her of her childhood. She said, "What's wrong?"

Mackenzie shrugged, a thin smile. "I don't like fights, I guess."

Then she turned to go to the sink, and Ingrid saw it: the way Mackenzie's shoulder twitched, as if an exposed nerve had been tapped.

She knew.

"Wait," Ingrid said, following her into the bathroom.

Mackenzie looked back.

"Raise your arms."

"What?"

"Raise them."

Unsure, Mackenzie raised her arms. When her elbows reached shoulder height she flinched but kept reaching until her arms were straight up in surrender. Slowly, Ingrid lifted her blouse. Mackenzie did not stop her, only stared down at Ingrid with those bloodshot eyes. By the time the blouse was up to her bra the bruises were exposed, running up and down the left side of her ribs.

"Jesus," said Ingrid. "I thought he'd punched the wall."

Self-conscious now, Mackenzie lowered her arms and pushed down her blouse. "Jesus had nothing to do with it."

Ingrid stepped back, feeling the past wash over her, seeing again the bruises that had been a familiar part of her mother's body. Here she was—those same bruises in front of her—and she felt as impotent as she had as a child.

No.

"I'm going to kill him," Ingrid said.

"You don't understand," Mackenzie protested. "It's not—he's not like that."

"He's not?" The anger was coming now, that sweet, warm anger. "What the fuck is your problem?"

"Get out of here."

"You're a pretty little idiot," Ingrid told her.

"Go!"

She didn't want to go; she wanted to beat the facts of life into this woman. But she'd been dragged too quickly into her past again; it had tongue-tied her. She knew she wouldn't be able to say anything of use, not now. So she went back upstairs and checked on Clare. Then she sat in front of the computer and stared at the swirling screen saver. She saw flashes of fists, drunk men and cowardly women. She saw the child she'd once been, hiding in her closet to save her own fucking skin.

She woke the computer and searched until she'd found a Tor client. She installed it and typed in the IP address that she and Martin Bishop had established back in July. It connected, but there was no one waiting on the other end. Not yet. There was just a blank space where her cursor blinked, waiting to be used.

"Hey," she heard, and turned to see Mackenzie in the doorway.

Ingrid turned away from the computer to face her. For a moment neither spoke, until Ingrid said, "Sorry. I'm pushy. I know that."

"No." Mackenzie came inside and sat on the corner of the bed. She first looked at Clare, arms and legs spread, softly snoring. The only sound in the room was the baby's breaths.

"My father was like him," Ingrid said. "My mother waited and waited for him to change. In the meantime, she went from bruises to broken bones to internal bleeding. I tried to talk sense to her, but she didn't listen. Maybe that's how it always is. So it went on. In the end, *I* was the one who broke. I was sixteen, and he was going at her in the living room. I went to the basement and got a shovel and knocked him over the head. He turned on me—I could see in his face that he wasn't really human anymore. The rage had turned him into a beast. Worse than a beast, because it wasn't about fear but pride. So I hit him again. Again." She inhaled loudly, remembering that moment. Mackenzie didn't move. "They don't get better," Ingrid said. "I would have killed him had it not been for my mother, who climbed over his body in order to stop me. Do you know what I felt then? Contempt. Not for him, though. For her."

Mackenzie turned away, unable to look into her face, focusing instead on Clare.

Ingrid said, "You're going to leave him."

"Eventually. Yes, probably."

"No, Mackenzie. You're leaving him tonight."

She finally turned back to Ingrid, a queer smile on her face. "That's crazy!"

"It's the only thing to do," Ingrid said as she turned back to the Tor client and, in the waiting space, typed "Circumnavigation." She pressed ENTER, then quit and trashed the application.

"What did you do?" Mackenzie asked.

"We'll find out soon enough." Ingrid stood. "Now let's take care of you."

13

IT WAS not Rachel's kind of place. The white-clad young man at the gate, once she'd given the name of the member who'd invited her, had pointed her in the direction of the clubhouse, an enormous white building that made her think of plantation houses in the antebellum south. When she drove up the rolling lane and looked across the lit grounds, sliced by a stone-edged canal, she thought that if she placed Jenny Mittag here the woman would probably die of a heart attack.

And what about Jenny Mittag now? Had she put the woman's life in danger by leading her pursuers to the Stayfair? She doubted it—she hadn't shared enough for Jenny to be enough of a threat. But they would ask her questions, and while Rachel had been careful to erase the history of her computer use, it wouldn't take long for Johnson and Vale to get a warrant for the neighbor's internet provider and uncover the tracks she'd left leading to Ashley, and to here, to Sam Schumer.

He was waiting in the Columbia Country Club's lush marble lobby. A mildly condescending smile crept into his face once he'd gotten a good look at her—after so many days and miles her jacket was wrinkled and soiled, while the blouse and long skirt she'd borrowed

He rocked his head, maybe wondering if he could trust anything she'd said. "You know, don't you, that I'll have to call the FBI for comment. And soon, if I want to make tomorrow's show."

"I hope you do," she said. "Just make sure you're not calling your other Bureau source."

He grinned. "You guessed it?"

"Owen Jakes was the only way you could have learned of Bishop's death that quickly."

He seemed very pleased by her detective work; then he signaled for two more drinks. As the waiter headed to the bar, Sam said, "You know you just threw the shit into the fan. Even if you change your mind right now, I'm going to follow up on all of this."

"I'm betting on it, Sam. If you don't, I'm a dead woman."

from Mackenzie's closet barely fit her. "Let's go to the bar,
"Darker there."

"What a gentleman."

"You said you wanted privacy."

Sam knew the staff by name, and as a rear table was being
they ordered drinks. When they settled down into the plush
Rachel feeling the full weight of her exhaustion, Sam furrow
brow. "Don't tell me we're friends again, Rachel. Don't shatte
entire worldview."

"I'd never do that," she said, trying to appear comfortable
all of this. "I just want to give you a story. If you're interested."

"I'm *always* interested." He reached into his pocket and place
spiral notepad and a fountain pen on the table. "But is this going
be business as usual? A little tantalizing fact followed by silence, mayl
some innuendo?"

She smiled at him. "Hope you haven't made other plans. This is
going to take some time."

Again, the furrowed brow, but he was interested. He opened his
hands. "For you, Rachel, all the time in the world."

Their drinks arrived. An old-fashioned for him, a Cosmo for her.
They both took sips, but she tried not to drink too fast. She didn't
want to fall asleep in the chair.

He put his hands together, prayerlike, and touched his lips.
"Shoot."

She'd had to take mental notes during the hour-and-a-half drive
from Waynesboro in order to organize her thoughts—keeping track
of the various players, noting inconsistencies, and constructing it so
that the evidence came before the sudden, and radical, conclusions.
Sam listened in a strikingly professional manner, breaking in only to
ask for clarification. He took notes. He probably went through thirty
pages over the space of two hours, and when she finished he sighed
and dropped his pen, then rubbed his eyes.

"So?" she said after the silence had gone on long enough.

14

SEBASTIÁN VIVAS insisted on paying for Kevin's flight out, but there was a catch: The Spanish government would only pay to return him to where he'd come from. Namely, London. So by Sunday he was back in Mattie's spare room, having bought a ticket to JFK for Monday morning. That evening, he drank beer with her and Elijah, the TV muted in the background. He listened to Mattie's stories about life in the islands before she married and moved to England. "There was no *time* there, you see? Morning, day, night was all we knew. The food—it came off the trees. Here? Every little second, they measure it. Your food comes from boxes. And always: money, money."

He'd written up a bare-bones Hushmail report for Rachel, giving her an account of Vivas's eye-opening yet unhelpful story of a secret CIA department, since disbanded, that had among its employees one Milo Weaver. Now working for the United Nations, Weaver had been in Bilbao when Martin Bishop appeared, still in shock from Berlin. "This Milo Weaver—he's also known as James Sullivan?"

"Just so." Vivas was amiable enough, once Kevin had agreed to leave.

"And why was he funding Bishop?"

A shrug. "That, my friend, you will have to ask him."

"I'd like to. Where can I meet him?"

Vivas laughed, patted Kevin on the shoulder, and pointed him to his gate.

On Monday morning, as he waited for Elijah to drive him to the airport, Kevin drank hot tea with Mattie in the living room. The television was on mute, but he noticed BBC News's bright red BREAKING NEWS chyron, and the words: FBI SCANDAL and OFFICIAL IMPLICATED. He set down his tea. "You mind if I turn that up, Mattie?"

What he heard stunned him. Sam Schumer, a right-wing commentator he'd never paid much attention to, had broken their story last night. BBC admitted that it was a long, detailed piece—as yet uncorroborated—but the essential details were that an FBI official named Owen Jakes was responsible for multiple outrages: the 2009 Berlin explosion blamed on the Kommando Rosa Luxemburg, the assassinations of three members of Congress and attempted murder of a fourth, and the murders of Martin Bishop and Benjamin Mittag. As if that weren't enough, there was an angle Kevin hadn't even considered: that Owen Jakes had been running Mittag as his own agent. The FBI, as yet, had released no statement. "As we said before, this story is developing and has not been confirmed, but it is causing enormous uproar in the United States at the moment."

Mattie saw the look on his face. "You all right, baby?"

On the drive to Heathrow, Elijah talked constantly, but Kevin heard little of it. He was trying to put together the knowns and unknowns. By then he'd watched Schumer's segment and read the accompanying article on his site, which went on and on, with some notable omissions. Milo Weaver wasn't mentioned; nor was Alexandra Primakov. Kevin wasn't named either. The story answered so much while leaving other questions entirely unasked. Though it was out now, he felt increasingly uneasy. This couldn't be the end of it. It was too explosive to be over.

The unease stuck with him the whole flight, and when the woman in the neighboring window seat struck up a conversation he was ready for a diversion. Her name was Linda, she told him, and she was an

investment banker coming back from a business trip. He was grateful that she didn't ask his line of business. She talked about the ways
in which London had changed over the years, and he found himself
drawn into her observations until, about an hour into the flight, she
said, "How about the news, huh?"

"What?"

"The FBI. Christ."

It turned out she'd also watched Schumer's report, and she was
working on theories to find the connective tissue between the dis-
parate facts. "Owen Jakes must have thought he had it all. He'd gotten
Ben Mittag right next to Bishop as the Massive Brigade grew."

Kevin agreed. Mittag had been Jakes's Kevin, his inside man.
Jakes had been able to keep an eye on Bishop from the early days,
but how was he supposed to know, back in 2009, what the Massive
Brigade would become? "Eventually," he told Linda, "the Brigade
had become so big that no one could get rid of it."

As if this question had just come to her, Linda said, "But why
didn't Jakes get rid of Bishop earlier? That would've taken care of
everything."

"Maybe he was afraid Bishop would reveal what he'd done in
Berlin. Maybe that was Bishop's protection."

"I mean kill him," Linda said. "He did it last summer. Why not
eight years ago?"

She seemed very interested in how he might answer that, but
to answer that he would have to delve into the mystery of Bishop's
guardian angel, Milo Weaver, who had not been part of any of the
reporting so far. So he shrugged. "I suppose they'll have to put that
question to Owen Jakes."

Linda looked back at him, eyes narrowed, and nodded.

When she left for the bathroom, he closed his eyes and remembered Mittag's wild anger after Bishop had been shot by that sharpshooter in that wheat field. Though he'd certainly reported Bishop's
location back to Jakes, it seemed clear to Kevin that Ben hadn't expected it to end in murder. It didn't matter that he'd always worked

at cross-purposes to Bishop; they'd spent years together. So what did Ben's next conversation with Jakes sound like? *I'm going to blow this wide open.* Yes, that's how Benjamin Mittag would have reacted in the heat of his anger. Hours later, a SWAT team had shot him dead.

"Excuse me," Linda said.

Kevin got up, and as she moved back into her seat he noticed the phone sticking out of her purse. "Is that a satellite phone?" he asked.

She looked confused at first, then realized what he was talking about. A cynical smile. "Bankers aren't allowed eight hours off the grid."

Linda laid off the Massive Brigade talk, and in fact seemed to sink into a quiet sort of depression. He wasn't sure if he'd said the wrong thing, but at least he could catch a couple of hours' sleep.

When he woke, they were breaking through the cloud cover above Long Island, and Linda had returned to her cheery self. She asked where he was heading, and he realized he didn't know. He was going to have to find Rachel, but now that the story had broken he no longer felt he was in a rush. "Hotel," he said.

"Need a ride into town?"

He considered it, but he didn't know how things would go for him after landing. Would the Bureau be waiting? A confrontation at passport control? He didn't want to drag her into it. "I've got a car already," he lied.

They touched down, and once they'd taxied to the gate he made space for Linda to exit first. He watched as she navigated the narrow space between the seats. The flight attendants gave them forced smiles as they passed, and he thanked them for . . . for what, exactly, he didn't know. There was a lot he didn't know, but that was nothing new. He remembered looking down Benjamin Mittag's gun barrel in that dilapidated farmhouse, Mittag accusing him of working for the Feds, and having no idea what would come next. Sometimes there was virtue in ignorance.

As he walked up the jet bridge, he saw Linda hurry past other passengers and take a right toward immigration control. She glanced back to meet his eye before disappearing, but instead of a smile of farewell she gave him a cold look, as if . . . what? Making sure he was still there? Then she was gone, and his scalp tingled. A moment of imprecise terror.

He slowed. An old woman grazed his arm as she passed, and he stepped to the side to let the other passengers move on. He looked back toward the plane, the exhausted faces of passengers heading toward him, oblivious. No, he couldn't go back there. So he again joined the stream of travelers, turned the corner, and found, on the right side, Linda standing with a sad smile on her face. Behind her, two broad-chested men—one white, one black—stood at attention. "Kevin," Linda said. "Let's not make a scene, okay?"

"Sure." As he followed her, the men walked on either side of him, their shoulders brushing against his.

There was a door with no handle in the white wall, and as the rest of the passengers passed, some glancing curiously at him, Linda knocked on the door and someone on the other side opened it. They entered a dim corridor that brightened at the next turn, then walked him into a windowless cell—table, chair.

"Pockets, please," said Linda.

On the table, he laid his wallet, house keys, passport, cigarettes, and phone.

"Freddy," she said, and the black Fed proceeded to pat him down.

"What's the deal?" Kevin asked her.

"Just want to have a conversation."

"I thought we did that already."

"I've got questions."

Freddy finished up and stepped back. When Linda nodded, Kevin sat in the chair, hands on the table. "Is it you asking these questions, or is it Owen Jakes?"

She blinked at the mention of that name. Even Freddy looked concerned. Something was up.

Linda said, "Last night, Owen Jakes made himself a nice hot bath in his apartment, then slit his own wrists." Kevin's emotions must have been apparent in his face, because she leaned closer, elbows against the table, and said, "It's all over the news."

"I've been on a plane the last eight hours," he said, then remembered the satellite phone she'd had with her in the bathroom. He cocked his head and looked right back into her eyes. "No wonder you went quiet, Linda. You must have been pretty freaked out."

15

IT HAD been a long time since she'd entered the Hoover Building. Crossing the threshold, she was faced with the wide lobby that smelled of dust. And there were the guards, one of whom—gray hair, saggy cheeks—she remembered from her old life, though he didn't recognize her as she went through the metal detector and placed her ID on the scanner to unlock the turnstile. Instead of a green light, she got a red one, and the guard came over, frowning.

"Hi, Nathan," she said, and he did a double take, but it still wasn't coming to him.

"Nathan," said another guard, and he looked back. "Four-one-seven."

Nathan's expression hardened as he reached for the pistol on his hip. Rachel raised her hands, smiling, thinking, *Do people get shot for simply entering buildings?* Then she remembered Jerome Brown. "I'm Special Agent Rachel Proulx," she said, quietly but clearly. "I'm at the Seattle office now, but I used to come in here every day."

Nathan's pistol was trained on her as the other guards came to join him. He said, "I don't care who you were, Rachel. I just care who you are now. Please lay on the ground, facedown, arms spread."

As she got down on her knees, she said, "I'm not armed," but no one cared. She wondered if she'd made a brutal miscalculation.

The feeling hadn't dissipated ten minutes later when she was sitting in a holding room in the basement level, where there was a single chair but no table. She'd been stripped of her phone and purse. The two-way mirror was as wide as she was tall, the better to let a whole crowd of gawkers get a good look. To the empty room, she said, "I'm here to talk to Assistant Director Mark Paulson."

The room did not answer.

She still hadn't caught up on her sleep, and was starting to wonder if she ever would. After meeting with Schumer she'd returned to Waldorf, planning to get five or six hours, but instead found Gregg sitting alone in an empty house, drinking. "Where are Ingrid and Clare?" she'd asked.

When he raised his glass of vodka she saw from his wavering arm that he'd been at it a while. "Vanished."

"What?"

He finished the glass and slammed it on the coffee table. "The fucking bitch. What did she say to her?"

"Focus, Gregg. What are you talking about?"

A fresh wave of anger gave him enough energy to stand up and point an accusing finger at her. "You. *You* brought her. Cunt."

He'd reached a state of fury that she'd once been familiar with, and even though it had been years she knew that these things didn't age well. So she left him to his misery and went to the kitchen, where she saw the note on the counter. It was from Mackenzie. She told him she was leaving him. She told him not to call. Then the back of Rachel's head exploded in pain.

Hours later, her skull was still tender from the punch he'd thrown after creeping up behind her. It was a sucker punch, because that was the kind of person Gregg Wills had always been.

But she'd had worse pain in her life, his fist nothing compared to a .357 slug in the leg. In the kitchen she'd spun, arms raised, and thrust an elbow into his neck and jaw. As he gasped, she caught his right arm and pulled, then swung out a foot to trip him up. His legs danced in the air as he fell through the doorway and crashed into the dining table. He slid off and hit the floor, groaning, and she thought of the punches she'd taken, and the ones she knew he'd meted out to Mackenzie—for why else would she have left him like this? She thought of the girls she'd never known, the ones he must have brutalized in his teens and twenties, because men like him start young. She thought about those schoolgirls in Nigeria, who had been taken by an army of men like Gregg Wills, and who were still captive months later.

Rachel gave him a swift, hard kick in the kidneys, then another one in the back of the head. And another.

She came out of her memory, her fists tight, when the door opened. Nathan was standing there with a younger guard. He looked more relaxed, and so she released her fists, wishing away the anger. "Special Agent Proulx," he said, "will you come with us?"

She would.

In the service elevator, he pressed number 6, and she leaned back against the wall to rest.

Do not sleep, she told herself.

No fear of that now.

The elevator doors slid open, and she let Nathan put a hand on her elbow as he and his partner led her down the corridor, where federal agents she had never met gave her the eye. Paulson's secretary was on the phone when they entered her office, saying, "She's here." Then she hung up and opened the door. Nathan and his partner brought her into Paulson's bright, sterile office.

"Rachel," said Paulson, standing, a stiff smile on his face and hands on the back of his high, padded chair. "Sit, please." As she took a seat, he waved the guards out as he sat down, too. "I think I can take care of myself, gentlemen."

Don't be so sure, she thought, realizing that she hadn't checked to see if Gregg was suffering from internal bleeding. When she'd left his house, he was still lying on the dining room floor, silent.

Once they were alone, Paulson moved into his chair. "You heard about Jakes?" he asked.

"This morning."

"Damn shame. I doubt his career would've recovered from this Schumer story, but taking your own life?" He shook his head. "That's just giving up."

She almost contradicted him. Maybe he hadn't given the order, and he didn't know. Maybe Johnson and Vale had taken it upon themselves to stage a suicide to clean up the Bureau's mess—were any Bureau employees that self-motivated? Jakes had been. Or at least he had appeared to be. "Yeah," she said. "A shame."

He looked at the cluttered surface of his desk like a confused old man. "I don't know how much of Schumer's story I buy, but if even a little of it is true . . ."

She didn't bother finishing his sentence.

He said, "The Germans are having a fit right now. They've given the legat office twenty-four hours to clear the fuck out."

"So I heard."

"And we picked up Kevin Moore at JFK."

She hadn't gotten any messages from Kevin since his return to London from Spain, and she'd worried. "Is he all right?" she asked, sitting up.

"Of course! Just debriefing him. But the question we're asking ourselves is: Who gave the story to Schumer? We're pretty sure he didn't."

"And you know I can't stand Sam Schumer."

"Right," he said, smiling. "That's right, Rachel. But it's all so elaborate, isn't it? It strains credulity. Jakes resurrected an applicant so he could secretly infiltrate the Massive Brigade?"

"To keep an eye on Bishop, yes. He had to protect his Berlin secret."

"But why didn't Jakes just get rid of Martin Bishop in 2009? Why waste time with Mittag, waiting until Bishop had become a national hero?"

"Because he couldn't. Bishop had a protector."

"A what? Schumer didn't report that, did he?"

She decided to ignore Paulson's questions. "He called himself James Sullivan, but his real name is Milo Weaver. I'm told he works for the United Nations, but I can't find his name attached to any departments. He used to be one of ours."

"Bureau?"

"CIA."

"*Fuck,*" Paulson said, spitting the word. "And what's the UN doing mixed up in this?"

She didn't know, and wouldn't until she'd met Weaver face-to-face. All she had to go on was what he'd said to her years ago, so she repeated it. "Fighting against the global power of corporations."

"You sound like you admire this Bolshevik."

She didn't know how she felt about him.

"Corporations, Rachel, are stability. You fuck with them, you fuck with our democratic way of life."

Until this moment, she hadn't been sure she would take the next step, but there was something in his tone, something privileged that rubbed her the wrong way. Maybe she'd spent too much time with Ingrid, and that was why she couldn't just let it go and take the comfortable route. She said, "The real question, Mark, is: Who benefited on July 4?"

"Not the American people, that's for damned sure."

Was he being purposefully thick? Perhaps. "The banks," she said. "One of the biggest laundering investigations in US history was buried. And everyone was so distracted by the Massive Brigade that they didn't even notice."

He pressed his hands together, as if in prayer. "What are you saying, Rachel?"

"I'm saying it's curious. The actions on July 4 killed or hospitalized the two people who were spearheading the investigation. What kind of leftist kills off politicians who are trying to break the banks? If Schumer's report is right, and Jakes was giving orders all along, then July 4 makes sense. Mittag's not crazy. He commits an act that he knows will ruin the Massive Brigade, and at the same time shield the financial sector from prosecution. He's following orders. He's a defender of your definition of stability."

She kept an eye on his face, the way he absorbed each little leap she was taking along the way. There, in his eye—a twitch. It could mean nothing, or it could mean everything, but the most important thing was that before coming to the Hoover she'd stopped at the Ballston-MU Metro Station and picked up Ashley's report on Owen Jakes's burner phone. Now, she took the three folded pages from her purse: times and numbers and coordinates. He noticed the pages but said nothing about them. Only: "Are you suggesting Mittag receive a Shield of Bravery? Maybe a Memorial Star for his mother?"

She flattened the pages on his desk and said, "Ben Mittag took his orders from his phone, which connected to Owen's burner."

"That was in Schumer's report, but we don't know what they said to each other."

"No, we don't. And we don't know why, if Mittag was working for Owen, he didn't hand over a list of safe houses rather than make us work to find them and shut them down. Owen didn't have a reason to hide that information from us."

Paulson seemed to find that interesting; he rapped his fingertips on the desktop. "Maybe the theory is starting to unravel."

"No, it's just a question."

"Do you have an answer?"

She shrugged. "I think it was hard on Mittag, maintaining his cover. Every day he listened to arguments against people like Owen, against us. He rationalized his behavior—we all do that. He would shoot some politicians for Owen because he thought it would also help the Revolution. But he wouldn't give away the safe houses. He tried to walk a line. Once Owen had Bishop killed, though, Mittag was probably too scared to commit to our side. So he chose the Brigade."

"You're twisting yourself into a pretzel trying to explain it to yourself."

She wasn't troubled by that, because Mittag's inner life was just another loose end, one of many that no one would ever be able to explain. "It doesn't matter," she said, then looked him directly in the eyes. "But you know what does matter? The phone records from Owen's burner. He didn't just use it for calling Mittag."

A sly grin from Paulson. "I'm in such suspense, Rachel."

"He also called a number that was triangulated to your house, Mark."

It meant something that Paulson held on to his grin, but it no longer looked like an expression of any emotion. It was frozen there, a mask to cover up whatever was going on in his head.

"Tell me, Mark. Which one of you ordered Sarah Vale and Lyle Johnson to execute me?"

His expression became pained, and he licked his teeth behind his lips. Finally, he said, "Jakes was an idiot."

"But useful for running Benjamin Mittag."

Now the grin was gone. "You think I was running Mittag, through Owen? That's insane."

She shook her head. "Owen was running Mittag long before you ever showed up. But you're not an idiot. You did some investigating. You discovered what Owen was up to, then decided to put his inside man to use for some of your friends. How are your Plains Capital shares holding up?"

"My *shares*?" His mouth worked the air, sputtering the word *"Really?"* His hands fidgeted, momentarily out of his control. "Christ, Rachel. You must think I'm a monster."

She wasn't sure what she thought of him, but nothing he had said was helping his case.

"What?" he asked her, his voice rising. "Would you rather a band of militants roam the country, blowing up shit?"

"They never blew up a thing," she said.

"Because we never let them."

Maybe, she thought, he really believed what he'd said: *Corporations are stability*. Or maybe it was only about his bottom line. Was there a difference? "It doesn't matter what I think, Mark. The optics matter, particularly for someone like you."

He exhaled noisily and looked around his office, at the photos of himself with politicians, with the president.

"Maybe you want to tell me about your friends, the ones you were helping out."

"Maybe you'd like to go fuck yourself," he snapped.

She couldn't help but smile. In the space of a few minutes he'd crumbled. It was almost too easy. She said, "And you can tell Johnson and Vale that getting rid of me—or anyone connected to this story—will only bring it out further."

Paulson gave her silence for ten full seconds, gradually settling down. Then: "You've got blackmail on your mind, Rachel. I can see it in your eyes." He shook his head, disgusted. "What is it you want?"

"Well, the first thing I want is for you to release Kevin Moore. And don't touch his passport."

"Done," he said, swiping his hand like an impatient magician making the unreal real. "Anything else?"

"Your job."

His fist dropped to the desk like a bird shot in midflight. "What?"

"You heard me."

"I don't *get* to choose my successor."

"You'll put in a good word with the director. The president's an old golfing buddy, right? I'll be charming in the interview. We'll see how it goes. The important thing is that you step down now."

"Are you really serious?"

"Try me."

More dismal silence; then the office door opened. It was Lou Barnes. When he noticed Rachel sitting there, he went slack-jawed, then closed his mouth. Something more urgent than a disgraced ex-colleague was on his mind. "Mark, you'll want to see this."

Paulson looked at Rachel, his face flushed, then got to his feet.

They followed Barnes through a crowd of employees to his glassed-in office, where everyone was glued to his wide-screen televi-

sion. The news channels were all reporting the same thing: Spontaneous demonstrations had appeared in twelve major cities, among them
New York, Los Angeles, Dallas, San Francisco, Seattle, Detroit,
Chicago, and Washington. Throngs of people filled the streets, hemmed
in by tall buildings, moving slowly toward major landmarks. "None
of these demonstrations has been cleared with local authorities," said
a newscaster. "The police aren't sure what to do."

"Oh shit, that's us," someone said when the image changed, and
Rachel saw that a loose crowd of a hundred or more people was standing outside the Hoover Building, with more people streaming across
the street to join them.

Rachel looked out of Barnes's office, past the gawkers. A dozen
agents stood at the windows in the front of the building, looking
down.

"They're not saying anything," said Barnes.

"What?" asked Paulson.

"No signs. Mouths shut tight. No demands. Not in any of the
cities. They're dead fucking silent everywhere."

"Circumnavigation," said Rachel, remembering.

Paulson looked very confused. "What?"

Before he could ask again, she left the office, pushing through
the crowd, and headed for the elevators.

On the ground floor there were employees hovering near the
entrance, others foolishly assuming that safety could be found by
standing out of sight and whispering into their phones. She saw
Nathan gaping at the windows, hand on his sidearm, and when he
saw her pass he said, "Agent Proulx, I wouldn't go out there."

"It's all right," she said, but she didn't know if it would be all
right or not. She didn't know anything, really, because she couldn't
see into the future. None of them could.

She pushed through the doors and stepped outside. Barnes hadn't
been lying—they *were* silent. A wall of mute people standing together
and looking at her. Just looking. No anger, no malice, just a thousand eyes that made her feel as if, from now on, she would never be

alone. It was terrifying. Her first impulse was to look away, but that made her feel ashamed, so she turned to look back at them all. It was hard, those eyes drilling deep into her, right to the center. The terror returned, and she walked hurriedly up the sidewalk. By the time she reached the end of the block, at the edge of the crowd she saw more demonstrators approaching on foot. Hundreds. Silent.

In the distance, she heard sirens. The police were on their way.

CIRCUMNAVIGATION

THURSDAY, MAY 24, 2018

1

IT HAD been two months since she'd walked through this city, overcome by hopelessness, back to Penn Station, thinking that it was all
over for her. Now it was a gorgeous day, warm without being oppressive. There was traffic, of course, and noise, and throngs of distracted pedestrians, but when she reached Bryant Park the green
stretch of nature was a relief, even populated by food carts, down-
and-outs distributing handbills, and New Yorkers spilled all over the
grass talking on their phones while nibbling on sandwiches and soy
snacks. Deeper in, she saw the young people—fifteen or so—dozing
under the sun beside a pile of protest signs. These days, everyone had
a reason to lift a sign. She found a bench and settled down to take it
all in.

She didn't see James Sullivan—more accurately, Milo Weaver—
until he was about ten yards away, taking off his sunglasses. His
suit, unlike back in San Francisco, didn't stand out here, but she remembered those bruised, melancholic eyes, and his flakes of gray that
had by now multiplied. And, she noticed, a silver wedding band. He
also wore a smile. She straightened as he reached her. "Mind if I sit,
Rachel?"

She tilted her head toward the empty space beside her, and when he settled down he placed his hands on his knees. Took a deep breath. "Congratulations on the new job."

She had taken over the assistant directorship three weeks ago. It turned out that, when motivated, Paulson was able to convince the director of even the most ridiculous things, like moving a special agent too many steps up the ladder. "Shaking things up" was how it had been described in the official statement. These days, she found herself at the head of the table in that noisy conference room, lording it over Barnes, Lynch, and Kranowski, still in awe of how their acting skills hid their contempt.

"Thanks," she said, then: "You know, it took some arm-twisting with your old employers at Langley, but we've collected a nice dossier on you. Father: the late Yevgeny Primakov, formerly of the KGB and FSB, and then UNESCO. Two sisters, one of whom—Alexandra—seems to do legal work for you. And you: Milo Weaver, once an agent of the ultrasecret Department of Tourism. After your father died, you moved over to UNESCO before eventually dropping off the official roster altogether."

"Gosh," he said, a smile on his lips. "Can't fool the Bureau, can you?"

He was already beginning to irritate her, so to get that smile off his face she added, "A wife, Tina, and a sixteen-year-old daughter named Stephanie."

Yes, that did it. The smile was gone. So she pushed on:

"Tell me what you really do for the UN. Tell me why the UN was funneling money to Martin Bishop, beginning in 2009. He came to you, broken, in Spain. And you encouraged him to work against the US government. Without you, none of this would have happened."

"Well, first of all," he said, stretching his arms out ahead of himself, "that wasn't UN money."

"Whose money was it?"

"Second of all, I didn't encourage him. When he came to Spain he connected with a friend of mine, who called me."

"Sebastián Vivas."

Weaver nodded. "Sebastián thought I could help. Once I heard his story, and had verified it, I tried to talk Martin *out* of doing anything. I told him that he'd get himself killed if he went back to the States and started speaking out, particularly about what had happened in Berlin. But I couldn't convince him. And I wasn't going to let him go back without some kind of support. So, yes, I set him up with some income. Not to work against the US government, though."

"No?"

He shook his head.

"And somehow Bishop survived, with your money, and for eight years Owen Jakes didn't kill him. He was under your protection."

"I met Jakes in a Berlin park much like this," Weaver told her. "He understood that if Martin was hurt or killed I would turn over the evidence of the bombing to the Germans. He kept to his end of the deal, but I had no idea he'd recruited his own mole. Benjamin Mittag was a surprise."

It was nice to hear that this smug man could be surprised now and then. "But you didn't keep your end of the deal," she said. "When Bishop was killed, you didn't tell the Germans about the bombing."

"Didn't I?"

"Did you?"

Weaver shrugged. "What makes you think the Germans didn't already know the story? How bad do you think their forensics are? Come on, Assistant Director. They knew all along."

"Now you're confusing me on purpose."

"Welcome to my world."

That was a phrase she would have expected to hate coming from his lips, but he hadn't said it as a boast. In fact, he acted as if the complexity of his world was a point of sadness.

He said, "The KRL had already humiliated the German government. The last thing the Reichstag wanted was for it to get out that an FBI agent had killed them, particularly when the reason was so sordid: getting the Germans to be more cooperative. All that would do was make martyrs of the KRL and encourage more radicalism."

She took her time, thinking through his explanation, holding it up against what she already knew. The explanation made sense to her, because like most mysteries it depended on the vagaries of human nature and a love of secrecy. That wasn't to say she believed it; believing anything this man said felt like naïveté. She said, "This is all very enlightening, Milo, but I almost got killed trying to put together the pieces. You could have passed me something."

"I'm sorry," he said, sounding like he meant it. "But this is bigger than Martin Bishop and Bureau corruption. It's bigger than banks helping launder money. Maybe you've noticed: The world is moving in a worrying direction."

"It's always moving in a worrying direction."

"That's a matter of perspective," he said, and flicked something off his pants. "The decline of the EU, the rise of nationalist movements all over the planet. Global fragmentation. This is bigger than Martin Bishop. It's bigger than America."

"This?"

Weaver hesitated, then: "My father once threw away his career and much of his life in order to try to make the world a better place. I'm not sure he succeeded, but I'm also not sure that mattered. The work he did gave him a reason to wake up in the morning."

"Is that why you're trying to destabilize American democracy? Because you have daddy issues? Or is it to push off thoughts of suicide?"

He grinned. "Destabilize democracy? Am I really that powerful?"

"Look, I can see protecting Bishop, but you actively funded him. You were funding terrorism."

"You're trying to get under my skin, Rachel. We both know he wasn't a terrorist. He needed support because he had a fight ahead of him. He was going against people with limitless resources. And after what he went through in Berlin he deserved a chance. So do you."

Weaver reached into his jacket, took out an envelope, and handed it to her. Unsure, she opened it and found five pages of spreadsheet filled with thirty-four-digit alphanumeric codes and dollar figures in the millions.

"What's this?"

"It's me helping you, Rachel."

"But what *is* it?"

"It's what you need to reopen and expand the investigation into Plains Capital Bank and *Investition für Wirtschaft*."

"Expand?"

"The banks don't matter. What matters is whose money was being laundered, and *why* it was being laundered."

"It was being laundered to avoid paying taxes."

He shook his head. "That's the clean story, and it's a pretty one—it's enough to interrupt the money flow for a short time. The important question to ask is where the money was headed once it was cleaned."

"Why don't you tell me?"

"Because I'm still figuring it out myself."

She refolded the pages, slipped them into the envelope, and pocketed it. She wasn't sure what she would do with the gift. She'd learned the value of holding on to incriminating information. She'd learned how to use evidence as a bludgeon.

As if reading her mind, he said, "You might want to just keep it for future use."

Though she'd thought the same thing, she said, "Why?"

He pursed his lips. "You remember those hundred and twenty girls who were kidnapped last year in Nigeria?"

"Yes, of course."

"I'm glad you do. A lot of people don't. Or they mix it up with some other school somewhere else. And if that kind of horror can disappear from the consciousness of people, imagine how quickly a case against some multinational banks will fade."

"You're saying I should choose the right moment, in order to inflict the most damage."

"Yes."

"What makes you think I want to inflict damage?"

He hesitated, then leaned back. Waited.

"Maybe I think the stability of Western civilization is a little more important than a handful of lives."

Milo Weaver rubbed the bridge of his nose. "Some might say that caring about a handful of lives is the *definition* of civilization."

Rachel turned to look across the park to where some demonstrators were waking from their afternoon naps, yawning. Beyond them, near Forty-Second Street, Kevin Moore was watching out for her, as were seven other agents. She felt protected and at peace, free to speak her mind. "You're full of shit," she told him. "People like you ignore the costs of blowing up hypocrisy. My job is to make hypocrisy and corruption function as well as possible, because that's what humans are—they're hypocritical and weak. Rip away the hypocrisy, and there's nothing left."

Milo blinked, looking across the park. She wondered if he, too, had his own heavies in reserve. He said, "You sound just like Mark Paulson."

She didn't bother replying to that. "Tell me," she said, "how much money did you funnel into the Massive Brigade?"

"It doesn't matter."

"Well, I hope you don't mind wasting that much money."

"You think it's wasted?"

"Martin Bishop is food for the worms."

He shrugged. "Take a look at the streets, Rachel. Walk downtown a little further. Melt into the crowds and listen. Then tell me if it's wasted."

2

"**PIÑA COLADA**, doll," said Francine, her loose jowls baking in the sun. "Coconut cream this time, okay? Those milk-coladas just don't do it for me."

"*Sí.*"

She watched the young waiter walk barefoot across the white sand back to the clubhouse, then turned to where Bill and Gina were huddled under an umbrella.

"*What?*" Francine asked them. "I'm too old to worry about my figure."

From behind sunglasses and a novel, Gina said, "I didn't say a thing," because she hadn't even been listening. Old age, it turned out, had robbed her cousin of the ability to shut up.

"What's his name? José? Jesus? He *is* adorable."

The ice in Bill's whiskey had melted, and the colored water was now beach temperature. He wished he'd asked the waiter for another, since he wasn't sure he could actually make the long walk to the bar. Eternal sunshine, which over that last nasty Jersey winter had sounded like God's Own Cure, turned out to have its drawbacks. Daily baths of sunscreen that stank up their condo, perpetual sweat, and the unending prattle of Francine's mildly racist banter.

"I bet he's got nineteen adorable brothers out there somewhere picking oranges. He's the lucky one."

"His name is Juan," Gina said.

"What?"

Bill had had his *Times* subscription rerouted south to him, and he was still making his way through yesterday's copy. As bad as it was, the life they lived here—sleeping in, the lazy wash of surf, and the drinks delivered on small circular trays—was better than the rest of the country, which was why he'd agreed to extend their stay another month. Tuesday had seen some of the worst of the demonstrations, with downtown Chicago turning up four dead in clashes between anarchists and police. Spontaneous demonstrations had brought Tribeca to a standstill, so that no one could drive anywhere in downtown Manhattan, and last week armed members of the resurgent Massive Brigade had taken over a derelict factory in Oakland and proclaimed themselves the Republic of the Bay.

All of it, Bill knew, was doomed to fail, and when it did there would be more bloodshed.

David had called a couple of weeks ago; his apartment was one epicenter of the organizing, and he'd been swept up by his students' enthusiasm. "What about Ingrid and Clare?" Bill had asked.

"I don't know" was his reply, but in that answer Bill sensed that, more than the students, Ingrid was the reason he had taken to writing daily dispatches posted to radical websites, chronicling the acts of civil disobedience that had, over the last months, become fashionable. *All you have to do is decide* was David's most-used catchphrase.

The waiter returned with Francine's drink and asked if they needed anything else. Bill didn't bother asking for the whiskey, because he'd become distracted by a second-page story of one of his ex-clients, a wildly popular actor who had expressed his solidarity with the Republic of the Bay. How many of his fans would now be swayed? How much would be destroyed before people came to their senses?

Francine took a sip and frowned. "I *told* Jesus to use the cream." She craned her neck. "Adorable but dumb as a post. Where is he?"

"You know," Bill said, unable to control himself, "when the Revolution arrives here, yours is the first neck adorable Juan is going to slit."

For the first time in history, Francine was speechless. Gina, laughing, lowered her book and turned to give him a grand smile. Then she took off her sunglasses, squinting past him. "Is that . . . ?"

He turned to see two figures, women, walking toward them along the shoreline. Initially, they were silhouettes, and then the sky's lone cloud shifted and he could make out details. "How about that?" he said as he grunted, pushing himself to his feet. He walked toward the woman he'd realized was Ingrid, who was holding a baby covered in a sheet as protection from the sun. Her hair was tangled and sun-bleached, but she looked healthy. With her was a taller woman, brunette, gorgeous. "Good Lord," Bill called. "Look at you!" Gina caught up to him and clapped her hands together.

"Who is *that*?" called Francine.

They walked together to meet Ingrid. After the kisses, Gina took Clare, and together they cooed at the baby. Mackenzie introduced herself and shook their hands; then Ingrid said, "Hey, you mind if we crash with you for a few days?"

"Thank Christ," said Bill. "A change."

ACKNOWLEDGMENTS

The Middleman took five years from idea to final draft, while my previous novel took only a couple months. Perhaps this is because it was my first book in a very long time to be entirely written in the United States, where the political and cultural noise is, for me, the most distracting. Perhaps it's because this was my first novel to focus entirely on American themes. Or—and this might be the most convincing—I simply didn't know what I was doing. At book number eleven, I can say that anyone who claims novel writing becomes easier with time is either lying or not doing it right.

Whatever the reason, the first draft required a serious rethink. While it juggled the same characters and much of the same story line as the version you're now reading, the tone was off by a mile, and the story was hobbled by poor choices. I was wrestling with subjects I knew well and cared about deeply but had never before fully committed myself to, and that inexperience showed.

My ever-patient editor, Kelley Ragland, who has shepherded every book of mine to publication, was sensitive to these problems, and, as always, was able to see the forest among the many misshapen trees. She saw that, for all its flaws, *The Middleman* had something to say about the world we were living in. She also knew that it would take time for me to draw that message out, and was perfectly willing to give me that time.

I stepped away from the novel in order to create a television show, *Berlin Station*, and by the time I returned to America the country had, on the surface at least, become a different place. The presidential election had exposed long-hidden fault lines, producing tectonic shifts not only in government but in how Americans spoke to and regarded one another. *The Middleman* was suddenly more timely that it had seemed a couple years before.

Upon receiving that first draft, a less perceptive editor would have said, "Hey, everyone writes a dud eventually. Why don't you try something else?" But Kelley's astute editorial eye saw what this book could be, and she had the wisdom to encourage me to continue.

After knowing her for fifteen years, both as an editor and a friend, none of this is a surprise to me, but it is no less appreciated.